FIGHTING FOR
FLIGHT

Also by J.B. Salsbury

Fighting to Forget
Fighting to Forgive

FIGHTING FOR
FLIGHT

J.B. SALSBURY

Fighting for Flight

J.B. Salsbury

Copyright © 2014 J.B. Salsbury

ISBN: 1482632462

ISBN 13: 9781482632460

Cover art by Amanda Simpson at Pixel Mischief.

Edited by Theresa Wegand

PROLOGUE

I have a brief moment to catch my breath before it's time to push again. My head lolls to the side, eyes fixing on the shape of a man. It's hard to tell through the blur of tears and sweat clouding my vision. The bright light illuminating my body is no help. Everything outside of its glow is darkness. But, even in the dark, I know who it is.

How long has he been here? In my labor-induced dementia I didn't see him come in. My skin crawls, each tiny hair standing on end. I squirm under the weight of his foreboding presence.

The vise grip on my midsection begins its violent compression. I lock eyes with the doctor between my legs.

"One more push, Milena. Take a deep breath." He wipes his brow with the dirty sleeve of his shirt. The smell of cigar smoke and liquor wafts from his body in nauseating waves. My stomach roils as my body tightens with a contraction.

"Good. Now, push!" I barely hear the doctor count to ten over my groaning.

My torso folds in half as the force of the contraction racks my body. I bite my lip and taste blood, refusing to give voice to my agony. Sweat beads on my skin. I grip the sheets against the unbearable pain. I want to give up, just lie back and sleep, but my womb is intent on purging this baby. A guttural sound rumbles in my throat. Searing pain. Intense pressure. I'm being ripped into two.

"Baby's out." The doctor announces to the room.

It's over. I fall back onto the bed.

The room is quiet except for my heaving breath and the clicking of the doctor's tools. I study the ceiling, not ready to face what I know is coming.

Exhaustion sets in and my eyelids slide shut, only to fly back open with the shrill cry of new life. Its stuttered vibrato pulls at something deep in my chest. My heart races.

The infant's scream calls to me on a primal level, begging for comfort only its mother can provide. My arms ache to cradle the baby to my breast. *It's okay, mommy's here.* The words coo in my head, but freeze at my lips. I can't get attached, not when his plan is to take it away to use it for his own purposes, like a bred work mule.

What kind of work will await this baby when it becomes an adult all depends on one thing. The nagging question picks at my mind.

Sitting up, I rub my eyes to clear my vision. He stands at the foot of the bed, no longer shrouded in the dark. Holding the baby in one arm, he hands the doctor a large wad of cash then flicks his fingers for the man to leave. The doctor scurries out the door like a mouse that just stole from the dinner table, and slams it behind him.

A devious glare catches my eye. "Well done, darling. She's perfect." His voice is a the smooth purr that haunts my dreams.

She.

Oh, God. No!

"Dominick, please, I beg you." I try to put authority behind my voice, but only manage a whisper. "Just give her up for adoption. She's an innocent—"

"Quiet!" His booming command echoes in the tiny room, making me flinch then cower. "She's mine. I'll do with her whatever I please." The fierce words cut through the newborn's cries and straight to my heart.

He runs his palm over the baby's head with the gentle grace of a jellyfish. Serene and lethal. "She has your dark hair, darling. I'll name her Raven." He steps to my bedside. "Would you like to hold her?"

My whimpered reply has him smiling. He knows what I've just done. Like laying out my cards in a high stakes game of poker, I've just shown him my weakness.

No, I can't hold her. If I do, I'll never let her go.

"I see." He keeps her in his arms and strolls to the single window. "You may raise her." His gaze slides back to mine. "But make no mistake, Milena, if you do anything to interfere with my plan, I will kill her. Then, you and I will start from scratch, and I'll not make it pleasant for you. Do you understand?" As if he can see into my soul and feel my fear, he smirks.

Revulsion courses through my veins like venom, making it impossible to speak. I close my eyes and nod, trying to force dry the tears that stream down my face.

If I could only take it back. The day everything had spun out of control. The moment Dominick Morretti ruined my life. Leaning against his car with his blond hair and those beautiful blue-green eyes, he looked like an angel. He spoke tenderly with sincere reverence and offered me a life I could only dream about. My heart wanted so badly to believe he was my savior: a heavenly messenger sent to wrap me in his embrace and whisk me off to my happily ever after. But he was no savior. He was my undertaker.

Realization hits: a heavy flood, drowning me in regret. Painful guilt eats away at my heart, slowly consuming what's left of my humanity. Dominick is nothing if not a man of his word. He's going to get his way, and there is not a thing I can do about it.

Hatred boils in my stomach. I want to lash out, attack the man who has taken my future from me. But I know better than to face off with him. I've seen what he does to girls who don't obey. They spend the rest of their days shaking, walking the thin line of their addiction, solely dependent on him, so desperate for their next fix that they beg for the gift of a quick death. Right where he wants them.

"Milena." His firm tone gets my attention.

Back at my bedside, he holds the bundle of blankets and baby for me to take. Raven. My daughter. *No. Not mine.*

Don't show him my weakness. Suffering in silence is torture. But he can't touch what I don't give him.

I wrap my arms tightly around my body, locking them in place. With the last pieces of my resolve, I shove the mother in me to the back corner of my soul and lock her there.

"Take her, darling." His words carry a heavy warning.

I shake my head.

He stands straight and studies me with narrowed eyes. "Very well." He turns and heads to the door. "I'll give you a few hours to come to terms with this. In the meantime," he looks at the rumpled bed and the floor, both riddled with the gore of childbirth, "clean this mess up."

Then he's gone, taking Raven with him.

I scan my surroundings, taking in the carnage: The product of the last twenty-four hours of labor; the bloodied result of an unsanitary home birth. Something deep down registers that mine are not the only horrors that haunt this room. I can almost hear the screams of the women who have been here before me.

My hand absently rubs my now soft belly. Once full of life and promise, and now, completely void. And through all this, I feel ...nothing.

ONE

20 years later…

JONAH

Well, shit. I didn't think the headache to fuck all headaches could possibly get worse. Between the strobe lights and the crappy music, my brain feels like it's twenty-four hours off a three-day bender. The stench of stale beer, sweat, and perfume swirl in the air, topping off my list of cranial irritants.

And add to that the gang of silverback gorillas at the table behind me. They grunt and holler at the stage, likely beating their chests for attention. *Amateurs.* I turn and give the frat-boy pussies a look that has them all sitting with their mouths sealed shut.

My head is going to explode, and it's putting me in a fucked-up mood. The only reason I agreed to come to the strip club was the hope that pounding a few beers might take the edge off the pile-driver in my head. So far, not so good.

With one long pull from the bottle, I check out the half-naked girl on stage in front of me. She's a typical Vegas stripper: bleach blond hair, dark tanned skin, and huge fake tits. There's an identical one for every slot machine on the strip.

"That chick's been eyeball-fucking you all night." Blake yells to be heard over the music. "You gonna hit that?"

I glare at my training partner. After all, it's his dumb ass that talked me into coming here tonight.

"May as well." Getting rid of this headache is my first priority. Since the booze isn't helping, maybe some female intervention will. "But only if she's off soon. I've got to get out of here. This place is killing my head." I attempt to rub the pain away with my fingertips.

Blake raises an eyebrow along with one side of his mouth. "I better get going too. I need my beauty sleep if I'm going to keep kicking your ass."

I give him the backside of my middle finger.

His knee connecting to my temple in training today is what got me in this brain-thumping predicament. I make a mental note to pay him back with a solid ball shot next time we're in the octagon.

"Right. You kicked *my* ass." I tilt my head, indicating his fresh black eye and bloodied lip.

Maybe I should feel worse about flipping the switch on him as I did. But he of all people should know better. He's seen what happens when I let the monster out. If I get hit hard enough, my brain goes into protection mode. I go feral. I can't help it.

I've learned to control it during training, for the most part. But Blake's knee hit hard out of nowhere and set me off. Luckily, I was able to rein it in before I really hurt the bastard.

"Hey, sexy," a seductive voice purrs in my ear.

Feminine hands run from my biceps, down my chest, and still on my abdomen. I turn to see the blond stripper from the stage resting her chin on my shoulder, biting on her cherry-red bottom lip. She slides her hands back up, skirting around to my front. Her long, naked legs straddle my thighs and she leans in close, placing her assets at eye level.

"I think I know you." Her hips undulate in front of me to the beat of the music.

I yawn. "Is that right? And where is it you think you know me from?"

I study her face, trying to pull up something familiar from my memory and coming up empty. There's no way I've had sex with her before. I would have remembered. And if I had, that would have a direct effect on how this night will end. I do not hit the same honey pot twice.

She allows her weight to drop so that she's sitting straddled on my lap. I feel the familiar stir of arousal as my body responds to the heat and friction, but nothing else. I know her type. They're all the same: fake—from their practiced, ditzy voices to their ass implants. These women are good for one thing, and she seems more than ready to go. *Perfect.*

"I've seen you on all the billboards."

My eyes roll to the ceiling then squeeze shut at the throbbing in my still-aching head. I don't have time for small talk. "You want to get out of here?"

Her face lights up and her eyes sparkle. "Sure."

What a surprise.

"Can we go to your place?" She's practically bouncing with excitement.

I can almost see the dollar signs flash in her eyes, she's so transparent. This chick is all about status, the money, and the right to brag that she bagged a fighter. She's looking to snag someone with cash that she can lead around by his dick. Her porn-star looks and willing sexual prowess turned on so bright, she's hoping to blind me so I'll *think* I'm in love. So fucking predictable.

"No. Yours."

I'd never take a woman to my place. Seems to me if a guy brings a woman home she suddenly feels like she can set up house. Before he knows it, she's making breakfast and stuffing his bathroom drawers with tampons. Poor shmuck looking for a one-night stand finds himself with a live-in wife. When she finally does leave, the guy's fucked because she knows where he lives. He never calls, but she doesn't care. She'll just show up at his house or, even worse, drive by or park across the street and stalk him.

No thanks.

"Fine." Her reply sounds deflated. The excitement tarnished, but I can tell, this chick doesn't give up. "I'll meet you out front. Give me five minutes?" She perks up, her thin eyebrows high on her forehead, anticipating my answer.

I nod.

With a long, firm grind of her pelvis on my crotch, she disappears into the crowd. Blake has his tongue down the throat of a busty redhead.

"Hey, bro. I'm gonna bounce." I say it loud enough for him to hear.

He doesn't break his lip-lock, but waves me off with one hand while skillfully sliding a fifty-dollar bill into the girl's g string. And they say they aren't prostitutes.

I down the dregs of my beer, throw some cash on the table, and head for the door. The club is busy for a Tuesday night, and the bar is three-deep, standing room only. People move out of my way a little quicker than usual, probably due to the don't-fuck-with-me look this headache is giving my face.

Shoving through the club's front door, I'm hit with desert air and cigarette smoke. The flashing neon sign makes everyone's skin look pink. I scan the parking lot and consider bolting. Maybe a hot shower and good night's sleep are all I need.

Just then, a small hand grabs my elbow. Too late. The stripper looks up at me from under her eyelashes. She licks her lips and presses her tits against my arm. She slides her hand into my palm and laces her fingers with mine. "I hope you're ready for some fun. One night with me and you'll be begging—"

I pull my hand from hers. "Where's your car? I'll follow you."

Her eyes flash with something that looks like disappointment. Chicks and their inflated ideas about romance. This isn't a date. This isn't an all-night sexual rendezvous. This is simple: Itch. Scratch.

She nods her head in the direction of her car. Feeling a little bad for my brush off, I walk her to it. *I'm not a complete asshole.*

She settles in and turns the ignition. I take off to my truck, telling myself that going home with ...*Ah hell,* I don't even know her name.

Oh well. Won't be the first time I bang a nameless face.

It's a short drive to her apartment. I back my truck into a spot in the visitor's section to ensure a quick departure. She waits for me at the bottom of the stairs.

"I'm right up here." She runs her hand down my chest hooking my jeans with her fingertips.

"Don't." I remove her hand.

Her eyes narrow before they soften into something more sexual. It's as if she wants to be pissed at me, but doesn't want to lose the prize.

"If control is your thing, sexy, just say the word." She spins around and I follow her up to her place.

Once inside, she throws her bag on the couch and walks back to what I assume is her bedroom. I head towards the glowing clock in her kitchen. It's almost midnight. Pulling a condom from my wallet, I vow to be home and in bed by one.

I walk down the short hallway to the room with the light on. She's lying on the bed, naked. The visual alone has my body charged and ready.

"You want to hit the light?" I work the button fly of my jeans.

Her face twists in anger. "What is it with you?" She props herself up on her elbows. "No touching. No foreplay. No lights! What do you think this is? Some quickie with the stripper?"

My hands freeze at my fly. Is she kidding? Of course that's what this is. I shrug. No use in leading the girl on. "Yeah."

Her eyes sweep my body from head to toe then back again. "Whatever." She rolls to the side and clicks the light, plunging us in darkness.

Much better.

I focus on the task before me: Meeting a need, no connection, no feeling anywhere above my waist. A goal set before me, a finish line that I'm racing to breach so I can go home and get some sleep.

She moves for a kiss, and I turn away. She tries to engage me in dirty talk. It's easy to ignore. Finally, she gives up, allowing our bodies to take what they want.

Still completely clothed, except for the fly of my jeans, I stand from her bed to leave. This girl probably has something more to offer a guy. But that guy ain't me.

Just the thought of having some needy chick hanging on my arm, making me buy her crap, taking up my time with her petty issues about girl shit makes me shiver. I need to get the hell out of here.

"Will you call me, you know, if you ever want to hang out again?" Her small voice reaches my now-sated brain.

Fuck. This is uncomfortable.

I grab my phone and press a few buttons. "What's your number?" *And your name.* She rattles off seven digits, and I pretend to program them into my phone.

"Right, I got it. Go to sleep."

I have a Jiminy Cricket moment with my conscience. "Thanks for …that."

She mumbles something I can't quite make out and I slip from her room.

—

RAVEN

"Holy crud." Shooting straight up in bed, I cover my ears. "Stupid thing." I pound quiet my obnoxious alarm.

Usually waking on my own, I forget how that thing buzzes like a swarm of bees with megaphones glued to their butts. Next paycheck I'm clock radio shopping.

The heels of my hands dig into my eye sockets to rub away my sleepy haze. *Why did I stay up so late?* I swing my legs over the side of the bed and push up with a big, feline stretch.

Coffee. That's what I need. I step in the direction of my kitchenette and kick the large wooden box on the floor.

"Ouchie, ouchie, ouchie." Cradling my injured foot, I give the darn box my most evil glare, the evidence of what kept me up so late, punishing me still.

The box is full of every *Car and Driver* magazine I own. I got sucked into some old issues last night and couldn't put them down until I kept falling asleep and face planting into the pages.

I shove the box under my bed and stir together my morning pick me up. A few teaspoons of freeze dried granules, cream, and sugar. *Voila.* A perfectly crappy cup of coffee.

I plop on the edge of my bed and gaze around my small but cozy home: four walls, one window, and one door. The doors to my bathroom and closet are nothing more than shower curtains on rods. Not my first choice, but the rent is cheap, and it's close to work—like right above it.

Work. I check the time.

"Twenty minutes? Plenty of time."

After sipping my coffee, I strip out of my PJ's and jump in the shower. The heat from the shower combined with the caffeine help to chase away the last of my drowsiness.

Wrapped in a towel, I open the top drawer of my dresser and gaze at my bra and panty collection. "Good morning, my pretties."

It's my little addiction. Over fifty percent of my paycheck goes toward my balance at Victoria's Secret. Vivid memories of my mom folding her laundry flicker before my eyes. Yes, her lingerie was appealing, but the reason why she—no. I shake the memories loose. Not going there.

My eyes scan each perfectly matching set. What color do I feel like today?

"How about you?" I grab the purple satin and lace duo and slide them on. Something about wearing beautifully sexy stuff under my uniform always brings a smile to my face.

With a quick dry of my hair, I pile it on top of my head. Throwing on a tank top, I slide my blue uniform coveralls up over my hips, tying the long sleeves around my waist. A swipe of mascara and a couple passes of cherry Chapstick and my look is complete.

Keys in hand, along with a small can of cat food, I'm out the door. Hopping down the stairs to the alley, I scrunch up my nose at the smell of rot and debris from the dumpsters.

"Good morning, Dog." In a crouch, I pet the black alley cat that showed up at my door months ago.

"You hungry?" I pop the lid and place the can of food on the bottom stair, smiling at his answering meow. Dog scarfs it down, as he does every morning, and I rub behind his ears.

"I still can't believe you like it out here." I won't try to take him inside. Last time he clawed my arms until they were bloody. Whatever terrible thing happened to him ruined him for others. I can relate.

"I've got to go to work. I'll see you tonight."

Leaving Dog to his breakfast, I round the corner of the building to face the garage front by the bay doors. Through the window, I see Guy sitting at his desk with a grim look on his face. Not unusual for him.

I throw open the door, hearing the bell jingle above head and getting Guy's attention.

"Mornin', Ray."

"Good morning, Guy. How was your night?"

"Shit! Got sucked into some stupid show about a bachelor and some bimbos who were all trying to get his rose. Those girls were pathetic. And drunk!"

I giggle at Guy's retelling the episode of The Bachelor, one of the few shows I get on my tiny television.

"Watched that stupid show for an hour, and that sorry sack still couldn't make up his mind."

"That's what happens when you give a guy a choice out of twenty-five beautiful women. Why choose one when he could have them all?" I shrug and grab the schedule for today from his desk.

"Them all? Hell, I couldn't stand to listen to just one of them talk for more than five minutes. They're irritatin'."

I didn't have the heart to remind him that he did, in fact, watch the entire hour-long show. How irritating could they have been?

He points to the schedule in my hand. "You got a couple oil changes waiting for you in the bay. You do what you can. I got Leo comin' in to close."

"No Mickey today?"

"Nah, he's got some shit going on at home he needs to deal with."

I throw my backpack into a locker.

"That's too bad. I hope everything's okay."

"Oh, he'll be fine. Little shit always works through stuff. Even when we were kids, our mom always said Mickey could shine his way out of shit storm. Anyway, better for you to work solo since you'll be taking over the place someday." He gives me a wink and goes back to the papers on his desk.

Butterflies dance in my stomach when I think about owning this garage. Guy has no children, and he's the closest thing I have to a father. He and his brother Mickey took over Guy's Garage from Guy senior when he got sick. Mickey's kids have fancy city jobs and want nothing to do with this place, so they've asked me to take it when they retire.

"I'll be in the bay if you need me," I call over my shoulder while heading out.

I take a deep breath, allowing the smell of gasoline and oil to soothe me. The garage has always been my sanctuary. I plug in the boom box and hear Stevie Wonder's "Superstition" fill the silence.

Lost in my work, buried under the hood of a '99 Ford Explorer, the rumble of a powerful engine draws my attention. A deep bass beat accompanies the engine's growl as it pulls up to the bay. I attempt to figure out what kind of car it is just by listening, one of my favorite games. My guess is a large—no, a very large—pickup truck. American made.

I hear rather than see Guy head out to greet the truck's driver. The engine and bass go quiet, and I faintly make out a deep voice. The low vibration sends a tingle down my body and goose bumps race across my skin. *What in the heck was that?*

I check my forehead. *No fever. Hm.*

"Ray! Ray, get out here!" Guy's beckoning call yanks me from my thoughts.

I grab a towel to wipe my hands.

"Ray! Now!"

Jeesh, he's impatient.

Walking through the bay doors into the Las Vegas sun, my eyes adjust to the bright light.

A monstrous, black, Ford FX4 pickup looms out front. *Ah-ha! I was right.* It's a twin turbo, kitted out with thirty-five inch wheels, black rims, and a six-inch lift. The limo-tinted windows and black headlights make it look alive. Whoever drives this beast has a passion I can relate to. My gaze swings to the truck's owner to commend his choice in automobile.

"Nice Ford—" I'm frozen, feet glued to the asphalt, voice stuck in my throat, and gawking at the Universal Fighting League's local-celebrity-hot-guy, Jonah Slade. *At my work!*

He's well over six feet tall, six-five if I had to guess. A jersey-like, sleeveless shirt hangs artfully from his broad shoulders. His well-muscled arms are covered with brilliantly colored tattoos that beckon to be touched. My fingers itch to trace each swirl, to touch him to see if he's real.

He clears his throat, making me lift my gaze to his face while continuing my appraisal. He's wearing a black baseball hat backwards with dark, almost black hair peeking out around his ears. His strong, square jaw frames the fullest, most sensual pair of lips I've ever seen on a man.

"Ray, this is Jonah Slade."

Yeah, no kidding.

My head tilts to the side at Guy's voice, but I'm physically incapable of taking my eyes off the man, no, the god, in front of me. I've seen him on posters and billboards all over town, but they don't compare to the breath-robbing, live version.

"He has an old Chevy he needs help fixing up. I told him you'd be up for the job."

I hear the smile in Guy's voice, but still can't move my eyes to look at him. Car. He said something about fixing up a car.

Pushing through my shock, I reach for my sanity. "What kind of—" My words break on a squeak. This is embarrassing. I clear my throat. "Car? What kind?" That sounds slightly better. I can—*Oh my gosh!*

Jonah Slade is smiling.

Framing his perfect straight teeth and his luscious full lips are two *freakin'* dimples. Sanity gone, fan-girl lust-buckets owning and operating my mind, I bite back an audible swoon.

He crosses his muscular arms across his broad chest, still smiling. "Ray? You're, Ray?"

He said my name. My cheeks heat.

"Raven. My name is Raven. Guy calls me Ray." My voice sounds weak and irritatingly pathetic. I try to sound more confident. "I guess it makes him feel better about having a girl working in his garage if he gives her a man's name." I study my feet and kick a pebble that isn't there.

"Raven. Great name." The compliment is said under his breath, almost to himself. "It's nice to meet you."

He's continues to smile. If he doesn't stop that soon, I'm never going to be able to concentrate on not making a fool out of myself. *More than I already have.*

His arm extends to shake my hand. I look at it like it's a live scorpion. Guy nudges me with his shoulder and motions for me to shake. I wipe my palm on my coveralls, hoping he thinks it's grease I'm removing, rather than my nervous sweat.

His large hand swallows mine in a firm handshake, the simplest gesture communicating strength and reliability. My shoulders relax, and I fall into the safety of the feeling. Static electricity buzzes between us. His thumb moves over my skin in the tiniest caress. *Or did I imagine that?*

I'm captivated. I'm unable to see his eyes behind his dark glasses, but I feel them boring into mine.

Without warning, his smile falls, and his eyebrows lower behind his shades. Oh, no. A simple handshake has now turned into holding hands. He thinks I'm weird. I pull back from his grip.

"You, um, have some grease on your…" He motions to his own forehead. "Here, I'll…" His hand moves toward my face. I lean back, but keep my feet firmly planted as he swipes his thumb across my forehead: once, twice, three times, leaving a trail of fire in its wake.

"Oh, yeah. I shivered earlier and…" I wipe my head, deciding not to disclose the fact that his voice made me feverish.

I peek at Guy from the corner of my eye and watch the corners of his mouth twitch. Glad someone thinks my embarrassment is funny.

"Your car …er …what—"

"Jonah here is restoring a '61 Impala." Guy shows me mercy and saves me from making things more awkward.

"That's great. Old Chevys are my specialty." I could dance with joy at my ability to speak in full sentences. "You want to bring it by?"

"Actually, I…" His voice cracks. With a fist, he taps his chest and clears his throat. "Sorry, what I mean is I was hoping you might be able to work on it at my house."

My eyebrows hit my hairline, my jaw loose and swaying in the breeze.

"I have a decent garage that has all the tools you should need." He must've read confusion on my face rather than the earth-shattering shock I'm feeling.

Guy nods with a Cheshire-cat smile.

"The thing is it isn't in running condition yet, and Guy said you get pretty busy around here. I don't live far. Come by and check it out tomorrow. I could really use your trained eye to tell me what parts I need."

My mouth hangs open.

Guy coughs away a laugh. "Sure, she can do that." He looks back and forth between Jonah and me, his lips rolled between his teeth. *What is so freakin' funny?*

"Okay. What time?"

He gives me the address to his house, and we agree to start at nine-thirty tomorrow morning.

I'm going to be fixing up a car with Jonah "The Assassin" Slade.

What have I gotten myself into?

TWO

RAVEN

"Jonah freakin' Slade? Are you shittin' me, Rave?"

I sip my overpriced cup of coffee to hide my smile. I decided rather than call Eve after work yesterday I'd wait for our coffee date this morning to tell her in person. I'm glad I did. The look on her face reminds me of a balloon that's inflated past capacity. She's about to burst.

"You and 'The Assassin'? Working together at his house? Like, alone?" Eve rattles off her list of questions, her last word ending on a squeal. I keep quiet. If I know Eve, she's only getting started.

"The tabloids call him The Las Vegas Casanova. He's a total skirt chaser. Oh my gosh!" She slams both her palms on the table, getting the attention of everyone in the small coffee shop. "He's totally going to hit on you. This is so exciting. I'm seriously going to pee my pants."

"Please don't." I try to keep my voice level but lose the battle as Eve's exuberance brings out my own.

She casually leans back in her chair while a wicked smile cuts into her perfectly made-up face. "Rave, you may be handing over your V-card by the end of the day." She flips her straight, long blond hair. "I think UFL actually stands for the Universal Fu—"

"Eve!" My eyes dart around the room. I'm hoping no one can hear my very loud, equally tacky friend.

She shrugs her shoulders, a smile splitting her face. "What? I'm just saying…" Her eyebrows bounce beneath her perfect bangs.

"Oh, stop it. He's like my boss or something."

"Or something," she mumbles through a chuckle.

Evil butterflies churn in my chest at the thought of being touched by Jonah again. A simple handshake had me drooling like a dog in heat. A kiss would probably send me into a seizure.

"It's no big deal. He's just a guy who needs help with a renovation." Now if I could just get myself to believe that.

My mind has been in a permanent state of shock since Jonah left the garage. I went through the rest of my day on autopilot as I tried to come to terms with what I'd agreed to do. I'm a bunny rabbit who's stumbled into a bear cave.

"No big deal? No big deal!" I'm in for it now. Her voice gets uncharacteristically serious. "You're going to be working side by side with Las Vegas' most eligible bad boy. He's been linked with every actress, model, and showgirl in town. And you are superduper hot, girl. 'The Assassin' is going to take notice of you."

"But like you said, he has every woman in Vegas at his fingertips." Jealousy flares in my gut at the thought of Jonah with a woman. "I bet he doesn't even notice women who aren't wearing miniskirts and six-inch heels." Beautiful, glamorous women whom any man would be proud to have on his arm. I take in my current wardrobe: nothing beautiful or glamorous here. Working on cars all day doesn't exactly call for anything other than denim and cotton.

"Just make sure he pays you." Eve's demand takes me from my self-pitying thoughts. "He can certainly afford to. No more working for free."

"I don't work for free." My words are laced with the acid of my envy.

Eve's eyes get soft. She leans across the table. "You know what I'm talking about. What about that guy who couldn't pay you to fix his alternator? Or the lady who couldn't pay you to rotate her tires and change her oil? Hmm?"

I roll my eyes and blow an errant hair from my face. "They didn't pay me money. They traded. The guy gave me my tattoo as payment, and that lady was a single mom." I play with the fraying threads on my jeans. "She gave me that chair in my apartment."

"I swear, Rave, you're good through and through. Not a bit of bad in that sweet ass of yours." She takes a sip of her drink. "Maybe you can pull out a little naughty for 'The Assassin.' Work out some kind of trade for your *services*." She waggles her eyebrows.

I suck in a breath on reflex. I know she's kidding, but the joke hits too close to home. I thought moving out of my mom's house would distance me from her line of work, but, apparently, geographical distance doesn't equal emotional distance. She reads my expression and mouths a quick *sorry*. I wave her off and smile. It's not her fault I'm damaged.

"So what time is 'The Assassin' expecting you? Wouldn't want to leave a hot piece like him waiting." She moans and rolls her eyes back in her head. "He's so sexy."

"Stop calling him 'The Assassin.' It's Jonah or Mr. Slade to you," I tease, kind of, and then slurp down the rest of my coffee. "I better get going. I told him I'd be there at nine-thirty." My stomach flips as my own words sink in.

"You better call me as soon as you're done." She flashes an evil grin and a wink. "And I want details."

JONAH

"You heard me, Blake. I'm not saying it again." I pinch the bridge of my nose, praying for patience.

"So, let me get this straight. You're cleaning your kitchen because a girl is coming over. Like a real one, over to *your* house. Is that correct?" His Perry Mason tone has me grinding my teeth.

"Yeah, bitch. Except it's not *a girl.* It's a mechanic who happens to be female." Why I'm even wasting my time to explain is beyond me. I remind myself to never answer phone calls from Blake again.

"Potato fucking poe-tah-toe. God, you're testy. Are you on the rag? I tell you what, grab a Midol and a brownie and call me in five to seven days." He's laughing at his own joke.

"Moron." I shut the dishwasher door and hit start.

"I'm just stating the facts. You never have chicks over. It's weird."

"News flash, pickle dick. The person who decorated my house was a girl. My cleaning *lady,* also a girl. This is no different."

"Then why are you cleaning your kitchen?"

Because this is different. And the reason why it's different kept me up all night. Every time I closed my eyes all I could see was her face. I would have brushed it off as a simple case of the I-wanna-screw-yous, but if that were true, I'd be picturing some other part of her anatomy. Not her face. Or the aquamarine color of her eyes, so unique, I had to fight from getting lost in them. Not the way she chewed on her bottom lip when she was thinking. And certainly not the way her cheeks turned pink when I touched her.

"I'm cleaning my kitchen because it's dirty." I wipe down the counters for the second time.

"Did my knee to the head do this to you? You got some kind of brain damage that turns you into a pussy?"

"You're hilarious, you know that?" Sarcasm laces my voice.

"I'm glad you think so."

I shake my head. "I've got to go. See you at training."

"All right. Let me know how your date goes."

"You never quit."

"That's what she said." His laughter sounds through the earpiece and I end the call.

I shove my phone in my back pocket and head to the living room for a last once-over.

This is ridiculous. I haven't gotten all stirred up over a girl since Samantha Salazar in the fourth grade. I did everything to get that girl to like me. Even changed the way I dressed, only to find out later that she was looking for someone to do her math homework. And I did for an entire school year before I figured it out.

That's the thing about women. They know what they want, and they use their pretty faces and hourglass figures to get men googlie-eyed and panting. Then they shred them of their pride, time, and bank accounts. I've seen it happen a million times, and I'll be damned if I allow that to happen to me.

Raven's probably no different. She practically radiates innocence and vulnerability. It's an act, I'm sure. A girl who looks like her can't be all that innocent. Just because she acts like no girl I've ever known before doesn't mean that she's not the worst of them.

Shit. Why did I invite her to my house? That certainly wasn't the plan when I went to the garage. I thought I'd have the Impala towed there and it would sit until Guy got around to it.

Then I saw her: The way she walked out of the garage all rolling hips and sex. Her coveralls tied at her waist, and tight tank top that hugged her delicious curves. I had to cross my arms over my chest to keep from reaching out to trace the dip of her collarbone. A groan rumbles in my chest at the memory.

She makes being a car mechanic sexy. Hell, she'd make collecting garbage sexy.

Her silky, dark hair was pulled up to expose her gracefully long neck. Every time she turned to look at Guy, I could see the hint of a black tattoo where her neck flared into her shoulder. The urge to run my tongue along the gentle slope of her throat, to feel her fluttering pulse beneath my lips and taste her olive skin overwhelmed me.

Yeah, this girl's trouble.

I need to work her out of my system, just like all the other girls I've been with. After sex, I'm done. I totally lose interest. I may have to find a new mechanic, but at least I won't lie in bed every night having fantasies about getting to know her better. *Wait, what? Getting to know her better?* I don't think I've ever fantasized about a woman completely clothed before.

Holy shit, Blake was right. I've turned into a pussy.

I'm shoved from my thoughts by the sound of music blaring. Is that …Johnny Cash?

I creep to the door and check through the side panel window. A jet-black Chevy Nova with a white ragtop and white-wall tires stops in the circle drive right in front of the door. Sweet ride. *Sweeter driver.* Time for my game face.

Raven sits, gripping her steering wheel. Her mouth hangs open as she stares at my house. One side of my mouth lifts into a smile. She likes my place. A rush of warmth engulfs my chest. *What in the hell is the matter with me?*

Minutes pass before she moves out of her car. She leans into her still-open door. I rake my eyes over the contours of her perfectly round ass. She's wearing hip hugging, low slung jeans with a rip in the knee and a bright blue tank top. I smirk when my eyes land on her shoes: black, low-top Chucks.

She's sexy in a way that lacks self-awareness, which only makes her sexier. Women in this town are overly aware of themselves. I know there are exceptions. But what are the chances that an exception who looks like a rule is about to push through my walls? *Walls? I mean, house. Dammit.*

She walks toward the door in a fluid way, as if her joints have been oiled. It's the same way girls walk when they know they're being admired. But Raven does it with no one around. Is it possible that she has no agenda? A slight breeze blows her long dark hair, and, at the moment, I feel like the dorky math nerd admiring the high school cheerleader from afar.

With my thoughts on her along with my eyes, I reach for the door. I pull it open. She jumps back with a squeak, her arm raised to knock.

"Wow, sorry about that," I say lamely. "I didn't know you were here. I was just going to check the mail." I make a show of opening the mailbox.

"Oh, no problem." She actually looks embarrassed, which is funny considering the ass I just made of myself.

"Did you find the place okay?" I hold open the door and motion for her to come in.

She lowers her head in an attempt to hide her face with her hair. She doesn't move fast enough, and I see a faint blush kiss her cheeks as she moves past me. The same blush that had me tenting my boxers all night.

"Yes, thank you." Her eyes go wide as we walk into the living room. "Oh, Jonah, your home is beautiful."

My pulse quickens at the breathy way she said my name.

Her head tilts as she peeks around the corner into the kitchen. "Looks like fighting pays well."

Ah-ha! There it is.

"You know who I am." Not a question.

"Of course, I do." Her eyes roll to the ceiling then fix on mine. "You're 'The Assassin'." She says my fighting name in an exaggerated announcer's voice.

Girls don't usually tease me. And they hardly ever look me in the eye. I try hard not to smile, but her easygoing nature is infectious.

"You're a local hero."

My nose wrinkles at her overestimation of my status. "I don't know about hero." My lips turn up in a half smile. "Wouldn't I need a cape for that?"

A cape? Smooth. This girl makes me feel like a love-sick schoolboy without even trying.

She quirks her lips and narrows her eyes in a way most women reserve for the bedroom. "Well, this is Las Vegas, Jonah."

God, my name sounds good on her lips.

"In the City of Sin, we can use all the good guys we can get, cape or not."

She obviously doesn't know my reputation. Many names have shadowed Jonah Slade, but good guy isn't one of them. Usually I would think she was just trying to flatter me, but there's a sincerity in her eyes that steals my breath.

I stare into their blue-green depths. Her thick dark lashes flutter before her gaze drops to my lips. I swallow hard, resisting the urge to show her exactly what I could do to her with my mouth. Blood races in my veins, shooting south with a vengeance.

"Is everything okay?"

No, everything is absolutely not okay.

"Yeah, of course." I force myself to turn away from her piercing gaze. One more second locked in those eyes would have me worshipping at her feet, begging for just the tiniest taste of her perfect mouth.

I need to pull my shit together, and fast.

As much as my body craves her, I can't seduce this girl. Sleeping with her will no doubt work her out of my system. But she'll most likely get clingy and annoying like all the others. Something deep down whispers that wouldn't be such a bad thing. Having a girl like this begging at my door might be fun. I shake off the visual of Raven's begging on her knees...

The resulting groan has Raven's narrowed eyes on mine. No, I can do this. She's here to help me restore my car. Surely I can handle being around her without throwing her to the floor and ravishing every inch of her beautiful body. Or at least, that's what I tell myself.

—

RAVEN

"How about a tour?"

Yes, please. Anything to distract me from his eyes. They're hazel, but not like any hazel I've ever seen. The brown is so light I can make out shards of deep green toward the pupils. The dramatic contrast makes it hard not to stare. "That'd be great."

It's taking everything I've got to keep my voice level and my hands from shaking. Even my grin feels off. My only hope is that he's used to people being nervous around him and doesn't notice that I'm about to jump out of my skin.

While he gives me a guided tour of his home, I take an unguided tour of his body. As extraordinary as his house is, my gaze is repeatedly drawn back to him. His towering frame is even taller than I remember. His thick arms are round in all the right places: t-shirt sleeves pulled taut around his biceps. As if it were sculpted from marble, his body is all muscle cuts and hard edges. His smooth sun-tanned skin is without blemish, except for the glorious bursts of colors that coat his arms from his wrists to beneath his shirt. I wonder how far they go? Over the bulk of his shoulders to his corded back to—

"Raven?" The sound of my name pulls my attention.

"Hmm?"

He's standing at a huge sliding glass door, smiling as if he's in on a joke I missed. "I lost you for a minute. Am I that boring?" His rugged physique is all man, but his boyish dimples and bright smile make my head swim.

"What? Oh, no, it's just I've never been in a house this big before." I make a show of casting my eyes to the rafters. *Wow, this place is huge.* I should have paid more attention. "It's a lot to take in."

A tiny grimace touches his face for a moment before it disappears. What did I say? I'm grateful to see his easy grin return.

"Oh, well then, let's get to the best part." He holds his hand out for me to take. "Shall we?"

I stare at it before my own lifts from my side. And like the bug that flies helplessly, drawn by the bright blue light that is Jonah Slade, I place my hand into his.

Not giving me a moment to soak in the contact, he turns and walks out the door. I'm not used to being touched, especially by someone like him, and it takes me a second to find my legs. I stumble once, thankful to catch myself before he notices.

We pass through his huge backyard. I see a pool in my peripheral vision. I would look directly at it, but I'm unable to drag my eyes away from our clasped hands. His hand is huge. Mine seems so small in comparison. His touch is strong and gentle at the same time. He could crush my bones with a flex of his fingers, but there's a security in his hold that feels safe. I'm smiling like an idiot. *Great.*

We stop at a large building off to the side of his house.

"Here we are." He swings open the door and leads me in.

There's no light, but the smell has my eyes roaming the dark. He drops my hand. I pout at the loss of his touch until he flicks on the lights.

I suck air on a quick gasp. "Oh my goodness, Jonah."

THREE

RAVEN

My mouth hangs open. I breathe in deep. The familiar smells of gasoline, oil, and rubber calm my nervous stomach. I'm in my sanctuary.

Jonah's garage looks like something out of *Car and Driver* magazine: The diamond-plated chrome and black metal cabinetry polished to a shine. Rows upon rows of drawers in different widths probably hold every tool imaginable. The floors are covered in a slick, gray coating that is so clean I could eat off it. He wasn't kidding when he said I'd have all the tools I need. There's even a BendPak hydraulic car lift.

"This is amazing," I whisper to myself, feeling completely relaxed and at ease. "Why do you have all this stuff?" My eyes continue to take in the surroundings.

"Hobby. I like fast cars, like to fuck around in here. Problem is I don't have time to learn the ins and outs."

"I could teach you." The words fly on a knee-jerk reaction. I scrunch up my face and sink into my shoulders, fighting my chagrin. I glance over my shoulder and find him staring at me.

His answering grin sends my gaze across the garage. I can't look at him when he's smiling at me like that.

It's then that I notice the truck he drove to the shop yesterday. I take a closer look. Walking around it, I study each component from the Pro Comp forty-inch tires to the RBP custom grille. I swear the thing looks like it'll growl.

Stepping deeper into what's at least a ten car garage, I see a gunmetal gray beast that makes my heart rate kick double time.

"That's a '68 Camaro." I tell the car. Jonah steps to my side from behind me.

Shoving his hands in his pockets, he nods. "I didn't fix her up. Bought her from a guy in Arizona."

I walk around, trailing my finger along her flawless gray paint. "What's she running?"

He doesn't answer right away, and his eyes are dark in a way that I feel deep in my belly. "572 big block."

I whistle low. "That's freaking spectacular." I'd do almost anything to get under the hood and fire this baby up. I bet she roars like—

Something sinister demands my attention. My arm shoots towards it, my finger pointing in accusation. "Harley Blackline!" My voice echoes through the space, allowing me to hear the embarrassing high pitch of my outburst. I'd care if I weren't so utterly beside myself with Jonah's collection.

"You into bikes too?"

"I'm into Harleys. I don't know how to ride them, but the power behind these babies deserves anyone's admiration."

He chuckles and shoves his hands in his pockets. "I'll take you for a ride sometime."

Go for a ride on the back of a Harley with Jonah Slade? His magnificent body between my knees, hands resting against his six-pack abs?

Yes, please. "Okay."

He hits me with his megawatt smile that has me fighting to breathe. "Come on. The Impala's over here."

I follow behind Jonah, my eyes firmly planted on the way his jeans move with every stride of his long legs as he leads me to the back of the garage. He stops and I almost slam into his back.

I step around him and there she is: the '61 Impala. Her classic blue paint still shimmers in places, like an old woman who insists on wearing her red lipstick. This old girl isn't going down without a fight. I study every inch of her frame, and assess how much work needs to be done. There's surprisingly very little bodywork outside of a couple rust spots and a dent.

"Oh, Jonah, she's beautiful." I check out the wheel wells, notice the window rubbers all need to be replaced, and make a note to order new taillight covers.

I pop the hood and lean in to take a peek. The engine needs new motor mounts, all new belts, and a good cleaning. It could be replaced with something bigger, but this isn't a muscle car. This car is for cruising. I need to take it apart piece by piece to see what can be salvaged and rebuilt. A moan from behind me cuts through my thoughts.

With a twist, I squint over my shoulder at Jonah standing a few feet from my back. My position, bent beneath the hood and reaching into the back, has my bottom out and up and right in Jonah's line of sight. His eyes are firmly planted and my face ignites.

With a speed I didn't know I was capable of, I straighten up and look to the floor, hoping to hide my embarrassment. Being in this place, my mind focused on the project, I almost forgot he was there. Almost.

"Sorry, I um…" I have no words. The heat from my cheeks crawls down my neck.

"Do you like rap?" He turns to nearby countertop.

"Huh?"

"Music." Jonah plugs his iPod to a space-age-looking dock and hip-hop beats fill the room.

I nod to his back. I'm not a rap music fan, but, at this point, I'd agree to anything that takes the focus off of me.

"Come over here and I'll show you where everything's at."

I exhale a breath. Thank goodness he didn't make that more awkward than it was.

After a short guide to his available tools, we get to work. I get into a zone and concentrate on the build. He asks questions, eager to learn the process. We talk about our jobs and friends, falling into comfortable conversation.

A few hours into breaking down the engine, we take a break. Jonah grabs a bottled water for me from the mini fridge. Its diamond-plated chrome covering matches the cabinetry. Fanciest garage I've ever been in, no doubt.

I work to unscrew the cap from my water. "So let me get this straight. You've been working out every day, letting your friends kick your butt, and taking any fight you can get, all for a big ugly belt?" I attempt to summarize the UFL 101 lesson Jonah gave me.

His eyes go wide and his mouth drops open. "They don't kick my butt."

Laughing at his defense, I struggle with the welded-shut water bottle.

He motions for me to hand him my water. "Here, let me."

Unscrewing the stubborn thing with ease, he hands it back.

"I loosened it for you." I drink deeply, hoping the cool water will quell my pounding pulse.

"Of course, you did."

"Okay, but really, the belt is ugly. What do you do with it once you get it? Do you, I don't know, wear it out to dinner or around the house? Do you, like, model it for your billboard ads?" Judging by the faint pink coloring Jonah's face at the mention of his ads, I bet he gets teased often.

"Maybe a black and white layout of you and your belt on a sandy beach for, say, a protein shake billboard?" Sucking both my lips between my teeth to hide my smile, I watch in fascination a shy Jonah. He recovers quickly and narrows his eyes on me. I'd worry that I'd offended him if it weren't for the humor lighting his face.

"Ha, ha, ha. Very funny," he drawls.

"What? You do *model,* don't you?" I tease doing my best Derek Zoolander face.

Exhaling, he throws his hand in his hair and drops his chin. Bringing his head back up, his eyes lock with mine. "Yes. I have sponsors that I've *modeled* for. Happy?"

I'm still smiling.

"You think that's funny, huh?"

"Well, yeah, I do. Don't get me wrong. It's not the modeling I think is funny. It's the look on your face when I talk about you modeling that's funny."

Tilting his head, I see something working behind his eyes. Then, to my surprise, he dips his finger in black grease and swipes my cheek. "There. You think that's funny?"

I stare silently, glaring in his direction. I snag the tin of grease, dip four fingers into it, and hold them up. "You're going down, Slade"

I lunge at him and make a swipe on his neck. My instincts tell me to be careful, reminding me that this is a trained fighter and that I'm a lanky, twenty-year-old girl. But a comfort that defies explanation has me trusting him.

Dipping both sets of fingers into the grease, he gives me a look that says I better run or else. I turn to bolt just as I feel two strong hands wrap around my biceps from behind. With a girlish squeal, I'm pulled, my back forced to the firm heat of his chest. I swallow a moan that almost escapes my lips at the feeling of his hard body pressed to the length of mine. His strong hands grasp my arms, rubbing the oil with one long stroke from elbow to shoulder, and igniting the blood beneath my skin.

"You're going to have to tap out. No way you're going to win this one." His words are spoken into my ear, making me shiver and practically sag in his arms.

"Oh yeah?" My question sounds weak in my own ears. *Darn it.*

"Mmm-hmm." The vibration of his low voice rumbles against my back.

If I don't get out of this hold soon, I may end up doing something stupid like rub up against him and purr.

I twist hard and he releases me. Darting around the Impala, back to the grease tin, I lather my hands up with ammo and slink towards him, hands held forward in warning.

He crooks his finger at me and lifts an eyebrow. I lunge again.

We chase and dodge, while laughing and throwing threats at each other, until we're out of grease and forced to call a truce. Our clothes and skin are covered in the oily evidence of our horseplay. Against a wall, I slide down to sit and catch my breath. He tosses me a stack of shop towels and goes to work cleaning off his neck and face.

"Okay, all fun aside, whose booty do you have to kick to get this belt?" I wipe grease from my shoulder.

He sits next to me, cleaning the muck from his fingers. "Victor Del Toro. He's the current heavyweight champion. No one's been able to knock him off the throne—until now, of course." The confidence in his voice makes it a statement of fact rather than a prediction.

"Hm. Well, good luck." A quick glance has me locked in his stare, fiery hazel pulling me in. "Not that you'll need it."

His eyes roam my face and neck. My defenses try to push my gaze to the floor, but I'm captivated by his allure. Awareness, like a silent confession, passes between us igniting my blood. I suck in air and roll my bottom lip between my teeth to avoid saying something I'll regret like *kiss me.*

A slow grin pulls at his mouth, his eyes sparkling. "You should come to the fight."

The way he's looking at me wakes the butterflies in my stomach. Come to the fight? I'd say yes to anything he asks. "Sure, yeah."

He's still staring, but his smile grows, his dimples forming bookends to his radiant smile. "It's September fourteenth at—"

"Shut. Up." My powerful response surprises even me.

"What? Why?" He's genuinely confused which only endears me to him more.

"Oh, no, I just mean ...shut up ...like ...no way ...My twenty-first birthday is September fifteenth."

"Wow, twenty-first. That's a big one. I remember my twenty-first." His eyes search the rafters, concentrating. "Actually, I don't." Shrugging one shoulder, he smirks. "I heard it was great though." He runs a hand through his hair with a shy grimace that I find completely sexy.

I fold the greasy shop towel. "How long ago was your twenty-first?"

His eyes narrow on mine. "Raven, are you trying to ask me how old I am?"

Heat warms my neck, rising up to color my cheeks.

"Five years ago. I'm twenty-six." Comfortable silence fills the air. "Anyway, you should come to the fight. I'll get you a ticket. Call it an early birthday present."

"I'd love that. Thanks."

———

JONAH

Thirty minutes with the heavy bag didn't make a dent in my attempt to exorcise Raven from my head. I thought for sure that spending time with her this morning would work in my favor. Figured if I got to know her better, I'd realize she's just like other girls. I was wrong.

From the moment she walked into my house to the moment she walked out, she held my rapt attention. Usually when women start talking I zone out, but this girl said things I wanted to hear. She talked about cars like they were family. It was captivating. If that weren't enough, working together was a breeze. We fell into easy conversation and comfortable silences, as if she were one of the guys—well, one of the guys in a supermodel package. *Damn.* What a package. Even the garage, with its twenty-foot ceilings, felt small with her in it. No matter how far away I would move, her perfect body seemed too close. Thank God I had to get to training or I'd probably fallen to my knees and begged her to have dinner with me.

This isn't good. With the title fight coming up, I can't afford any distractions. Maybe I should put the restoration on hold until after the fight. That should give me time to forget about her. Or maybe I should pull my shit together and stop acting like some teenager with perma-wood.

I can't blow her off now. I promised her tickets to my fight, and I can't go back on a promise. Comfort washes over me at the thought of looking out from the octagon on the biggest fight of my life and seeing Raven standing in my corner. This shit is not cool. I'll get one of the guys to give me a thorough ass kicking before I leave for being such a pansy.

But pansy or not, I'm drawn to her by some unseen force. Everything from my thoughts to my dick gravitates in her direction. Like getting caught in a rip tide, one minute I'm swimming, free to go in any direction, and then I feel a tug. I'm kicking and flailing my arms and legs toward shore while the invisible pull takes me in the opposite direction. No matter how hard I swim, I keep going further and further out to sea.

Yeah, that's how it is with Raven. One minute I'm free, navigating the waters of my life, and, now, I feel a tug.

"What's up, man? Where is everyone?" Rex calls as he makes his way to the mats to warm up.

"They should be here." I answer absently, still trying to pull my head out of my ass. "Yo, T-Rex. You missed a couple." I motion to my eyebrow and lip.

"Shit, man. Thanks." Rex removes the small barbell from his eyebrow and ring from his lip and places them on the bench.

I stretch my arms and roll my neck. "Where's Caleb?"

"He's here, just wrapping his ankle in the locker room." Rex motions over his shoulder where I see Caleb making his way to the mats.

"Y'all talkin' about me?" Caleb's telltale, country-boy accent echoes off the walls. Owen sneaks up behind him, and smacks the back of his head. "Ow, dick!"

Owen ignores Caleb's pained remark. "You done wrapping your ankle, sweetheart?"

Caleb rubs the back of his head.

"You guys get warmed up, and we'll break into teams for grappling." Owen's order is all business. He's one of the best coaches in MMA, and when he gets down to it, he doesn't fuck around.

"You bitches ready to get your asses handed to you?" Blake strolls toward the mats. Late.

The group grumbles and throws back a number of different taunts and insults before we pair off and take our places. This title fight is an accumulation of everything I've been working for since I started fighting. It's the single biggest accomplishment of my life. And I'll be damned if a girl is going to rob me of my goal. Never.

A few hours into training and I'm breathing deep. Sweat coats my skin, proving without question that I worked hard. I welcome the burn of my muscles and the flood of endorphins that blur the thoughts of a certain female.

Owen calls time. "Take five and we'll hit the bags."

We all grab our waters and stretch on the floor.

Caleb flops down next to me lying flat on his back. "Where are we watching the game this weekend?"

"Not my place." I swig from my water bottle.

"Jonah's it is." Owen decides for the group.

I scowl at him and contemplate sweeping his legs. "The fuck you say?"

He shrugs in my direction.

Blake's standing, grabbing his ankle to stretch his quad. "Sweet. I'll bring the pizza."

"I'll get the beer." Rex's voice calls out from behind me.

"Shit, no. I said *not* at my place."

Caleb nods to Rex. "Game starts at three so we should be there by two."

"Fucking assholes." It's like I'm not even here.

Rex's dumb ass looks right past me. "Don't forget, I have a show that night. Sound check's at seven. Ghost Bar. We can all head over to the club after the game."

"You guys want me to bring the Wii?" Caleb puts on his gloves, his eyes darting from dickhead to dickhead, overlooking me.

"No. No fucking Wii." What started as watching a game at my house has turned into a party, and knowing these guys, they'll stay all weekend.

"Oh come on, *Vajonah*." Blake's cocky smile makes me clench my fist. "You worried we might dirty your kitchen?" He lifts one eyebrow.

I spear him with a glare. As if one douche bag giving me shit isn't enough, I don't need the group giving me a hard time.

"All right, fine. But no pizza. I'll throw something on the grill. I can't eat that shit this close to the fight." Defeated and pissed as hell, I strap on my gloves.

"If you're going to grill, I'll bring Nikki. She can whip up some healthy shit in the kitchen and sit by the pool."

Owen's wife Nikki is a nutritionist and kicks all kinds of ass in the kitchen. That alone makes this worth it.

"Sounds like a plan. I'll bring some girls so Nik will have chicks to hang out with." The group goes still, staring at Blake. "What?"

Everyone knows the kind of girls Blake keeps company with. I'm not interested in having a bunch of jock-sniffing groupies around, and Blake travels with a fucking harem.

Owen looks at Blake, a grin pulling at his lips. "This should be interesting."

Blake glares at Owen. "That was a long time ago, man. You two weren't married yet."

"Nah, but Nikki sure didn't appreciate your bitches rubbing up on my shit." Owen laughs and shrugs.

"How can you laugh?" Blake throws his arms out to his sides. "Nik broke that chick's nose."

Owen's laughter answers Blake's question.

I cross my arms at my chest. "I don't want a house full of your knob polishers."

"Hey, a player needs lovin' too."

"No more than two, Blake. I'm serious," I warn.

"Yeah, I got it." He dismisses me with a wave of his hand.

He doesn't get it.

I tilt my head, feeling the side of my lip curl into a smile. "Say it, Blake. Say, 'I promise, Jonah, I won't bring more than two chicks to your barbeque'."

Blake's eyes narrow. "Are you fucking serious? I said I got it."

"Say it."

"Shit. Fine. I won't bring more than two chicks to your bar-beque." Blake's jaw is so tight I'm surprised he doesn't bust a tooth. This guy is so easy to mess with.

"You forgot, 'I promise, Jonah'."

Umpf!

My breath is knocked from my lungs as Blake tries to take me down to the mat …unsuccessfully.

FOUR

RAVEN

It's day three working on the Impala: seventeen hours and thirty-eight minutes to be exact. I keep track of the hours spent at Jonah's for my time card, not because I mark every minute with him, committing it to memory so that when my work here is done I have something to remind me of our time together.

I've got the engine out and apart. Going through it piece by piece, I set aside the things that can be salvaged while Jonah disassembles the inside. Perched at a workbench, I sort through the motor brackets.

Out of the few restorations I've done over the years, this one is by far the best: high-end tools at my disposal, clean working environment, great company …and the view. Like the one I have right now.

Jonah is lying on his back across the front seat of the car, his head underneath the dashboard. His t-shirt slid up, exposing a few inches of his firm stomach. A strip of dark hair trails from his belly button and disappears beneath his saggy jeans. His strong legs are open in a V to brace his weight against the floor.

"Ouch, gosh dang it!" I grab my bloody finger, more worried about bleeding on Jonah's stuff than the extent of my injury.

"You okay?" Jonah rises from his sexy pose and stands across the workbench from me, worry etched on his perfect face.

"Yeah, it's fine. Stupid rusty bracket." I move to stick my finger in my mouth when he grabs my hand.

"No, don't do that. Germs."

Heat rises up my neck and into my face. "Oh, you're right." I rub my forehead, hoping that I can cover my embarrassment with my free hand. "Mouths are dirty."

He lifts his gaze from my wound, but I avoid his eyes. "Not germs from your mouth. Germs from your hand. Who knows what kind of shit is living on that thing." He motions to the offending bracket. I peek up at him and watch a smile tug at his lips. "From what I can tell, you have a very clean mouth." He flashes one dimple, before his gaze drops to my lips.

I roll them together, wetting them with my tongue. My chest rises and falls in erratic bursts and heat floods my body.

"I've got something for that." The deep timbre of his voice draws me closer until I'm leaning toward him over the workbench.

I swear the man could bed any woman with one look. He releases my hand to walk to the nearby cabinets. I slump forward, bolstering myself against the tabletop to keep upright.

I'm no idiot when it comes to lust. I've seen it in men before. But I've never felt it: The burning need pushing against my chest; the building tension that coils in my belly; my blood racing in my veins, flooding my head with visions of his hands on my body. Desire fires my skin, flushing my cheeks. I look around for something to use to fan myself.

"Here ya go." His voice is right at my side, and I push back the urge to rub up against him as Dog does when I'm holding his food.

He lifts my hand sending delicious tingles down my arm. With a quick squeeze of ointment, he wraps my finger in a

Band-Aid. His hands are surprisingly gentle for their size, and I wonder how many women have felt their tenderness in better places than their hands. Thousands would be my guess. My stomach twists with painful jealousy.

"You're good at this. I guess you'd have to be in your profession."

"Yeah, I get a lot of practice." He finishes with my hand and throws out the wrappers.

I want to thank him for taking care of my wound. I've been on my own for so long I don't remember the last time someone took such care with me. The gratitude I feel for his kindness makes me want to throw myself into his arms and kiss him. *Gratitude, yeah right, that's what I'm feeling.* Instead, I change the subject.

"What got you into fighting? Were you a wrestler in high school?"

He clears his throat. "No, I started street fighting first."

With his knuckles on the workbench, he drops his head for a moment before bringing his eyes back to mine. For the first time, there's sadness there.

"My dad died when I was twelve." The words come out forced, like he's not used to the feeling of them on his lips. "I became the man of the house way before I was ready. I started getting in fights at school, getting in trouble all the time. My mom," he pauses to run both hands through his hair, "she was destroyed when my Dad died. I just made things worse."

His dark eyebrows furrow over his deep-set eyes as he looks past me.

"At fifteen, I got busted while kicking some kid's ass at a park by my house. The cop pulled me aside and said that if I didn't get my shit together I'd end up in jail. He told me I could use my anger to better my life." He shakes his head with a wistful smile. "It didn't make sense at the time." His last words are said under his breath.

He's next to me physically, but his eyes are far away. "He gave me the address of a Boys' Club, told me they taught karate, jiujitsu, boxing—stuff like that. The way I saw it, beating the shit out of people wasn't doing anything but making my mom cry. May as well take his advice."

He shrugs and his eyes meet mine, no longer troubled. He studies my face

"I'm sorry about your dad. You must really miss him." *I know the feeling.* Although, how can I miss what I never had? I banish the thought as soon as it forms.

"Yeah, he was cool. He worked hard, but found time to throw the ball with me or get down on the floor with my sister and play Barbies." His lips upturn warmly and his eyes go soft. "He was a big guy as you can imagine, so that was no small task."

My heart swells with appreciation that Jonah was able to experience a good dad, even if only for twelve years. The fact that he has good memories to carry with him is more than I could hope for. "He sounds amazing."

"He was."

"How did he die?" The question is airborne before I realize the boldness of my intrusion. I drop my gaze, immediately wanting to take it back.

Silence fills the space between us, sucking the oxygen from my lungs. I shouldn't have asked such a personal question. Knowing someone for three days hardly constitutes this type of soul exposing confession.

"I'm sorry, it's none of my—"

"Hit by a drunk driver."

I meet his gaze and almost stumble backwards at the agony in his eyes. He's not angry. He's heart broken. My eyes burn and I swallow hard.

"He was killed instantly. I was so pissed off. It seemed so unfair. I thought if I could beat the shit out of someone, make them hurt as badly as I was hurting, I'd feel better." Shaking his head, he takes a deep breath. "Didn't work."

My hands itch to soothe him with my touch, even if only to grab his hand and let him know I'm here and that I understand.

According to the local media, he's a private guy. He never exposes information about his family or personal life. Sharing that with me took a lot of courage. For all he knows, I could run out and sell his story to the papers. But he trusted me. And the best way to pay him back is to trust him in return.

"My mom moved here from Colombia with her parents when she was eight." I clear my throat. I'm nervous. I've only told this story to Eve and Guy. My palms sweat and I busy my hands picking at a shop towel. "I guess they came here for the job opportunities that Las Vegas had to offer. My grandparents were working at the MGM when a fire broke out in one of the restaurants. Back then, there were no sprinklers in that part of the casino. Eighty-five people died, including them."

"I've heard about that fire. They call it the worst disaster in Las Vegas history."

"Yeah, that's the one. My mom was fifteen. She had no family here and wasn't a legal adult so she had to go live in a group home. At eighteen she had to leave and find a job and somewhere to live." I take a deep breath as I prepare for the final blow.

"That's when she met…" I'm afraid to say his name. If Jonah knew whose blood runs through my veins, he'd probably never speak to me again. Deep down I know that our working relationship will end someday, but I'm not ready to give it up yet. "She took the first opportunity she could find."

"Oh, did she get a casino job like—"

"My mom's a prostitute." Hearing the words out loud sound so much worse than they did in my head. I drop my gaze to the floor, afraid to look up and see the disappointment—or worse, disgust—in Jonah's eyes.

Seconds pass. He's completely silent. So much for not losing his friendship.

——

JONAH

"Sorry, I didn't mean to just throw it out there like that." She laughs uncomfortably and studies the ends of her hair.

Hearing *those* words come from *this* girl? I'm in shock.

Living in Las Vegas, prostitution is fairly common. It's illegal outside of a licensed brothel, but that doesn't stop a few key players from maintaining the business. But to think that this beautiful woman, so innocent and unaffected, was raised in that world.

I shake my head. "I don't know what to say."

She waves her hand dismissively. "Don't worry about it. I understand. You probably shouldn't be associating with people like me, what with your big fight coming up." She turns away from the workbench and grabs her backpack. *Is she leaving?*

My mind scrambles for the right thing to say, but a frantic need to keep her here moves my body first.

She heads for the door and I grab her arm. "No, wait. Don't go."

She's silent, her back to me, head drooping between her shoulders.

"I didn't mean to make you feel bad or ashamed. I'm just surprised that someone as innocent and open as you could have been raised—"

"By a hooker." She tugs against my hold, but I don't let go. Her head drops even lower. "Just say it, Jonah."

Pain twists in my chest at the demoralized sound in her voice. She sat and listened to me talk about my family and share my pain, but the second she opens up, I treat her like a leper.

"Look, Raven, I'm not good at this ...relating to people and sharing. *Fuck*." I breathe deep and search for the right words to keep her from pushing me away. "I think you're amazing." Her muscles tense beneath my hand. "It doesn't matter how you were raised or who you were raised by. All that matters is who you are now."

She turns toward me, her eyebrows pinched and her mouth in a flat line.

I release her arm and shove my hands in my pockets to keep from grabbing her and kissing that look off her face. "The woman I see right now, she's something special."

Her pinched eyebrows dissolve into wide eyes, and a dazzling smile threatens to send me to my knees.

"Thank you." Her words are said in that breathy way that I want to feel against my lips.

We stand only a foot apart, lost in the intensity of what we've just shared, giving each other a little piece of ourselves. I'm balancing on the edge of something huge. I try to push back, clawing my way to solid ground, when everything in me screams to swan dive off the precipice.

My emotions swirl in a cocktail of confusion, desire warring with self-preservation. But through this, one thing is clear. There is no working this girl out of my system. From the moment she walked out of Guy's Garage, she burrowed in deep. This whole time I've been kicking and fighting against her pull. What if I just let go?

I've been avoiding this since the day I left home, not wanting to be responsible for another person's happiness and wellbeing. But locked into the aquamarine eyes of the woman in front of me, I realize I'd give up everything for the chance to take care of her.

I have a choice to make, and screwing her out of my system isn't one of them: face my fears and take a shot at a relationship or let her go. She'll go on living her life until someone worthy of her love comes along.

Oh, hell no!

My teeth clench and possessive fury twists my gut. The thought of her loving some piece of shit with her gorgeous body, some other guy's hands tangled in her hair as he devours her mouth, brings a growl from my chest.

"Do you have a boyfriend, Raven?"

"What? No!" Her response comes out fast and defensive.

Well, thank fuck for that.

My lips curl so hard my cheeks ache. Decision made.

"What are you doing tomorrow?"

She chews on her lip and looks to the floor. "Um …tomorrow is Saturday. I'm off."

I step closer—so close that I can feel the heat coming off her body. Her breath catches and I detect the unmistakable lust in her eyes. "Jonah?"

The way she says my name saturates my blood with arousal, and I fight to keep my eyes from rolling back in my head.

"Come over tomorrow. I'm having a barbeque. I want you there." My voice sounds deep and gravelly in my own ears. I'm not taking no for an answer. I can't. I want her, and now that I've stopped fighting it, I can't get her soon enough.

"Okay."

I grin at her simple answer to what wasn't a question. I cup her face then slide my hand back to fork my fingers into her hair at her nape. Her eyes flutter closed. Warmth explodes in my chest, flooding my veins and making my heart race. As much as I want to kiss her, I force myself to step back.

"Let's get back to work." I turn back to the Impala.

The tiny whimper from her gives me hope. She's just as wound up as I am. If the sexual tension is already this high, what will the sex be like?

I freeze as dread drops in my stomach, heavy and unwelcome. I've never slept with the same girl more than once. I lose interest seconds after I orgasm. What if I lose interest in Raven?

I turn to look at her over my shoulder. She's at the workbench, sorting through engine parts. Her eyes look up from beneath the canopy of her dark lashes and she gives me a shy smile.

I'm completely fucked.

FIVE

RAVEN

"Whoa, Rave, that's the one. Get that one." Eve points to the coral-colored string bikini. "That color will compliment your skin and make your eyes totally pop."

I'm grateful to have Eve with me on this last minute shopping trip. Jonah's barbeque is today. After his impromptu invite that left me grinning like an idiot, he told me to bring a bathing suit. I thought, and Eve agreed, that the possibility of swimming at a celebrity's house called for a new suit.

I pay the swanky boutique's cashier and figure I'll have to get Dog generic cat food for the next six months to make up for the money I just spent. He lives in a dumpster. He won't mind the cheap stuff.

We pop into a little coffee shop to grab a latte when my cell phone rings. I check the caller ID. Butterflies stir in my belly.

"Oh my gosh, Eve, it's him." I hold my phone out to her, thinking that she might answer it for me.

I've been working for Jonah all week, and he's never called me. *How does he know my number?* He gave me his number the day he came to the garage, and I programmed it in my phone in case I couldn't find his house. And why am I so nervous? Sweat slicks my palms, making me almost lose the hold on my phone. Or maybe that's the shaking.

Eve leans away from me, shooing the phone to my ear with a few quick flicks of her wrist. "Uh-uh, girl, we're not in grade school. Now answer your damn phone."

I step out of the ordering line and head to a table at the back of the coffee shop. I can't sit as nervous energy keeps me pacing.

With a finger pressed to my ear to drown out the chatter, I drop my head. "Hello?"

"Raven, what's up? It's Jonah."

"I know …I mean I have your number in my phone, you know, from that first day, and it came up on the—"

Eve elbows me in the ribs and shakes her head. And thank God. Who knows how long I would have rambled.

His low chuckle vibrates the phone against my ear, sending goose bumps down that side of my body. He's even sexy through the telephone. "Right. Where are you?"

"My girlfriend Eve and I are having coffee at…" I stare at the coffeehouse sign. My face heats immediately and Eve giggles. "The Bump and Grind."

He laughs again, just as low and sexy as the first, but louder. "Only in Vegas, huh?"

"Yeah, God forbid there be a Starbucks around." I roll my eyes, even though he can't see me.

"I wanted to touch base and make sure you were coming by this afternoon."

"Of course, four o'clock, right?"

"That's it. And, Raven?"

"Mm-hm?"

"Bring Eve along."

My eyes dart to Eve who is standing nearby hanging on my every word. I smile at her. "Bring Eve? Okay, sure." Her face splits into a smile, and she fist pumps the air.

"Great. See you in a few."

The phone disconnects, and Eve and I stare at each other for a few wordless seconds.

"We're going back to the boutique." Eve grabs my arm and pulls me out the door. "I need a new suit too if I'm going to meet 'The Assassin.'"

I stop walking. "Please, whatever you do, do not call him 'The Assassin' to his face. That would be so embarrassing."

She lifts one side of her glossed lips like I just gave her a fantastic idea. *Oh, great.*

"You know, there'll probably be a few single guys there tonight." I ask the silent question with my eyes.

Eve is gorgeous, and she gets plenty of attention from guys, but her taste is selective. She only dates complete jerks.

"We'll see." She shrugs. "It would take someone pretty special to turn my head at this point." A sly smile spreads across her face.

Eve has a secret. I look around before pulling her from the sidewalk to a bench.

"Who is he?" Excitement must show in my expression and Eve's face lights up.

"Oh, Rave! He's amazing. I met him at work. He came into the restaurant for dinner, and he was so sweet." She has a dreamy look that I don't see often on my cynical friend. "He asked me out and I said yes," she squeals.

"That's great. When's the date?"

"Oh, it was two weeks ago." Guilt laces her voice. "We've been hanging out almost every night since."

My brows drop low. I try to justify why my best friend has been dating a guy for two weeks and this is the first I've heard about it. We tell each other everything. Just last week Eve called me at midnight to tell me that Donny Osmond came into her restaurant and told her she had great bone structure. And for two weeks she's been keeping her mystery boyfriend from me?

This can't be good. History proves that she attracts the meanest most abusive guys Vegas has to offer: usually verbally, sometimes physically, and always emotionally. I tell myself that she doesn't know better. Growing up in that environment, she obviously sways toward her idea of normal. But surely she doesn't want the life her mom had.

I've been running in the opposite direction of my mom's life since I knew she was a prostitute. I'm a mechanic and a virgin. Can't get more opposite than that.

"I'm sorry I didn't tell you. He's really …um …private. He told me he wasn't ready for anyone to know about us. Things are getting pretty serious though, so I'm sure you'll meet him soon."

"I'm really happy for you, Eve." The hurt in my voice contradicts my words.

Her smile turns sad. "Hey, I'm sorry."

"It's fine, really."

She hops to her feet and grabs my hand. "Come on. Let's go get me that suit. Just because I'm officially off the market doesn't mean I'm not going to enjoy the view tonight. These guys work hard for their bodies." I stand and she links her arm in mine. "I intend on showing my appreciation."

A couple more hours of shopping and we head back to my house to freshen up. At three forty-five on the dot, we leave for Jonah's. I toss my backpack into Eve's car just as Guy calls to me from the open bay doors of the garage.

I pop my head in the car door. "Give me a minute? I'll go see what he wants."

I jog to Guy who's standing with Leo and Cane, two other mechanics in the shop. "Hey, guys. What's up?"

Their eyes travel from my neck to my toes and back again. They don't look happy about what they see.

"Where're you going dressed like that, Ray?" Guy motions to my halter dress bathing suit cover up.

"I'm going to a barbeque pool party thing." I hook the string of my bikini top with my thumb and hold it out. I mean, isn't it obvious. And why are they looking at me like I'm wearing raw meat?

"There gonna be dudes at this party?" Leo's protective tone isn't the least bit surprising. He's got three daughters and five granddaughters.

"Yes. There will be guys there."

Cane, the newest mechanic at the shop, laughs hard, making his big belly shake. Guy and Leo aren't laughing.

"Whose party is it? And please, don't tell me it's at one of them titty pools all the casinos are opening," Leo says, sending Cane into another fit of laughter.

"You guys, it's fine. I'm going to Jonah's."

No one is laughing. Not only are they not laughing but they're frozen. Completely still. Oh no, this can't be good.

Guy breaks the silence. "Ray, don't be a dumb shit."

"I'm not." Falling for a guy who will most likely break my heart? Maybe I am. "Er ...I'll try not to be a dumb ...um ...what you said."

The man, who has been like a father to me, must read my face. "You're wearing a dress." He makes a tsking sound and shakes his head. "Known you since you were fourteen. Ain't never seen you in a dress." Guy's probably right about that.

He was my shop teacher in high school, and I never wore dresses to school.

Oh, wait.

"What about graduation?" I put my hands on my hips to force some attitude into my declaration. "I wore a dress to graduation."

"That was a graduation gown."

Darn, that's right.

"Whatever. This isn't a dress anyway, it's a cover up." I smooth the soft fabric over my stomach. "It's new. Now, if you guys will excuse me—"

"You seriously gonna let her go?" Leo's question is directed at Guy.

"She's a grown woman."

"And he's nailed more women in Vegas than Barry Manilow."

"Ray's a smart girl. I trust her not to fuck up." Guy's eyes swing to mine. "Right, Ray?" His question reeks of warning.

I nod.

"You call us if you need anything. Don't drink booze. Say no to drugs. And whatever you do, do not take a drink from a stranger or leave your drink unattended. You gotta piss, you take your cup in the john with you." Leo's instructions are given with a firm point to my face with each one.

"Got it. Can I go now?"

They shake their heads and turn back into the garage grumbling. I practically skip back to the car with a cheek-cramping smile plastered across my face.

—

JONAH

I'm antsy as hell. I hit the gym, went for a run, worked on the Impala, and nothing seemed to help. Needing to hear her voice, I finally broke down and called her. She seemed nervous on the phone, which was something I haven't seen from her in a while. In the garage, she works with the cool confidence of a seasoned mechanic, but outside of the garage, she's shy and nervous. And both are hot as hell.

Raven is nothing like the girls I'm used to. She's not arrogant or overly aggressive. She doesn't try to mind-fuck you into submission. With her, you get what you see. No twisted facades or acts of desperation. She doesn't expect anything from me. It's refreshing. And because of that, I'm completely at ease around her.

I've known her for a week, and I'm spilling my guts about my dad like a pigtailed girl at a sleepover. The words I'd been holding in for years just poured out, and rather than making me feel weak for my admission, she gave right back.

I miss her when she's not around. I never miss women. Hell, I go months without seeing my mom and sister. Never bothers me. Raven's been away from me for twenty-four hours, and I'm going nuts, as if something valuable were missing.

When she was here yesterday, I was shocked at how quickly I gave in to the urge to touch her. We stood so close at one point our eyes locked in a lusty stare down. I was ready to explode. Then she had to go and lick her lips. I would have kissed her if I thought I'd be able to stop there. The way I was feeling, I would have taken her on the hood of the car. Mental images assault my brain, eliciting a groan from deep in my chest. She'll be here soon, and here I'm mentally fucking her on my car.

The doorbell rings, shaking me from my fantasy. She's here. I adjust my board shorts before I throw open the door to the object of my obsession. My smile falls.

Owen pushes past me with bags of what I assume is food. "Good to see you too."

"Hey, Nik." I kiss Owen's wife on the cheek.

"Jonah, how are you?" She gives me a quick hug. "Owen baby, just throw that stuff in the kitchen."

Nikki is the resident chef at all our barbeques. She knows her way around my kitchen, so I leave her to it.

Owen drops the bags then walks straight to the backyard bar. He angles his barstool to face the sixty-inch flat screen and turns on *Sportscenter.*

I join him outside, grab a beer, and settle in. Halfway through my first beer, Caleb and Rex show up. The guys argue whether the San Diego Padres will go to the World Series. Owen says it'll be the A's. I'm sure it'll be the Yankees, but I stay out of the conversation. Nikki's voice, along with a couple other female voices, cuts through the conversation.

"Jonah, your guests are here," she calls from the sliding glass door.

Her announcement silences the baseball talk as everyone turns to see who it is.

Holy fucking shit.

It's Raven.

And she's wearing a dress.

Thankful for my sunglasses, I let my eyes roam her body freely. Her dark hair is braided to the side, the thick chocolate rope lying against the swell of her breast. My gaze lingers on her cleavage, the dress accentuating her already perfect form. The flowing fabric ends well above her knees, exposing her long, toned legs.

I vaguely notice the blonde at her side. That must be Eve.

As they walk toward the bar, I can't take my eyes off Raven. She glides across the yard in that unconsciously sexy way of hers. A deep moan from one of the guys at the bar has me turning my head. They have their greedy fucking eyes locked on my girl and her friend.

My girl?

Possession flares, having me step away from the bar to meet them, effectively cutting the girls off from the ogling, lecherous dicks behind me.

"Is this a joke?"

"Didn't see this coming."

I hear the mumbled comments from the numb-nut gallery, and ball my fists to keep from flipping them off.

"Ladies, glad you could make it." I'm impressed that my voice didn't crack under the pressure.

"Hey, Jonah." Raven tilts her head, motioning to her friend. "This is my friend, Eve. Eve, this is Jonah."

"Hi, Jonah." Eve shakes my hand and peruses the backyard. "Nice digs."

"Thanks. Come on. I'll introduce you to the guys."

I direct the girls to walk ahead of me with the idea that I can place my hand on the small of Raven's back. It's a gentle way of claiming her in front of the guys. It's either that or plunge my tongue down her throat in front of everyone, and something tells me she's not quite ready for that.

She brushes past. Her delicate pear fragrance fills my lungs. I bite my lip and lust saturates my brain. My fingers burn to bury themselves in her hair and pull her to me.

I place my hand where the slope of her spine flows to her ass and nearly stumble over my feet. There, on the backdrop of her perfect olive skin, is the tattoo that has been taunting me for days. A flock of blackbirds serpentine from her shoulder, dipping below the fabric of her dress. From the scale of the tattoo, I'd say the birds start at her hip.

The view evokes images of her laid out naked before me. Running my tongue along my lip, I imagine what it would taste like to kiss her from one end of her tattoo to the other. To feel her skin, warm, soft and sweet against my lips. I'm already hard as a rock, and I haven't even seen her in her bikini yet. I go over baseball stats, trying to ease my raging need.

"This is my friend Owen." Raven rakes her sunglasses up on her head. "The pierced one is Rex, and the one who looks like he just jumped off a tractor in Idaho is Caleb." She nods through the introductions. "Guys, this is Raven and her friend, Eve."

I watch closely as my friends size up the girls. It's not wasted on me that they seem to find the two women attractive. But they linger a little too long on Raven's eyes.

"Damn, girl. You got some wicked peepers." Owen's observation has the rest of the guys agreeing in grumbled affirmations.

A familiar blush lights her cheeks. "Thank you. It's nice to finally meet you guys."

"Finally?" Rex's shit-eating grin tugs at his lip ring. "How long have you and Jonah been hanging out?"

Raven's attention slides to me, her eyes wide. "Oh, we're not hanging out …er …we work—"

"What would you girls like to drink?" I redirect the conversation and smile at the relief I catch in Raven's expression. Why does it feel as if we're hiding some deep, dark secret?

"Water would be great," Raven answers and Eve nods.

"You girls up for baseball?" Most girls wouldn't be interested in the game, but, then again, most girls aren't car mechanics.

"Baseball?" Raven scrunches up her nose and shakes her head. *So damn cute.*

I motion to the loungers set up poolside. "Would you rather get some sun?"

She studies the double lounger and looks at Eve. They both smile big. "Yes, please."

I set them up with towels and a lounger, placing them close enough so that I can admire Raven, and go back and forth from them to the game easily.

With a fresh beer in hand, I relax against the bar and settle in for the game. So far so good. I have a girl, *a date*, over at my house. The guys are being semi-respectful. The girls are laughing and talking comfortably. What could possibly go wrong?

"Let's get this party started, motherfuckers!"

Oh, shit. Blake.

SIX

JONAH

My glare sharpens toward the sound of his voice, and it takes everything I have not to punch something.

"Fuck me," I whisper to the floor.

Blake isn't alone. He has *three* girls with him. Two of them I've seen before. One is the red-headed stripper, and the other is the blond stripper I slept with a week ago.

Girls I've slept with don't come over. Ever. What the hell is Blake thinking?

I drop my head into my hand. *Dammit.* Blake doesn't know I slept with her. He was too busy inspecting the tonsils of that redhead when I left the club.

"Jonah." Blake saunters up, a girl under each arm. "You remember Selena." He motions with his chin to the girl with unnaturally bright red hair. "And Candy." He motions to the blonde.

Her name is Candy. Typical.

"And this lovely lady here is Fiona." He motions to the dark-haired girl with gigantic breasts shoved into a tiny top. Won't have to worry about her sinking in the pool.

Candy slides out from under Blake's arm and steps into my space. Too close. I straighten from my leaning stance at the bar to gain some distance.

"Nice to see you again, Jonah." Her very white teeth dig into her plump lower lip. She finger walks her hand up my chest to wrap it around the back of my neck. Her other hand lies flat against my stomach.

"Candy, get your hands off me." I command in a low voice to avoid making a scene in front of Raven.

I'm grateful to see her engaged in conversation with Eve and Nikki who joined them by the pool.

Candy follows my gaze and sneers in Raven's direction. "Oh, I get it." She looks back at me and pulls her hand from my neck, making sure to drag her long fingernails against my skin. "Fresh meat." She looks back to Raven before spinning on her high heel. Her short, tight skirt looks more like a belt as she swings her ass. "You'll be back. Can't live on SPAM forever."

Her sidekicks squeal with laughter, and I glare at Blake. He shakes his head and throws his hands in the air mouthing, "I didn't know."

I'm not familiar with the sick feeling that gnaws at my insides. From the hateful look Candy gave Raven, there's no way she'll keep her mouth shut about our night together. My reputation is no secret, but having it confirmed is unsettling.

It shouldn't matter because I slept with Candy before I knew Raven, but the thought of Raven knowing the intimate details of my sexual history makes me insecure. I want her to see me as worthy. And sleeping around, especially to the daughter of a prostitute, doesn't say ideal boyfriend material.

Is that what I want? To be her boyfriend?

It's on this eye-bulging thought that Nikki walks up with Raven and Eve flanking her.

"Blake, I see you've brought the entertainment." Nikki's smile is the farthest thing from friendly.

"Oh, come on, Nik. Don't hate the player; hate the game." Blake laughs and the tension rippling off Nikki intensifies.

Raven and Eve, eyes wide as saucers, look back and forth between the two.

Owen stands from his barstool and grabs his wife by the hand. "Nik, baby. Inside. Now."

She allows herself to be led away, but maintains a death glare on the strippers until she's out of sight.

Blake's eyes follow Nikki into the house before he sets his sights on Raven and Eve. He pushes past his dates. "And who do we have here?" His cocky-ass smile has the girls giggling.

Fucking Blake.

I give a quick growled introduction.

"It's nice to finally meet you." Raven extends her hand graciously. She motions to me with the hand that Blake is *still* holding. "Jonah mentioned you the other day."

My eyes burn at their connection. I try to figure out a way to get him to let her go without breaking her hand in the process.

"Raven. Why haven't I met you before?" Blake's gaze leaves Raven to narrow on me.

Raven shifts at my side. I spear Blake with a glare. He gets the message and lets her go. *Smart man.*

"Raven's helping me with my Impala."

Blake throws his head back, roaring with laughter. Raven stiffens at my side. I drape my arm over her shoulder, and she presses softly into my hold. Her body feels so small and delicate under my arm. The intimacy of her bare shoulder against my shirtless torso has me gathering her deeper into my side. Her mild fruity scent combined with the comfort of her body calms my nerves. I resist the urge to bury my face in her hair.

"Dude, you have a smokin' hot mechanic. What the hell?" He's back to looking at Raven, and as his eyes dance up and down her body, I thank God she's still in her cover up. "Gives a whole new meaning to the term body shop." His eyes settle on her legs. "Nice legs, what time do they open?"

"Watch your fuckin' mouth." My jaw locks down. A warm, familiar buzz stirs in my head. My hand squeezes Raven's shoulder on reflex.

Silence hangs thick in the air as everyone stares between Blake and me. Even the Stripper Sisters have ceased their obnoxious babbling.

Blake focuses on me, his eyebrows low and questioning.

A soft giggle breaks the silence. In unison, all eyes move to Raven.

"Thanks for the compliment, Blake." Raven rolls her lips between her teeth, her face red with withheld laughter.

The buzz in my head retreats.

"Jonah didn't tell me you were so funny." She loses the battle, a burst of laughter escaping her lips. The melodic sound further calms my temper.

Small talk erupts all around me, but I don't hear a word. I'm stuck analyzing what the hell just came over me. I never get possessive over girls. I was half a second away from giving my best friend a beat down.

Raven and Eve go back to the lounger, and I throw Blake a chin lift. He responds in true Blake form, cocky smile and the middle finger salute.

The Stripper Sisters saunter to one of the lounging areas and whisper back and forth to each other. I relax seeing they've decided to sit on the opposite side of the pool from Raven and Eve who are back to their loungers by the bar.

Damn, I need a beer.

I walk behind the bar where the guys are camped out in front of the television.

"What the hell was that about?" Blake shoves a handful of popcorn in his mouth.

I shake my head. "I don't know."

"You almost flipped the switch on your boy for spewing the kind of shit he says to every girl he meets." Rex laughs and rubs the back of his neck. "One more word and I'd have been pulling your ass off him."

I nod and grab a beer. No doubt in my mind I would have beaten Blake for disrespecting Raven.

"Never thought I'd see it." Owen's back from settling down his wife and caught up on recent events. "You got it bad, my man."

Dress removed, I'm staring at a bikini-clad Raven. She's not covering or sucking in her stomach. No bashful body language that would expose her insecurities. Her olive skin glistens in the sun as she laughs and talks with Nikki and Eve. She looks so natural and at ease in her own skin in my backyard, hanging out with my friends, as if she's been doing it for years.

"Hey, Jonah." Owen calls my attention away from the girls. "She's one fine piece of a—"

A growl rumbles deep in my chest.

The guys explode into laughter.

Owen smacks me on the back. "Yep, you're hooked, brother."

RAVEN

The murmured voices and rhythmic thumping of rap music lull me into semiconsciousness. I close my eyes and relax, soaking up the last warmth from the sun before it drops behind the mountains. Male laughter erupts. I turn and watch Jonah with his friends, his dimples highlighting his bright smile. I slide my sunglasses down my nose for a better look. He's stopped laughing, but still smiling as he engages Owen.

I track his movements while he walks around the bar to sit on a barstool. His back muscles flex powerfully, as he brings his drink to his mouth. Brightly colored tattoos decorate his arms from his wrists to his shoulders with one flowing over and onto his chest. I want to get a closer look, run my hands along his arms as I study his body art. I wonder if his skin is as soft as it looks. If it tastes like he smells. Citrus and spice.

"This place is sick, Rave."

I jump at the sound of Eve's voice. Shoving my sunglasses up my nose, I pat my cheeks to bring down the heat. Eve is on the lounger with me, a gossip magazine resting against her thighs.

"Yeah." I clear the lusty sound from my throat. "I'm always in the garage. I didn't know all this was back here."

I scan my surroundings. The modern outdoor kitchen and bar, flat-screen TV, lagoon-style pool with Jacuzzi, and a fire pit. But the best parts of the backyard are the loungers. They're made for two, complete with large queen-sized mattresses and outdoor pillows.

"When you guys make it official, you have to have me over … like a lot." Eve looks at me over the tops of her sunglasses with a smile lighting her face.

My eyebrows pull together. "Make it official?"

"Yeah, you know, admit you dig each other." She shrugs before licking her finger and turning another page.

"Whatever."

It's all I can say through the full-on grin I'm sporting. As much as I wish I didn't, I feel something for him. What girl wouldn't?

Even the women Blake brought seem to fall into a trance when Jonah's around—not that I blame them. A swell of nausea threatens at the thought of Jonah with a girl like that. Their huge, clearly medically enhanced, breasts and lips push up and out for anyone's attention.

"What's going on over here, baby girl?" Blake plops down at my hip.

There is something about this guy that goes beyond his super-hot, bad-boy, fighter good looks. That alone would make any girl fidgety. His light brown hair is buzzed short, drawing all the attention to his bright green eyes. His looks alone are enough to leave a trail of broken hearts in his wake. But it's his composure, a slight expression he wears, that makes him dangerous, like his eyes hide a dirty secret he masks with a friendly smile.

"If I flip a coin, what are the chances I'll get head?"

Eve turns to Blake, her jaw wide open, and closes her magazine with a smack.

"Eww, Blake. That's gross," I say through a fit of giggles. "Please tell me that doesn't actually work on girls."

"You see how many dates I have at this barbeque. What do you think?" He turns his attention to Eve. "How about you, Barbie? You up for a game of naked leap frog?"

"Ugh! I'm going to get a drink. Rave, you want anything?"

"No thanks."

Eve gets up, and Blake is not shy about watching her butt until she disappears behind the bar.

"Is it something I said?" His crooked smile tells me he likes making girls uncomfortable.

The fact that he can talk to women like that and still get dates is a testament to how incredibly attractive he is.

I catch Jonah at the bar from the corner of my eye. He's watching Blake and me, the weight of his stare makes me shift in my seat. I don't want a repeat of what happened earlier.

"Shouldn't you be getting back to your dates? I don't want to get you in trouble."

Blake looks to the girls, but quickly dismisses my concerns with a wave of his hand. "Nah, they're cool. And if they're not, fuck 'em." Blake rubs his hand back and forth a few times on his buzzed head. Turning his head slightly, he fixes his cocky half smile on me. "You into my boy?" he asks cryptically.

I prop myself up on my elbows. "Huh?"

Leaning forward, he looks me in the eyes. "Jonah tried to take my head off back there. You want to know how often I've seen him do that when I put the moves on a girl, even a girl he's going home with?"

"How many?"

He makes a circle with his finger and thumb. "Zilch. Never."

I stare at Blake, trying to figure out exactly what he's telling me and hoping like heck I don't misunderstand.

"We're just friends." Thankfully, I'm wearing sunglasses so he can't see my eyes betraying my words.

"Just friends, huh?" He rubs his chin then shrugs. "Perfect. I'll see if a couple of my dates want to hang with Jonah tonight after the barbeque." He braces his hands on his knees to stand.

No. "Wait." Reflexes have me grabbing his arm. My heartbeat throbs with panic.

He looks at me. "You got something you wanna say, baby girl?"

I like Jonah.

The words are there, but I can't bring myself to say them. What if he doesn't feel the same way? I won't be able to work with him after suffering that kind of embarrassment. Putting myself out there like …No, I need to keep my feelings private. His friendship means too much to me. And really, what kind of chance do I have with a guy like Jonah Slade?

"Yeah, I just wanted to say…" I let go of Blake's arm and lean back on my lounger. "Go ahead. Jonah's free to date, er, um, *be* with whoever he wants." *Gosh, that hurt.*

Blake studies me for a second before leaning in. "Jonah's a lot of things." He looks around the pool then back at me before sliding his sunglasses over his eyes. "But from what I've seen tonight, he's not free—at least, not anymore."

He struts away, acting completely unaware of the shock-and-awe devastation he left behind. "Raven, a little later we can play Titanic," he calls over his shoulder. "I'll yell ice burg and you can go down."

A laugh rips from my chest, fueled by giddiness from Blake's admission.

He's not free …not anymore.

Could Blake be right? Is it possible that Jonah could be feeling the same thing I'm feeling?

Eve comes back from the bar and sits at the spot Blake just vacated. "Finally, he's gone. He's a sweet piece of eye candy, but the second he opens his mouth…" She shakes her head and takes a sip from her water bottle. "Why do you think he's so funny?" She points her grimace in Blake's direction.

"I think he's hilarious."

I lie back, a face-splitting smile aching my cheeks that has nothing to do with Blake.

SEVEN

RAVEN

"My woman can cook," Owen bellows from the doorway of the kitchen as he brings in a stack of dirty and very empty plates.

Nikki takes the plates from his hands and kisses him lightly on the cheek. "Thank you, baby. Now get out of here before I put you to work."

These two look like a famous Hollywood couple. Owen has deep mocha skin and short cropped hair. His body is similar to the others: athletic, bulky, and the perfect mix of captivating and terrifying. His rugged masculinity is a contrast to his wife's caramel-colored skin, soft curves, and long, wavy hair. He gives her a playful swat on the bottom, making her squeak and jump, her light brown eyes sparkling.

She drops the plates in the soapy water. "Thanks for helping me clean up, girl. I'm usually the only other female around that does more than stick my tits out." She rolls her eyes at the obvious reference to the women Blake brought with him.

"It's the least I could do. That was one of the best meals I've had in a long time. You're an incredible cook." I rinse out a huge bowl that once held a delicious fruit salad.

"Thanks. I get a lot of practice hanging around this group."

That doesn't surprise me. The guys alone ate enough to feed a small country. I think Jonah grilled an entire cow.

"Nikki, where do you want me to put these?" Eve asks from the doorway, her arms filled with more plates.

Jonah follows behind her, a few bottles of condiments in hand. He walks to the fridge to put them away.

My gaze is soldered to his form, and I nearly slice open my finger with a soapy steak knife. It shouldn't be legal for him to walk around without a shirt on. Reckless endangerment.

"You girls don't have to do this. My cleaning lady comes in the morning."

"Like dealing with your dirty drawers isn't enough, you're going to make that poor woman clean up after the five of you? Uh-uh." Nikki turns Jonah around and shoos him from the room.

"All right, all right, I'll go." He wraps Nikki in a one-arm hug.

She leans in with a grin.

His eyes find mine. "But, Nik, don't work my girl too hard. She needs to take care of those hands. Can't have tools sliding from her grip because you overworked them." He hits me with a wink and walks away.

Nikki chuckles. "Damn, girl. He's sprung."

Eve snickers in the corner, stacking clean dishes to the side.

I can't believe he just called me his girl! And something about the way he talked about tools sliding in my hand. Sure, it sounded like simple shop talk, but the way he held my eyes made me feel like he was as if her were talking about using my hands for something entirely different. First Blake and now Nikki. Could they be right? They've known Jonah a lot longer than I have. Is it possible that he could be feeling something? For me?

I rushed through the rest of the dishes, anxious to get back to Jonah. The kitchen is spotless in record time.

"Well, girls." Nikki wipes her hands on a dishtowel before hanging it perfectly on the rack. "I think we've just earned ourselves a little hot-tub time."

Minutes later, I'm submerged in liquid heaven. I lean my head back as the warm bubbles caress my body. Everyone around is either in the water or sitting on the edge, dangling in their legs. Conversation hums around me. Relaxing, I allow my eyes to slide shut, a soft moan drifting from my lips.

"...then tell her to swallow." Blake's punch line has me giggling despite the fact that I didn't hear the joke.

Eve's responding snort drags me from my relaxed state and has me laughing harder.

Feeling eyes on me, I turn my head away from Eve and Blake. My laughter dies instantly.

The carnal stare from Jonah's eyes has me mesmerized. I'm unable to look away from the smoldering hazel. My blood heats and pounds in my ears. A yearning, deep and delicious, stirs in my belly. The intensity making it hard to breath, my chest rises and falls erratically. He tilts his head as his eyes travel from my face to my breasts and back again. I suck my bottom lip into my mouth, and my mind conjures images of him coming at me from across the warm water. I squirm.

"I'll be right back," I mumble to whoever's listening and excuse myself from the hot tub.

I push up and swing a leg over to jump out. A hiss sounds from behind me, like someone sucking air through his teeth. I turn and find Jonah with an expression that looks like pain mixed with something new I can't name. Whatever it is makes my stomach plummet and land low. Really low. I grab my towel and head for the bathroom.

Locked inside, I flip the toilet seat closed and sit. *What was that?* I fan my flaming cheeks. What that was, was hot. And it had nothing to do with the water temperature. It's happening more often: our eyes lock on each other, and the world around us fades away. But why? I can't explain it, only that he must feel some attraction or ...God, what is wrong with me?

I step to the mirror and let down my hair, running my fingers through the tangles. This is crazy. I have a major crush on a UFL fighter who probably looks at me and sees nothing more than a score: a naïve girl who will fall for his charm and meet some need on a physical level. If that's true, why hasn't he made a move? What would I do if he did? My lips curl and my stomach flips.

Fed up with staring at my goofy grin, I wrap my towel around my waist to head back to the party. I duck my chin to my chest as I push through the door, hoping to shake my lovesick-puppy smile before I face Jonah.

"Raven, right?"

I jump at the sound of a female voice. The blond girl who came with Blake is standing just outside the bathroom. Her arms are crossed at her chest as she glares in my direction.

My smile fades. "Yes?"

She looks me up and down as if I'm covered in cockroaches. Her lips peel back in disgust. This feels so much like high school. I curl into myself.

"I'm just trying to figure out what Jonah would want with a little grease monkey like you." Her icy stare continues to scrutinize me from bare feet to bikini top. "What are you? Eighteen? Do you really think a silly little girl like you could satisfy a man like him?"

I jerk from the truth in her statement.

The words *he's just a friend* itch at the back of my throat. Something tells me we're more than that, but uncertainty seals my lips.

But she's right. I'm inexperienced and young. Men want women who are confident and know how to please them. My shoulders sink as I consider all the ways I'm not good enough for Jonah. Maybe she's right and I've been misreading things.

"Jonah and I …We're just friends. You want him, he's yours." My voice is dull, and my heart sinks like a lead balloon.

I push past her with every intention of getting as far away as I can before I do something stupid, like cry. A firm grip on my elbow halts my getaway. In shock, I lean away from the blonde, who is sneering inches away from my face.

"Want him?" She flashes a heartless smile that tells me she's going to enjoy whatever she's about to say. "I've had him. He fucked my brains out last week."

I turn my face away, trying to escape the vulgarity of her words.

"Yeah, that's right. And he screamed my name, begging me for more." She leans in so close I can smell the liquor on her breath. "He said I had the sweetest pussy he's ever tasted."

My eyes burn, tears threatening to spill.

"Keep your filthy fucking hands off of him. He doesn't want you. You're nothing but a worthless piece of white trash, and he—"

"Who the *fuck* do you think you are?"

An enraged male voice breaks her concentration. In unison, we turn toward the source.

Oh, crud.

"Jonah." His name escapes on a whisper.

His jaw is tense and ticking, his fists balled at his sides. The fierceness in his stare is terrifying, and it's not directed at me.

"Get the hell out of my house," he spits out through clenched teeth while glaring at Candy.

"Jonah, honey, I don't know what you thought you heard." Like a sneaky little viper, she tries to backpedal. "We were just having a little girl talk." She releases her hold on me and brushes my hair over my shoulder.

Jonah's eyes dart to mine then move back to glare at Candy. "Out. Now." His voice trembles with rage.

Candy lifts her head and squares her shoulders. Lithely, she moves past Jonah, stopping to look him in the eye. "You're really going to pass this up?" She looks down at me from over her shoulder. "For *that*?"

Her reference to me being an object rather than a person has me studying the concrete at my feet.

Jonah grumbles a reply I can't make out. Whatever he said makes Candy finch before she struts away.

My heart is beating out of my chest. I peer at Jonah from behind my hair. His head falls forward, hands resting on his hips. I hear the sound of him breathing deep and blowing air from his mouth as if he were trying to calm down.

He looks up at me, concern etched on his face. "You okay?"

"Yes." I'm unable to control the quiver in my voice.

He steps to me and interlaces his fingers with mine. "Come on."

He leads me into the bathroom and locks the door behind us. Releasing my hand, he leans against the door. My arms wrap protectively around my body in an attempt to hold myself together. His face is more relaxed, but his eyes are still angry.

"Raven, I owe you an apology."

I stumble back a step. An apology? I wasn't expecting that. "No, Jonah you don't owe me—"

"I slept with Candy."

My body stills along with my words. I close my gaping mouth, surprised at his honesty. "Um, I know that."

He shifts on his feet and rubs the back of his neck. "I slept with her." He takes a deep breath. "Why is this so hard?" He mumbles to the floor before his eyes meet mine. "I slept with her a week ago."

This, too, I already knew because of Candy's less than lady-like admission. "Okay."

Is that all I can say? Okay?

"I didn't invite her here. I'm not interested in her." His eyes study my face for a few silent seconds.

"Jonah, you don't need to explain—"

"There's something else." He takes a step toward me.

I pull in a large breath through my nose and blow out my mouth. Can I handle his something else? I nod.

"I can't stop thinking about you."

Yes, I can handle that.

My cheeks hurt as I wrestle against an embarrassing grin. "Okay."

He takes another step in my direction. "You're unlike anyone I've ever met."

My breathing picks up, my heart pounds, and something begins to unfurl and flutter in my chest. "Okay."

"I want to be with you."

Is this really freaking happening?

"Okay."

He closes the final few feet between us. His arms surround my waist and lock at my lower back, forcing my hands to his bare chest. The heat from his skin ignites a fire in my palms that shoots down my spine and awakens my senses. The gentle rise and fall of his breath, the rhythmic beat of his heart, all magnified. My bikini-clad breasts brush against his rib cage. The friction makes me shiver in his arms.

He slides his hands up my back, trailing his fingers across my skin. Goose bumps skate across my flesh. A bright smile lights his face at my response to his touch. His eyes become hooded. His hands rest against either side of my neck, rubbing my jaw with slow swipes of his thumbs. I watch in amazement as his eyes travel from my eyes to my lips before they drop to the side of my neck.

"I've wanted to do this since the first day I met you."

Bending forward, he brings his lips just a breath away from mine. I lean in and close my eyes, expecting to feel the warmth of his mouth. He uses his hold to tip my chin down and kiss my forehead. I sigh and melt into the tenderness of his touch.

Gently, he runs his nose down my hairline to my ear. "Mmm, you smell so good."

My fingers flex against his firm chest at the husky sound in his voice. A second chill races through my body. Heat floods my system. I welcome every new feeling, every fragile emotion that courses through me.

He makes a fist in my hair and tilts my head. The soft heat of his lips brushes against my earlobe then my neck, trailing kisses to my shoulder. He lingers there, licking and nipping with his teeth. The abrasive stubble of his chin against my collarbone electrifies my body. I press my aching breasts into him as my bones liquefy beneath his touch. His hard, strong body accepts my weight, and a moan tumbles from my throat.

I feel him smile against my skin. "You like that, baby?"

He called me baby! I'm thankful he can't see my eyes as they stare at the ceiling, wide in shock.

The silky moisture from his open-mouth kisses at my neck have my eyelids falling shut. "Sweet, just like I knew you'd be." His breath tickles my skin.

Something coils deep inside, a damn on the verge of collapsing. "Jonah…" My mind scrambles with how to communicate everything I want from him right now. His lips on mine, the weight of his body, his hands…

He places a final kiss against my neck and pulls his head up. My eyelids, suddenly heavy, fight to stay open. My body trembles with a raw need I've never felt before. And our lips haven't even touched.

"I want to take you inside," he whispers, through a dark, sexy smile.

"Okay."

"Send Eve home. You're staying with me tonight."

His proposition douses the fire raging in my body.

"You want me to spend the night?" Panic creeps in.

His lips curve at the ends. "Yeah, you can borrow something to sleep in."

I try to think of something logical, some reason why I can't spend the night, but with his hands running up and down my back, it's hard to concentrate. How can I say no? Jonah Slade asks for a sleepover, the answer is always yes. It's in the female handbook. She says no, she gets her membership revoked, right? If not, she should.

"Okay."

The corners of his mouth twitch. "Raven, you gotta give me something besides okay."

Here he just confessed to having feelings for me and asked me to spend the night, and he want's something besides okay? My brain is on overload, not to mention the other parts of my body that have just woken up for the first time in …well, forever. They may even short circuit if he gets anywhere near them with that skilled mouth of his. I laugh inwardly at the thought of Jonah's vast experience with women compared to my complete lack of experience with men.

Oh, no.

"I can't have sex with you." I blurt out the words, my hand covering my mouth too late.

I'm an idiot.

His eyes light up, dancing with laughter, making my idiocy totally worth it.

"That's all right. I'm not asking you to stay over so I can have sex with you." He lifts one eyebrow and gives me a one-dimpled grin. "Can we make out?"

Heat bursts against my cheeks and floods down my neck. I bury my face against his chest to hide my embarrassment. "Okay."

He throws his head back and laughs while holding me to him. Instantly, his touch calms my nerves and my lungs take in a full breath. His warm skin smells like coconut sunblock mixed with his usual masculine spice. I relax deeper into his hold.

"Jonah?'

"Hmm?"

"I like you too."

He pulls back just enough to see my face, determination flashing in his eyes. He leans down and, knowing what he's after, I lift up on my toes. Our lips touch for the first time in a soft caress. I've wondered what it would be like to kiss Jonah, and even my best fantasies weren't this good.

His full, strong lips mold to mine. A slow sweep of his tongue has me opening to him. What started off teasing turns hot and urgent as he pulls my lower lip with his teeth, coaxing my tongue to explore. His hands grab at my hair and mine wrap around his biceps.

The kiss turns demanding as he possesses my mouth. His muscles flex against my palms. I struggle to keep myself on my toes, his expert mouth making my legs completely useless. I slide back down on flat feet, dragging my breasts down his chest as I go. He releases his hold on my hair and cups my bottom with his hands, pulling me against him.

My gosh, that feels good.

With what seems like great effort, he ends the kiss, gently nibbling and tasting my lower lip. His hands give me a squeeze before sliding up and resting on my lower back. He bends down and presses one last kiss on my neck before looking into my eyes.

Amazing. In this moment, after that kiss, he's no longer Jonah "The Assassin" Slade, celebrity bad-boy. Looking at him now, he's just Jonah.

"Don't worry about tonight." His words are said in a way that makes me feel like I might be more to him than a hook up. "I'd never push you further than you're willing to go."

My stomach twists with anxiety. He has no idea.

EIGHT

JONAH

After my talk with Raven in the bathroom, I have one objective—get these people out of my house. Pronto. With the taste of her still on my lips, I let the guys know that the party is over.

It's just past ten as I wave off the last of my friends. I watch from the front porch as Raven says goodbye to Eve. The patio light illuminates her face as she laughs hard at something Eve must have said.

Damn, she's gorgeous. I always knew she was beautiful, but getting her alone in that bathroom, her body trembling in my arms, her breathy moans, and flushed cheeks. *Perfect.*

And that kiss. I'm not big on kissing, never have been. But Raven's sweet lips, so tentative at first, only to turn greedy and demanding—a few more minutes of that and I'd probably bust in my shorts like a teenage boy.

She walks toward me, her backpack slung over one shoulder, Eve's taillights disappearing down the driveway.

"Come here." I brush her hair aside and lean in. Before I'm there, she tilts her head, offering her throat to me. *Fucking perfect.* I hone in on my spot: the blackbird's wing that peeks at the base of her neck. First, a quick press of my lips, then I part my mouth to taste her tender flesh. She hums low in her throat and leans into me.

"I like your tattoo." My voice against her neck makes her to shiver.

"I like yours too."

I force myself back a step. "Everything okay with your girl?"

"Yes, she's happy I'm staying here. She hates my place, thinks it's not safe." She picks at the frayed strap of her backpack.

"Why is your place not safe?"

She looks up at me and rolls her eyes. "I live in a studio apartment."

Okay. That doesn't sound so bad.

"Where?"

She blows out a long, defeated-sounding breath. "Right by the garage."

She shifts on her feet, and I know she's holding something back. I tilt my head and wait. Her eyes grow a fraction. *That's right, sweetheart. I'm on to you.*

"Well, actually…"

"I'm listening."

"I live above the garage." She's back to picking at her back-pack strap.

Nope. I must've heard that wrong. "You live above Guy's Garage?"

She nods.

A wave of anxiety floods my body. "Raven, there's nothing over there but warehouses and vagrants. There's not a decent human being within a ten-mile radius after business hours."

Thinking of her all alone at night in that part of town makes my muscles tense. My mind imagines all the things that could happen to an innocent girl in that part of town after hours. The alley behind the garage is a festering crime spot. There's probably all manner of piece-of-shit lowlifes lurking in the shadows. I'll never be able to sleep knowing she's over there alone. No.

"From now on, you stay here with me," I blurt.

Her eyes flash in shock and her lips part.

I just took this too far.

"What did you say?" Her voice is barely a whisper.

I run my hands through my hair, trying to figure out what the hell is going on in my head. I'm having a hard time believing my own words. Did I just ask her to move in with me? I want this girl, more than I've wanted any other girl. There's no denying that. The protective instinct stirs in my chest, something I've never felt for any woman outside of my mom and sister.

"You heard me."

"Jonah, I'm not staying with you every night. That's absurd. You barely know me. I mean…" She studies me, and I can't help but think how her confused and shocked expression adds a cuteness to her already gorgeous face.

"I just want to keep you safe, and I can't do that if you aren't with me." I take a deep, steadying breath. That felt okay. Not awkward, like I thought it would. "Besides, you work on the Impala most mornings. It'll save on gas money." It's a stretch, but I'm desperate—also a new feeling for me.

"That's really sweet of you, b-but I can't." Her expression relaxes, and she puts her hands on her hips. "I have to feed Dog."

This is interesting. I can't think of a single girl, not one, who would argue with me at my offer to have them sleep in my bed. And did she say she has a dog?

"Dog?"

"Yes. Dog." Her shoulders square off and she lifts her chin.

She thinks something like having to feed her dog is going discourage me? She needs to get to know me better, which is exactly what I plan on doing once this conversation is over.

"Bring your dog." I shrug.

"Bring my ...but ...I don't have a dog." Her forehead pinches between her eyebrows, and I fight the desire to kiss the skin smooth.

Damn, she is really cute.

"You said you had to feed your dog."

"Right, Dog. My cat. Well, not *my* cat. The cat that lives in the alley."

I roll my lips between my teeth to keep from laughing. "Let me get this straight. You feed an alley cat that you've named Dog, and that's why you can't stay with me."

"Exactly." She throws her hands out like she's just made the point of the century.

I lose the battle against my laughter and nearly double over with it. "You're, without a doubt, the most amusing girl I've ever met, Raven ...uh..." I'm not going through this again. "What's your last name?"

Her expression falls and her face goes pale. *What did I say?* She rolls her bottom lip into her mouth, raking it across her teeth. My laughter dies and instinctively I pull her into my arms.

"Baby? You okay?"

She exhales and wraps her hands around my waist. "I'm fine. You just caught me off guard." Her arms grow tight as she hugs me to her. "I guess you'll find out sooner or later."

What the hell? What could possibly be so bad about her last name? I guess it could be Manson or Bundy.

"Morretti. My full name is Raven Morretti." Her words are dull and lifeless.

Morretti? I look past her, squinting into the darkness. Why does that name—*Holy shit!*

Dominick Morretti. Las Vegas's most infamous pimp. And her mom's a prostitute. It all makes sense.

Not only have I seen his mug all over the news but I've actually met the scumbag. I've seen him at all our fights, working his girls. He tried to get us to throw down some cash for a night with a Morretti girl.

Raven looks nothing like him with her dark hair and olive skin, but those eyes. It's amazing I didn't make the connection before. The color is so unique, but, where hers are cool pools of Caribbean water, his are death by drowning. My mom always said, "The eyes are the windows to your soul," and looking into Dominick Morretti's eyes, it's pretty clear he ain't got one.

"Jonah?" Her arms grow impossibly tighter around my waist.

She's got to know I know who her father is. Everyone in town knows who her father is. He not only runs the biggest prostitution ring in the state, allegedly, but he also owns half the real estate in town. *And she lives in a studio above a garage?*

"Yeah, baby. Let's get you inside."

I grab her hand and lead her into the house. Not letting go, I lock the door and take her to the couch. I sit down and pull her onto my lap. She stiffens and avoids my eyes.

"Your dad is Dominick Morretti."

Dropping her forehead, she simply nods.

I take a deep breath and look to the ceiling. "I know him, Raven. I know your dad—"

"He's not my dad." Her harsh glare locks on mine before her expression softens. "I mean he's my biological father, but he's not my dad. I don't have a dad."

I pull her to me, and she nestles into my chest, her arms wrap around my waist.

"Well, whatever he is to you, he's no good. I don't want you around him."

She laughs humorlessly. "You don't have to worry about that. He hasn't wanted anything to do with me in twenty years. I doubt he ever will. I'm pretty sure whatever happened between him and my mom was a mistake …you know, me." Her final words are barely audible as her voice is muffled in my chest.

Anger pushes its way through my concern for her. I place my hand under chin and force her eyes to mine. "I can't see your life ever being considered a mistake."

Her sad smile rips through me.

"My parents never had a relationship that I know of. I'm not close to my mom, so she's never told me, but it's pretty obvious they have nothing beyond, um, a professional relationship."

Her bright eyes look away for a second as she blows a piece of long hair from her face. "Anyway, can we talk about something else now?"

Her full lips lift into a smile that doesn't reach her eyes. I'm left with a million questions tumbling in my head, but I don't want to ruin the night by bringing up painful memories of her past.

"Yes, we can." I stare at her lips, hungry to taste them again. But there's one thing I need to say before I can put this subject to bed. "Promise me you'll stay away from Dominick Morretti."

"That, I can promise." Her eyes move down my face and settle on my mouth.

I shove both hands into her hair and bring her lips to mine. She eagerly complies, wrapping her hands behind my neck and holding me close to her. She tilts her head and our tongues slide together. Her body shifts on my lap and I moan my approval. Just days ago I thought I could walk away from her. And now, I don't want to spend one night without her.

—

RAVEN

The marble flooring is cool under my bare feet as I stand, looking at myself in Jonah's bathroom mirror. Something's different. I can't put my finger on what it is, but I know I've never been able to see my molars before when I smile. I have a serious case of the perma-grins.

I look down at the cotton t-shirt and sweat pants lying folded in my hands. It hits me again, with no less intensity than before, that I'm spending the night with Jonah Slade. Now my cheeks actually hurt.

Checking out his dark brown, granite counter top with double sinks and mahogany cabinetry, curiosity pushes at me. I question whether or not to snoop in his medicine cabinet. I chew on my lip, staring at the mysterious mirrored door. Just one peek won't hurt.

I cautiously pull open the door as if something might jump out at me: deodorant, shaving cream, razor, all the typical man stuff. Grabbing his cologne, I press it to my nose and take a deep breath. My eyes almost roll back in my head at the woodsy smell that his skin has hinted at before. He never smells coated in fragrance, more like an underlying flavor that runs beneath his natural scent.

Snooping complete, I move to close the door when a gray box catches my eye. I squint and lean forward to read the label: condoms. Wow, extra-large, lubricated, jumbo pack. I slam the door shut and stare at my reflection.

"Well, what did you think you would find?" I hiss to myself. "You know his reputation." I stand back and shrug. "You need to tell him."

Hey Jonah, guess what? Now that you know my mom's a hooker and my dad's a pimp, I have one more bomb to drop on you. The V-bomb. Surely if he can look past the first two bombs that last one should be no big deal. It's not as if I'm not open to eliminating the issue. Candy's words come flooding back. *Stupid little girl.*

I push the feelings of unworthiness to the back of my brain and head for the shower. Stripping down, I hear my inner fourteen-year-old fan-girl screaming, *You're naked in Jonah Slade's bathroom! Squee!* She's not wrong, I think while covering my mouth to stifle my laughter.

Stepping under the water, I close my eyes to enjoy the calming spray. After a minute or two, I grab Jonah's body wash and take a deep breath. It smells like citrus and spice and man all mixed together. I wash up slowly, taking the time to enjoy being covered in his smell and nothing else. While rinsing my hair, I notice just how different our realities are. He has a rain shower head and marble tile, and all my shower boasts is mildew stains and a slow-moving drain.

After towel drying, I finger comb my hair and slide on a fresh pair of panties from my backpack. I pull Jonah's t-shirt over my head. It's huge and hits me just above the knees. I pull on the worn sweat pants, and they slide back down my legs. Frowning, I pull them back up and roll the top in an attempt to tighten them. Still too big. The shirt covers enough, so I ditch the pants.

Slipping out from the bathroom into Jonah's room, I'm met with a vision that has me locked in place. He's shirtless with his back against the headboard. His navy blue pajama pant-covered legs are crossed at the ankles, and the remote is in his hand. He exudes casual confidence.

My eyes consume his body from his colorful arms to his bulging chest and settle on his face. He's staring at me with a hunger that charges the air between us.

"Hi."

"Hi." His eyes narrow on my bare legs.

"The pants were too big." I tug at the hem of the shirt.

Silence.

"So, I decided the shirt would be long enough."

Still silence.

"I thought it covered as much as a dress would, so—"

"You look amazing in my shirt." I shift uncomfortably at the gravely sound in his voice. "You're safe with me."

I let his words wash over me as my shoulders relax and I take a deep breath.

"You want to watch some TV?" He gives me a one-dimpled smile that sucks the breath from my lungs.

Forcing my gaze to his enormous television that hangs on the wall, I step closer to see what he's watching. "Sure. What—" I gasp and race toward it, stopping only a foot away from the screen.

"Raven—"

"That's Chip Foose!" I point at the screen while looking back at Jonah who is smiling huge. "I've read about this show in *Car and Driver Magazine*. It's called Overhaulin'. They take old cars from people…" The sound of Chip Foose's voice calls my attention back to the show. "'57 Chevy, Bel Air, two door, hardtop," I mumble to myself, captivated by automotive brilliance.

A pair of strong arms wrap around my waist. "Come back and sit on the bed, baby. You can watch it from there." A hint of humor laces his words.

Flaming embarrassment. Here I get the chance to be in bed with Jonah, and I'm stuck to a television screen, watching a reality show about cars. *How very sexy and feminine of me.*

He pulls me a few steps backward to the bed. I don't take my eyes off the screen as he hauls me to the headboard, tucking me into his side. My head against to his chest, I slide my hand over his bare abs and bite my tongue to keep from *Oooing*. His hand moves up my arm and stops to toy with my hair. I sigh in contentment, but quickly remember the heavy weight I need to get off my chest.

"Jonah?"

"Hmm?"

"I need to talk to you about something."

He lifts the remote, pressing a button that freezes the screen.

"I know your, um, reputation." His body tightens beneath my cheek and his hand stills in my hair. "Nikki told me that you've never had a girl over. Is that true? It's just, you've obviously had your fair share of, um, female companions, so I assumed—"

"Yes. It's true. You're the first girl I've had in my bed."

I take a deep breath and try not to chicken out. "Um … well, there's something you should know about me."

He doesn't say anything, and I can't see his face, but his chest has stopped moving.

I squeeze my eyes shut and shove the words out. "I'm a virgin."

Holding my breath, I bite my lip and await his reaction.

I'm not a total prude. I dated Billy Dryer, and he was the most popular kid in school. We made out a few times until he broke up with me. Guess his parents told him who my mom was, so he thought I'd be easy. I'll never forget him trying to pull my pants down. When I refused, he said he knew I was a lesbian. A girl working on cars all day had to be gay. He stormed off and left me there under the bleachers alone. I decided I'd rather be a virgin lesbian than the slut daughter of a prostitute.

I'm tossed from my thoughts by the shaking of Jonah's silent laughter, and my eyes pop open in surprise.

"Are you laughing?"

His reaction turns into uncontrollable hilarity, not the response I was expecting.

I push myself up and take a minute to enjoy his dimples, wide smile, and shining eyes. "What's so funny?"

"Raven," he says between chuckles. "You said yourself I've never had a girl over to my house before. Yet, here you are, in my bed, wearing my shirt, cuddled up in my arms." He tucks a piece of hair behind my ear. "You don't get it, do you?"

My confused face confirms that I, in fact, do not get it.

"You, Raven Morretti, are mine. Doesn't matter if you're a virgin or an alien. What you've told me changes nothing. Not. One. Thing."

Stunned into paralysis, I let his words take root.

"How's that possible? Were you not listening when I told you my mom's a hooker and my dad's a pimp?" I'm processing his reaction aloud and can't seem to stop. "Candy was right. I'm a grease monkey, and, considering what my parents do for a living, I'm trash. I'm inexperienced, young, and a virgin."

Good job, Raven. Talk him out of liking you. Why don't you go ahead and make him a list of all your unlovable qualities.

It happened so fast I barely registered the movement. Jonah hauled me up the length of his body and sat me face to face with him, straddling his hips. My face dwarfed by his big hands, he holds me until I meet his eyes.

"Don't ever speak about yourself like that again." His deep, firm command makes me drop my eyes. "Look at me, Raven." I do as I'm told. "You're unlike anyone I've ever known. You're kind, smart, funny, gracious …hell, you even laugh at Blake's jokes. I want *you*. And that includes everything that makes you who you are."

He wants me. This amazing, powerful, beautiful man wants me. Have I ever felt wanted before? A lone tear rolls down my cheek. His words are a warm blanket wrapped around my heart. Leaning forward, he brushes his lips across the corners of my eyes.

Will he ever understand how much his words mean to me? I've never felt important enough to anyone or good enough to deserve this kind of affection. Just days ago, I felt a fissure in the wall I had erected around my heart. With those simple words, he busted it down.

It's crazy and it makes no sense, but there's no doubt in my mind. I'm madly in love with Jonah Slade.

NINE

JONAH

I wake up with something soft and warm pressing against the length of my body. My left arm lies flat against the bed, tingling, a sensation like tiny ants tunneling through my veins. My right arm is comfortable and pressed directly against the soft heat. Taking a deep breath, I smell the faint pear fragrance and smile. *Raven.*

So this is what it feels like to sleep with someone. Her back pressed to my front, I nestle my face into the silky waves of her hair and pull her body deeper into mine. What the h…? I flex my hand against a heavy weight in my palm. The feeling registers, immediately making my body tense.

Ah, hell.

Sometime in the night, I shoved my hand up her shirt and am now cupping her left breast. All I need is for her to wake up to me perving out on her in her sleep. I slip my hand slowly from her chest. My fingers skate down the soft skin of her stomach and settle there. Her legs slide against mine as I draw lazy circles at her belly button.

She moans and presses her bottom into my groin in a tiny stretch. I bite back my groan at the feel of her round ass against my throbbing crotch. I don't think I've ever had a hard-on for this long.

Last night, after Raven confessed her virginity, there was no way I could make out with her. At least, not the way I wanted to. The tears in her eyes as she ripped herself apart verbally sealed it for me. I needed her to know that I respect her and that she's more than a shallow one night. We'd kiss during commercials, and at times I thought I could have gotten away with more, but last night was about getting her to see me differently. It was about getting her to trust me with more than her painful family history, with her body as well. And to do that, I had to hold back my appetite for her. Way back.

Besides, holding her against my side with her head on my chest while she watched Overhaulin' was entertaining as hell. She went back and forth between mumbling to herself and giving me a detailed history of Ford Motor Company. She'd talk to the television, making her suggestions as to what should be done, and made it clear when she disagreed. I enjoyed watching her as much as I did the show. And the show was cool as shit.

I introduced her to the DVR, showing her how to record the entire season so she can watch them whenever she wants. She rewarded me with a shining smile that I felt in my toes. Her sparkling eyes lit up like I'd just given her keys to a Lamborghini. The fact that I could make her light up like that filled me with more pride than winning my first fight. I spent the rest of the night figuring out ways to earn that smile again.

"That tickles," she whispers with a giggle as she stills my hand at her stomach.

"Good morning." I push my luck and glide my hand up her body to her rib cage just shy of the underside of her breast.

A sharp intake of air and she relaxes.

"How did you sleep?"

"Mmm, really good." She rolls over to face me.

I prop up on my elbow, my head in my hand, and run my fingers down her ribs to where the sheet lies at her waist and back again.

She touches my cheek with a barely-there brush of her fingertips. "I like these," she whispers, tracing my dimples.

I roll my eyes.

"What? They're cute."

She did not just say that.

"Cute? I don't want to be cute."

I didn't think her giggles could get any sweeter, but her scratchy morning giggles are the best.

"Well, too bad, because you are."

My smile widens at the compliment. It's not that I've never had a girl tell me I'm cute, but everything means more coming from Raven's mouth.

Her eyes move to my arm as her finger slowly traces my tattoo.

"This is really beautiful. Ryan Allen Slade." She reads the scripted name. "Is it a tribute to your dad?"

"Yeah, he loved the ocean so I thought it fitting that the cross rises up from it."

Her fingers outline the swirls of waves then the cross at my bicep, moving up to the sky and clouds. Leaving trails of fire against my skin, her finger follows the pattern to the angels at my left pec. She looks up at me, her piercing aquamarine eyes heavy with sleep, her eyebrows raised in question.

"Katherine is my mom. Beth is my sister." The words come out rushed. I don't want her to think the women's names inked on my body are past lovers.

"And why the blank spot in between them?" Her finger brushes at the unmarked skin over my heart, teasingly close to my nipple.

"I'm saving that for my future wife."

She pulls her hand away like it's been burned and ducks her head. I curse myself for ruining the moment.

I roll to my back to expose my right arm and point to the fiery phoenix.

"This one here I got for a two reasons. First one is obvious." We've talked about me being from Arizona and moving to Vegas after high school.

She lifts her head and nods. I'm thankful to see the awkward moment pass.

"Second is because after my dad died, I was destroyed, like I'd lost everything, not just my dad. Then I started fighting and..." I pause, remembering the lost boy I was and comparing him to the man I am now. "It gave me something back. Not so much reborn, but redirected. It gave me purpose, a reason to wake up every day."

Her thoughtful eyes study mine, her eyebrows pinched in concentration. "You found a way to deal with your pain in a healthy way that improved your life."

"Yeah, I guess. Although sometimes it feels like fighting found me, ya know? I could have gone either way. Jail for assault or the UFL."

She sighs and rolls to her back, eyes to the ceiling. "If only everything were like that. It's not easy to do: owning and accepting the pain of our past, the heartbreak, our misgivings, and using them for good. Make our lives better not in spite of it all ...but *because* of it."

Her whispered words are directed at no one, and I wonder if they were meant more for me or for her. I watch her profile as she continues to inspect the ceiling fan.

It's not the first time that the girl beside me has knocked me stupid with something that comes from her beautiful mouth. As I sit dazed by her brilliance, my mind attempts to piece together what she's been through. Being the daughter of a pimp and a prostitute in Las Vegas couldn't have been easy. Her dad was hawking women's bodies and profiting from it, even the mother of his own daughter. Revulsion stirs in my gut.

We lie in silence for several long minutes, me lost in thoughts of her, her just looking lost.

Huffing, she turns her head with a sweet smile. "I need caffeine."

And just like that, she's back. These last few days, Raven has opened up to me on her own, always changing the subject when she's done sharing. I want to know more about her, but I'll let her set the pace.

"Are you always this pushy in the morning?" I tease.

A soft pink kisses her cheeks as she buries her head in my chest. I run my hand up her back into her hair.

"I don't think I'm pushy in the morning, but then again, I've never slept over with a boy before."

"Boy, huh?"

Rolling her to her back, I climb above her and bury my face in her throat. Her hands slide into my hair, and she holds me to her. I nip at her neck, eliciting a soft moan that vibrates against my lips. It takes every ounce of my control not to flex my hips into her accepting body. I pull up the hem of her t-shirt and rest my hand against her ribs.

"Jonah, is that your phone?"

I ignore her breathy question as my fingertips brush against the underside of her breast.

"Jonah, I think you should get your—"

I silence her with my mouth, swallowing her unspoken words. She hums and tilts her head, allowing me to delve deeper. I do just that, driving my tongue against hers. As slow as I can manage, I move my hand up until it's overflowing with the weight of her breast. She presses into my hold, molding my hand against her.

"What if it's an emergency?" She breaks the kiss to speak before pulling me back to her lips.

I smile at her eagerness before sucking her full bottom lip into my mouth. Her hands slide from my neck down to my chest as she explores my body with her touch.

"You taste fucking fantastic." I trail my tongue from her lips to her neck with every intention of tasting her breasts.

"The phone. It could be …a family emergency." Her clipped words come out between needy pants. Her hands run up again and into my hair sending the opposite message of her words.

I'm kissing her shoulder, her chest heaving against mine. There isn't much that could drag me away from her willing little body. But she's right. And I'm pissed.

"Fuck." I kiss her hard and suck her tongue deep into my mouth letting her know there's more to come. "Later."

With a quick push up, I'm off the bed. She whimpers, her face flushed, a shy smile tugging on her swollen lips. Her face is free of makeup, and her hair is tossed around the pillow in a wavy halo. *Seriously gorgeous.*

"I'm going to kill whoever that is."

Her laughter fills the room making it hard to stay mad. I follow the sound of my ringing cell phone to the living room, hoping the distance from Raven will calm my racing pulse and dull the throb in my pants.

Nabbing my phone off the table, I check the caller ID.

Yeah, he's dead.

"This better be good," I growl.

"Oh shit. Either you didn't get laid last night, or I interrupted your morning piece of ass."

My teeth grind together and I grip my cell. Blake has no idea how close he is to a beat down.

"Blake, you ever talk about Raven like that again, I will rip your balls off and shove them down your throat. I won't tolerate anyone disrespecting her. We clear?"

Is he fucking laughing? What the hell.

"No shit, man." The way he says it, I'm surprised he doesn't follow it with a "Duh!" He chuckles. "Pretty obvious after watching you two last night. Oh, and for the record, I approve."

"Great. Don't know what I'd do without your blessing." I force sarcasm into my words, but can't suppress a smile.

"'The Assassin' settles down. I can see the headlines now. Women around the greater state of Nevada flood the streets with tears."

"I'm not settling down. We're just hanging out." I grimace at the sour taste of those words from my mouth.

"Right, dude. Whatever you say."

Subject change, ASAP. "You called for a reason?"

"Well, besides calling to find out if you dipped your—"

"Blake." My tone is heavy with warning.

He's laughing. "Training today is moved to eleven."

"Got it."

"Oh, and, Jonah, I want details."

"Keep dreamin'."

His laughing is coming through the phone in loud bursts. "Just hanging out, my ass!"

"You're an asshole."

Hitting end, I toss my phone to the kitchen island, making it skid. I grab the coffee pot and turn to see Raven leaning up against the kitchen doorway. She tilts her head, flashing me a sexy half-smile. How long has she been standing there?

"Let me guess …Blake?"

"Yep, Blake." I fill the coffee maker with water. "How'd you know?" *Or better yet, how much did you hear?*

"I heard the a-hole part when I walked in."

Good. I'm glad she didn't hear the part about us just hanging out. I know it's more than that, but Blake's nosey ass doesn't need to know.

"He really knows how to get you going, huh?"

"It's safe to say Blake knows how to get everyone going." I scoop coffee grounds into the filter, spilling some on the counter. "Except you, you actually laugh at him."

Most girls who laugh at Blake are trying to get him take them home. No way Raven has feelings for Blake. Jealousy, mean and ugly, twists in my gut.

"He's funny." She says it like it's the most obvious thing in the world.

I stop what I'm doing and turn to her, arms crossed at my chest. "How funny?"

She shrugs and comes to me from across the kitchen. "Really funny."

The urge to beat the snot out of Blake comes out of nowhere. A need to protect or mark what's mine overwhelms me. Something primal and male pushes my feet to move across the room and make a point.

I close the space between us, grab both hands full of her ass, and fuse my lips to hers. Her body tenses for a moment, probably shocked by my sudden need, before her muscles melt against mine. She clutches at my shoulders with a moan that settles behind my ribs. I use my hold on her backside to lift her up on the counter and step between her legs. The heat from her skin sears mine as she presses in close. My hands tangle in her hair, gripping tight and pulling back, opening her to me. Her body relaxes, giving me control. I growl in victory before I break the kiss: no slow sweeps of my tongue to bring her back, just a quick nip at her lower lip.

"Wow." She straightens out of my hold. With her hands locked behind my neck, she leans her forehead against mine. "What was that for?" She pulls back, her eyes searching my face. "Wait, was that …are you jealous?"

She knows? Of course she knows. I acted like a complete animal.

"I had to be sure."

"Be sure?"

"Yeah. Be sure that I do it for you."

Her eyebrows pinch together. "And?"

"Baby, the way you just gave yourself over to me? No question."

Her eyes grow wide and her face gets red, but she doesn't deny it. Yeah, I totally do it for her. Blake can live.

I run my thumbs across the heat of her blush. "Do you work today?"

She blinks as if she's just been released from a spell before her shy smile is directed at me. "I'm on call."

"I'll finish up the coffee. You check in with Guy and find out if he needs you in today. If not, I want you to go to training with me."

"Training with you?" Her hands tense behind my neck. "I mean, won't you get in trouble if you bring a friend?"

I tuck her loose hair behind her ear before cupping her jaw, my thumb skating along her lower lip. My eyes follow the path of my thumb, remembering what she tastes like. "Friend? Is that what you are?"

She tries to drop her chin. I hold her face to mine, locking her eyes.

"No, at least, I hope I'm more."

"Yeah, baby, you're definitely more. So, the answer to your question is no, I won't get in trouble if I bring you to training.

We can swing by your place, feed Dog the cat, you can change and grab some of your stuff for the next couple days."

A slight tremor runs through her body. "Days?"

I ignore her question. After last night and this morning, with her sexy warm body pressed against mine and waking up to her giggles, her throaty moans, and my hand up her shirt, she isn't going to be sleeping anywhere, but my bed in my arms from now on. *Or as long as this lasts.*

"Come to training with me. You'll like it. You might even pick up on a few things."

"Don't think I need MMA skills in my everyday life at the garage."

"True," I say, twisting a piece of her soft hair around my finger. "But it wouldn't hurt to know how to break someone's arm."

I laugh at her horrified expression.

"You can do that? Break someone's arm?"

"Come to training and I'll show you."

A quick call to Guy confirms that she's free for the day. She had a hard time explaining why she was over at my house at nine o'clock in the morning, but it seems he bought her excuse that she was here working on the Impala. Their close relationship puts me at ease. In the short time I've known Raven, I haven't seen her talk on the phone to anyone outside of Eve and Guy. She's mentioned that she and her mom aren't close. I remind myself to ask her about that later.

Ready for the day, me showered and dressed, Raven properly caffeinated, we head to my garage. She walks to the truck and waits for me to hit the locks.

"Which one do you want to take?" I motion to all of the available forms of transportation.

Stunned, she looks up at me like a kid who just walked through the gates of Disneyland.

"I get to pick?"

"Sure, if you want to."

"Heck yeah, I want to!"

She walks to the Harley without hesitation and hits me with the stupefying smile she did last night. So open, and trusting but also something beyond that. Believing.

I try to ignore the tightening in my chest. "The Harley it is. Grab a helmet."

We climb on, and I try hard not to smile like a complete jackass as she wraps her arms around my waist. The weight of her head touches my back, and I could swear she was hugging me.

There's not a guy out there that wouldn't list having his girl on the back of his bike as one of the best feelings in the world. Her knees are at my hips and the heat of her body at my ass. Yeah, I'm smiling like a jackass all right. At least she's behind me so she can't see it.

TEN

RAVEN

Fan-freaking-tastic. That's the only way to describe riding on the back of a Harley Blackline with my super-hot, badass boyfriend. The words tumble around in my head, making my stomach flutter, or maybe it's the adrenaline from the ride. My guess is a combination of both.

The sun is shining, and there's a comfortable breeze from the speed of the bike. Jonah's massive body commands the incredible piece of machinery as we twist and turn through the Las Vegas streets. I can't help but wonder what it would be like to drive it myself. I make a mental note to ask Jonah if he would teach me.

He takes the long way to my place, making sure to hit some of the most beautiful parts of town. On a particularly long stretch of road, I loosen my hold on his waist and tighten my knees at his hips. With a quick prayer, I throw my arms over my head, completely free, and howl like a wild dog. Jonah's body shakes with what I assume is laughter, but I can't hear over the roar of the bike. A little embarrassed by my blissful liberation, I wrap my arms around his body and hug him to me.

We pull up to Guy's Garage, and Jonah parks the Harley right next to my Nova. I swing my leg over the bike and dismount while he holds it steady. Pulling my helmet off, I smooth the tussled ends of my hair. Kickstand down, I admire him as he comes off the bike. He exudes confidence and stability, like a man well aware of his body and its capabilities. His red t-shirt hugs his torso, and his jeans are baggy but tight in all the right places. He removes his helmet and walks around my car checking it out. He's seen it plenty of times from a distance, but never close-up.

I study the look of concentration on his face. "Well, what do you think?"

His gaze snaps to mine. "What do I think? I think it's amazing." He bends at the waist with his hands on his hips to look in the driver's side window. "Original interior, stock shifter, steering wheel ...Raven, baby, you did this?"

I'm back to perma-grin status. My chest swells with pride at the surprise in his voice.

"Yeah, it took me two years saving money for parts and working on it in my free time."

He closes the space between us and wraps his arms around my waist, placing his hands on my bottom. Just like in his kitchen, the simple touch ignites my blood and I feel something I don't feel often. Sexy.

"I'm so proud of you, babe. This," he gestures to the car with a nod, "is incredible. *You* are incredible."

His words penetrate deep into my soul, shaking the useless rubble of the protective wall he destroyed just last night.

Pushing up to my toes, I place my hands on his chest and slowly brush my lips against his. His grip flexes against my bottom. I make another pass at his lips, and another, then open my mouth and allow the tip of my tongue to drag against his full lower lip. He reaches into my hair and tugs gently, angling me to him and taking no prisoners. His lips cover mine, tongue thrusting into my mouth. A groan rumbles against my palms, sending my blood soaring. His kiss is possessive and dominant, and I moan into his eager mouth. Without warning, I feel the sunbaked metal of my car against my back as Jonah pins me there. He grinds his hips into my belly and my legs go weak. Time passes, minutes or hours I'm not sure, as I lose myself in his kiss.

"We need to slow down before we get arrested for indecent exposure." His wicked grin and hungry eyes have me thinking it's worth the risk.

He holds me firmly against the car until my breathing calms and I regain the use of my legs.

"You okay?" he asks, a wolfish smile tugging at his lips.

"I'm good."

With two steps back, he releases me from his hold, but grabs my hand.

He shrugs one shoulder. "Show me your place."

I head for my apartment in a Jonah-induced fog. Will I ever get used to being with him? Or will I be stumbling over my feet every time we're together.

"Ray!"

Just steps from the alley, I hear the unmistakable call. Guy is standing in the bay, his glare so tight I can't see the color of his eyes.

"Um, I'll be right back." I let go of Jonah's hand only to feel him hold on tighter.

"No. I'm coming with you." His expression is relaxed, but determined.

This should be interesting. Guy has never seen me with a man before, mainly because I've never dated one. And now here I am, walking hand in hand with The Las Vegas Casanova.

"Hey, what's up?" My unusually high voice has Guy's scowl narrowing.

He looks back and forth between Jonah and me, his eyes darting from our joined hands to our faces. "What's going on here?"

"Oh, uh …well, we just—"

"Raven and I are dating, sir."

Guy's face goes from pinched and small to wide and slack. "Dating."

"Yes, sir." Jonah pulls me to his side, letting go of my hand and throwing his arm over my shoulder.

I smile up at Guy, who's back to glaring. This time, it's aimed directly at Jonah.

"Didn't know you were the dating type, son."

My heart races at Guy's blunt confrontation of Jonah's reputation.

"Never was. I am now." Jonah's answer is accompanied by a firm squeeze.

I want to jump up and down at the certainty that laces Jonah's words. Instead, I wrap my arm around his waist and hug him to me, smiling huge at Guy.

His face relaxes, the corner of his mouth twitching. "Right then." He points in Jonah's face, putting on his best fatherly expression. "Behave yourself."

Now it's Jonah who's fighting a grin. "Yes, sir."

With a curt nod, Guy walks back into the garage. I exhale the breath I was holding and lead Jonah to the alley. That went well, but if I know Guy, we'll be talking about it later.

We take the stairs to my door, and I watch the playful humor slide from his face. I grab my keys and open the door.

"This is it." I motion for him to enter.

He glowers around the 500 square feet. "It's …cute."

I'd be embarrassed if I thought his distaste was due to my poverty, but it's clear in the way he checks out the street lights and the locks on my door that he's concerned for my safety. My heart beats a little faster.

"Make yourself at home. I'm going to change and grab a few things."

Thankful that I hit the laundromat a couple days ago, I pull a black lace bra and panty set, my favorite jeans, and a black tank top into my arms. I step into the bathroom and slide the curtain closed. Changing quickly so that Jonah doesn't have to wait, I brush on some mascara and swipe on lip gloss. I grab my toiletries and walk back out into my room.

On the way to my backpack, I freeze and bite back my smile. Seeing a UFL Heavyweight on my tiny twin bed makes it look like a Twinkie. I lose the battle and a laugh shoots from my throat. He looks at me like he knows what I'm laughing about and totally agrees.

"Can you imagine both of us in this bed? Or hell, just me?" He looks perplexed while he studies the bed from top to bottom, which sends me into full-fledged hilarity.

"If we stay here, you'll have to sleep on the floor." I manage to say through my giggles.

His hazel eyes darken, his amusement replaced by something tangible and consuming. "Not sleepin' on the floor, babe. I'm starting to think of a few different ways we could fit."

I suck in a breath and try not to fidget as electricity vibrates between us.

Breaking the moment before we set something on fire, I shove things into my backpack. Jonah gets up from the bed and goes to the small bookshelf in the corner of the room. I do a quick mental inventory of what's there, hoping he doesn't find anything embarrassing. Thank God, I got rid of the Kama Sutra book Eve gave me on my last birthday as a gag. Other than a Bible, some romance novels, and a few pictures, there's nothing much to see.

"That's insane," he says with wonder in his voice.

He picks up a small framed picture that I know is of my mom. It's the only picture I have of her. I took it before I moved out, wanting to keep something of her, even if she wanted nothing to do with me. I remember catching her on the couch after she worked late. She had taken a long, hot shower, as she always did after work. She had on a pink, cotton, floor-length nightgown. She was listening to The Temptations, staring out the window at the distant lights of Las Vegas Boulevard with a lost look on her face. I'll never forget how her beauty clashed dramatically with the ugliness she held in her eyes. I grabbed my throw away camera and snapped the shot. She was in such a daze she didn't even flinch. That was two years ago. I haven't seen her since.

"Raven, you look just like her. She's gorgeous."

"Yeah, she is."

My chest burns with heartbreak like it does every time I think about my mom. I absently rub my chest in an attempt to push back the pain. I can't do this right now, going from the extreme high of the last twelve hours with Jonah to this extreme low.

Anyone up for a ride on the bi-polar coaster?

He puts the picture back and turns toward me. There is a kindness in his eyes that makes me feel vulnerable. I look away.

Grabbing my stuff, I remember the can of cat food and head for the door. "Ready?"

He's standing in the same place, his hands shoved into his pockets. I watch as something works behind his eyes, like he wants to say something but he can't sort it out.

With a long breath, he nods and smiles. "Yeah."

Walking up to the UFL Training Center doors, my stomach flutters with nerves. The idea of being inside a room filled with guys just like Jonah is daunting and intimidating as heck.

He holds my hand as we push through the entrance and I grip him tighter.

Air conditioning and heavy metal hum through the lobby. Bright red couches and sleek side tables line the dark gray walls. At the far wall sits a desk with a striking strawberry blond woman sitting behind it.

Jonah tosses the lovely lady a quick chin lift. Her perky smile fades as her eyes hit me. I give her a small wave of my fingers and suppress the urge to throw her my middle one. I chalk up my aggressive attitude to all the testosterone that drips down the walls like honey.

We make our way down a hallway lined with doors. As we near the end, I hear the vibration of male voices. They get louder and louder until we emerge from the hallway into a massive room.

Clean sweat and the unmistakable smell of man fill the room along with the called-out directions of trainers and grunts of fighters. I slow my pace until a tug on my hand has me moving. He leads me towards the center of the gym where roughly a dozen men are grouped off in various forms of fighting. Some are fighting on a mat while others are punching and kicking bags. A few are taking a break, soaked in sweat and sucking down water, some are on the floor stretching. There is a large octagon in the middle of the room where two men are boxing. The combinations of voices and metal music bounce off the concrete walls and high ceilings, putting a palpable energy in the air.

"Give me your backpack. I'll put it in my locker." I hand it to him without looking away from the activity on the floor.

Slowly, the action stops and the room goes quiet. It's then that I notice all eyes are on me. *Crud.* I look for Jonah but catch his back as he passes through the locker room door.

Facing the room, I lift a hand to wave, my expression probably as awkward as I feel.

"Who are you?" a handsome, older man calls out to me.

I clear my throat. "I'm Raven." I try unsuccessfully to control the shake in my voice.

"That's Jonah's girl. She's cool."

I exhale in relief at the sound of Blake's voice.

He makes his way over to me, and the rest of the guys stare for a minute longer before they resume their training.

"Hey, baby girl. Where's Jonah?"

His shirt is off and his skin glistens with sweat. Yesterday at Jonah's party, he never took his shirt off. I stand staring at the military tattoo that takes up one whole side of his chest, but avert my eyes to his face before I can make out what it says. He's smiling at me in his usual charming way.

"He went to put some stuff in his locker." I chew the inside of my cheek. "Is it okay that I'm here? I wouldn't want to disrupt or cause any problems."

"Are you kidding?" He looks at the guys over his shoulder and back to me. "You just gave these butt holes a reason to show off. They'll probably have the best session of their lives with you here to put up for."

My lips twitch, fighting my smile.

"You laugh even when I'm not trying to be funny. What'd I say?"

I cover my mouth to muffle my giggles. "You said butt holes."

He shakes his head, looks to the floor then back at me. "You ever cuss, Raven?"

My laughter dies as I contemplate his question. *Of course I cuss.* What adult doesn't cuss? Ugh. Who am I kidding? I totally don't. It's not as if I haven't tried. It just always sounds so stupid coming from my mouth.

"Of course I cuss," I lie.

He glares at me with a playful glint in his eye. "Really?"

"Psht. Yes." My palms sweat, and I wonder what it is about this guy that makes me so nervous.

"All right, fine. Hit me with one right now. Give me your nastiest curse."

Rocking back on his heels, he crosses his bulging arms over his muscular chest waiting.

My mouth falls open at the ridiculousness. I snap my mouth shut and square my shoulders.

"Okay, I will." I race through my mind pulling up some of the least offensive curse words I can think of, all of them sounding lame even in my head. "It's just I'm not mad right now and I never cuss unless I'm mad." I hold my head high and pray like crazy that he'll be intimidated by my integrity and leave it alone.

His eyes narrow, and his smile grows by the second. "You can't do it, can you?"

Apparently, my integrity doesn't intimidate; it instigates.

"Yes, I can." I say in a high voice that doesn't even sound like me. What is my problem? Why can't I just friggin' cuss? I am not going to let him get the best of me. No way.

"Go for it, baby girl. I'm waiting."

Girding my proverbial loins, I go for it.

"Shitass!" I blurt then quickly cover my mouth with my hand. My face feels like a Molotov cocktail as the blush takes over my cheeks and neck.

Blake's face is stoic for two beats before he throws his head back in a booming laugh that gets the attention of every guy in the room. This, of course, does not help my situation. It's possible, I discover, to have a full-body blush.

"That was fuckin' awesome." He bends over, sucking in breath.

"What's going on over here, Blake?" Jonah's voice demands as he marches up to us. "Why does my girl look like you just flashed her?"

"Dude, she said, 'shitass.' I've never heard a *sweet* curse word before."

He puts his arm around my shoulder and pulls me to his side. "Of course, it's sweet. She isn't capable of anything less."

My body melts into him, and my blush recedes at the safety of his touch.

"Right. You ready to warm up?" Blake says, a whisper of amusement still lighting his face.

"Yeah, let me get Raven set up and I'll be right there."

"Cool." Blake's eyes move from Jonah to me. He shakes his head. "You're something else, baby girl." Walking away, I hear him mumble something that sounds like lucky bastard.

Jonah's body tenses at my side, drawing my eyes to him. He looks down at me, and I watch the tension leave his face. "You all right?"

"Of course." Thanks to him.

"Blake's not so funny anymore, is he?"

I shrug, slide my arms around Jonah's middle and rest my cheek against his chest. "No, he's still funny."

He chuckles and tugs me to move. "Come on. Let's find you somewhere to sit."

We walk to a row of chairs, and he tells me to take a seat. A firm kiss on the lips, then one to the side of my neck, and he moves to meet Blake and Owen in the octagon.

Taking in my surroundings, I notice gigantic posters on the walls, each depicting a different fighter. I make my way past each one, studying the fighters I recognize until I land on Jonah's.

His poster is by far the most enticing. The photo was taken at an angle, his head turned to face the camera. His eyebrows are dropped low making his eyes look black, and I'm transfixed by the fierceness of his face. No dimples or sexy grin, just pure focus. His lethal arms, posed in punching position, look huge as the vibrant colors of his tattoos intensify the cuts of his muscles. A shiver runs through my body and I turn away to find my seat.

I take a chair up close and set my attention to Jonah in the octagon. It doesn't take long before I'm gasping for air with my hand covering my mouth to keep from crying out. Watching Jonah in action is terrifyingly beautiful. He moves like a predator, graceful yet powerful. His punches and kicks are controlled as he commands his body. On the mat, as he rolls in a tangle of arms and legs, there's no doubt he was born for this.

"Baby! Come here." Jonah's command is terse with loss of breath.

I look up in horror and point to my chest. *Who me?*

He smiles, nods, and waves me over.

"This is going to be embarrassing," I say to no one in particular as I push myself up and head his way.

"I'm going to teach you an arm bar."

Owen leaves the octagon, giving me a sweet smile. "Good luck, princess."

My eyes find Blake who is covering his mouth, but his eyes give away his amusement. *Oh, real nice.*

Jonah and Blake demonstrate a few times, both of them explaining each step in detail with the clarity of professional fighters. I hang on every word, determined to get it right and not make a complete idiot out of myself.

Their instruction complete, they call me over to try. Lying with my back to the mat, I do exactly what I'm shown. After a few minor adjustments, I have Jonah's forearm in my hands. His arm runs the length of my body down through my legs. His shoulder rests between my thighs and my calves are locked around his torso. I thrust my hips forward.

"Fuck." He makes a pained grunt, but I continue to hold him in place. "You got it."

"I did it!" I could break the arm of a man at least twice my size by a thrust of my hips.

Power surges through me and I'm suddenly flipped. Jonah has his huge body wrapped around me like a boa constrictor, his mouth at my ear.

"Yeah, baby. You did it. I'm proud of you." He whispers before nuzzling my neck and dropping lingering kisses on my earlobe.

I shiver.

"That's my girl." He releases me and pulls me to my feet.

Blake is off to the side of the mat. "This," he indicates by waving his hand back and forth between me and Jonah, "is freaking me the hell out." He waves us off then stalks away.

I shrug my shoulders and look to Jonah who has both dimples out in full force.

"You're not the only one," he mumbles.

"What?"

"Nothing."

ELEVEN

JONAH

"Still with the same girl. Gotta say, brother, I didn't think you had it in you."

Owen and I are in the kitchen at the training center, shooting the shit and powering down protein shakes.

"I wasn't sure I had it in me either, but here I am, one full week." Pride warms my chest every time I think about the longest and only relationship I've ever had. It isn't at all like I thought it'd be. She doesn't bug me to buy her shit, ask me to get her into the most exclusive clubs, or fill my bathroom with her girlie crap. I can't even get her to leave clothes at my house. She's always tossing clothes in and out of her backpack.

After that first night, she put up a fight about staying over the next two. Until I told her that I'd personally go and feed Dog every morning if it meant having her warm body in my bed every night. And every night since, she tries to leave again, only agreeing to stay once I kiss her until she surrenders.

"You still haven't slept with her."

Bringing my cup to my mouth, my arm stalls out in midair and I glare at my friend. "How did you know that?"

He swallows a gulp of his shake. "I didn't." A grin spreads across his face. "But I do now."

Fuck.

"Figured you're keeping her around for a reason. What's the hold up?"

"None of your fucking business."

Owen's deep laughter bangs against my every nerve. I could lie. Tell him that she's a virgin and I'm holding off until she's ready. The first part's true. The last part's the lie. She's ready. Her words haven't said it, but her body has screamed it.

"I'm just surprised, man. You have her in your bed every night. How can you, of all people, not fuck her?"

"Owen." The caution in my tone forces him to roll his eyes before he studies me silently.

"That's it, isn't it?" His words are almost a whisper. "I had a feeling, but I wasn't sure."

I toss my empty cup into the sink a little harder than I need to. This entire conversation is pissing me the fuck off. "Sure about what?"

"You love this girl."

Irritation is sucked from my body along with my breath. *Love her. Do I?*

"As long as I've known you, you've never even taken a girl out unless it was something UFL related. You use woman to get off, move on, and never look back. And now here you are, looking like you're about to take me out for asking why you haven't fu—*had sex* with her yet."

I'm hearing his words, but still processing his earlier statement. I remain close-lipped.

He starts laughing, then harder, and points at my face. "Yeah, man. That's the face. You love her."

"But it's only been a week. People don't fall in love in a week."

"The hell they don't? I knew I was in love with Nik on our first date. No question."

We've been spending a lot of time together. Mornings are spent working on the Impala until she goes to Guy's garage and I go train. Nights, she's back at my house where we cook together, eat together, watch television together and—*Holy crap.* We're my parents.

Maybe I do love her.

I wipe the sweat from my forehead, feeling suddenly faint. Must be from the intense training session. Yeah, that's all it is.

"So now that we've established that, what's the real reason you're holding out?" He leans against the counter.

He'd never understand why I haven't slept with Raven. Hell, I'm still trying to figure it out. It's not that I don't want to. I want to, badly. So badly, I've had to sit in a cold shower for forty-five minutes after making out with her. Every time we get close, I hold back. The rejection I see in her eyes when I shut her down makes me want to kick my own ass.

"What if I …I don't know, screw things up?"

Owen's eyebrows hit his hairline. "Dude, if practice makes perfect, you should have your PhD in sex. Pretty sure you won't screw it up."

"That's not what I meant, fuckwad."

He pins me with his stare. "You're afraid you're going to lose interest after you do it."

I blink my eyes, absorbing his words, and conclude that my friend is a genius.

"Yes, exactly, I'm afraid my fucked-up head will ruin things with Raven."

"This is different though, Jonah. I'm telling you the way you feel about Raven you might as well be a virgin too. This is going to be a first for both of you. Be prepared to have your mind blown, my brother. There is nothing like making sweet love to the girl you feel it for."

I remain silent, mulling over Owen's revelation. He's right. I have a problem with getting attached to people on an intimate level. I always assumed that my hit-'em-and-quit-'em mentality was intentional. That I never sleep with the same girl twice because I don't have to.

But I'm seeing things more clearly. A deep dark part of me whispers that it's because I lost my dad. That getting close to someone is a risk because of the potential pain in losing them. And having sex with Raven, combined with the fact that I'll be her first, will be devastating. She'll probably see it as solidifying our relationship, and I'll subconsciously put her in the I-came-I-conquered file.

Unless Owen's right. *Could it be different this time?* It sure as shit feels different. Fighting has always dominated my brain space, until her. I have to believe my old ways won't fuck this up for me. I have to.

—

RAVEN

On an impulse, and an urgent need to update my lingerie collection as new boyfriend status dictates, I talked Eve into meeting me at the mall. Browsing around Victoria's Secret is a new experience now that I'm shopping with someone in mind. Every piece I pick up, I imagine Jonah's reaction to it. I can picture myself in each one, and in doing so, practically feel his eyes on me.

Things with Jonah have escalated physically, but not to the level I'd hoped. It seems like every time I'm about to beg him to make love to me, he freezes up. He's nothing like his reputation, at least, not with me. I tell myself it's because I mean more to him, but a small voice in my head tells me it's because I'm a virgin. An even smaller, but no less influential, voice tells me that he's not sure about us or more specifically, me.

I hold back a frustrated growl and move to a table covered in panties.

"You're staying at his place again?" Eve pulls out a pair of blue leopard-print hip huggers and tosses them in my arms.

"Yeah. He wants me to stay with him every night."

"You're so lucky. The guy I'm dating won't even invite me over."

I look over to see her wiping her eyes with a pair of cotton bikini underwear and then tossing them back on the display table. We've been at Victoria Secret for almost an hour, and I've been so wrapped up with Jonah, I never even asked about her boyfriend.

"I'm a jerk. Sorry. Here I'm going on about Jonah, and I never asked about, um, what's his name?"

She bursts into tears. I drag her back and lock us into a dressing room, dropping my arm full of stuff and pulling her into a hug.

"Eve, what is going on? Did you guys break up?"

"No." She sniffs, and wipes her nose on a pair of panties I *was* going to buy. "I think he's into me. I mean he tells me he's in love with me every time we have sex."

Envy creeps in at the thought that Eve's getting sex and I love you. To be fair, I've known that I'm in love with Jonah since my first night in his bed, but haven't told him. Could it be possible that he feels it too, but just hasn't said it?

"So then, why are you crying?"

She looks up at me, and I can see the pain in her eyes. "He's so secretive. I've asked him if he's married or, like, I don't know, a member of the Secret Service, but he just laughs and swears it's just because he's skittish about relationships." She straightens her shirt and checks her make up in the mirror.

"I'm sure he's not married. Hasn't he gone into your restaurant on the nights you're working? Surely he wouldn't show up at the restaurant his girlfriend manages if he wanted to keep the relationship a secret."

Her eyes drop to the floor. "He only came in the one time. Now we just hang out at my house."

That doesn't sound good.

"I wouldn't think the worst yet. Give him some time. If things don't get better in the next few weeks, break it off."

She nods and takes a shaky breath. "Yeah, you're right. Sorry." She manages a sad smile. "You want to try any of this on? Might as well since we're in here."

I study the pile of lace and satin at my feet. Maybe one of those will be the pair to finally break Jonah's iron restraint. "I'll just get them all."

JONAH

I'm pulling swordfish out of the fridge to throw on the grill for dinner. Raven says she can't eat anything that isn't microwavable at her place. Since she's been staying with me, I cook almost every night. With my strict training diet, eating out is next to impossible.

Raven's recent text said she was on her way, and I want to get dinner going so she can eat when she gets here. I shake my head, contemplating what in the hell has gotten into me. I told myself I'd had enough of taking care of people when I moved out of my mom's house. Nothing will shove you into a lifestyle of partying and irresponsibility like becoming a man at twelve. When I moved out at eighteen and came to Vegas, I was like a big kid in an adult candy store.

The sound of my phone bumps me from my thoughts. I check the caller ID.

"Hi, Mom."

"Hey, Joey, how are you?"

Rolling my eyes at her nickname for me, I wonder why she didn't just name me Joey. "I'm really good. How about you?"

"I'm great. Just got back from spending time with Beth and the boys. They're getting so big."

I rub my forehead, reminding myself to call my little sister Beth. She lives in Phoenix with her husband Rick and twin boys. Things have been so hectic I haven't stayed in touch.

"Yeah, I need to make a trip out for a visit. I'll do that after the fight."

"Oh, that would be great. She'd love to see you. What have you been up to lately?"

"Just training, getting ready for the fight. I've been working on the Impala I bought last year. I found a great mechanic who's been coming over every day helping me take it apart, clean it up."

I feel guilty keeping Raven a secret from my mom. She's not some dirty indulgence or a passing good time. Even though I've never talked to my mom about the recreational girls in my past, with Raven, things are different.

"Mom, I want to tell you I met someone. It's the mechanic who's helping me with my car. Things are getting serious between us, and I thought you should know."

Silence.

"Mom?"

I check to make sure our call didn't get dropped. Nope, still connected.

"Mom, you still there?"

She clears her throat. "Yes, Joey, I'm here."

Why is she acting so weird? I know I've never had a serious girlfriend before, but I thought she would be off the wall about my finally settling down.

"What's wrong? I thought you'd be excited about my being in a serious relationship."

"Oh, honey, I'm very happy for you. It's just …I guess I thought …Well, it's just a shock, that's all. I always thought you liked girls."

My eyes bug out of my head and I choke. I cough to clear my voice. "What? Of course, I like girls. Wait, Mom, Raven *is* a girl! Shit, you thought I was telling you I was dating a guy? Fuck me."

"First of all, Joey, you watch your mouth. Second, what was I supposed to think? You told me you were dating your mechanic!"

I laugh so hard that it brings tears to my eyes.

"No. Raven is very much female." My laughter calms. "You'll meet her when you come out for the fight. She's been staying with me, so I guess that will give you guys a chance to get to know each other."

"Oh, honey, that would be wonderful. I can't wait."

"Shit, Ma! You thought I was gay! Fuckin' hell."

"Jonah Ryan Slade, you watch that mouth!"

After giving her the details I've arranged for her flight, I finish up with my mom and go back to preparing dinner. While pulling out some vegetables to grill, I hear the front door open.

"Baby! I'm in here," I yell from the kitchen.

The soft beat of her Converse against the tile floor has me smiling. Her chest presses into my back as her arms wrap around my waist.

"Hey," she says softly into my back, and bringing on an even bigger smile.

I turn around and wrap my arms around her, placing a wet kiss against my spot over the tattoo on her neck. The pear scent of her hair, combined with the sweet taste of her skin, is a heady mixture. I trail kisses along her jaw then pull at her lips with mine. After a little coaxing, she tilts her head, always eager, but making me work for it. Perfect. My tongue explores, gliding against the roof of her mouth and her teeth. Sucking on her lips, I slowly pull back. We lock eyes, panting and hungry, giving our blood a chance to cool.

She looks past my arm at the fish. "Mmm, is that swordfish?" Her voice carries a different kind of hunger.

"Yeah, you ready to eat?"

"Mm-hmm."

I grab an iced tea for her, and we head out to light the grill. We settle ourselves at the bar. It's getting warmer, but the outdoor misting system and ceiling fans make the temperature perfect for eating outside.

"How was shopping?" I grab myself a Muscle Milk from the outdoor cooler.

"Good. How was your day?"

I pop the top off my drink, take a swing, and lean a hip on the bar. "Infinitely better if those bags I heard you drop at the door are pink."

"How did you know?" She sips her tea that I've sweetened and added lemon to, just like she likes it. "Mmm." She takes another sip.

"Babe, if you keep this up, you're going to have to take on a sponsor. And I'd like to be the first to volunteer."

"I only buy the stuff that's on sale." She sets down her drink and traces patterns into the condensation on the glass. "I know I don't make much now, but I will. I have a plan."

Why am I not surprised? I take a few steps to the barstool next to her and drop down. "What's your plan?"

She shrugs and drops her eyes to her lap. Her delicate hands knot together, something I notice she does before she opens up about something personal, so I wait patiently.

"Guy said when he retires he's handing ownership of the shop to me. He has no children of his own, and he knows I love the garage."

"Really?"

"Yeah."

"Wow." I lean back and prop my feet on the bar.

She fixes me with a glare, but the shadow of a smile plays on her lips. "Wow? Is it that hard to believe?"

"Not a lot of women dream of owning their own auto body shop."

"I don't know if you've noticed," her shoulders slump and she picks at her nails, "I'm not like most women."

"No, baby, you certainly are not."

She peers up at me from beneath her eyelashes. "It would be nice to own a business, make my own hours. If I'm ever lucky enough to get married and have kids, it'll make things easier." Her cheeks turn pink and she hides behind her tea.

My mind conjures up images of Raven, her belly swollen with a baby. And like the flicker of an old home movie, pictures flash of her cradling a dark-haired infant. Scattered visions of dark pigtails, training wheels, and ballet recitals manifest behind my eyes.

"Holy shit." I grind my fists into my eye sockets, rubbing out the fantasy. That has never happened to me before. Never.

"You okay?"

I shake it off, pull it together, and attempt to hide the full-fledged freak out that's bubbling to the surface.

"Yeah, fine. Just a-a weird headache or s-something." *I'm fucking stuttering!*

Time for evasive maneuvers. I breathe deep, and fix my eyes on hers. The concern in her face dissolves into an easy smile. I smile back, making sure it's bright enough to expose both dimples. It's a desperate move, but it works. She licks her full lips, slowly rubbing them together in anticipation of what's coming. As I'm leaning in, happy to give her what she wants, the muffled sound of her phone fills the air.

"Whoops, sorry." She grabs her phone from her pocket. Glancing down at the caller ID, her eyebrows scrunch and mouth goes tight.

"Who is it?"

"I don't know. I don't recognize the number."

"Answer it, baby."

She nods and hits the answer button before pressing the phone to her ear.

"Hello." Her pleasant smile quickly fades. Her body shoots ramrod straight, and the color drains from her face.

TWELVE

JONAH

What the hell? Blood pumps in my ears, and a mild buzz starts at the base of my neck.

"I'm fine." She's being polite to the mystery caller, but her voice is completely void of its usual spunk.

Alarms fire in my head.

Her eyes snap up to mine and widen a fraction. "Meet with you tomorrow?"

I'm up from my barstool and standing at her side. Less than a foot away, I'm able to make out the voice coming through her phone. I can't hear exact words, but the low mumbles are undoubtedly male. *Fuck.*

"Um …I don't know. I mean, why now?" She looks at her lap and rubs her forehead with her free hand.

The man on the phone mumbles on, and she worries her bottom lip. Her eyes hit mine, and a tiny spark of my Raven is back. "Okay, see you then."

She hangs up the phone and stares at it in her hand as if she doesn't know how it got there. Then she looks up at me.

"Who was that?" My voice is calm, but not in a way that provides comfort.

She places the phone on the bar like it's made of glass. "That was Dominick."

Adrenaline rocks my body. My muscles tense. The buzz in my head intensifies with every hammer of my heart.

"He wants to meet with me tomorrow at ten a.m."

"No fucking way."

She pins me with a glare. "Why not?"

How can she ask me that? I told her she needed to stay away from that guy.

"Because I said so." I annunciate every word slowly to avoid roaring in her face, but she still flinches.

"I told him I'd go. I'm going." She says it with such conviction I can't decide if I want to shake her or kiss her.

"Fine. I'm going with you." This woman is infuriating. Why can't she just do what I say? I pinch the bridge of my nose and close my eyes, trying to numb the all-consuming buzz that makes me want to rip Dominick Morretti apart.

"No, he said I have to come alone."

My eyes shoot open before they narrow in anger. "What! Why? Who says that unless they're up to something?" I don't mean to yell, but my fight or flight reaction is kicking in and flight is *not* in my vocabulary. "What the fuck, Raven? I told you I don't want you anywhere near that guy, and you promised you'd stay away from him!"

"I know, I promised but—"

"But what? Do you have any idea what this guy's like? Word around town says he's got his hands in everything, not just prostitution. He's been questioned for murder, drugs, weapons. Shit, Raven, he's only walking free because he's got his money so far up law enforcements ass I'm surprised they don't shit gold."

"Please, stop." She whispers to her lap.

"Stop! Stop what? Your psycho dad calls and wants to meet with you *alone,* and you want me to sit here on my fucking hands and do nothing? God, Raven! This guy's a criminal." I pace the around the bar to burn off some aggression. The last thing I want to do is scare her, but fuck. "If you think I'm going to let you meet that dickhead alone, you're crazy."

She sniffs and wipes her eyes. *Ah, crap.* I breathe in and out of my nose and count to ten. My heart rate slows enough that it's no longer throbbing in my ears as I wrangle my wild impulses.

"Baby, I'm sorry." I smooth her hair behind her ear. "I didn't mean to scare you. I just lost it for a second."

She wipes the tears from her cheek. "You don't understand."

Closing the space between us, I pull her chin up to look in her eyes. "Explain it to me."

"Ever since I was a kid, I'd dreamed that one day he would come along and ask for me. Even after I found out what he was, I still wanted him." Her eyes look away, but I don't release her chin. "I still wanted a dad."

Her words shoot through my rage, straight to my heart. I wouldn't give up the twelve years I had with my dad for anything. And as painful as it was to lose him, I had a dad who loved me. Raven's never felt that.

Who am I to say that Dominick's intentions aren't good? Maybe he does want a relationship with Raven. I'd bet my balls that's not true, but if I don't allow her to find out for herself, if I stand between her and the possibility, she'll never forgive me.

I brush my thumb along her lower lip, feeling it quiver beneath my touch. "Okay, baby. I get it."

Her eyes smile through her tears and she kisses my thumb.

With a tug, she's up from her barstool. I wrap my arms around her waist. She locks her hands behind my neck, holding me to her.

"You'll call me when you get there." I'm so close to her mouth, I can smell the sweet tea on her breath.

"Yes." Her answer is breathy and full of need.

My girl. Always so responsive.

She puts pressure on my neck to bring me to her, but I'm not finished.

"And you'll call me when you're finished." I slide my hands down to her ass, drawing her hips closer.

"Mm-hmm." Her answer comes out on a moan.

"Not when you get in your car, not when you get home, but when you're walking away, you call me." I tighten my hold to make sure she understands. I'm not fucking around.

"Yes, Jonah, I'll do anything. Just kiss me, please."

"That's more like it."

I drop a soft kiss against her lips. She pushes up on her tiptoes, pressing hard against me searching for my lips, but I hold back. She whines adorably, and I reward her by feathering another kiss on her lips.

"Please."

Her final plea shatters the last of my control. I cover her mouth with mine. My hand slides up her shirt along her spine, desperate to feel her skin. She arches her back, and pulls me in, shifting her weight so that our torsos are touching from chest to hip.

With her body soft and pliable in my hands, the taste of her tongue flooding my mouth, my chest tightens with feelings I'm only beginning to name. She owns me completely. The pull I felt toward her when we met, waking up with her in my arms, my conversation with Owen, my compulsion to protect her, everything jumbles in my head until need coils in my sternum. Not the usual need that rips at me, but something stronger. It's been seeping in slowly and now crushes me from the inside out.

I hold her to me, hoping the strength in my arms will give me the power to do what I've never done before. Breaking the kiss, her eyes lock on mine, questioning. Even through my nervousness, in this moment, nothing has looked as clear or as obvious.

"I love you, Raven."

She gasps and her body jerks. She looks at me as if seeing me for the first time. Her shaky hand covers her mouth. Her head rocks back and forth slowly in what looks like disbelief. She doesn't say it back and I don't care. I love her. If she's not there yet, I'll wait as long as it takes until she is.

Without warning, she launches into me, our lips fusing together in wild passion. Her tongue slides into my mouth along with a soft moan that shoots to my throat. I tilt her head to plunge in deep, walking her backwards to the closest lounger. I crave Raven in a way that makes the dozen yards to the house seem like miles.

Laying her back, I brace my body above hers to keep from crushing her. I flex my hips into the warmth between her legs. She grinds into me, and I fight the urge to claim her here by the pool. Not like this. She deserves better.

I move to my spot at her neck and feel her racing pulse against my tongue. Her hands slide from my lower back to my stomach where she runs her fingers along the waistline of my shorts. She pulls at my zipper.

"Not yet, baby. Soon, but not tonight," I whisper against her skin before nipping at her earlobe.

Her hands fall away on a hopeless sigh. I nuzzle her neck to avoid the look of rejection that I'm sure colors her face. My body screams to join with hers. To show her how deep my feelings run. But I'd never forgive myself for taking her in my backyard like a cheap party date.

"Baby, I'm sorry. I want you, I do. But you deserve—"

"It's okay. But you said soon. Promise?"

I grimace at the dejected sound in her voice.

My lips skate along her jawline to her mouth. "Yes. I promise."

Sliding my hand against the smooth skin of her belly, she writhes against me. I pull her shirt over her head and take in her bright green bra. My thumbs make firm passes over the sensitive tips through the silk. Feeling isn't enough. I need to see them. I tug the fabric down, releasing her full breasts to the tepid night air. *Fucking gorgeous.*

I kiss the valley between them, breathing in her subtle sweet fragrance. She arches her back in a silent plea. I smile against her eager little body before taking her breasts into my mouth, first one and then the other. The sweet taste of her delicate skin increases my appetite for more.

I pop the button of her shorts, and she lifts her hips for me to slide them down her legs.

"Good girl."

"Jonah—"

"Don't worry, baby. I'll take care of you."

Her eyes flare and she bites her lip. I take a deep breath and remind myself to take it slow. This isn't the *get in, get out* operation I'm used to. For the first time, I'm not thinking of my own needs. Only about taking Raven's body to new places, to express what I feel emotionally through loving her physically.

Her lips curl in a wicked grin as she shimmies off her matching lace panties. I watch in awe as she reveals her perfect body to me. Sitting up to unhook her bra, she removes the last scrap of covering, my gaze held firm by her seductive show. She's completely exposed, and I stare in wonder as she falls back on the lounger, legs parted.

"You're stunning." My voice sounds heavy and rough with desire.

I rip my shirt off over my head and toss it behind me. My lips ache with the urge to taste every inch of her olive skin.

"Hmm, I was just thinking the same thing."

I run my hands along her thighs, her knees falling wide open in response. "Raven, I need to taste you."

She nods her head once, her body yielding to my every touch. *Perfect.*

Taking my time, I kiss the tender skin of her inner thigh. With teasingly long swipes of my tongue, I give her a sample of what's to come. Her heels dig into the lounger, and she pushes her hips up, searching for contact. Just the invitation I need.

I take my first taste and growl in pleasure. *So sweet.* I fight the urge devour her, wanting to take my time and make it last. She moans and rolls her hips. I look up the length of her toned stomach to see her eyes squeezed shut. *That won't do.*

I back off. "Baby, look at me."

Her eyes lock on mine, passion swirling in their blue-green depths. I slow down, but maintain eye contact. Every hitch of her breath stimulates my need to please her.

This is so different. And more arousing than anything I've experienced in the past. My love takes a front seat to my body's desire for release.

I stare, absorbed in the visual of her mouth dropped open as she pants for breath. Her bare chest heaves with every flick of my tongue. Moans turn into desperate cries and her legs quake. Slow is no longer an option. I want nothing more than to hold her, to feel her against my lips while she falls apart for me. Her hips push and roll, seeking. I lock my hands on her hips, holding her still, and give into her body's demands.

She grabs a fistful of my hair, holding me to her, pressing me deeper. Her voice catches and she calls out my name in release. Moans of pleasure fall from her lips, and the sound sends shockwaves straight between my legs. My stomach tightens, and I flex my hips into the lounger, groaning at the relief in the friction. I continue until she squirms, unable to give her up. With a final, tender kiss, I pull away. She falls back, her body sated and limp.

My girl. Her eyes are closed, and I'm entranced by the rise and fall of her breasts as she breathes. I gently press her legs together, removing myself from in between, to climb in next to her. Moving her hair from her damp face, her eyes flutter open.

"That was amazing." I marvel in the beauty of her satisfied expression.

"I thought that was my line." Her sexy post-orgasm voice vibrates in a way that I feel in my shorts.

I grab a towel from the table next to us and cover her naked body.

"Do you want to go inside?" I trace the delicate angles of her face with my fingertip.

Her mouth tilts to a grin. "I have a better idea."

She pushes herself up off the lounger, leaving the towel behind. With her back toward me, I admire the luscious curves of her bare flesh in the moonlight. She winks at me over her shoulder and, with a small bend of her knees, she jumps into the pool. *Skinny dipping? Hell, yeah!*

Kicking off my shorts, I jump in after her, keenly aware of my killer hard-on that even the cool water won't tame.

She floats on her back, and I shamelessly gawk at her perfect breasts poking out from the water. Catching my stare, she swims over to me in the shallow end.

"It's your turn," she says as she pushes me back to the steps of the pool.

My heart pounds in my chest. Does she mean what I think she means?

"Sit." She directs me to sit on the top step where the water is the shallowest.

Eyes still locked on mine, she pulls my legs apart and crawls between them. Her soft, slick body brushes the insides of my thighs, heating my oversensitive skin. With her knees on the step below me, she props herself up to meet my eyes. Her breasts drip with pool water and sex appeal.

"I've never done this before, so don't expect much." Even in the dim light, I catch the red that colors her cheeks.

"Raven, you don't have to do this."

She places her finger against my lips, silencing further protest.

Was I just talking her out of giving me a blow job? That's a first.

"I'll just, um, go for it, but if I do something wrong, will you show me?" Her innocent eyes implore mine.

"No way you could do it wrong, baby. I'm almost there just listening to you talk about it."

With a nod and a smile, she sits back on her heels. Her wet sexy body glistens in the dark, and I know I'm not going to last long. She looks down and licks her lips, then takes me into her mouth. Sucking in a breath, I dig my teeth into my lower lip to keep from groaning in pleasure. My hands fist in her damp hair, not to control her speed or caress, but in pure animal possession.

To think that I could experience this all-consuming lust, as well as the soul-shackling love that I would die to keep, is life changing. This tiny girl who works on cars, laughs at stupid jokes, and blushes at the slightest flirtation is mine. There is nothing I wouldn't do for her. I would spend the rest of my life making her happy if she'd let me.

So this is love.

My life will never be the same.

I pull her hand from my thigh and wrap it around myself, guiding her strokes before leaving her to it. Her velvety touch striking deep in my core, my hips push off the step. She leans in, the silky push from her breasts at my thighs dropping my head back. Sensations combine with hunger and love, and *fuck*—My stomach tightens, my release coiling in my abdomen. I've got seconds.

"Baby, stop." I lose her mouth as a delirious groan falls from my lips. I unravel in her hand. Her tight little fist continues to pump and the euphoria intensifies. *What the hell?* I'm panting, colors swirling behind my eyelids. My legs tense as I'm rocked with aftershocks. "Oh shit." I blink open my eyes, fascinated that Raven's first blowjob is the most consuming sexual experience I've ever had.

"I'm sorry. Did I hurt you?" Her arms are wrapped around her chest, a concerned expression on her perfect face.

I fight what could very well be a goofy smile, and lose. "Hurt me?" I lean in, elbows to knees. "Does it look like that hurt me?"

Pushing off from the step, I meet her in the shallow end. I walk her back to the side of the pool and gather her in my arms. Her muscles relax against my own.

"Baby, this has been the most amazing night of my life. Everything about it is perfect, including that kick-ass blow job you just gave me."

Her giggles erupt against my chest, and I kiss the top of her head.

"I love you, Raven," I say into her hair.

She tilts her chin up, resting it on my chest. Her wet hair is slicked back, black eyelashes thick with water, and her lips deep red and swollen from taking me. Her stare bores into mine, and I watch something heavy working in her aquamarine eyes.

"I love you too."

THIRTEEN

RAVEN

I'm pulling out of Jonah's garage at exactly nine twenty-eight a.m. I'm second-guessing that third cup of coffee, my hands shake on the steering wheel, and my empty belly churns. There's no way I can eat until this meeting with Dominick is over. Trying to calm my angry stomach, I roll down the window for some fresh air. My mind wanders back to last night in an attempt to soothe my nerves.

Lying in bed, wrapped in Jonah's arms, I found the courage to tell him why I have to meet with Dominick. As a little girl, I'd daydream about him pulling up to our house. He'd have a big box in his hands, wrapped in pink paper. I pictured him kneeling down and telling me how much he missed me. That he'd made a huge mistake in severing himself from my life, and that he was going to make up for lost time. He would beg for forgiveness. I'd finally get the dad I needed.

It's because of that dream that I have to meet with Dominick. Even if it's on his terms, I'll do it. I owe it to that little girl.

Lux, the high-rise condominium just off the strip, comes into view. I take a right into the circle driveway. A valet scurries to my door. On his heels is a tall, broad man, in a black suit. His formal attire at ten in the morning is unusual for a summer in Las Vegas. Is he a lawyer? He looks more like a hit man.

I ignore the valet's proffered hand and step out of my car.

Suit guy steps to me, a forced-looking smile plastered across his wide face. "Good morning, Miss Morretti."

My eyes narrow at him. *How does he know me?* "Um, good morning."

"Mr. Morretti is waiting for you." He motions for me to follow him into the building.

Pushing through the rotating door into the lobby, the smell of floor wax and fresh flowers fills my nose. The intricate-carved, dark wood reception desk and marble floor scream money. I smooth my cotton shirt in response.

We reach the elevator that has only one button with the letters 'PH' on it. As we ascend in silence, I take in the man in front of me. He must be a bodyguard. He isn't as tall as Jonah, but he's almost as wide. Every one of the light brown hairs on his head is stuck in place by a decent amount of hair product. The diamond earring in his left earlobe is far too big for a man's ear.

The elevator comes to a stop and the doors slide open.

"After you." He says it in a way that would be polite if his tone wasn't so condescending. Without reason, I'd say this guy doesn't like me. Now I'm really nervous.

"Thanks."

Stepping through the elevator doors, I find myself in another lobby. This one is smaller, but no less extravagant. At the opposite end is an enormous double door that probably cost more than my car. As I walk towards it, I notice the etched glass doors depict a holy war with angels and demons swirling in a vicious battle. The visual puts a looming dread in the air.

Bodyguard guy knocks twice on the thick glass, making me jump. *Calm down, Raven.* I'm freaking myself out. The door opens, and a petite blond girl wearing a skintight tank top dress and no shoes lets us in. I try to greet her, but her gaze is locked on her feet. I'm taken to an office where I'm told to sit and that Mr. Morretti will be with me shortly.

A large desk looms in the back of the room, only one chair in front of it. *Guess that's for me.* I sit and stare out the floor-to-ceiling window behind the desk. I bet the view from here at night is one of the best in the city.

Minutes pass and my knee bounces. The heel of my foot pounds a fast, rhythmic beat into the floor. It seems like I've been waiting an eternity. My nails are chewed to the quick before I hear the door open behind me. The air gets heavy and the room seems smaller. I don't have to turn around to know that Dominick is walking in behind me.

I haven't seen him in five years, and even then, it was only for the minutes it took for him to drop off a package to my mom. I expected him to look older, but he's exactly the same. His blond hair and familiar aquamarine eyes are set off by his dark tan. A radiant smile lights his face, a charming façade that manipulates without effort.

"Raven, darling, you look exquisite," he says like a proper gentleman.

Warning signals blare in my head, but I brush them off as nerves. "Thank you."

He walks around his desk and sits in his chair opposite me. "You met Vince?" He nods toward the man over my shoulder.

I turn and see bodyguard guy standing in front of the closed doors, blocking any escape. My pulse races.

I should have listened to Jonah. Unease advances into fear. But why? He may not know me, but that doesn't change the fact that he's my biological father. I'm safe. Then why do I feel like running?

I need to get to the point so that I can get the heck out of here as soon as possible. "You wanted to see me?"

"Yes." He clears his throat. "I have a job offer for you."

"I have a job, but thank you." I stand to leave.

"Sit!" he barks, making me feel like a misbehaving dog.

Oh God, this is bad.

"I have a job offer for you, Raven. And you can't say no." His previous soft tone is now forceful.

"I don't understand."

Everything I know about Dominick is corrupt. What could he possibly want with me?

"You know, Raven, when I first started in this business, I was around your age. I was young, rich, and drunk with power." He rolls a gold pen between his fingers. "I got bored easily. I knew from the moment I saw your mother she was something special. Everything about her screamed sex: the way she moved, the way she spoke. I'd never met anyone like her. It's as if she were made for the singular purpose of pleasing men. I had to have her." Depravity shines in his eyes.

Saliva rushes into my mouth and panic grips my insides.

"I had to have her, Raven, for two reasons. First, to capitalize on her God-given gifts for profit." He spears me with a glare. "And second …to *breed*." The last word he stretches out as a snake would if it could talk.

Breed? Like a dog? I know then I'm looking into the eyes of the devil himself.

"So that's what I did. I used your mother to create another like her. The next generation, if you will, to meet the growing demands of my business."

I don't want to hear anymore. Tears pool in my eyes as I realize what kind of job he's offering me.

"You want me to be a hooker for you." This can't be happening. He wants to sell my body for sex? My own da—no, I can't bring myself to *think* of him as that.

"Hooker is such an ugly word," he tsks. "I prefer escort. But, yes, that's what you were created for. That's why I made you. It's time you fulfill your purpose."

"No! I won't do it. You can't make me do it!"

Tears trail down my face, and I'm pissed he sees me weak.

"I *can* make you do it and I will. I'll give you a couple weeks, say, until your twenty-first birthday. That should give you enough time to tie up any loose ends. Then you'll be moved into one of my apartments," he declares with a wave of his hand like a king on his throne of immorality.

"Fuck you!" I'm scared out of my mind and a little bit crazy, because as the fierce curse flies from my mouth, I can't help but think Blake would be proud.

"Hmm, you're feisty. You must get that from me. Your mother never argued, never fought, and never said a word really." He thoughtfully rubs his chin. "Let me put it to you this way. You will do as you're told, or I will slowly pick off every single person you love."

No, no, no, no!

"You're a monster."

An evil smile curls his lips. "I'll start with that sweet little friend of yours, Eve." My hands and feet tingle and then go numb.

"Then, I'll work my way to Guy and your mother."

Numbness moves up my arms and legs to my abdomen.

"And last, but not least," his voice carries a sing-song tone, "I'll end with that Neanderthal you've been living with, Jonah."

The final blow.

Heart, mind, and soul. Numb.

I'm no longer crying as my body and mind assimilate information. His words spin in my head over and over like a tilt-a-whirl: breed, hooker, everyone I love.

The predicament hits me like a hurricane. In danger of passing out, I grip the arms of my chair. *This isn't happening.* I lean forward and put my head between my knees, hoping to gather my bearings.

"This is Las Vegas, darling. You know how easy it would be to make someone disappear? Bury them in a dirt hole out in the desert? Although, I won't make it quick, I'll have my fun with them first."

"Stop, please. Just please …stop." I rock back and forth, my hands fisted in my hair. I hear a low keening sound, and realize it's coming from my mouth. I pinch my eyes closed tight, praying to wake up from this nightmare.

And here I thought he might want to know me. That maybe he missed the daughter he never knew. *How could I be so stupid?*

"Why now? Why not when I turned eighteen?" My voice is pleading and desperate for answers.

"In my business, it's important the girls are of legal drinking age. This helps to avoid unwanted attention from the local authorities. But more importantly, I needed leverage. You're quite the loner, darling: never had a boyfriend, very few friends. I had Guy and Eve, but they weren't enough. Once you starting practically living with the Slade boy, it was time." He straightens his cuffs and twists their links. His gaze swings to mine. "Do you love him?"

I roll my lips into my mouth, refusing to answer him.

"Ah, yes. And it seems you're still a virgin as well."

From behind me, Vince muffles his laugh. Mortification and anger mix, igniting my face in a furious blush. I'm appalled that he could speak so freely with his own flesh and blood.

"Don't look so shocked. Sex is my business. I can tell by your blush you still retain your innocence. That will work well for me and my business."

Bile burns my throat. I wish I had eaten so I could vomit all over Dominick's pretentious Oriental rug. I hate him for what he's proposing and for what he did to my mom. I want to pounce on him and fight like a maniac. Adrenaline fills my body as I contemplate the risks involved with taking him on here in his office.

Is today a good day to die?

He leans forward, resting both elbows on his desk. His eyes bore into mine, making me recoil.

"Raven, if you fight me, I'll shoot so much heroin in your arm, you won't know what day it is. I'll keep you so addicted you'll be begging for it. You'll live out your days on a street corner, sucking off frat boys for twenty bucks a pop. You come peacefully and be a good girl, you'll have a life very similar to that of your mother. I suppose I could make it even better, seeing as you are my daughter."

"I'm not your daughter!"

He looks down his nose, studying me like a piece of art he's considering buying. "No, I suppose you're not. More like the product of a perfectly executed experiment."

"I would rather die a slow, painful death than work for you." My hands are wrapped so tightly around the arms of the chair that my palms burn.

"Well," he sits back, checking out what I assume to be freshly manicured nails, "that, too, can be arranged," he hisses with contempt.

A defeated whimper bursts from my lips. The horrific sound confirms my lack of options. I don't have an out.

"So you agree? The day after your twenty-first birthday, I'll send for you."

"I thought…" My whispered words aren't meant to be heard.

"You thought what, darling?"

I look up from my lap and stare at the man who's just ripped my heart out and stomped on it for sport. "I hate you."

A slow smile stretches across his face. "Very well. I've always been a sucker for a challenge."

I have no memory of how I got back in my car. I don't remember walking, but I don't believe I was carried. All I know is I'm sitting in the valet driveway, stone still, staring straight ahead, wondering where to go and what to do.

And just like that, right when my life starts looking beautiful, it disappears like a mirage in the desert.

———

JONAH

"Aw fuck, not again!" Blake throws his arms into the air, and stomps to the bench.

Two o'clock. No missed calls. *Shit.*

Something's not right.

I've checked my phone every thirty minutes for the last three hours, and still no word from Raven. I agreed to let her go meet with Dominick alone this morning, even when everything in me was screaming it was a big mistake.

"I'm done for the day," I call out to whoever's listening, not bothering to look up from checking for text messages.

"Good. You haven't really been here anyway. You got that fuckin' phone stuck up your ass when we're supposed to be training."

Usually I would jump all over Blake and his attitude. Not now.

I lean against the octagon chain link and try her cell. Straight to voicemail. My team files out and toward the locker room, each one grumbling.

Owen lingers, his eyes on me. "Yo, Jonah. You all right, man?"

"Huh?" I look up from my phone into the concerned eyes of Owen then back and hit send. "Oh, yeah. Fine."

"What's going on? You're preoccupied. Everything okay with Raven?"

Just hearing her name makes me break out in a panic-induced sweat.

"Um …I don't know. She met with her dad today, and they don't really get along. I haven't heard from her. I'm worried."

"Oh, that's it? I'm sure she's fine, probably just got to talking and reminiscing about old times. I mean how bad can he be that—"

"It's Dominick Morretti."

Owen's easy demeanor disappears as his dark skin drains of color. We lock eyes. Yeah, now he gets it. Everyone knows Dominick Morretti would walk over the dead bodies of his own children to get to a dollar.

"Let's go." Owen's storms from the octagon.

"Wait! Where are we going?"

He doesn't slow his pace. "We're gonna find her. I say we check her place first."

"I'll grab my keys."

—

We pull up to Guy's Garage and I see Raven's car in the lot. *Thank you, God.* I pop my head into the garage and ask Guy if he's seen her. He tells me she showed up a few hours ago but went straight to her place saying she wasn't feeling well.

My feet move like they're on fire to the alley. I jump up the stairs, taking three at a time. My fist pounds on the door as adrenaline courses through my veins. I need to see that my girl is okay.

"Raven, baby, you there? It's me. Open up."

Nothing.

I knock again.

"Open up, Raven!"

Nothing.

Panic surges and the buzz at the base of my neck shoots to my brain, clouding rational thinking.

"Raven! Open the fucking door!"

I'm about to flip the switch and rip this piece of shit door down with my bare hands, when a firm hand on my shoulder directs me to step aside. Owen is there and he takes my place.

"Princess, it's Owen. You don't open up this door, I'm gonna kick it down. We need to get to you."

Nothing.

Shit! I'm in full freak-out mode. I know Owen feels it rolling off me in waves by the way his eyes dart from my fisted hands to my clenched jaw. I roll my head around on my neck, preparing to bust open the door. Owen takes one step back.

Boom!

Splintering wood flies all around us, the result of Owen's front kick. He steps in and pushes aside the flimsy door that hangs lopsided from its hinges. I push past him and into the studio.

I stop short upon entering and hold my breath. In the middle of her bed, curled up in the fetal position, is Raven. I'd think she was sleeping if not for her soft guttural moans.

Seeing her so broken sobers the raging beast in my head. I go to her and climb in behind her, my front to her back. Wrapping my arms around her tiny body, I bury my face in her hair.

"Baby. Shh, it's okay. I'm here now."

Her body goes solid for a second or two before it's wracking with sobs. Her cries of anguish make me hold tighter as if I can somehow take her pain away by the sheer strength in my arms.

"Raven? Shh, it's going to be okay. I'm here. You're safe. I love you, baby. Come back to me."

My eyes start to burn. The pain in her cries is tangible, making the air thick and hard to breathe.

"What happened? Talk to me."

I kiss her tenderly and encourage her to turn and face me. She does, but only to bury herself in my chest and cry harder. The sight of her tear-streaked face and red-rimmed eyes make me downright homicidal. From the looks of it, she's been crying for a while.

I'm going to kill that motherfucker!

I don't know how long I lay there with Raven in my arms. Her breathing evens out, and she takes a long shaky breath.

"It's over." Her voice is quiet and devoid of emotion. "My life, no matter what happens, is over."

"What do you mean?" I smooth my hand through her hair. "Your life isn't over."

She pushes herself up on the bed. I look to the door and see no sign of Owen.

"What happened?" My voice is sharp with worry. I fight the roaring in my head and focus on keeping my cool. "What did he do to you?"

I swing my legs over the side of the bed and something crunches under my feet. It's a broken picture frame. In the mess of glass and shattered wood is the picture of Raven's mom.

What the hell is going on?

I pull Raven into my lap, and she curls into my body like she was made to be there.

Then, she starts to talk.

FOURTEEN

RAVEN

My head throbs as I blink open my swollen eyes. The room is dark except for the dim light that shines through the window. It's evening. I roll from my side onto my back and know instantly that I'm in Jonah's bed. My hand reaches for him, but the cool sheets tell me he's not there. He brought me here after I'd cried myself dry in his arms, snuggled in tight to the safety and warmth of his touch, holding me as if I'd float away if he didn't ground me.

Thoughts of Dominick invade my mind, like an army hell bent on eradicating my hope. Shame and embarrassment strangle any pride I have left. I bury my face in the pillow, pressing in deep, robbing myself of oxygen and welcoming the ache in my lungs. The life I'd built for myself, friends, Jonah, all of it was erased in less than an hour. I'm chained to the ugliness, caged in a nightmare with no chance of escape.

I become a prostitute, or everyone I love dies.

I turn my head and gasp for air, sucking the life-giving oxygen into my lungs. Rubbing my eyes, I try to erase the memories of the pain I saw in Jonah's face. He told me we'd figure it out, that, together, we'd come up with something. *Impossible.*

Reaching over, I click on the lamp. There's a glass of water on the bedside table along with two Tylenol. I grab the pills and toss them to the back of my dry mouth. I swallow against the sting in my aching throat as it draws my attention away from the pain in my heart. The glass drained, I push my legs over the side of the bed, giving my body a second to acclimate to being upright. I'm no longer wearing my jeans and shirt, but I'm in one of Jonah's t-shirts. I pull the fabric to my nose and breathe in deep, his scent a reprieve to my anguish.

Tying my hair in a low knot, I head out to find Jonah. I freeze in the hallway at the sound of two male voices. Jonah's voice is as recognizable as my own, but who is the other? I tiptoe closer and make the voice out to be Owen. Veiled in the shadows, I listen in.

"I have too much to lose. I can't afford to lose everything."

"Dude, I get that, I do. But just give it some time. You might find a way to figure something out."

"What other choice do I have? I have to end this."

"You're going to hurt her."

Silence, then, "I know."

"I don't like it, Jonah. She's been through so much already. She's not going to handle this well. You have to know that." Silence. "All right, at least do it sooner than later. Like pulling off a Band-Aid, just get it over with."

"Yeah, I will."

My heart plummets into an icy black hole. It's impossible to breathe past the constricting burn in my chest. I bend at the waist, hands on my knees, trying not to pass out. My head pounds with the beat of my racing heart. I pray that the numbing will come and ease the ache, but my body takes no prisoners as my stomach coils in agony. I lean my back against the wall, pressing my fingers to my sternum, as if I could physically push back the pain. The slight sting is on my cheeks from the tears I didn't know I'd cried. Hearing about the pain of a broken heart doesn't do justice to feeling the crippling devastation. *This* is a broken heart.

Of course, he's leaving me. Why wouldn't he? Everything he's worked for his entire life is waiting for him. His career is taking off, the title fight only weeks away. That's his priority.

The voice in my head reminds me of what I really am. I'm the daughter of a pimp and a hooker bred for a lifestyle of meaningless sex and money. It all makes sense now. My mother never saw me as her child …as a child at all. I'm nothing more than a prized animal—a product they can profit from. Who was I to think I could have a future with Jonah? My future is in that world, not his.

"Hey, how long have you been standing here?"

Long enough for you to destroy me. "Oh, um, I don't know. Not long." My voice sounds like it's been trampled by a herd of buffalo.

He cups my face, wiping away my tears with his thumbs. His warm eyes and empathetic smile threaten to burst the floodgates, so I look past him.

"Baby, you're crying." He dries my tears with his thumbs.

I shrug and force my mouth into a smile.

"Come on. Let's get you something to eat."

He hugs me to his side and guides me into the kitchen. My muscles relax and my pulse slows, comforted by his touch. Apparently my traitorous body isn't aware that Jonah's done with us. Leaning down, he kisses tenderly his favorite spot on my neck then pulls back a fraction to my ear.

"I love you." His warm breath combined with the power of his words make me tremble in his arms.

I finish his declaration with an unspoken, *but we can't be together.* "I love you too."

And I do. That's why I don't mention the conversation that I overheard. I know love doesn't conquer all, that it's not always enough. I know that Jonah has to look out for himself. He can't afford to be wrapped up in my life, and part of me is at peace about that. I want him, but more than that, I want him to be happy—to have a life with a woman who can love him the way he deserves to be loved: a woman free from the ugliness of my reality.

"How you feelin', princess?" Owen asks.

"I've been better."

His dark eyes study mine. "Right. Well, I'm gonna take off." He steps to me and tugs me from Jonah's hold for a hug. His arms linger a little too long, making it feel like a long-term good bye.

He releases me with a final squeeze. I don't miss the look he gives Jonah or what it communicates. He's not happy that Jonah's breaking up with me, but he understands.

The rest of the evening passes like a dream. Only half-conscious most of the time, my mind pounds away at Dominick's words. Plans to escape my fate form in my head, but they all end in one reality. I can't protect everyone. And losing anyone I love is a risk I'm not willing to take.

Jonah treats me like I'm made of glass. He feeds me, bathes me, and dresses me for bed. He holds me in the dark, whispering words of comfort while twisting tendrils of my hair around his fingers.

I want to tell him that it's okay, I understand why he has to let me go, but words fail me. Physically incapable of walking away from him, I choose to take this moment. I wrap myself up in it, absorbing all the love I can from his touch, hoping it will be enough to last me through a lifetime without him.

———

I open my eyes to a new day. The sun bathes the room in yellow, but I refuse to move. For the first time, I don't feel Jonah behind me as I do every morning. I try not to think about what's ahead, but live in the moment. And this moment sucks.

Staring at the digital clock on the bedside, I watch the minutes tick by. Sooner or later, I'm going to have to get up and go to work. But leaving Jonah's bed, knowing it may be the last time I'm here, is a mountain I'm not ready to face. I sigh, long and hard.

"You awake?" His voice comes from my back, but he's across the room.

I squeeze my eyes shut tight. Do this for him. Don't make it harder than it has to be.

Rolling over, I see him in the club chair across the room.

"Good morning." I say, my voice feeling a little stronger than yesterday, but no less scratchy.

"Good morning, beautiful."

I sit up and notice that his hair is damp from the shower and he's dressed for the day. "Where are you off to so early?" My heavy heart drops to my stomach like an anvil.

He stands and makes his way to the bed, plopping down beside me with a huff. "I have some things to do today. Just, um, work stuff."

He's avoiding my eyes. This is it. He's breaking up with me.

"Oh, but I thought you had today off?" I want this to be easy for him, and I know I should just nod and let him walk away, but instinct has me clamoring.

"Yeah, well, I got called in for a meeting. With the fight coming up, there's a lot of publicity stuff." He pushes his hand through his hair then rubs the back of his neck. "I wanted to know if you could stay with Eve tonight."

And there it is.

I swallow a whimper that threatens to shoot from my lips. Blood rushes in my ears distorting his words as he makes excuses about training late.

Unshed tears burn my eyes, but I refuse to let on. *Make this easy for him.* He deserves that much.

"Sure, that won't be a problem. But really, I can stay at my place." *You won't be around to protect me anymore.*

His expression hardens, making his jaw tick. "Raven, promise me you'll stay at Eve's. I can't sleep knowing you'll be alone at your place."

With a nod and a smile, I agree. I have no intention of staying at Eve's, but if it makes what he's doing easier, he can believe I am.

Leaning in, he brushes his lips against mine then kisses my neck at his spot. He pulls back to look me in the eyes and I see something there. Regret? Loss?

"I'll try to call you later."

Try?

"Okay."

Standing with purpose, he walks away.

"I love you, Jonah Slade." My whispered words are said to the door that he closes behind him.

———

JONAH

"Come on, Blake, answer the door!"

I've been knocking on his door for the last ten minutes. I know he's home because I saw his Jeep parked downstairs.

I bang on the door again. "Blake, open up!"

I hear him fumbling with the lock and the door swings open. Blake is standing in the doorway, wearing nothing but his boxer briefs. His eyes are half shut and his face puffy with sleep and a possible hangover.

"Fuck, man. Where's the fire?" His voice is rough and laced with irritation.

"I need to talk to you about something. It's important."

"What?" He yawns, scratching his chest. "Dude, it's like six o'clock in the morning."

"It's ten o'clock, idiot."

"Oh, well then, come on in." He gestures dramatically with his arm, and I push past him into his place.

"What the hell happened to you? You look like shit."

"You don't want to know," he says on a groan.

"You alone?"

He stares at me and his eyebrows drop low. "No. Why?"

"I need what I'm about to say to be kept private." My eyes dart to the hallway that leads to his room, then back to him. "You mind sending your sleepover guest home?"

"Fuck. Yeah, hold on."

He disappears down the hall, and I walk to the other end of his living room. Last thing I want is a front row seat to the dismissing of his overnight guest. I watch out the ten-foot-tall window of his modern townhouse and shudder at the show his neighbors must get most nights.

"But, I thought you said you'd make us breakfast," a female voice whines from the hallway.

"Yeah, you said you'd feed us your sausage," says another.

Fucking Blake.

"Change of plans, ladies. Maybe next time."

"Aww." The disappointed reply sounds in unison.

Blake walks to the door with two girls. One stumbles, trying to slip on her high heel, while the other shoves a wad of lace and silk into her tiny purse. I recognize them immediately as Octagon Girls. And I am intimately familiar with both.

"Hey, Jonah." The tall blonde calls out as she passes me in the living room.

I nod.

The brunette tosses me a wave. "Hi, Jonah."

"All right, ladies, thanks for last night …and this morning."

He all but shoves them out the door, slamming it behind them.

"Screw you later," he mumbles.

I shake my head. "You're a pig."

"So were you once." He plops down on the couch, still in his underwear.

"You want to get some fucking clothes on?"

He looks at me like I just asked him to wear a dress. "You want to tell me why you're beating down my door at the shit crack of dawn?"

Dropping down in the seat across from him, I fill Blake in on my situation. His jaw locks down as I tell him every detail of Raven's meeting. A whispered curse breaks free when I tell him about how I found her after.

"That motherfucker!" Blake jumps up from the couch to pace the room.

"I have a plan, but I need your help. I know Dominick is part owner of Zeus's. I need you to get with one of the girls and find out when he goes in there."

He's still pacing and hasn't acknowledged that I've said a word.

"Blake. Can you do that?"

He stops and turns toward me. "Abso-fucking-lutely."

Grabbing his phone, he takes his seat back on the couch, this time not slumped over, but tense and leaning forward. "You're not meeting with that asswipe alone. I'm going with you."

"No, I have to do it alone. I won't drag you into this."

He pins me with a glare. "Drag me into this?" His arm shoots out to point a finger to his wall window. "That girl's cool as shit." He points at me. "She's your girl. That makes her my responsibility too."

"Blake, anything could happen. You sure you want to get messed up in all this?"

He coughs out a laugh. "Let me ask you something. What're you going to do when Morretti makes some comment about Raven taking cock for cash, huh?"

I suppress a growl. A low vibration in my spine amplifies to a buzz. My teeth grind together and I scowl at Blake.

"That's what I thought. You're going to flip the switch on that dicklick and he'll shoot your dumb ass and claim self-defense. And where does that leave Raven, hmm?"

I narrow my glare on him.

"Exactly."

The cocky ass is right. Dominick will most likely try to get me riled up, and I can't be responsible for what happens if he disrespects Raven.

"You're right. I'll need you there. How soon can we get the ball rolling?"

Blake already has his phone to his ear. "Selena, baby, it's me. I got a question for you."

FIFTEEN

RAVEN

The bay doors slamming shut pulls me from the wiring of a '57 Chevy. The halogen lights of the garage replace the sun that shone in when I started this project.

Where did the time go?

Drowning myself in work is a good distraction from the chaos in my head, but I've lost an entire afternoon.

The awareness of time brings pain to the gaping void in my chest. I haven't heard from Jonah all day. I didn't expect him to contact me, but I hoped he would. I check my phone again. Nothing.

"Wrap it up, Ray."

I grab my tools and find Guy in the back, putting things away.

"Who's on tomorrow?" I ask, tossing my set on a workbench.

He doesn't look up from an assortment of wire terminals. "Cane. Why?"

"I thought I'd come in, you know, um, help out—"

He bangs closed a metal toolbox. "What's goin' on, Ray?" He studies my face. "You've been zip-lipped all day, and from the look on your face, I'd say someone died."

That's what it feels like. I shrug and pick grease from my nails, avoiding his eyes. "Nah, just thought I'd get some extra hours."

"You hurtin' for money?"

"No, it's not that." I just need to stay busy so I don't have time to …feel.

His bushy, gray eyebrows drop low, making the wrinkles around his eyes more pronounced. "You and the boy havin' problems?"

I exhale, annoyed at my transparency.

"You could say that. He has a lot on his plate with the fight coming up." Guilt washes over me as I lie. I can't tell him the truth. It's too real.

He leans against a workbench and crosses his ankles. "He tell you that?"

I shake my head. "Our lives are too different."

"And different is a bad thing?"

"You don't understand," I mumble to my feet.

"I'll tell you what I do understand. I see a boy who's lived his life in the public eye for just shy of ten years. He's made his taste in women obvious: quick, easy, and disposable. You step on the scene, he drops it all, stands toe to toe with me, and makes his intentions clear. Differences be damned. The boy's crazy about you."

"Some differences are too big."

"You listen here, Ray. I'm no expert on relationships. Only been in love once. That was over thirty years ago. But I know it when I see it."

"You were in love?" I stare in shock at the self-proclaimed, lifetime bachelor.

"Yep, fell in love with an angel." His eyes get soft. "But she was engaged to someone else."

I don't know what to say, but I want to hear more. I nod for him to continue.

"You know what I did to mess it up?"

"What?"

"Nothin'. And that's how I lost her." He reflects in silence for a beat, studying the garage walls. He shakes his head. "I didn't fight for her. I could have fought, tried to get her out from under her obligation, but I didn't. Biggest mistake of my life."

"But she was engaged to someone else. How do you know she would have left her fiancé?"

His face falls, eyebrows low, and he studies the floor. "I'll never know. That's what kills me."

The pain in his voice has me blinking back tears. "Was there never anyone else? After her?"

"I love her. She's it for me." He's not speaking in past tense.

I can't decide if that's the saddest or the most romantic thing I've ever heard, and yet I'm destined for a similar fate. There will never be another love for me, not like Jonah. I can see how Guy would close himself off, subject to a lifetime sentence of loneliness for one girl. But the difference is that Guy's love was worth the fight. He didn't fight for her, but he lives with the regret because she was worth that. Not me.

"Not everyone's worth fighting for."

He steps close and places his hands on my shoulders. His blue eyes look deep into mine. "I've seen you two together: the way he looks at you when you're not looking, like you're the sun and he's happily stuck in your orbit. Never seen you with a boy before so I can't be sure, but seein' you messed up in the head about it, I'm guessin' you feel the same way. You guys got something special, Ray. Fight for it. It's worth that."

His words rock me to the bone. Something deep and instinctual recognizes Guy's words as truth, but I can't get past my head: Jonah's conversation with Owen, him pushing me off on Eve, not calling all day. All arrows point to a broken heart.

My head throbs, and I have an overwhelming urge to be alone. "Thanks, G."

"You're welcome. You don't want to be me, lookin' back on your life, wishing you could have another shot at something sweet." He ruffles my hair then steps back. "Now, go get some sleep. You look like hell."

He throws his arm over my shoulder and walks me to the foot of my stairs. Departing with a wave, I watch him until he disappears around the corner.

The weight of today pressing down, I drag my body up the stairs. A hot shower sounds better and better with each step. The motion light above my door flicks on, and I freeze as my foot hits the top step. Holy crud.

The old door to my apartment is gone, and in its place is a solid, dark wood one with an enormous platinum handle. My jaw falls open as I study its features: a peep hole and three gleaming locks. I grab my keys and finger through the set to find … Yep, there it is: a shiny new silver key. Jonah must have slipped it on my key chain this morning. The corners of my mouth lift as I examine the product of his overprotective nature, and just as quickly as the smile comes, it fades. How will I live without him?

I'm able to get myself inside before the tears start to fall. Crawling onto my bed, I bury my face in the pillow and sob. I have to believe there is a tiny chance that Jonah doesn't want to end things. I can't go on any other way.

But hope is such a dangerous thing. My heart dared to hope that Dominick would one day come banging on my door, begging for forgiveness. But instead, he killed every dream of a future I had. Hope. It has sustained me through my darkest days, but it also lifted me up only to drop me, breaking me into irreparable pieces. Could I live through that kind of fall again?

Crying jag over, I pull myself up and into the shower. I move through the motions, numb and absent. Dressed in drawstring fleece pants, a tank, and flip-flops, I check my phone. No missed calls.

I haven't heard from Eve all day, and although I'd planned on ignoring Jonah's request that I stay at Eve's, I could use the company. It must be the new boyfriend that's keeping her busy. Except for the occasional text message and a couple morning phone conversations this past week, she's been unavailable. The few talks we've had have been one-sided. She asks me about Jonah, and I talk forever, but she never talks about herself outside of what she's up to at work. Just thinking about her now is making me miss her terribly.

I dial her number and listen as her voicemail tells me to leave a message. With nothing better to do, I decide to drive over and drop in on her. If she's not there, I can always try her work.

Grabbing my keys, I head to my car with the hopes of finding Eve and keeping my mind off Jonah. I relax as the hum of my Nova and the warm air that whips my hair envelop me. Elton John blasts in my ears, and in that moment, I'm just some girl, not the daughter of a prostitute and a pimp, bred for—Ugh! I slam my hand on the steering wheel and focus on the crooning voice of Sir Elton. I punch the gas, singing at the top of my lungs and hoping to chase away the worst of my demons.

As I pass a strip of fast-food restaurants, I'm hit with the smell of hot oil and french fries. My stomach rumbles its complaint. With everything that's been going on today, I've forgotten to eat. I try Eve's phone again. Voicemail. I redirect my car to hit my favorite drive-thru.

Turning left towards the lights of the Vegas strip, I head down Tropicana. The flashing neon of a club up ahead gets my attention. There's a line of people wrapped around the building. I recognize it immediately as Zeus's Playground, one of the high-end strip clubs in town. Stuck at a stoplight, I look at the club, shaking my head at all the men who are about to drop a week's pay down the panties of a stripper while the little woman is probably home taking care of the kids. Pathetic.

My gaze moves back to the road in front of me when something catches my eye. In the parking lot of the club, I would recognize it anywhere. I squint hard. My head gets light, and the blood drains to pool in the pit of my empty stomach. I fight the impulse to vomit or pass out.

Jonah's truck.

I blink, hoping to clear the optical illusion. The honking of a car horn startles me and causes me to look ahead. The light's green, and I need to drive, but I can't get my limbs to cooperate.

He said he had a meeting.

A quick shot of anger brings my body around, and I press the gas to get through the intersection. With trembling hands, I pull off to the side of the road. I take another hard look. Blake had mentioned this place at the barbeque. It was where he met the girls he brought. All of them, including Candy.

Jonah's in there with Candy.

And just like that, hope has dropped my sorry butt off a cliff.

Panic floods my veins. My breathing is labored, like I'm sucking air through a straw. I shake out my arms, trying to rid them of the numbness taking over, but movement only pushes the sensation into my torso. My heart beats fast—too fast. Terror spreads through my body. I squeeze my eyes shut.

"Oh please, God, not now." I pray aloud with hopes of divine intercession.

An anxiety attack grips my body. Tears stream down my face, and I struggle against the lost feeling that threatens to overtake me. I push against my sternum, willing my heart to slow.

"Come on, Raven. Talk yourself down." I take a breath. "I'm in control."

My eyes fly open at my pitiful lie. Control? That's the last thing I have. My hands grip either side of my head and I rock back and forth.

Of course, he's there. Why would he want to be with me, the future hooker? I close my eyes tightly. The daughter of a pimp. My body shakes. The grease monkey, tomboy. My head pounds. The virgin.

I need to calm down. Stop acting like a helpless little girl. I breathe in deep through my nose and out my mouth, until my mind slows enough for me to think straight. I need to decide what to do now. Should I go confront him? Why? So he can tell me to my face, with Candy straddling his lap, that he doesn't want me? I pull back into the street, almost hitting another car, and speed to Eve's.

Throwing my car in park at the curb outside her house, I walk up the front path. I'm shaking, but still. Pained, but numb. Bleeding, but alive. Consumed with confusion and contradictions.

I reach her door and knock as hard as I can. After a few clicks of the lock, the door opens to expose a very skimpily dressed Eve. Through the small crack in the door, I can see lit candles in the background.

"Raven, what are you doing here?"

"I called. You didn't answer." It's all I can manage without breaking out in a full-body sob.

"Oh, yeah, sorry. I've been …busy." She looks guilty and a little ashamed.

Her eyes seem sketchy as she looks over my shoulder to the street behind me. I look to see what's stealing her attention. There, parked in the street, is a black H2. My eyebrows pull together.

I must have missed it when I pulled up. I guess seeing my boyfriend's car at a strip club where his ex-hook up works when he told me he had a work meeting made me unobservant. My arms wrap protectively around my chest and my shoulders curl forward, holding myself together. I might dissolve completely at the slightest breeze of pain.

"Eve, who's at the door?" a deep voice beckons from behind her. My wide eyes lock with hers in shock and silent apology.

"Oh, Eve, I'm so sorry. You have company. I'll go."

Wait, why does that voice sound familiar?

"No, Rave, wait. You look horrible. Have you been crying? What's going on?"

She still hasn't opened the door anymore, but her face shows concern. A large hand curls around her waist from behind, and a tall man comes into view over her shoulder.

Holy shit!

——

JONAH

It's nine forty-five and the club is getting crowded. Even from my seat at the bar, it's hard to see through the bodies filling the place. The girls finally got the hint that we aren't here for entertainment. Their advances went beyond annoying to borderline hostile in the last hour. Blake and I finally had to tell them to back off and get the hell out of our way.

"Can I get you a drink, man?" the bartender asks for the third time, irritation lacing his voice.

This kid is pissing me the fuck off. My head swivels in his direction and I drill him with my stare. A beer would do wonders to calm my urge to kill, but there's no way I'll be anything less than one hundred percent coherent when I face Dominick.

He throws his hands up and takes a step back. "Whoa, I don't want any trouble. But you can't sit here all night and not buy a drink. I'm just following the rules."

I pull a hundred dollar bill from my pocket and toss it his way.

"On second thought," he nabs the cash, "enjoy your night."

I go back to surveying my surroundings.

No sign of Dominick. Selena told Blake that he usually comes in around this time of night to work some of his girls. We've been here for an hour and he's a no show.

"How long do you want to hang out?" Blake asks, his eyes scanning the room.

"As long as it takes. Raven's with Eve so I have all night."

I have fight-night focus. My senses are sharp. Every male voice draws my attention along with every opening door. Adrenaline runs high, as does my determination. I will not leave this place until I meet with Dominick.

I swallow a growl when I feel a small, feminine hand move up my shoulder. Can these girls not take no for an answer? Turning towards its owner, I cringe. I don't need this shit.

"Hey, stranger," Candy purrs, with her fake, over-affected seduction.

I jerk my head in acknowledgement.

Leaning forward, she brings her lips to my ear. "I told you, you'd be back."

"Not in the mood for your games tonight, Candy."

She gasps when I remove her from my shoulder and go back to scanning the room.

"Don't tell me you're still with that trashy little girl," she scoffs.

What did she just say? My gaze swings toward her.

Her puffy lips lift into a satisfied smile. "You never gave me the chance to show you what I could do for you, lover." She runs a sharp nail from my shoulder and down my arm, her eyes following its path. "I'd do things to you that would make you forget that dirty skank's name." She swings a leg over my knee, rubbing against me like some pathetic animal.

I stand and she stumbles back, my sudden movement throwing her off balance. She looks up at me and her eyes grow wide. I would never hit a girl, but this bitch is pushing my buttons. I'm already walking the fine line of my temper. She picked the wrong night to fuck with me.

"One night, Candy. That's all we had and that's all we'll ever have. You need to squash these deluded fantasies you have about us. It ain't gonna happen. Ever. Understand?"

She opens her mouth to speak, but I'm not finished.

"And if you ever speak about *my girl* like that again, I will ruin you. You won't be able to move far enough away to escape the reputation I'll give you. Only job you'll be able to get is shit-pumping port-a-potties. We clear?"

Her eyes narrow and her mouth moves, but for the first time the bitch is speechless.

"Now, leave me the fuck alone."

Face flushed, she spins and storms off.

I lean against the bar and go back to scanning the room. If that speech doesn't get Candy off my back, nothing will. It's then I notice a new group of men standing around a table. One of them has blond hair, but his back is to me, so I can't see his face.

Blake grabs my arm and grins his cocky smile. "It's go time."

He jerks his head in the direction of the light-haired man. A slight shift in the man's position and I see his face. Dominick Morretti.

A low hum of energy coils in the back of my head. My legs move me forward while my mind visualizes taking this prick-ass down. Pressing in through the crowd, I force back my protective instinct and wrestle with reason. I focus on my breathing and remind myself to stay calm. For Raven.

Don't kick his ass. Not here. Not yet.

An aggressive presence prickles from behind me. I look over my shoulder to see Blake, his jaw clenched and his fists tight at his sides. He's ready to throw down, and I'm grateful that he has my back.

I approach Dominick while he's chatting with a group of businessmen. I catch a second of the conversation that clearly involves selling a few of his women for the night. Imagining for a moment that it's Raven he's selling, the buzz in my head explodes. *Fuck that.* My arms burn to reach out and break this fucker's neck right here and now.

"Lock it down, man. For her."

Blake's words push me forward.

I take the last step, placing me a foot away. "Dominick Morretti. I need a word."

He swivels around and meets my eyes. I'm taken aback by how much his look like Raven's. There's no doubt this is her father. My stomach roils. I don't smile, and I can only imagine that my face looks about as friendly as a rabid pit bull.

"Why if it isn't 'The Assassin.'" He sneers. "Gentlemen, what a treat we have tonight." A slow clap of his hands has the men at the table's attention. "The undefeated contender."

The men at the table acknowledge me, but my eyes burn into Dominick.

He must sense I'm not here for a meet and greet, and he leans in so no one can hear him but me. "I have a feeling I know what, or should I say whom, you want to have a word about."

Blake steps close, placing his shoulder between me and Dominick and making him lean back.

169

"You want to go somewhere private or would you rather have it out right here? I'm cool either way," I spit through my teeth.

His face turns to stone, his previous bravado gone. He nods to a man who takes his place and excuses himself from the group of patrons. I follow him toward the back of the club.

We're in a dark hallway with doors running along its sides. I follow Dominick to the very last door and into an office. He doesn't move to the desk chair, but instead stays in front of it, leaning against it. There's shuffling behind me and I hear the door close. Two men stand on either side of Dominick against the wall. My senses go on high alert. They're here to protect him against us. Smart.

"Have a seat Mr. Slade and…" he looks to Blake with raised eyebrows. "Mr. Daniels."

"How the fuck do you know me?" Blake says from my side.

"I know *everything*, Mr. Daniels. Now, sit."

"We'd rather stand," I snap.

"Suit yourself." He grins and I don't miss his eyes darting to our fisted hands. "What can I help you with, boys? Looking to set up a date? I've got some beautiful girls who would love to spend some time with you, for the right price." Locking eyes with me, his lips curl back from his teeth. "If you'd be willing to wait a few weeks, I can arrange for you to have a new girl. She's never been used before. She'll cost a little extra, the virgins always do—"

"Shut the fuck up," I roar.

"You son of a bitch!" Blake yells at the same time.

Blood drums in my ears. He's obviously provoking me, trying to get me to attack him so he can take me out, leaving Raven defenseless so he can pray on her like the scavenging fuck that he is. I fist my hands against the urge to destroy him. My hands flex so tight, I feel the bite of my nails breaking the skin. The buzzing in my brain is nuclear. I push through the fog and focus on Raven. My muscles twitch with unbridled fury.

"What do you want, Dominick? For Raven? I'll give you whatever you want in return for her freedom."

Dominick leans back and props his expensive loafers onto the desk.

"Whatever I want, huh? Don't think you have anything I want, Mr. Slade."

"Name your price."

"You don't have enough."

"Try me."

He stares at me in silence while spinning his gold pinkie ring with his thumb.

"Ten million dollars, cash."

Shit. That's a lot of money. My chest constricts. This is a lost cause. I can't afford that. If I sell my house, my cars, everything I have in savings …dammit, that's still not enough.

"Or," he looks at Blake then back to me, "we could make this interesting." He taps his bottom lip with his finger.

I'd give anything to bust that lip open.

"I'll tell you what. You want to win my daughter? Throw your title fight."

His words suck the air from my lungs.

"Fuck me," Blake whispers.

"You boys must be aware of the odds in this fight. You're the favorite to win. If I put enough money on Del Toro, and he wins, I could become a very rich man. You lose that fight, I'll release Raven."

"Done." My answer bursts forth without hesitation. I would give up anything for her, including my life's dream. She's my dream now.

"I have one stipulation. The fight must go three rounds. You can't just walk into the octagon with your hands at your side. Make it believable, as if you're fighting to win."

Blake steps close and Dominick's bodyguards follow suit. "That's impossible. He goes out there to fight. Del Toro's down."

Dominick's eyes stay focused on mine. "That's what makes it a challenge. Are you up for the challenge, Mr. Slade?"

"I'll do it." I can do anything if it means being with Raven.

Blake murmurs a string of foul words while depraved satisfaction shines in Dominick's eyes. He reaches out to shake my hand. I hesitate.

Rage rides me hard, and I know if I touch this man I may lose it. I picture Raven's smiling face and take a deep breath. I force my hand forward and shake his, harder than necessary.

"It's a deal," he says. "Are we done here?"

"No, one more thing." I place both palms on the edge of the desk and lean forward, looming over Dominick. His bodyguards step up close, flashing their weapons under their suit coats. "You stay the hell away from Raven. I don't want you to contact her, threaten her, or even *think* about her. You got someone on her, you call them off. She's mine. I'll do whatever it takes to protect her. Whatever. It. Takes."

The all-consuming buzz has me shaking with the need to fuck this guy up. Blake reaches from behind me and pulls me back by my biceps. I lean forward on pure instinct.

"Come on, man. You got what we came for. Let's get outta here." Blake drags me backwards, my piercing scowl locked on Dominick.

Yeah, good idea, before I kill this bastard.

I rip free of Blake's hold and leave the room.

"Good night, gentleman." Dominick's cackling laughter fades as we walk down the hall.

I'm a bomb, live and loaded, ready to rip the shit out of anyone that looks at me wrong. My muscles coil, pulse racing.

I shove the front door open and hear the satisfying smack as it slams against the exterior wall of the club.

"Easy, man," some douchebag college kid says standing with a group of his pissant friends.

I stalk over and step right up in his face. "The fuck you say?"

"Nothing. It's cool." The kid shifts and steps back into the safety of his friends, unaware they've all backed up a good ten feet.

My lips curl. I advance a step.

"Come on. Don't make the poor bastard crap his pants in front of his friends." Blake's tone is joking, but he doesn't move to touch me. He knows better than to put a hand on me when I'm this close to lighting shit up.

Dropping the little punk will make me feel better. Nothing satisfies the beast within like a good street fight—until recently. There's one thing that works even better.

I turn away and hear him exhale a "Thank you, Jesus" as I head to my truck.

"Breathe, brother." Blake's voice comes from behind me.

"Raven. I need her. Now."

SIXTEEN

RAVEN

In shock, I stare silently as Eve tilts her head, smiling with affection to the man at her back.

"Raven, this is the guy I was telling you about, Vince. Vince, this is my best friend, Raven." Eve introduces us like we're at a dinner party.

Vince leans forward, sucking Eve's earlobe into his mouth. Her eyes flutter closed and a soft moan escapes her lips. His eyes lock on mine as his lips peel back over his teeth, and he sinks them into her ear.

Eww.

"Nice to meet you, Raven. Eve has told me *a lot* about you."

That's why he looked at me so familiarly yesterday. He's been feeding information about me to Dominick. No doubt Eve has told him everything. I groan as I think of all the things I've told her, things I confided in her about my life.

I bet he's the one who told Dominick that I had fallen in love with Jonah, that I was staying with him every night, that I was a virgin.

Vince is Dominick's Ass-In-The-Hole.

He had this planned: having Vince stalk me, violate my personal life to gain leverage against me, taking advantage of my best friend, her loving heart and beautiful body, to spy on me. I lock eyes with Vince, but talk to Eve.

"I just needed to make sure you were okay. I hadn't been able to get ahold of you and I worried." The words flow without emotion. My mind churns, processing how *wrong* this is. "I'll let you guys get back to it."

"Wait, are you sure you're okay?" Her words come out on a moan as Vince cups her breast right in front of me. I have to get away from here.

"Yeah, I have to go." I run to my car, wishing I had the strength to tell Vince off. His blatant attempt to make me uncomfortable worked.

"I'll call you tomorrow, Rave!" Eve yells and I slam my car door shut. My hand hits the lock button and I fire up the engine, my tires squealing as I pull away.

Shaking with uncontrollable force, I grip the wheel tighter. Just when I thought things couldn't get any worse.

I want to tell Jonah about Vince and wrap myself in the safety of his strong arms until the hurt goes away. I crave his touch like an addict. It doesn't make any sense. He's with another woman. How disgusting can I be? Pining after a man who has lied and cheated?

I hate myself for what I am and how I feel. I'm Dorothy, skipping happily down the Yellow Brick Road of self-loathing. Blasting the radio, hoping the comfort of the music will be a decent substitute for the man, I grimace. Skeeter Davis sings "The End of the World," and for once, I understand her pain.

Waves of despair wash over me. The negative emotion, from my childhood until now, bears down. I want it to end, desperate to release my tortured soul from this doomed life I was born into. I would gladly give up this fight. Maybe Jonah and I aren't that different. I've been a fighter all my life too. But I don't fight against people. I fight against feeling worthless, ashamed, and unlovable. I'm sick of it, and at this point, I'd welcome death.

Morbid thoughts swirl in my head when I hear the faint chime of my phone. I dig it out of my backpack, grateful for the distraction.

One new text.

> Raven, I need to see you. Tried calling but
> no answer. Call me ASAP. xJ

He must have called me when I was at Eve's door. But why? What could he possibly want after a night with *her*? My phone rings in my hand.

In no shape to drive while talking on the phone, I pull over and check out the caller ID. Tears spring to my eyes as I read the words, "Jonah Calling".

I should throw my phone out the window and go home, but I can't. The pitiful girl in me wants to hear his voice. And why is he calling me now? The phone continues to ring. He could be calling to confess, to end things officially. Or …what if he's changed his mind?

Hope creeps back in, an energy that ignores my misery.

I have to know.

I squeeze my eyes shut and press the phone to my ear. "Hello?"

"Baby, hey." I relax against the soothing tone of his words. How did I think I could live without this? "I need to see you. Are you at Eve's?"

"Oh, um, no, she uh, had a date. I didn't want to intrude."

Silence.

"Jonah?"

"You're at your place? Alone?" I hear the accusation in his voice, chasing away the calm. Bitterness burns in my chest, squashing optimism and reviving my broken heart.

How dare he act like I'm a child. He was at a strip club. With Candy!

"No, I'm not home. I'm out. Why?" My clipped words come out harsher than I intend, but oh well.

"Where are you? I need to talk to you."

"You've got me on the phone. So talk."

More silence. I wait.

"Raven, what's going on with you? You sound, I don't know, pissed or something."

Is he joking?

"How was your *meeting*?" I say, my voice laced with acid.

"It was good." He draws out his words cautiously.

Yeah, I bet it was.

"Oh, yeah? Good, huh? I bet it was. I bet it was *real* good." The sarcasm in my voice is so obvious I sound completely ridiculous.

"That's it, Raven, where the fuck are you? I don't know what's going on, but this attitude you're throwing is pissing me off."

"Oh, God forbid."

He growls, and I know I've upset him. *Ha!* Now he knows how it feels.

"You want to know how my meeting was? It was perfect. Better than perfect. That's what I want to talk to you about."

Did he just say that being with Candy was perfect? Better than perfect? That jerk!

"You're a liar!"

"What? What the fuck are you talking about?"

I'm breathing heavy, and anger keeps me from articulating an answer. All I want to do is scream.

"What is it, baby?" His words drip with sarcasm. "You run out of shit to talk? Those sweet little lips of yours can't keep up with you being a bitch—"

I gasp. Loud. "*What* did you call me?"

"Fuck. That's not what I meant—"

"No, Jonah. You just called me the b-word. I can't believe you just called me that!" The tone in my voice is so high I'm surprised my windows don't burst.

"Baby, calm down."

"Do *not* call me baby. Not after what you've done. Not after tonight." A whine slides up my throat and I burst into tears.

"Raven, you're scaring me. Where are you? I'll come to you."

I whimper and sob, knowing I should hang up, but lacking the power to say goodbye.

"Please don't cry. Look, I'm sorry. It's just been a long day, and I need to see you."

I take a deep cleansing breath as Guy's words flood my mind. This is it. The moment he was talking about. I swallow a shaky breath. I have a choice to make. Fight or give up.

I love Jonah with all my heart. As disgusting as it is, I would take him even now after he's been with Candy. But what kind of a future do we have? Putting his life at risk isn't an option. And fighting for our love will only be prolonging the inevitable. Dominick has me. Besides, the fight takes energy. It takes words and emotions that I've run clean out of. I'm drained in every possible way.

I have no fight left.

"Goodbye, Jonah."

JONAH

"Fuck!" I launch my phone across the room. It shatters against the wall. I've just destroyed my only way of getting in touch with Raven.

My ass drops to the couch and I rest my elbows on my thighs. I run my hands through my hair like my head is a genie's bottle and I'm begging for my three wishes.

What in the hell just happened?

You called her a bitch, asshole.

What was I thinking? I was pumped up from my meeting with Dominick and sick of being away from Raven all day. I've never seen that attitude from her before. It caught me off guard, and I slipped. But she was pissed before that.

Growling in frustration, I sit back and stare at the ceiling in my living room. This isn't over. I'm not letting her get away with a simple fucking hang-up.

No. She will talk to me and tell me what the fuck is going on. Jumping up from the couch, I grab my keys. I'll drive every street of this city until I find her.

My truck thunders through the streets of Las Vegas. I check everywhere. First Raven's studio, then Nori Pizza where Eve works. The hostess gave me Eve's address so I could check there. After I talk to Raven and give her a firm spanking, I'm talking to Eve. Employees shouldn't be giving out addresses. The way the girl acted, I probably could have gotten her bank account and social security numbers if I'd asked.

No sign of her Nova anywhere. After an hour of circling the city, I go back to her place and wait.

Parked out front of Guy's Garage, I replay my conversation with Raven for the millionth time. She usually answers the phone with a smile in her voice. This time she was pissed from hello. What could I have done to upset her from the time I left her in my bed this morning?

I watch the numbers on the clock climb. It's just after one in the morning. Rubbing the exhaustion from my eyes, I hear the familiar rumble of Raven's Nova. She's driving like an Andretti. Her car screeches through the turn into the parking lot. I jump out of my truck as she throws the Nova into a spot sideways. She slams shut her car door, muttering something about reinforced steel walls.

I make it to her as she's turning around. She jumps and stops herself just short of running into my chest. I reach to pull her to me. She stiffens, dodging my embrace. Her eyes avoid mine, but I can tell she's been crying.

What the fuck?

"Baby, don't close me out. I don't understand what I did—"

She silences me with a piercing glare.

"Okay, I called you a bi—uh, the b-word. I'm so sorry for that. If I could take it back I would."

I cup her cheek and pray she doesn't push me away. The moment my skin connects with hers, she presses into my hold and closes her eyes. A lone tear makes a path down her face, pooling at my hand.

"Baby, talk to me. What did I do? You were pissed before I called you. When you answered the phone, I could tell you were mad." She leans into my hand. "What you said about my meeting—"

She snaps out of my hold with wide eyes and stands to her full five foot eight inches. Her face is hard, the softness she showed earlier completely erased.

"What's wrong? You want to know what's wrong?" she says with a shaky voice and cold, hard gaze.

I've never seen her like this. She's furious. I reach for her again and she shoves my arms away. I step back.

"I'll tell you what's wrong, Jonah. I was told yesterday by my biological jerk-wad that he bred me for prostitution. Then, my boyfriend took better care of me than I've ever been taken care of in my life, just to turn around and break my fucking heart!"

I flinch at her curse. "Broke your heart?"

"Do you know what it's like to go your entire life never being touched? Never being told that you're loved?" She laughs and her lip quivers as she wipes her tears. "No one was ever there for me. Not when I was sick. Or sad. Never. Can you even fathom the effect that has on a person? They have a term for it. It's called Failure-to-Thrive Syndrome."

She exhales and her shoulders slump. "You want to know the first time I heard the words 'I'm proud of you'?"

My heart cramps with every broken word.

"March 16, 2007. Sick isn't it? I remember the exact day. I was fifteen years old. It wasn't my mom or my dad who said it. It was Guy. My high school shop teacher."

Her eyes glisten with tears. I picture a little dark-haired girl crying alone with no one to comfort her. My hatred for her parents roots deep in my soul. Even now, it's not my Raven standing before me. It's that sad little girl who desperately wants to be loved. Who craves the touch and comfort that only a parent can provide. I want to reach out and hold her, but her arms wrapped around her body in a protective shield.

"Then you come along." Her voice is softer now and she meets my eyes.

I am undone, powerless against her pain.

"You hold me, protect me, worry about me ...tell me you love me. And the sun shines on me for the first time in my life. I look beyond your past, your reputation, all because I'm so desperate for what you give me. I fell so deeply and madly in love with you I couldn't see straight."

I watch the clear waters of her eyes turn stormy and cold. "And then you find out what I really am and you run to her. Not even twenty-four hours after you left me warm in your bed, you go to her!" Her last words break with the cries that assault her body.

Her? I don't have any idea what she's talking about, but I hate myself anyway for hurting her like this.

"Raven, baby, you have to listen to me. I don't know what you're talking about. Her? Her who? I didn't run to anyone. I'm right here with you."

I brave a touch and wrap my hand around the nape of her neck. Bending down so she can look in my eyes, I flex my fingers into her skin. "Raven, look at me."

Her eyes come to mine. The brokenness of her past shines through their aquamarine depths.

"I love you. You're the only girl I ever want to run to."

Her eyes narrow, but this time not in anger. This looks more like confusion. "But …I saw you. You were there at her club. I saw your truck outside in the lot."

Shit. I study my feet, but keep hold of her neck. She knows I was at Zeus's. She thinks I ran to Candy because of everything that happened with Dominick.

It upsets me that she doesn't believe my feelings for her are stronger than what Dominick has planned. But I know that's not what made her believe I would run to Candy so easily. Her lack of self-worth is ingrained. My hate for her parents festers and spreads.

I'll explain, get on my knees and beg if that's what it takes for her to understand. I'd do anything if it means I get to keep the lost girl I hold in my hand.

"I was at Zeus's Playground tonight, but it wasn't for the reason you think."

Her face is still hard, but the muscles in her neck relax a fraction.

"Blake and I had a meeting there." I pause a second to make sure she's still with me. "We met with Dominick."

"Jonah, why?" She steps close and grabs the wrist of the arm that's holding her. "He could have hurt you. Are you okay?" She runs her hands over my chest, arms and up to my shoulders, searching for physical damage.

My skin tingles at the touch I was afraid I might never feel again. I take advantage and wrap my arms around her waist to pull her closer.

"Yeah, I'm fine, but can we talk about this inside?" I look up towards Raven's studio and picture trying to cram myself into her bed. Nope, not happening. "Or better yet, can I take you home now? I'll explain everything there."

Her eyes drop to her feet, and she sucks her bottom lip into her mouth.

Please say yes.

She sniffs and wipes the tears from her cheeks. "Okay."

I exhale the breath I was holding and pull her into a deep hug. Placing a quick kiss on her head, and inhaling the smell of her hair, my heart slows its frantic pace.

Not wanting to let her out of my sight, I walk her to the passenger side of the truck and usher her in. Then I snag her backpack from her car, shut and lock her doors.

The ride to my house is silent. I notice Raven still looks confused, and I grab her hand to rest on my thigh. Her expression softens as I gently run my thumb along the smooth skin of her wrist.

Once home, I open her door and help her out. I swing my arm over her shoulder and she leans into my touch. From my garage, we walk up to the house side by side. I tell myself to give her some space, but I'm not ready to let go of the comfort her body gives mine.

Settling on the living room couch, I bring her a glass of water and sit next to her. She's turned toward me with her legs bent, knees to chest, arms wrapped around her shins.

I run a hand through my hair. "I'm sorry I lied to you. I was afraid if I told you the truth you'd worry or try to talk me out of it. After seeing you yesterday and last night," my jaw involuntarily tightens at the memory of her hurting, "I had to do something. I had to try."

She nods, but remains silent.

I tell Raven about the meeting, careful to expose every detail. When I finish, she stares past me, as if she's seeking counsel with some unseen force just over my shoulder. I allow the silence and give her time to process all the information.

"So, you're going to lose your fight? On purpose?"

"Yes."

"But ...you've been waiting so long for this fight. How can you give it up so easily?"

"Simple. I've been waiting longer for you."

The best thing that ever happened to me shows up in coveralls and a pair of Chucks when I least expect it. I'll do whatever it takes to keep her.

I lean forward and un-wrap her arms from her knees. Holding her hands, I press them to my chest. "You feel that? Every beat pounding away? You do that to me." I want to groan. I'm so frustrated. How can I get her to understand how much she means to me? I squeeze her hands. "You're part of me now. I'd do anything for you. I'll fight for your life as I'd fight for my own."

Wonder colors her face. She throws her body into mine and tucks in tight on my lap. I wrap her up in my arms and hold on. I almost lost her.

"I'm so sorry, Jonah. Please forgive me. I had no idea. I thought you had lied about the meeting and that you were leaving me. I heard you and Owen talking about you breaking up with me, and I thought it was because—"

"Hold on." I lean away to look in her eyes. "I never told Owen I was breaking up with you. Where did you hear that?"

"You guys were talking when I woke up." Her gaze swings toward the kitchen then back to mine. "I heard you."

I think back to the conversation and start to laugh. Raven wrinkles her nose, which makes me laugh harder.

"Why are you laughing?"

"Baby, we weren't talking about me breaking up with you. We were talking about my plan to meet Dominick. I knew I was going to have to lie to you about it. Owen wasn't happy about that, thought you'd already been through enough. And he was worried about me coming face to face with him."

The corners of her mouth lift slightly before she burrows back into my chest. "I swear you find the strangest things funny."

"Oh, that's rich coming from you."

"Blake is funny," she says like a petulant child.

I hold Raven, her body relaxed and nestled into mine. I think of how she was neglected as a child. I smooth her hair and kiss her head, wishing I could be enough to fill that void in her soul.

I can't change her past. But I'll damn well keep her safe in the future. After she hung up on me tonight, not knowing where she was, I was driving all over town worried she'd been in an accident, or worse. That shit ain't happening again.

"Baby?"

"Yeah?"

"That stunt you pulled on the phone with me tonight?"

Her body curls deeper into my lap. "Um, which part?"

"You should know tonight won't be the last time I fuck up. I'm new to relationship stuff, so you can plan on getting pissed at me a lot. But from now on, when you're pissed, you do it where I can see you."

She pushes herself up, her hand on my chest. "See you?"

"You can put up walls and not talk to me, call me every name in the book, throw shit at me, I don't care. But you'll do it *with me* and end every night in my bed."

"But, but—"

"No buts." I wrap my hand around the back of her neck and give her a squeeze. "I've been in fights with guys twice my size, been locked in holds so tight I didn't know if I'd survive, but I've never been as scared as I was tonight."

"Jonah—"

"Driving around town, looking for your car, knowing that Dominick has his sights on you…" I slide my hand up and grab a handful of her silky hair. "I can't lose you."

She blinks once then again. "I promise. You'll never lose me, Jonah." She rests her forehead against mine. "Never."

I pull her to my chest and she nestles in.

"No more hanging up on my ass either," I say while I rub her back.

"Okay. As long as you never call me the b-word again."

"Deal."

She sighs and nuzzles her face against my neck. I feel the brush of her nose under my ear. As if touching isn't enough, she breathes in deep, taking a little bit of me inside her. I stifle a groan.

Shifting on my lap, she tempts me with her sexy ass. The sweet fragrance of her shampoo combined with the feel of her soft body permeates my brain. I'm overwhelmed with the burning desire to be inside her. My blood races. The primal man in me wants to stand up and beat his chest, knowing that he's found a woman to claim, to mark her as his own, going places with her that no man has gone before.

"I love you, Raven."

She tilts her head up to look at me. "I love you."

I brush my knuckles against her cheek. "Can I show you?"

Her eyebrows drop low.

"Make love to you, baby." I answer her unspoken question.

Her body goes rigid in my arms and she studies my face. Whatever she sees seems to agree with her. A sexy smile pulls at her lips and damn if that doesn't seal the deal.

Nodding her head slowly, I stand with her still in my arms. She cups my face, her thumbs at my dimples, and places feather light kisses against my mouth. I race to the bedroom, her giggles bouncing against my lips the entire way.

SEVENTEEN

RAVEN

Locked in Jonah's bathroom, I stare at myself in the mirror. My hands grip the counter and I lean in to study my face: red-rimmed, bloodshot eyes and a wild mane of dark hair framing my pale face.

"Lovely. I look like a zombie. Real sexy, Raven," I whisper to myself.

Even though I took a shower a few hours ago, I decide another one might help to rinse the dead, decaying look from my face. I pull my hair into a messy bun to keep it dry, and stand under the warm water. A good scrub of my face has me feeling human again. I hop out and the reality of what's about to happen has me patting my body dry faster than usual. Butterflies swirl in my belly along with eager anticipation.

A smile pulls at my cheeks, flooding my body with warmth. I push the obstacles from today to the back of my head and lock my worries away. They'll still be there tomorrow. Tonight, it's just us.

I brush my teeth and throw on a new pair of panties I bought on my last Victoria's Secret shopping spree. After I slide the bright blue lace up my legs, I check out my reflection from all angles.

This particular style is called The Cheeky and while checking out my backside, I can see why. The low slung, hip huggers are made of delicate lace that cut up dramatically in the back accenting the full curves of my bottom. I bought these with Jonah in mind. He can't seem to keep his hands off my booty, and I can't wait to see what he thinks of these.

I forgo a bra or tank and decide topless is the way to go. I run a brush through my hair and allow the messy waves to fall in haphazard disarray.

A quick peek into the bedroom reveals lit candles, soft music, but no Jonah. I race to his bed, arms crossed at my chest, and crawl on top. Lying on my stomach, I take deep breaths to calm my nerves.

He has so much experience with sex. What if I disappoint him? He's used to sexually confident women who probably hang from the rafters or stand on their heads. I can't compete with that.

"Stop it. It's going to be fine. You can hang from rafters," I whisper. Muffling my giggles into the pillow, I picture myself in some ridiculous position which only antagonizes my nerves.

Think sexy. No giggling.

I breathe deep, and visions of Jonah quiet my thoughts. I welcome the sultry voice of Ella Fitzgerald and the smell of lightly scented candle wax to soothe my frazzled nerves.

I hear the click of the bedroom door as it opens then softly closes. Still on my stomach, my arms folded under my head, I turn to see him and almost choke.

Jonah's in nothing but a pair of black pajama pants. They hang low on his hips exposing the v of his lower abdominal muscles, dusted with dark hair. *Holy crud.* His inky black hair is spiked with moisture. He must have taken a shower in the guest bathroom. Kaleidoscopic arms, bulging with muscle, tense at his sides, I gawk at his masculine body then settle on his smiling face. His hazel eyes move over me in a visual caress, causing a tremor of need to vibrate beneath my skin.

"Fuck. You look so sexy right now." His deep voice and dirty talk have me trembling.

My eyes lock on his as he crosses the room to the bed.

"You take my breath away." His penetrating gaze roams over every inch of my form. "Don't move. Stay just like that."

I obey, and he disappears to the foot of the bed. What's he doing?

The mattress dips at my feet just before I feel the warmth of his hands cover my calves. Using them to guide him, he slowly climbs up my body until he straddles my hips. The fabric of his cotton pants brushes my exposed skin. I take a deep breath and relax as the tips of his fingers run along the edge of my panties at my back.

"These are my favorite." His fingers trace from one hip to the other.

"I bought them just for you. I thought you'd like them."

"I fuckin' love 'em." He flexes his hips into the space between my legs, his blatant arousal making me gasp. "Can't you tell?"

"Um, yeah, I can." Nervous giggles creep up from my chest and tickle my throat. *Don't giggle!*

He traces the line of my tattoo from my hip to my shoulder. My skin tingles and goose bumps break out across my flesh. The bed dips by my head, and he nips at the shell of my ear. I inhale citrus and spice, swirling my senses and igniting a fire in my belly.

"Have I ever told you how much I love your tattoo?" His mouth travels along the side of my throat where he kisses at his spot.

My head tilts to the side to welcome his attention. His soft lips follow the line of birds, gently kissing and licking until he's back at my hip. A pleasured moan rises from my chest.

"You like that, baby?" he asks against my skin.

I arch my back, lifting my bottom up and into his chest. He slides his hand beneath the lace and cups one cheek, squeezing and molding it in his hand while his mouth continues its torture.

"Jonah, I want to see you." My words finish on a whimper.

"Not yet. I'm not finished playing with you."

I'm so turned on already I can't imagine what it's going to be like when he's finished playing with me.

His large hands move back up to massage my shoulders with gentle pressure. Having never been touched this way before, my body responds in new and unfamiliar ways. I melt into the bed. A glorious tingling starts at my chest working its way through my veins and heating my blood.

His slow powerful strokes work down my back. I feel small and delicate under his expert touch. Hands, lips, tongue, and teeth, all stimulate my hunger. I'm panting and greedy. My moans combine with the soft music filling the room, creating an erotic symphony.

"Jonah, I can't take much more." I move to roll over, but Jonah presses his chest into my back, caging me to the bed with his weight. His arms rest close to my face and I barely hold back the desire to lean over and trace the tattoos on his biceps with my tongue.

"My girl's eager." He rocks his hips into me.

An embarrassing whine flies from my lips, and I grind back into him. Intimate parts of my body request, no, beg for his attention.

"You keep that up. This will be over before it begins." He nips at my neck, soothing his tender bites with slow sweeps of his tongue. "Don't worry, baby. We'll get to that. First, we need to talk."

My body freezes and I twist my neck to look at him.

"Talk? I don't want to talk." I sound like a child forced to eat her vegetables.

How sexy is that?

He bites his lip, fighting a smile. "We have to. I know you're on the pill, so birth control is taken care of, right?"

My face falls into my folded arms to hide my pink cheeks.

"Yes. How did you…" Stupid question. He's seen me take them. "Never mind."

The only parental thing my mom ever did was take me to get put on the pill at sixteen. She probably thought I'd end up just like her. *Gah! I don't want to think about this now.*

"Here's the thing. I've never had sex without a condom. I've also never made love to a woman before. How would you feel about me not wearing one?"

"Ugh! Jonah, you're seriously killing the moment here." I speak my muffled complaint into the pillow.

"What? I'm being thorough. It's your first time and I want it to be good for you. I think going bareback would be better. But I won't do it without your permission."

"Bareback?"

"Without a condom."

I've had fantasies about what my first time with Jonah would be like. In all my versions of this moment, I never had a conversation that involved the word bareback. This reminder of Jonah's sexual experience to my lack thereof is off-putting. But I love him and I believe he loves me. There's no doubt in my mind that he has my best interest at heart. He always does.

"I trust you."

His weight lifts and he falls to my side. I prop myself up on my elbows and look into his handsome, smiling face.

"All right, no more talking."

On a growl, he leans over and possesses my mouth. His tongue glides along mine, rekindling my need. I tilt my head and press in deeper. My toes curl and my back arches in an attempt to get closer. He sucks my tongue into his mouth and runs his teeth along it as I pull it back. The simple scrape turns my insides to liquid.

More.

The word echoes in my head, sending the message to every nerve cell in my body. He's consuming me, and I want nothing more than to crawl inside him. His hand curls around the back of my head and he rolls. My legs open to him, cradling his body. He hovers over me, the hard plains of his chest cushioned against my breasts. Flexing his hips, he grinds into me with solid steel and I swallow his moan.

His hands dig into my hair, grabbing it firmly at the roots. A slight tug opens my mouth further and he plunges deeper. With firm pressure he continues to rock against me, building my impending release. My stomach flips with the promise of what's to come.

Breaking free for air, he kisses down my neck, leaving me panting for breath. His warm mouth closes over the firm tip of my breast. Electricity shoots down my torso to my womb. He switches back and forth, sucking on one while rolling the tip of the other between his finger and thumb. I slide my legs against his, restless and impatient.

"So fucking responsive," he growls, the rumble of his deep voice against my chest vibrating down my body. "God, you taste so sweet." He licks and pulls at my breast. "I want to taste the rest of you."

His words are rocket fuel to my libido. I'm writhing and panting. His hands roam down my torso to between my legs. My body bows off the bed. If I wasn't so wanton, I'd be embarrassed at my lack of control.

He runs his lips down the length of my body, pausing only to nip at my belly button.

"Mmm, Jonah…" I want to say something to communicate how good he feels against my skin, but I'm too lost in the sensation.

Hooking his fingers into the fine lace of my panties, he shreds them with a firm tug. I moan, lifting my hips, and he tosses the flimsy lace to the floor. I'm all feeling and emotion, completely void of rational thought.

He lifts his head and gives me his sexy, one-dimpled smile. This one is similar to the one I've gotten before, but better. Way better. His lowered lids and dark glare turn this smile into something different all together, and I'm gone. Completely owned with one look.

I tremble as he places himself between my legs. His eyes lock on mine seconds before he dips down. His mouth presses against me in a probing thrust. My head falls back. Every nerve fires and I'm overcome with desire. His hands still my hips in a display of full carnal domination. Gripping the sheets, I dig my heels into the mattress and push my hips up begging for more. His mouth commands my body, pulling my strings and pushing me on. He slides his hands beneath my bottom to tilt my hips, delving deeper and thrusting harder. Euphoria swirls behind my eyes with every abrasive scratch of his stubble between my legs.

"Jonah, I'm gonna…" My words fade into a glorious moan and I bit my lip.

He pulls back, the cold air hits me hard. I open my eyes to see him braced above me looking intently into my face.

"Why did you stop? I didn't …I was almost …there." My voice whines with disappointment.

"You're ready."

He's not asking, but I nod.

Yes! I'm ready!

He kisses my chin. "You sure about this? Cause, fuck baby, I *need* to be inside you." He runs his tongue along my bottom lip. "Deep inside you."

I push my hips up and dig my fingernails into his arms.

"Yeah, my girl's ready."

He slides his pants down and kicks them to the floor. I stare openly at his arousal.

This is going to hurt. Bad.

"Don't worry, baby. I'll go slow."

My eyes dart to his face. *Did I say that out loud?*

He crawls up my body, eyes fixed on mine. His hands push my arms above my head, weaving our fingers together. In this position, his weight against me, his huge body forcing my legs apart, I'm completely at his mercy. Helpless against his invasion. And totally safe. Warm, silken heat nudges its way in, slowly pressing, forcing me open. Instinctively, my body resists and I press my knees into his sides.

"Deep breath." He brushes his lips against my jaw. "Relax."

Taking a deep breath, I concentrate on relaxing my muscles. He pushes in further.

"I love you." He speaks the words against my neck, feathering kisses against my skin.

He releases my hands, and I brace them against his ribs. His pulse races against my palms. His hazel eyes darken and worry crosses his face.

"What's wrong?"

"This is it."

"It?"

A deep pink blush colors his cheeks. My eyes widen.

Oh, IT.

He looks conflicted. "I don't want to hurt you."

I wrap my legs around his hips and use my heels to press him to me. "I'm ready, Jonah. I want this. I want you to be the one to do it. I love you." The confidence in my voice mirrors the feelings in my heart.

He smiles so sweetly that I'm forced to catch my breath.

"Okay, baby. Take a deep breath and blow it out slowly."

My eyes lock on his in determination. Taking a deep breath through my nose, I hold it and nod. I blow the breath out slowly, and when I'm almost out of air, he buries himself completely. A hiss shoots from his lips as he pushes past the final barrier of my virginity. My eyes slam shut at the searing pain.

"I'm so sorry, sweetheart. I love you." Tender brushes of his lips trail from my jaw to my shoulder.

After a minute, I release his hips, my legs no longer able to hold him with their quivering muscles. The burn recedes, leaving behind a delicious fullness.

Past the pain, I focus on Jonah's face: both dimples, full teeth, and shining eyes. Pure male pride.

He cups my face, running his thumbs along my cheeks. "Feel okay?"

"Perfect." I rake my hands into his hair and pull him in for a deep, wet kiss.

"My girl."

His movements start slow, dissolving my discomfort and awakening my hunger. I scrape my nails along his scalp, grasping in desperation. Closer, deeper, harder. More. I don't know what's come over me. All I know is that I need Jonah more than oxygen.

"Jonah, I—"

A gasp robs me of my words as he rocks into my body. Ripples of pleasure shoot up my torso and coil in my chest. I grip his backside with two hands, feeling the flex and release of his muscles as he moves between my legs.

Possession pushes below the surface of my skin. An animalistic satisfaction at being marked, permanently changed by the man I love.

"More." The simple spoken word has him rolling his hips deeper, and thrusting harder.

Yes!

I groan as the tension builds, churning low and ready to burst.

"You're perfect. So hot, and fuck, so tight," he growls into my mouth.

I'm hot and writhing, his words and body mastering mine. Every angle winds me tighter, pushing me higher. I buck against him, searching for release.

A shift of his hips in the right spot and sparks fly behind my eyes. I suck in a lungful of air, my release shooting through my body. My nails dig into his biceps and I call out his name against his lips. He continues to rock into me. And just like an expert guitar player hitting the perfect chord, another explosion of pleasure pushes through me. My heels dig into the bed, riding out my climax. Blissful satisfaction washes over me in waves. I labor for breath, floating down and sinking into the bed.

Is it always like this?

My body hums. I blink away the post-orgasm fog. My limbs fall to the side, sated and heavy.

It's only then that I notice Jonah still moving above me. His colorful arms flex and pulse. His eyes lock on mine, and he bites his bottom lip. I can't resist the urge to taste it myself and push up to pull at the soft flesh with my teeth. He releases it and I suck it deep into my mouth.

He quickens his pace then growls his release. Heat fills my body where the sting has died to a dull ache. I lick and suck at his lips and tongue until his movement slows. He collapses onto my body, and I wrap my legs around his waist, my arms around his neck. We breathe heavy, chest to chest, hearts pounding against each other, until we calm.

"I'm not ready to give you up," he says against my skin while moving gently inside me.

"I'm not ready to be given up."

We kiss, this time absent of the heat from earlier. Only gentle touches and whispers of affection.

"Thank you, Jonah. That was better than I imagined."

His lips brush mine once more before he rolls off of me. I wince as he pulls free from our connection. He falls to my side and wraps me in his arms.

My head on his chest, he takes a deep breath. "Baby, that was incredible."

We lie in silence, Alicia Keys singing "How it Feels to Fly" and soothing the aftershocks of our lovemaking. The lyrics send goose bumps racing across my skin. Lying here in Jonah's arms, having given him the only thing of worth that I have to give, I've never felt freer. Tears sting my eyes, and I swipe at one that rolls down my cheek.

"Ah, shit. I'm sorry. Was it too rough? Are you okay?" Jonah's hands are at my face, wiping at the moisture beneath my eyes.

Propping myself up, I look at him and smile. "Do I look okay?"

"No. I mean, of course, you look amazing. But you're crying."

He continues to dry my wayward tears. I stop his hands with mine. "I'm fine. It's been an emotional day." My fingers trace the tattoo on his chest. "Was it, um, okay? You know, for you?"

He throws his head back in a quick burst of laughter. "Shit, let's put aside the fact that I'm in love with you. Let's also not count the fact that being skin on skin, no barrier between me and your hot, wet, gripping—"

I smack him playfully in the arm, my lips upturned and cheeks cramping from the glowing review he's giving me.

"Okay, all that aside, the way your body responds to mine, the slightest touch or shift in my position …Moans of pleasure coming from those gorgeous lips ...Baby, that was the hottest..." His eyes dart to the side as if he's having a hard time putting words to his feelings. "What we did tonight was more beautiful than anything I've ever experienced."

"I feel the same. I'm glad I waited for you, Jonah. You deserve to be my first—"

"And your last."

My jaw drops open before I catch it and slam it shut.

Could he really mean what he just said? I've heard men do that, say things they don't really mean after sex because they're caught up in the moment. He doesn't look uncertain. He's not smiling, his mouth isn't twitching uncomfortably. His eyes are fixed on mine and his face is soft. I don't have much experience in this area, but if I had to guess, I'd say he looks like a man in love.

My rational side busts out a checklist. He replaced my door, risked his safety to talk to Dominick, hunted me down after I hung up on him, and tonight he loved me, mind, body, and soul.

How could I take advantage of his love by allowing him to give up his fight for me? There has to be another way. My mind is slow with fatigue and sexual satisfaction, but I scroll through possible alternatives. Beyond ending my life, which isn't an option, there's only one other thing I can do.

"Jonah?"

"Yeah?"

I clear my throat, my mouth suddenly dry. "I could run."

Silence.

"I could just take off and drive to New York or Florida. I'll change my name and find a job that pays cash. After a while, you could come visit me. You wouldn't have to throw your fight. I could even get—"

"No." His answer isn't angry, but absolute. "That's no way to live. We'd have to move every few months, constantly looking over our shoulders."

"You don't know that. He might just give up when he can't find me locally."

Hooking his hands under my arms, he pulls me up his chest and we're face to face.

"You think Dominick is the kind of man to let go of something he wants? You know he'd come after you, Raven, for no other reason than he doesn't like to lose. I want you free from all ties, and throwing the fight is the only way. Money is the only language Dominick understands."

Hot tears pool in my eyes and cool as they cascade down my face. "I'll never be able to re-pay you for all you're giving up for me. I'm afraid that, in time, you'll resent me."

"Impossible. The title will always be there. The fight is replaceable. You're not."

Closing my eyes, I bury my face in his neck. "I love you." It's the only thing I can think of to communicate my appreciation. But it's not enough.

"I love you too." He repositions me at his side.

I lean up and give him my lips. It's in this kiss that two truths penetrate and soak into my soul.

First, Jonah loves me.

And, second, I don't know what the future will bring, but whatever happens, I won't be facing it alone.

EIGHTEEN

RAVEN

I shiver as cool air washes over my back all the way down to my thighs. Surfacing from my deep sleep, I reach for the blanket to ward off the cold when I feel something warm pleasantly teasing my hip. Little by little, the cold is chased away and a tingling heat moves through my body. I blink my eyes open, aware of the slight shifting of the bed and the soft touch that makes its way up my back. *Jonah.* Like last night, he's kissing a trail along the path of my tattoo.

Last night! My eyes pop open as impassioned memories tear their way through my sleep. I lost my virginity. A giggle erupts from my throat.

He smiles against my shoulder. "Tickle?" His deep, gravelly voice against my skin raises goose bumps down my arm.

"Mmm, no. Feels good."

"You're laughing."

Shaking my head, I refuse to divulge my schoolgirl thoughts.

"I didn't think waking up to you in my bed could get any better. But waking up to you, with your hot little body, naked and pressed against mine?" He nibbles and licks at his spot on my neck. "The shit dreams are made of." Groaning, he pushes himself up to my ear. "I hate to leave you like this, but I have a phone interview. Go back to sleep, baby. I shouldn't be long."

"Interview? But it's still dark out."

"Mm-hmm." His face is buried in my neck and his fingers graze my breasts.

I moan and arch my back, pressing into him.

"Fuck." The word rumbles against my skin. "Don't move. I want to get right back to this when I'm finished."

With one last kiss to my shoulder, I feel him get out of bed. I hear him slide on his drawstring pants. "Stupid fucking interview." He shuts the bedroom door behind him.

One deep, contented sigh later, my eyes drift close.

—

JONAH

"This sucks," I say under my breath as I drop down into my desk chair in my home office.

I check the clock. Five fifteen in the morning. I sip my coffee and curse my publicist for setting up these interviews.

I'm at my desk when I should be wrapped around Raven. My girl's flawless bare body molded to mine, surrounded by her smell, it was nearly impossible to walk away.

I log into my email and open the one from my publicist. This is the absolute worst part of being a fighter, the publicity shit. Some guys get off on it, but most of us hate it. The radio station interviews are the lesser of the publicity evils. At least I get to do it from home in my flannel pants. If I had my cell I could do this from my bed with Raven in my arms. I shake my head and make a note to get myself a new phone first thing.

Scanning the email, looking for the number, I notice I'm fifteen minutes late. I shrug. Fuck 'em. I made love for the first time in my life to the girl of my dreams. They can wait.

I punch in the number listed on the email. I give the producer my name and wait, my thoughts drifting back to last night. I've never had a sexual experience like that. Owen wasn't fucking around when he said sex was different when you do it with someone you love. And Raven, the girl had zero experience, but damn if she didn't light up like a fucking Roman candle. Those panties, her moaning, body arching, begging for my attention. I groan and readjust my pants.

And here, I thought I'd lose interest? Once would never be enough—shit, a lifetime would never be enough of Raven. She just gave me a taste of what she has to offer, and I'm famished, completely starving for more.

"To all our radio listeners out there, we have a special treat for you today." The voice on the phone rips me from my happy place. "Jonah 'The Assassin' Slade is taking a break from his rigorous training schedule to give us an exclusive interview. His fight with Heavyweight Champion Victor Del Toro for the belt is September fourteenth at Mandalay Bay. Jonah, thanks for taking the time to talk to us."

"Of course, thanks for having me." I roll my eyes.

"Victor Del Toro has been the reigning Heavyweight Champion for over six years. Are you confident that you can beat him?"

"Absolutely. I think my record speaks for itself. I haven't lost a fight yet and don't plan on losing one now." I grimace at my blatant lie because that's exactly what I plan on doing.

"Del Toro has what you call a glass jaw. Can you explain what that is to our listeners?"

"Sure, glass jaw refers to someone who gets knocked out easily. It's Del Toro's Achilles' heel. But the guy is the reigning Heavyweight Champion and has been for six years, so he's no pansy. Weak jaw or not, the guy can fight."

"Now, you, 'Assassin,' have a mean right hook. We can assume that your powerful right hook combined with Del Toro's glass jaw means he has very little chance of winning this fight?"

"No, not necessarily. The key to a great fighter is to know your weakness. He trains to protect his jaw at all costs. I could throw a dozen killer right hooks, but they only work if I land them. He'll be on guard the entire fight."

"Last question, you have a reputation of being …how should I say …friendly with the ladies? Rumor has it you've been seen around town with a sexy brunette. Our sources say it's Raven Morretti, a local car mechanic." The interviewer and his co-host laugh before finishing. "Is 'The Assassin' settling down?"

No, he fucking did not.

I grind my teeth and my muscles tense. Leaning forward, resting my elbows on my desk, I speak clearly to keep from being misunderstood.

"Not gonna discuss my personal life, guys, but I will say this." My voice sounds low and menacing even to my ears. "You talk about Raven, I'll pay a personal visit to your studio and we'll have words. You get me?"

"Whoa! You heard it here, folks. Sounds like The Las Vegas Casanova is finally settling—"

Click.

Shit. How did I not think about this? This fight is huge for Vegas. She's going to get thrown into the middle of the media firestorm. As if the girl doesn't have enough to deal with already. I need to protect her. But how? I'll make sure we lie low until the fight's over. Briefing Raven on the situation should help to prepare her for what she's up against.

Running away with her and living out the remainder of our days on some deserted island doesn't sound like a bad idea after all.

I make a few more calls: two for interviews and one for a new cell phone to be delivered to my house. It's eight fifteen, and I haven't heard a sound come out of my room. Raven must still be asleep. I plan on crawling back in bed with her when I hear the water running in my bathroom. Or a shower? I smile as visions of shower sex with Raven infiltrate my mind.

"Don't be an insensitive prick." I shake the wet fantasy from my head. She's got to be sore. I can't have sex with her for a day ...or two. Okay, a day. Give her a chance to recover.

No way can I go in the room when she's wet and naked in my bathroom. I won't be able to give her a break if I see her like that. Killing time, I pay a couple bills online, check my email, and play a game of solitaire before I head back to my room.

I stroll down the hallway with purpose and a smile. Sex might be off the agenda for today, but I can think of plenty of other things we could do to occupy our time.

—

RAVEN

I open my eyes to bright sunlight. Stretching my arms above my head, my muscles object. *Gosh, I'm sore.* I roll to my back as a smile tiptoes its way across my face.

"This is awesome." I stomp my feet on the bed under the sheet.

The faint smell of coffee crashes my private party. I throw my legs over the bed, gripping the sheet to my naked chest. I search the floor for my panties, and remember that Jonah destroyed them last night. My lips roll between my teeth to muffle my excited squeak. I'll make sure to fit a panty-replacement shopping spree into my schedule this week. Maybe I'll get a few extra pairs of those—

A warm rush of heat seeps from between my legs. My jaw drops open as my hand flies to my mouth.

"Oh no! My period? Crap!"

Wrapping the top sheet around my body, I run to the bathroom and jump in the shower. I do the mental math while scrubbing my body, making sure to be gentle with the tender areas. Ten days early? Impossible. I haven't missed one pill—my breath hitches.

Not my period! No, that would be embarrassing enough. What just happened, on Jonah's fancy sheets no less, is a direct result from last night.

"This is so humiliating."

I can't imagine what the proper protocol is for a girlfriend who bleeds virgin blood on her boyfriend's sheets. One thing's for sure, I need to get those off and get them in the wash before he sees.

Dressing quickly in one of Jonah's T's, I throw my wet hair up in a towel and put Operation Virginity Devastation into action.

I race around the bed and toss the comforter to the ground. Ripping pillowcases off one by one, I pile them on the floor along with the sheets. I'm frantically scooping up the soiled linens when I hear the bedroom door open. Frozen in place, I squeeze my eyes shut.

Darn it!

Head down, I sneak a peek, silently hoping I'd imagined it.

"Hey." He studies the load in my arms, eyes lingering a bit on my legs.

Nope. I'm caught. I hop to standing, losing a few pillowcases on the way, and force my most innocent grin.

"What's going on?" He tilts his chin to the sheets in my arms. "I have a maid for that."

His sexy half grin almost makes me forget my all-consuming embarrassment. Almost.

My mind spins, trying to come up with a plausible reason why I'd be doing Jonah's laundry. His gorgeous body, uncovered from the waist up, does nothing for my concentration. I run my hungry eyes over every muscular curve.

I blink in a flutter, clearing the optical orgasm. *Concentrate, Raven.* "I, uh, thought I'd help out. Um, do my share since I've been living here?" My excuse comes out a question.

Jonah reads me with narrowed eyes. He knows I'm lying.

My eyes dart around the room unable to focus on his penetrating gaze. On a sigh, I drop my shoulders along with the sheets, defeated.

I can't lie to Jonah. "This morning, when I woke up, I, uh…"

He lifts his eyebrows for me to continue.

"When I sat up, I guess gravity or something took over and I …um…" I drop my face, concentrating on the floor in front of me. "Bled …on your nice sheets." I confess and rub my forehead to avoid eye contact. "I'm sorry. I'll wash them, and if it doesn't come out, I'll buy you new ones."

I don't hear him move, but his bare feet move into my line of sight. Standing less than a foot away, he pulls me into his arms. They flex around me and he places a kiss on my head. I relax and snuggle into his hold.

"Let me take care of the sheets. You go get some coffee, and I'll throw these in the wash."

He leans back, searching for my eyes. I direct my stare past his shoulder. He cups my cheek, holding my face prisoner, demanding my attention.

"I love you, baby, but I don't love you thinking that I care about some stupid sheets. I hope it does stain so that every time I sleep on 'em I'll be reminded of our first time, not that I'll need the reminder. Last night is burned into my brain, permanently."

He did not just say that. My cheeks heat and my nose wrinkles. "Eww. That's gross."

"What? That last night is burned in my brain?"

I break eye contact to focus on his neck. "No, that you'd want to sleep on sheets stained with my blood."

His fingers bring my chin up as he bends down. "Not gross to me, baby." His voice is close and rough. "It's sexy." His breath caresses my lips and smells like coffee. My tongue darts out to see if I can taste it. His eyes focus on my mouth and I watch his eyelids drop.

Oh boy.

"I need you to walk away now. Go get your coffee."

I nod, but my body pushes closer to his.

"You're probably sore from last night, and I want to give you time to heal. If you stay here, looking at me like that, smelling the way you do, inches from my bed, I won't be able to let you."

I shiver.

"That's right, baby. Coffee. Now." His demand is gentle, but still no less a demand.

I blink my eyes quickly. "I'll go get my coffee."

"That's my girl. I'll be there in a few."

Moving past him, he lightly smacks my butt. Shaking my head, but smiling ear to ear, my mind processes his words.

Not gross to me, baby. It's sexy.

He really must love me.

NINETEEN

JONAH

Raven left for work a few minutes ago. And with her absence came my crushing reality.

My scalp is numb from fisting my hands in my hair. Sitting at my breakfast bar, I stare mindlessly at the black granite countertop, as I attempt to sort out the jumbled thoughts in my head.

Throwing a fight isn't as easy as it sounds. I can't just walk into the octagon and stick my chin out. I have to fight. Just not fight good enough to win.

How the fuck am I supposed to do that?

I'm undefeated because I go ape shit when I get hit. It's impossible to reason with the primitive part of my brain. That, along with the roar of the crowd and shouts of encouragement from my team, is a violent combination, a winning combination. Fuckin' hell, if that isn't the problem.

I'm going to have to be completely retrained. I have one week to figure out how the fuck to lose a fight.

I grab my new cell phone that was delivered and punch in a few numbers.

"Blake, meet me at the training center in ten."

Ending the call, I head out.

Blake is a red belt jiujitsu master. He earned the name Blake "The Snake" at seventeen when he constricted a guy in a cage fight and had him out cold in less than thirty seconds. If he can't help me, I'm fucked.

I pull up to the UFL training center right behind Blake.

"Hey, man. You ready to figure this shit out?" He heads my way through the lot.

"Yeah. I have a few ideas. Wanted to go over a couple techniques with you. That cool?"

Blake shrugs his shoulders. "Whatever helps. This shit's fucked. Still can't believe you're," he looks around to make sure we're alone in the parking lot, "really gonna do this."

I lean against my truck. "You sure you're up for this? I don't want to drag you into my shit. Not gonna lie though, I could use your help."

He rips his sunglasses from his face and leans in. "Don't start this shit with me. You fuckin' know I got your back. I'll give you that one, but you say that kinda fucked up crap again, I'll kick your ass myself."

I suppress a grin. "Then let's do this." I give him a chin lift and we walk to the center's doors.

Once geared up, we hit the octagon. It's quiet, just a few guys working at the heavy bags a dozen yards away.

"The key is to avoid this motherfucker's jaw like a two-dollar hooker," he says, then cringes. "Sorry, bad joke."

I shake my head, thinking I may just have to slide one solid punch in during this training session.

"Right, I know that, fuckwad. What I want to know is how the hell do I keep from flippin' the switch on his ass when he punches me?"

"Easy. Submissions. Take him to the ground and lock him down. Milk the clock until the ref breaks it up."

That's not a bad idea. If I can get him in a solid hold where he can't get the ground and pound, I should be able to buy some time.

"That might work. Let's work on some submissions that keep his fists away from my face."

Blake nods.

Without time on our side, we get to it. Modifying a few key holds isn't easy, but we manage to come up with a couple strategies. A few take-downs and pinning techniques will help, but I'm going to need more.

"I need to go at least three rounds, and I can't just sit on the mat holdin' him like a newborn baby. The fans are expecting some stand-up. If I keep my punches to body shots during the stand-up, that should help."

Blake shakes his head. "Yeah, until he strikes back and hits you hard enough to bring out the beast, but not knock you out! I'm telling you I've seen you fight. You need to stay grounded as much as possible. Protect your head, and keep that fine piece of ass in the forefront of your mind. Then, pray for a miracle."

And now, I remember why I'm friends with Blake.

After a couple hours of training, I hear a voice call my name. I peer through the octagon chain link to see Taylor Gibbs, the owner of the UFL. He's in his usual dark suit, wearing his usual schooled expression.

"Taylor. What's up?"

"Need a word with you in my office when you're done."

"Give me five."

He nods and walks away.

I turn to Blake. "You know what this is about?"

Blake looks at the space Taylor recently vacated then back to me. "No clue." He shrugs.

We make plans to continue training tomorrow, and I head to Taylor's office.

He probably wants to talk to me about the fight, but I feel like a kid called to the principal's office. There's no way he could know about my deal with Dominick. Dominick isn't stupid enough to go flapping his gums. Blake and Raven are the only other ones that know. Blake seemed just as caught off guard as I was, and Raven, well, there's no way she's talking.

His no-good assistant isn't at her desk, so I walk in his office without knocking. It's an asshole thing to do, but I don't have the patience for social politeness.

Taylor looks up from his computer screen. "Jonah, have a seat."

I stay standing. "What's this about?"

He lifts his eyebrows and nods to the chair in front of me. I sit.

"We just signed a deal for a joint campaign with the female MMA fighting league."

"Okay. What does that have to do with me?"

"Not much, just a few cross promotions, photo shoots, magazine covers—stuff like that."

I nod. It's not uncommon that the UFL use me for promotional shit. I still don't see why this warrants a visit to the boss's office.

"I'm going to need you to be seen with their headlining fighter, Camille Fisher. Won't be much, just the pre-fight formal dinner, and we'll get her seats by your corner for the title fight. After that, a few sightings out at the clubs ought to do it."

Pretending to date a girl I don't even know so that the suits can pull off a campaign? Hell no.

"No. I'm not doing that."

His eyes narrow and he leans forward, resting his elbows on the desk. "No? Why not."

"I'm dating someone. I'll be bringing her to the formal dinner, and she'll have my seats at the fight."

With a chuckle, he leans back into his chair, relaxed. "That it? Surely a few dates with another girl won't bother her. Tell her it's for work. Besides, have you seen Camille? She's hot. I'm doing you a favor, my friend."

What kind of man does he think I am? The kind that fucks girls whose names he doesn't know without a second thought. Not anymore.

"Look, Taylor, I want to help you out. I'll do photo shoots, press junkets, whatever, but I'm not cheating on my girl even if it's staged for publicity. Have Del Toro do it."

"She doesn't want Del Toro. She's requested you personally."

I shake my head, completely solid, unwavering.

"Who's this girl who's got you by the balls?" he asks with genuine curiosity.

My head tilts slightly as I fix my stare on him. "Don't see how that's your business."

"You've been fighting for me for eight years, and I've never even heard a rumor about you getting serious with a girl. Now, just weeks before your title fight, a fight that is going to make me a lot of money, you get serious?"

I shrug. Where in the hell is he going with this?

"No bullshit, I'm worried. I need you on your game, no distractions. I think it's in the best interest of the organization for you to put your relationship on hold until after the fight."

I sit forward, leaning one elbow on my knee. This guy's got his head shoved up his own ass if he thinks I'd give up Raven to please him.

"Haven't had a dad since I was twelve, Taylor. Managed to make it this far without one. Don't need one now."

"I'm not speaking as a parent, Jonah. I'm speaking as your boss."

"Don't remember seeing you dictating who I date in my contract."

"I can't force you, but I can advise you."

"Consider me advised. We done?"

"No. Don't forget about the press conference."

"That's what I have a publicist for. Now, we done?"

He studies my face for a few long seconds then shrugs.

I stand to leave, but turn just before walking out the door. "Let your assistant know I'll be bringing a date to the pre-fight dinner."

His eyes dart to mine and narrow a fraction. I smile back before walking out.

Who the fuck does he think he is?

—

RAVEN

"Hey, Dog." I place his food on the bottom step and scratch behind his ears. He purrs as he eats. I smile at the content sound, knowing I'd be making the same one if I could.

After last night, I've been walking around in a perpetual state of contentment, robbing me of my focus.

"Yeah, I know how you feel. Feels good to be taken care of." I rub Dog from head to tail and back. "Good kitty."

My phone rings, scaring Dog and sending him down the alley and behind a dumpster.

"Hey, Eve." I take the conversation inside, hoping my absence will bring Dog back to finish his food.

"How are you? I'm so sorry about last night, I felt like shit after you left. It looked like you'd been crying, and I should have sent Vince home and had you stay. What happened?" She speaks quickly, whether from guilt or concern, I don't know.

"Oh, um," I clear my throat, "Jonah and I just had a little fight, but we're okay now. Just a misunderstanding."

I bite my lip and contemplate telling her about Vince. My loyalty to her is warring with my need to protect her.

"Oh, phew. I was so worried after you left. I called your cell, but you didn't answer. Vince kept telling me that you were probably okay. He said if you weren't you would call."

Nice of daddy's little henchman to comfort my best friend.

"How are things going with you and Vince?" I wait for her answer, ready to read into every word, to feel her out before I decide on full disclosure.

"Pretty good. He's still so private about stuff, but now that he's met you, I think he'll start to come around."

Private or big fat, disgusting liar?

I can't sit back and watch her get used. She needs to know. "Eve, there's something I need to—"

"I know what you're going to say, Rave. He's really affectionate, and …sometimes it comes across as kinda pervy or whatever. I'm sorry if he made you uncomfortable last night. He says he can't keep his hands off me." I can hear the smile in her voice.

Yuck. I fight the urge to shove my finger down my throat like a surly twelve year old.

"That's not what—"

"Enough about boys. I need my girl time. We're going out tonight. My old waitress from Nori just got hired at Club Six. She said she'd put us on the list and told me if I slip the bouncer a fifty he'd let us in without ID's."

"Tonight? Um—"

"Come on! I'm so sick of the under twenty-one clubs. This is our chance to go to a real club!"

"Okay." Unable to think of an excuse fast enough and also missing my friend like crazy, I agree to go out with her.

"Come over after work and we can get ready at my house."

This has play-dress-up-with-Raven written all over it.

"Sounds great," I say with the enthusiasm of a snail.

"Whatever, Debbie Downer. It'll be fun and besides …I miss you."

"I miss you too. See you after work."

Perfect. I'll tell Eve about Vince after she's had a couple drinks. That'll help soften the blow. And being in a public place should keep her from getting too emotional. *Ugh, who am I kidding? This is going to be a nightmare.*

TWENTY

RAVEN

"Time to lock up, Ray!"

At the sound of Guy's voice, I slide out from under the Honda CR-V. Shifting my eyes to the clock, my jaw drops at the time. Six o'clock. *Darn it!*

It got busy at the garage, and I never got a chance to text Jonah to let him know about my plans for tonight. He said he had to train, but that he was looking forward to having me back in his arms. My body warms all over at the mere thought of more sex with Jonah.

I grab my phone and see I have one missed call and a text.

Training then phone interviews all afternoon. Quick meeting then I'll be home. See you tonight. xJ

"Ray! Quit draggin' ass. Shut 'er down."

"Yeah, G. I heard you."

Shoving my phone into my back pocket, I close down the garage and race to my studio.

I throw my dirty coveralls in the hamper and strip down to jump in the shower. My foot taps impatiently, waiting for the water to heat.

Crud! I didn't call Jonah. I wrap a towel around my naked body and fish my phone from my coveralls.

Sitting on the bed, I press send and place the phone to my ear.

"Hey, baby. Where are you?" His deep voice comes through the phone and a smile pulls at my lips.

"Hi. I'm at my studio. It was crazy busy at the garage today, and I didn't get your text until just now."

"That's cool. Grab your shit and come over."

My finger traces the swirling pattern of my towel at my thigh. "I won't be able to come over tonight. I made plans with Eve." My stomach bottoms out. I do want girl time, but I'd be lying if I said I didn't want Jonah time more.

After explaining the evening's agenda, I sit patiently waiting for his response.

"Club Six. Just you and your girl." He's not asking. It's more like he's saying the words so they sink in.

"Yeah. I'll stay with Eve tonight because we'll probably be out late, and I don't want to wake you."

"Hm."

Is he mad?

"Look, here's the deal. I'm stoked you want to hang with your girl tonight. But you at some nightclub, looking as hot as you are, dressed to kill, without me? No. I'm also not thrilled that you're putting yourself at risk by going to a club when you aren't twenty-one. And there's the DomiDick shit we have to worry about."

His possessiveness is fierce and I freakin' love it. My entire body floods with the warm gushy feeling that makes my toes curl and my belly flip.

As a child, no one ever cared what I did. Never cared where I went, who I was with. I never had a curfew, never had the sex talk, the don't-do-drugs talk. I was treated like an adult on my own ever since I could remember.

"Baby, you still there?"

"Yeah, Jonah, I'm here." The low hum in my voice reminds me of Dog's purr.

"Damn." His rough and sexy tone vibrates the phone at my ear. "I've been thinking about last night all day. Now I get you on the phone and you say my name like that. I have a mind to drag you to my house and hold you hostage. You and Eve will have to reschedule."

"Jonah." My voice is thick with arousal.

He groans then clears his throat. "Get dolled up, go out with your girl, and have a good time. Call me when you're done and I'll pick you girls up, drop Eve off at her house, and you come home with me. You're in my bed tonight. Deal?"

Um, gee, let me think.

"Deal."

"Oh, and there's something you should know. Your name came up during interviews today."

My body shoots ramrod straight, and I grasp my towel at my chest. Now my belly flips in an altogether different way. "What! Why?"

"Big fight, lots of publicity. People talk, you know how it is. It'll die down after the fight, but don't be surprised if you get approached by paparazzi. Just ignore them, don't answer any questions, and if you're alone or scared, you call me."

Well, crud. This night just went from bad to worse.

———

We pull up to the front of Club Six and climb out of our taxi. The front walk is lined with people awaiting entrance. Pounding music charges the air as we step up to the VIP line.

Waiting our turn, I fidget with nervous energy and catch my reflection in the window. My strapless, black mini dress hugs every contour of my body. The strappy heels cage my feet up past my ankle, making my legs look impossibly longer. I can't see my face, but it's framed by long silken strands of dark hair, flat ironed to perfection. Eve did my make-up heavier that I usually wear, the smoky dark shadow bringing out the strange color of my eyes.

I'm Ravenstein, put together and brought to life for a night of shenanigans.

"Stop freaking out. You look gorgeous," Eve says close to my ear.

"Ladies. You on the list?" says a large man with a clipboard.

Eve exchanges words and a handshake with the purpose of palming him a fifty dollar bill. The man smiles and looks us both up and down before stepping aside. We're in.

The strobe lights and black lights make it hard to see, and the booming bass makes it impossible to talk. Guiding me through the crowd, Eve leads me to an outside patio bar. The music is muted out here so we don't have to yell. We belly-up and order two Cosmopolitans.

"So, how are you and Jonah?" Eve wags her eyebrows.

"Better now." I can't control the heat that rises to my cheeks.

Eve narrows her eyes and swivels toward me on her barstool. "Oh my gosh. You did it." A slow smile creeps to her face, and she starts clapping and bouncing on her seat. "You fucking did it …like literally!"

I cover my face with my hands and nod my head. This information will surely find Dominick's ears in the next day. *So much for your plan to make money off my virginity, eh?*

"Eeeeee!" Eve jumps from her stool and wraps her arms around my neck. "My girl lost her virginity, everyone!"

Mortification overtakes me as my eyes dart around the bar. Other than a few smiles, almost everyone ignores us.

"Eve, please! Be quiet!" I hiss.

She sits back in her seat and takes a huge swig of her drink. I follow suit.

"Rave, you gotta give me details, girl. Did it hurt? Was he good? Is he …big?" With eyes as wide as gas caps, she waits for my answer.

"He's amazing in *every* possible way."

She stomps her foot and slaps her knee. "I knew it! I knew he was big."

I roll my eyes and suck down the rest of my drink. Apparently embarrassment makes me thirsty. I order another.

Details of my night with Jonah begin to flow out at the same pace the liquor flows in. I imagine steam shooting from Dominick's nose like an angry bull when Vince relays the information. Satisfied with what I've given, I decide it's time to broach the subject.

"What about Vince? What does he do?"

"He's a consultant. I don't know what he consults on. Like I said, he's a private guy."

More like private eye, I joke to myself and fight the urge to laugh.

"Does that bother you? That he's a private eye …um, guy?"

Whoops, almost turned my private joke public. My tongue feels bigger in my mouth as my words start to slur. I wave my hand to the bartender and motion for another round.

"Yes. It does." Her face falls and she dabs the corner of her eye with her cocktail napkin. *Here we go again.* Apparently, I'm not the only one feeling the effects of our drinks.

I spin my barstool so I'm facing her. "Eve, aren't you sick of crying over this guy? The only time you don't cry about him is when he's got his tongue in your ear."

Perfect transition into bad news. I mentally pat myself on the back.

Her arms fly out to her sides. "Ugh! It's just I feel so close to him, you know?"

Okay, this is good. Let her vent and then I'll go in for the kill. I nod while gulping the last of my drink.

"I get the feeling that I'm more into him than he is to me. He never talks about himself. I know nothing about him." She sniffs. "Fucking men!"

Sick of the mastodon in the room that's sitting right on my lap, I grab a stack of cocktail napkins and slap them down in front of her. Here it goes.

"Eve, there's something I need to tell you. It's about—"

"Holy shit, Rave! This is our jam!" Her shoulders bounce to the beat of the music. "Come on, let's dance!"

"Wait, I—"

She drags me to the dance floor and the familiar voice of Dev singing "Bass Down Low" makes even me squeal.

Darn alcohol has me acting like a stupid girl.

I've only been drunk a few times, and the familiar floaty feeling taking over my limbs tells me I'm there. I close my eyes, absorbing the beat of the music, and move with the rhythm. The bass pulsates around me, every tiny hair on my arm responding to the call of the music. I slide my hands from my hips, up the sides of my body and into my hair. I imagine being here with Jonah, his hands all over me. Grinding against each other as the music throbs around us. Kissing in the middle of a crowded dance floor, and tasting the sweat that beads off each other's skin. So lost in each other that we're oblivious to everyone around, I skate my fingertips down my neck, imagining that they're his. Remembering his touch on a cellular level, goose bumps race across my flesh. Flashes of him above me, memories from last night, have me gripping my hair.

There's no place I'd rather be than in Jonah's arms, in his bed. It's time to go.

I open my eyes to see Eve is few feet away. She has become the meat in a dance-floor sandwich. I move to pull her away when hands grip my hips and heat hits my back. I react on instinct, pushing away from the grip and turning around to face the jerk.

A man in a pink golf shirt stands before me. His lips move, but I can't hear what he's saying over the music. Realizing that, he motions for me to come to him. I shake my head and turn to get Eve.

My heart is racing and I stumble, the alcohol making it difficult to control my body. I can't believe I drank so much that I lost myself in my surroundings allowing a strange man to press his crotch to my backside. I'm anxious by the time I pull Eve from between the two guys she's dancing with.

"Whad'da fuck, Rave! I was 'aving fun." Eve speaks to my shoulder with a heavy slur.

I guide her to the bar, and order us two waters. Buzzed and freaked out by the forward guy on the dance floor, I trash my plan to talk to Eve about Vince and grab my phone to call Jonah for a ride.

"Can I get another Cosmoplothian, pleeese?" Eve's attempt at cunning falls flat.

"I think we should call it a night."

"No!" Her enthusiasm gets the attention of two guys nearby.

I give them my best don't mind her, she's just drunk smile. Mistaking my smile for an invitation, they walk to us. As they get closer I recognize the guy from the dance floor.

Crap.

Tapping Eve on the knee, I alert her to our unwelcome guests.

They're good-looking guys. Not hot-tattooed-fighter good-looking, but more like successful-banker-golfer good-looking.

I try to politely brush them off while Eve gives them death stares, mumbling something about asswads and pricks. It's bad enough that we're in the club at all, but getting kicked out for public drunkenness is sure to draw unwanted attention.

Punching a quick text to Jonah that we'll be out front in fifteen minutes, I look up to see Eve with her arm slung over banker-golfer number one. She teases her finger at the collar of his perfectly pressed shirt. *Guess her anger at men is over.*

"Eve, our ride will be here any minute. What do you say we hit the ladies' room and make our way to the door?"

Totally ignoring me, she runs her hand into Number One's hair and leans in to whisper in his ear. Pink Shirt steps in my space, pressing me back into the bar and blocking my chance for escape.

I flatten my palm to his chest. "Can you please step back?"

"You ran away from me earlier. Can't let that happen again."

The smell of his breath makes my stomach clench. My spinning head, combined with fear and a belly full of liquor, has me tasting bile.

I try to implore Eve for help, but she's face to face with Number One.

Pink Shirt hooks a piece of my hair with his finger. "You're gorgeous." He motions to his friend with a tilt of his head. "My buddy and I have room at Trump. Looks like your friend and my friend are hitting it off."

He's right. Number One has his face buried in Eve's neck.

He steps closer so that I'm arched back over the bar, my head turned away. He leans to my ear. "What do you say you and me—"

"What the fuck is going on here?" The voice comes from down the bar, but it's unmistakably male and mad.

Pink Shirt steps back, freeing me, while Number One is yanked violently backwards. Eve shrieks and falls back onto her barstool.

Pink Shirt looks like he's about to run, but sways as if he doesn't know if he should attempt to help his friend.

Number One's down. A man wearing all black holds him by the neck of his shirt and shouts in his face. I can't hear what he's saying, but from the look on the poor guy's face, it's terrifying.

The man in black shoves Number One hard to the ground and turns to Eve. Only then do I catch the face of our knight in shining armor.

My heart races and I break out in a sweat. Stalking towards us with a murderous look on his face, he gets right into Eve's space. Nose to nose, he stares her down as she looks up at him doe-eyed.

"You trading me for a pussy-ass, country-club boy, Eve?" Vince's body trembles with rage.

Terror works behind Eve's eyes as she shakes her head.

"Vince, she didn't do anything wrong. Those guys wouldn't leave and—"

He rakes his eyes over me, and my mouth slams shut.

"Mind your own fucking business!" All pleasantries from our first two meetings are gone.

"Vince, please, look at her. You're scaring her," I whisper, trying to control my voice. She's not the only one who's scared.

"Look, you little slut."

I flinch as his insult cuts deep.

"I told you this is none of your business. You wanna make it your business, I can do that. You two are coming with me, and I'll be happy to make it your business …all night long."

"You wouldn't …I mean …Dominick…" The vicious smile that breaks his angry expression tells me everything. Dominick doesn't care about me. As long as I'm able to solicit myself for him, he could give a rip about what Vince does to me.

Tears burn my eyes as the reality sinks in. I'm breathing rapidly. The hurried beat of my heart pounds in my ears. I should run, but I can't leave Eve.

He eyeballs me from my boobs to my shoes and licks his lower lip. He wraps his arm around Eve's waist, pulling her from her seat. Her eyes are unfocused as he tugs her close to his side. His free arm shoots to me. The impact of his grip throws my body forward. He drags us through the club. I stumble to keep upright. The crowd of gyrating bodies part as he storms through the dance floor to the club's exit.

With a firm kick, the double doors fly open, and we're in the secluded alley behind the building. I take a sobering breath of fresh air to clear my head. I need to get us free so we can run. But how? Looking around frantically, I search for a way out, knowing I have only seconds before we're locked in his car.

My mind surges with questions. What would Guy tell me to do? What would Jonah tell me to do? And with that comes my answer, loud and clear.

Fight.

Adrenaline floods my veins. Energy strengthens my muscles as I struggle in his grip. I pull against his hold, digging my heels into the pavement. His eyes shoot towards mine and narrow. His grip gets tighter and Eve whimpers.

I twist my arm as hard as I can, and his hold begins to slip. Twisting and pulling, a sharp pain shoots through my shoulder. Desperate to free myself, I push through the ache. Vince stops walking and I yank down. My arm slips from his hand. He grabs hold with his other hand. *He let Eve go.*

"Eve, run! Run!"

Blinking wildly as if she woke up from a trance, she takes off. Vince has my back, his arm locked around my waist, hand gripped on my throat. Screaming is out of the question as his crushing embrace robs me of breath. I struggle to get free and my vision starts to recede. The sound of heavy footfalls pounding the pavement behind us has me jerking in his hold.

My vision goes black as two words scream in my head.

Help me!

TWENTY-ONE

RAVEN

One minute I'm choking, desperate for air, and the next I'm on all fours sucking precious oxygen into my lungs. Hearing a scuffle, I turn to see what freed me.

Shock freezes my body. Vince is on his back and Jonah is straddling him. His fists are pounding Vince's face. His colorful arms are blurry with the speed of each blow. The sickening thud of each blow is a drastic contrast to the beauty and fluidity of his movements. Jonah's arms swing with deadly accuracy. But Vince is out, his body flopping from side to side with the power of each punch.

"Jonah, stop. You'll kill him." My burning throat makes my voice a little more than a whisper, not enough to penetrate Jonah's rage.

I crawl to him with trepidation and place myself by Vince's bloody face.

"Jonah, stop. I'm okay. I'm right here. You have to stop now." My voice is gentle, and it's then that his arms slow their gory punishment.

Jonah's body stills, but his chest swells and deflates with deep breaths. Reaching forward, I place my hand on his forearm. His head jerks, and his eyes connect with mine, wild and distant. He blinks a couple times and I see my Jonah return.

"God, baby, are you okay?" His words falter with the power of each breath.

Jumping off Vince, he pulls me to my feet. His eyes move over my body along with his hands.

"I was out front. I saw Eve run from behind the club. I ran as fast as I could. He had you …Shit, are you okay?"

"I'm fine. Just a little scared. Where's Eve?"

"I told her to go to the truck and sit tight." He looks back at an unconscious Vince. "Who the fuck is that piece of shit?"

I drop my eyes to the ground, wanting to slap myself. I never told Jonah about Vince. "That's Vince, Eve's boyfriend," I take a deep breath, "and Dominick's right hand."

His eyes grow narrow and his muscles tense. "That motherfucker!"

An echo of Jonah's curse rings off the walls of the alley. The H2 I saw at Eve's the other night is parked there, hidden in a service entrance of the warehouse next to the club. Without a soul around, I'm thankful no one was a witness to what Jonah did to Vince. But I can't help but wonder what would have happened if Jonah hadn't shown up when he did.

"We need to get out of here." I rub my neck and wince as my shoulder protests the movement.

Jonah looks undecided as to whether he should finish the job he started on Vince or get us to the truck. Moaning drifts from the bloodied piece of meat beside us, and that seems to force Jonah into a snap decision. He wraps one arm around my shoulders and the other around my stomach, supporting my weight, and we hurry to the truck.

It's a silent ride to Eve's house except for her occasional apologies for Vince's behavior. I see hurt in her eyes, but not hurt that she just found out her boyfriend is abusive. The pain in her eyes is that of a girl with a broken heart. Will she always be attracted to men who hurt her like her father did? God, I hope not.

We drop her off at her insistence. She wants to be alone, and I don't blame her. She has a lot to think about. Jonah walks through her house, turning on all the lights and making sure she feels safe before she locks herself inside.

Safe in the cab of the truck, I allow myself to feel the weight of what happened. I turn my head to face out the window, not wanting to give Jonah any more to worry about. A silent sob rips through my body as tears of fear, guilt, and anxiety flow down my cheeks. The driver side door slams shut and a warm hand covers mine. I interlace our fingers, hold on tight, and vow to never let go.

JONAH

"That son of a bitch!" Blake's response to my re-telling of the evening's events mirrors my own.

I grip my phone tighter before loosening my hold, remembering what happened the last time I took out my anger on my phone. To avoid putting my fist through a wall, I force myself to my bed.

"You told him at Zeus's Playground to pull his tails on Raven. I was there. I heard you!"

I don't know if calling Blake was the smartest choice. Talking shit out with Blake usually helps me decompress. Right now, he's just getting me worked up. I sit back and stare at the ceiling, hoping I can calm my ass down before Raven gets out of the shower. The poor girl has had a round trip ticket to hell and back. The last thing she needs is her raging boyfriend climbing the fucking walls like a caged animal.

"I almost killed him. I swear if I hadn't heard Raven's voice begging me to stop, I would have. Seeing that motherfucker with his arms wrapped around her..." My sentence trails off as my jaw clenches so tight I'm spitting words through my teeth.

"Sounds like it's time for another meeting with dear ol' dad," Blake says, his voice holding a hint of excitement.

"Yeah, I have to talk to my girl first, get the story on this Vince guy." My head falls to the backboard and I rub my eyes with my free hand. "You should see her arm. All dressed up, lookin' hot as hell, with a fucking bruise in the shape of a man's hand on her arm." The calm that had been slowly moving through my body dissolves into anger. "He had her fucking neck!"

"At least you taught that fucker a lesson. Don't think he'll be messin' with Raven again after you flipped the switch on his ass."

He's got a point. I had to trash one of my favorite shirts because it was splattered with his blood.

"Look, the fight's this week. You and Raven lie low until then. You don't need any more publicity than you..."

My attention is drawn from Blake to the sound of the shower being turned off.

"What the fuck is Eve thinking?" His angry question jerks me back to the conversation.

"Don't know, don't fucking care. This douchebag's been on Raven's ass from the get-go. I'm putting this shit to an end."

"Fuckin' A, brother," Blake says under his breath.

The bathroom door opens and Raven walks out in nothing but a towel. My mind clears of everything that happened tonight at the sight of her wet skin. I imagine drying her with my mouth as my eyes devour her legs and move over her towel to her arms. Her arm. The angry bruise brings me back in a violent rush.

I glare at the color on her arm. "Gotta run. I'll talk to you tomorrow."

"Right. Tell your girl to stay strong."

"Will do. Later."

Tossing my phone on the bedside table, I watch Raven put on a short pair of drawstring sleeping shorts, no panties, and a thin tank top. Blinking, I tell myself that my body can wait but the conversation we need to have cannot.

"Baby, come here."

I make room for her on the bed, and she quickly takes her place at my side. Her cheek is pressed to my chest and her finger traces lazy circles on my abdomen. My dick responds immediately. I place my hand over hers to stop the stimulation before I forget my own name and bury myself inside her.

"Um, you're going to have to stop that so we can talk. Shit happens to my body that short-circuits my brain."

I feel her smile against my chest. She pushes her hand out from under mine, down past my belly button. I groan as her delicate fingers slip beneath my shorts.

"I, ah…" My mind goes fuzzy and my heart pounds in my chest.

Her soft hand grasps me in a firm hold and my hips jerk in response. *Fuuuck.*

"I know you want to talk, Jonah, and we will. But right now, I need you."

I can't remember what we were going to talk about, and I don't care.

Her hand picks up its pace and pressure. My eyes fix on her forearm as her lean muscles flex with each stroke. The fruity smell from her clean hair makes my mouth water. My lips burn with the need to kiss her.

"Baby, I want your mouth," I say, panting.

She kisses my neck, a tease with her full wet lips that has me achingly frustrated. I wrap my hand behind her neck, sifting my fingers through her hair, then grip tight. She moans.

I bring her luscious lips to mine, taking what I want. Our tongues crash together as I convert my anger from earlier into passion. The feel of her teeth as she nips impatiently at my lips makes me think she's doing the same. My mouth is flooded with her pure, clean taste. I flex my hands in her hair as her sweet mouth moves against mine in a sensual rhythm.

She presses her breasts into my chest and her stroke quickens. I'm fighting not to roll my eyes at the perfection of her touch. Reaching down, I release my button and zipper, freeing myself for her. She smiles against my lips then sucks on my lower lip. I can't help but imagine she's sucking on something else, and I groan.

She breaks the kiss and locks her blue-green eyes on mine. Her eyebrows raise a fraction as if she's asking a question. Then her hand releases me just enough to slide her hand lower.

"Mmm…" My head falls back and my eyes slam shut. She's never done this before, and I marvel at her growing confidence. Her gentle play and tender touch are both teasingly sweet and erotic as hell. My stomach muscles contract as I let her explore.

Desperate to feel her, I slide a hand beneath her tank top. Her soft skin is pliable against my rough hands. I cup her firm breast then knead, rolling the tip between my thumb and forefinger. Her sexy curves push and rub against me, enticing my body.

"I want you naked," I growl.

Pushing myself up, I straddle her knees, and pull her tank top off. She sucks in a pained breath and falls back to the bed.

"What's wrong?"

"My shoulder," she says with a grimace.

"Shit, baby. I don't want to do this if it's going to hurt you." The thought alone is like dumping ice cold water on my crotch. "I already feel like an asshole not giving you more time to heal after last night." I sit back on my heels and pray she doesn't want to stop.

"I can't explain it," she says and pushes herself up on one elbow. "All I know is that, after everything I went through tonight, I want to feel safe and cherished. Protected."

I look into her eyes and watch them brim with tears.

"I want you …I *need* you to love me. Please." She's beautiful all the time, but the vulnerability in her eyes as she pleads robs me of speech.

I lean forward and she lies back. My tongue licks at the crease of her mouth, requesting entrance. We have plenty of time for rough passion. Tonight, I want to love her at a deliberate pace.

I slip my hand beneath the drawstring of her shorts and she breaks the kiss, gasping at my contact. Her hips move in rhythm with my fingers. I brace myself above her on one elbow, mesmerized by her response: her lip sucked into her mouth, moaning. White knuckles grip the sheets as her hips push and roll against my hand.

Perfect.

Her hands move to her shorts, and, with a lift of her hips, she pulls them down. I do the same, ridding myself of the stifling confinement. She's naked before me, chest rising and falling erratically, and knees wide in invitation. I caress her thighs, taking in all that is mine. Only mine. She stares openly at my hard-on, making it twitch, and I watch her eyes widen.

From my kneeling position between her legs, I grab her hips and pull her up so her ass is resting on my thighs. I spread my knees, bringing myself lower and pulling her higher until we meet. Her legs wrap around my waist, and I slip my hands below her ass and tilt.

"Jonah." There's an edge of concern in her voice.

This is a new position for her, and I'm sure she's nervous. My chest swells with the knowledge that every position will be new to her and I'm the one who gets to teach her.

"Don't worry, baby. I'll take care of you."

Her expression relaxes with a tiny smile.

I push forward, and just like last night, my stomach is gripped with the urge to thrust. *Slowly.* I repeat it in my head. Inch by inch I ease into her. My eyes take in the sight of our bodies connecting. The silky heat, gripping pressure, and visual stimulation turn me into an emotional live wire. I pull out an inch and push in two more. Over and over, slowly until I'm buried deep. I pause and fight the explosion coiling in my body. Think of something else. I go over a list of choke holds. Triangle choke, gator roll, rear naked choke …Oh, no, not that one.

The image of my body connected to Raven's becomes too much. I fall forward, bracing my weight with my arms and straighten my legs. Raven immediately responds to the closeness of our mouths by devouring mine. I move above her in lazy strokes, taking in each sensation. My chest brushes against her breasts with each painstakingly slow thrust. She squirms with impatience beneath me.

"Faster, Jonah. Harder," she says, grasping at my ass.

"Baby, you're sore. I need—"

"Take me, please. I want you to." Her words are breathy and hot as hell.

My body responds by thrusting in deep. I bite my lip to keep from calling out in blissful satisfaction as her gripping heat pulls me in. *Fuck.* She gasps against my neck. I check her face to see it's not pain she's feeling. It's pleasure. Pulling out slowly, I push in again, harder this time. She moans and coaxes me on.

My girl.

Overwhelming emotion and raw need push my hips deeper. I keep my eyes locked on hers and roll my hips. The sounds coming from deep in her chest take me to the edge of my control.

A familiar twinge in my chest warms my skin as I continue to love Raven. My strokes increase in strength and her fingernails dig into my ass. She meets each thrust with a push of her own. Her dark hair is splayed wildly around her face. She arches back in the way that I know is her signal. She's close.

Not ready for this to end, I roll to my back, keeping our connection. A light sheen of sweat clings to our bodies, her torso lies atop mine. Her face is buried in my neck where she kisses and licks below my ear.

She pushes herself up, straddling my hips. Her eyelids are low, and her lips part as she seems to absorb the sensations of the different position. My eyes roam her body from her hips, up her slightly rounded feminine stomach, to her perfect full breasts. Gloriously naked and towering over me like an angel without wings.

I circle the tips of her breasts with my fingertips, teasing the sensitive flesh. She presses them into my hands and sucks in a breath. Her heavy-lidded eyes sparkle and she begins to move above me.

Her hands brace at my chest, and I continue to caress her breasts. I watch in amazement as she commands her body with practiced ease. She moves with confidence and control, and it's hard to believe she was a virgin a day ago. Her pace quickens. She rolls her hips in bliss-ridden waves. I fight every urge to flip over and pound into her. She shifts, searching it out, desperate for the perfect combination.

I'm so close. Her cries alert me to the fact that she is too. I flex my hips into her. She grinds down hard against me. My toes curl and my stomach tightens.

"Fuck, baby…"

"Me too, Jonah…"

We're panting and pushing. Grinding and moaning. Her beautiful eyes lock onto mine and bore into my soul. Wound tight, we reach together, pushing toward the edge. Her mouth drops open, and I bite my lip, our orgasms ripping through our connection together.

The shockwaves push through my body, lifting my shoulders from the bed. Her hands move to my knees, bowing her back. I hold her hips in place and continue to grind into her. She throws her head back, calling out my name as we ride out our climax.

Fucking amazing.

Her body falls forward against my chest, pressing her warm, balmy skin to mine. Heavy from the aftershocks of our love-making, we lay silently, breathing as one, our hearts beating together.

"Wow," she mumbles against my neck.

"Mmm."

She pushes herself up, resting her elbow on my ribs, and her chin in her hand.

"Is it always like this?"

Beautiful and cute.

"No. It's never been like this. And, yes, with us, it'll only get better."

Her eyes grow a fraction before her lids drop lower. "Really?"

I run my fingers through her hair, from root to tip, the long strands falling against my chest. "Yeah, baby."

She bites her bottom lip and softly moans. Her hips start to move again.

I smile. "My girl wants more."

"Yeah, Jonah," she says in that breathy way that makes me instantly hard.

"I aim to please."

———

After another round of lovemaking, Raven is curled in my arms. Her head rests against my chest and her leg is thrown over my abs. I run my hand through her long, silky hair, twirling it around my finger. My other hand lazily traces patterns on her hip while her finger outlines my tattoo.

"You loved up enough to talk now, or do I need to give it to you one more time?"

She smiles, but doesn't laugh. "I would love to do it again, but I'm too tired." The yawn that follows confirms her words.

"Tell me about this Vince guy."

She huffs out a frustrated breath. "I met him that day I went to see Dominick. He acted like he knew me, but I didn't think much of it. Guess he'd been milking Eve for information about me for weeks. Then I ran into him at Eve's. I wanted to tell you, but forgot with everything that was happening with us."

This all makes sense. Now for the tough question. "What happened tonight at the club?"

She cowers against my chest.

What the fuck?

"We were at the bar after dancing. We had a little too much to drink, and before I knew it, these guys were harassing us—"

"Harassing you? Fuck, Raven! Why didn't you call me?" My words are flying before my brain has time to consider what I'm saying. *And I wonder why she's cowering?* Not wanting to lose my shit, I push my anger down and take a deep breath. "Sorry, baby. Go on."

She continues to tell me about her night. I try not to dwell on the motherfucker that put his hands on my girl then pressed her up against the bar. I swallow the angry retorts that bubble up from my all-consuming frustration. I nod and listen, unsuccessfully suppressing the occasional growl.

"Did he say where he was taking you?"

"No, he called me a slut and told me it was none of my business. He said that if I didn't shut up, he was going to make it my business, um …allnightlong." Her chin drops again as she ends the sentence in a whisper.

Did she say all night long? He called her a slut!

My head starts to buzz. "He's fucking dead," I say with a calm I am not feeling.

"Um, I'm pretty sure you got him back. I didn't even recognize his face when you were done with him."

Her body shivers in my arms. I hold her tighter.

"I can't let this go, Raven. I'm going back to talk to Dominick. If he doesn't get his boy in check, we're going to the cops."

"Jonah—"

"I'll do this Dominick's way. I'll throw my fight. He'll get his money. But the moment his goons put their fucking hands on my girl…"

What? I have no options. I'm the one with everything to lose, not Dominick. The fucker's backed me into a corner and he knows it.

"We can't go to the cops. Even you said he's got them on his payroll. If Dominick feels threatened, he could leak to the media that you agreed to throw your fight. Even without evidence, the rumors could get you banned from the UFL."

Fuck. She's right. My mind spins with unanswered questions. The most important thing is to keep Raven calm and safe. That's where my focus needs to be, at least until this shit is over.

"I'll talk with Dominick again. He wants his money. I'm sure he's not pleased that his boy got his ass handed to him tonight. Don't worry, baby. I'll take care of this."

She nods into my chest. "Please be careful."

"Always. Now go to sleep. We can talk more in the morning."

"Okay, Jonah. I love you," she says through another yawn.

"I love you too, baby."

After shutting off the light, I stare into the dark room. Raven's breathing shifts to the rhythmic cadence of sleep. I hold her a little tighter, absorbing the contentment I feel from having her safe in my arms.

This clusterfuck with Vince has complicated my deal with Dominick. He needs to know now, especially after I turned Vince's face into ground beef, that I'm not going to allow him to fuck with Raven. There's no way—

My thoughts are redirected by the sound of my phone ringing. With a slight lean, I grab my phone from my bedside.

I don't check the ID, but instead hit answer and bite out a quick, "What!"

Raven stirs, and I rub her arm reassuringly.

"Mr. Slade."

Adrenaline floods my bloodstream, making my head buzz. "Dominick."

TWENTY-TWO

JONAH

I kiss Raven's head before slipping out from under her and into the hallway.

"I see you and Vince had a little difference of opinion this evening," Dominick says, sounding bored.

"Difference of opinion? He assaulted her! He was taking her to God knows where to do God knows what! You call that a difference of o-fucking-pinion?"

The usual buzz in my head has amplified to a roar. I'm vibrating from head to toe.

"I've taken care of him. I'm not happy with what transpired at the club."

"I told you to pull your tails. That was part of our agreement."

"Yes, well it seems Vince has grown fond of this Eve girl. You can't blame a guy for sticking around for a little easy pussy. I'm sure you of all people can understand that."

"I could give a fuck what Vince does with his dick, but I swear to God, if he comes near Raven with it or with any other part of his body again, I will kill him. You get me? I hope like hell you do because I've never been more serious about anything in my life." I pace the living room, trying to keep my voice down.

"I won't apologize for Vince's behavior."

"You want Raven so bad, but you'd let that animal put his hands on her?"

"Vince knows the girl needs to remain unharmed. Whatever his plan was, I'm confident it wouldn't have left any permanent—"

"You sick motherfu—"

"Our deal is still as it was agreed upon at Zeus's."

"Only if you and your men agree to leave Raven alone."

"Mr. Slade, you are in no position to make threats."

"The fuck I'm not. Say it!"

"I will protect what's mine."

"She's not yours!" The intense buzzing between my ears travels down my arms to my fists.

"We will see, Mr. Slade. We will see."

The phone disconnects. My call log lists the number as *unknown.*

"Fuck!" I throw my phone into a club chair across the room. It lands with an unsatisfying thud.

My appetite for beating Dominick to a bloody mess claws at my nerves. I fall to the couch with my head in my hands, fisting my hair, and will my heart to slow.

Fear from tonight comes rushing in. Flashbacks of Vince's arms around Raven flood my mind. What if I hadn't gotten there in time? I shove the question back, resisting the thought of losing her.

She's safe in my bed, where I should be.

I stalk down the hallway to my room and throw open the door. It slams against the wall, making Raven jump then settle.

Shit. Calm the fuck down.

I fight the buzz in my head and crawl into bed with Raven. Her soft body, warm with sleep, curls into mine. A gentle hum vibrates from her lips, the soothing scent of her skin a salve to my fury. My heart rate slows and the riot between my ears recedes. I haul her deeper into my arms, silently promising to keep her safe and make her mine. Forever.

—

RAVEN

"Hand me the wrench?" Jonah's big hand reaches out from beneath the Impala, and I slap the wrench into his palm.

We've been working on the Impala all morning in an attempt to take my mind off the fact that I haven't heard from Eve. Hours pass, and still no word. *I can't just sit here and do nothing.*

I'm assembling the new engine parts when I gather the courage to broach the issue with Jonah.

"If I don't hear from her soon," I scrunch my nose and pinch my eyes closed, "I'm going to her house."

The metallic clank of a tool hitting the concrete floor bounces off the walls. My eyes remain fixed on the project before me.

I hear him slide on the dolly out from underneath the car. "Over my dead motherfucking body."

I brace myself for an argument. With a determined scowl, I bring my eyes to his, steel in my resolve.

Worry and concern mask his usual easy smile, shattering my will. My shoulders slump and I lean on the workbench. "I'm worried about her."

He stands and closes the space between us. "I know, baby. But I can't let you go to her house alone. If you insist on stopping by, I'm going with you."

I need to tell Eve about Vince, and I don't want her to get embarrassed having Jonah there. Not to mention he turned her boyfriend into road kill just hours ago.

"No. I need to go alone."

He wraps me in his arms and I go limp against his chest. "No way."

I exhale, frustrated, but not surprised. "Jonah, I understand why you're worried. But really, what're the chances that Vince will be at her house? He's probably hiding away with a tube of Neosporin and an ice pack after what you did to him."

His arms tighten at the mention of Vince. "You aren't going."

Why does everything have to be so hard?

I tilt my head to see his face. "What's the big deal? All I'll be doing—"

"The big deal?" He lets me go and takes a few long strides back to the Impala. His hands spear through his hair. "The *big deal* is that the last time I let you go somewhere on your own, against my better judgment, you came back *destroyed*." He leans into the car's hood, arms bracing his weight, head down.

I step to the front fender. "Jonah."

He turns his head, a tortured expression on his face. He's right. I promised him, the night we made love for the first time, I'd never put him through that kind of worry again.

"Okay. I won't go."

With a murmured curse, his body weight collapses, and he pushes off the car.

"To her house. I'll go to her work." My determination is back, and he must see it in the seconds he studies my face.

"Fine. But only to her work. With plenty of people around. And call me before you walk in and the second you walk out. Understand?"

I grin, overwhelmed by how much I love my protective Jonah. "Okay."

"I'm serious, baby. If you see—"

My phone chimes with a new text.

Just got your message. I'm fine,
just slept in. Come on over. Eve.

I text her back and ask her what time she has to work. We agree to meet there a half an hour before her shift starts.

Jonah's not satisfied with the plan, but at least he's not chaining me to his bed for safekeeping, as he threatened. I promised him I'd meet him at the training center after I met with Eve so he could see with his own eyes that I'm okay.

He takes me to work to check in with Guy, looming in the background the entire time like some Adonis bodyguard. We hit my studio to feed Dog and pack some things. He finally left my side so I could meet with Eve, but only with the promise that I'd see him in less than an hour.

I pull into the parking lot of Nori Pizzeria right on time. Walking from my car to the front door, I notice Eve's 2010 blue Mustang. I do a quick scan for Vince's H2 and exhale in relief to see it's not there.

I push through the front doors, and the aroma of garlic and butter make my stomach growl. Wax-covered Chianti bottles sit atop tables dressed in white butcher paper. A few waiters mill about, but no Eve.

"Raven! Hey, haven't seen you here in a while." Stephanie's eyes dart around and behind me before landing on my face. "Where's the hottie you're dating?" The enthusiastic hostess flashes a hopeful smile. "Did you guys break up?"

She's a cute girl, and I've never considered myself the jealous type, but my hand tingles with the desire to backhand that ready-and-willing look off her face.

"Mmm, nope. We didn't break up." I lay my forearm on top of the hostess stand and lean in. "We're still very much *together*, if you know what I mean." I give her a wink and watch the enthusiasm drain from her face.

Yeah, take that!

"Eve in the back?" I don't wait for an answer and head to the kitchen with pep in my step.

She mumbles something I can't quite make out as I push through the kitchen doors.

At the closed office door, I pause to refocus before knocking. I have no idea what kind of mood Eve will be in, and I can only hope she takes what I'm about to tell her well.

"Eve? You there?" I rap my knuckles against the door.

Her soft voice tells me to come in.

The room is dark except for a dim desk lamp. She's sitting in her chair with her elbows on the desk and both hands on either side of her head. Not good.

I take the seat across from her. "Hey, Eve. How are you doing?"

"Humph."

"That bad, huh?"

She doesn't reply only drops her forehead to her desk.

"Look, about last night, I'm so sorry—"

Her head flies up, and she locks me in a narrow glare. "Sorry? What do you have to be sorry about? This whole thing is my fault. I keep telling myself that *this guy* will be different. *This guy* won't hit me or talk shit to me. They all seem so normal in the beginning. Or so I think." Her head is back in her hands as she rubs at her temples. "God, Rave, I'm so fucked up."

"Eve, you aren't …effed up."

Her puffy eyes narrow on mine again, and I decide this is a good time to shut up and listen.

"You know what I did last night after you dropped me off? I lay in bed all night with my phone on my chest, hoping he would call me. I wanted that piece-of-shit to call me and tell me that he was sorry, that he would never scare me again. If he would have shown up on my doorstep, I would've taken him back." She falls back into her chair. "Still think I'm not fucked up?"

No, that sounded pretty screwed up to me. But, I wasn't going to tell her that.

She's beating herself up about Vince, feeling as though this is all her fault. If she knew that she was nothing more than a job to him, maybe it would help her to let him go and let herself off the hook.

"Listen, I tried to tell—"

"He held onto you," she says with a distant sound to her voice.

"What?" I whisper.

"You were pulling away, almost out of his grasp. He *let go* of me. He *held on* to you." She looks at me with tears pooling in her eyes and shame on her face. "I was jealous." The tears burst free, creating rivers of pain down her face. "I'm *so* fucked up."

She buries her face in her hands as her body shakes with sobs. I walk to her side of the desk and kneel down.

"Eve, there's something I need to tell you. I didn't tell you before because I was trying to protect you. But, you need to know now. None of this is your fault."

Her bloodshot eyes lock on mine as I explain about Vince. I tell her about Dominick and what his plans are for me. I keep Jonah's fight a secret, but I do tell her that Jonah, Dominick and I are working something out so that I don't have to prostitute myself for the rest of my life. I finish by making it clear that, although I'm sure Vince has feelings for her, his intentions from the beginning were getting information to Dominick, and his holding me last night probably had something to do with that.

The silent minutes tick. Eve stares at the wall just over my shoulder. Her lips are moving, but no sound comes out. Sitting back on my heels, I wait for her to register the gaggle of putrid information I dumped on her.

"That fuckingpieceofshitmotherfucker!"

Stunned by her sudden outburst, I rock back, throwing an arm behind me to keep from falling to my butt.

"Fucking men! Piece-of-shit, no good, dick licking, mother-fucking men!" She shoots out of her chair and paces the small space of her office. "That's it!" Locking her wide eyes with mine, she throws her hands in the air. "I'm done. I'm switching teams. I despise men and from now on will only date women."

"I don't think that's necessary—"

"Urrggh! My dad, your da—um, Dominick, Vince, every other sick fuck that came before him! I'm so fucking mad!" She's back to pacing.

"Yes, I can see that," I mumble.

I listen as Eve comes up with every possible combination for every possible curse word, and even some she invents on the spot. Having finally exhausted the English language, she sits back in her chair.

"Are you going to be okay?" I'm grateful to see her previously purple face fade to a splotchy red.

"Me? Hell yeah, I'll be okay. I'm a lesbian now. I think the question is, are you okay?"

I think about how to answer, wanting to be as honest as I can.

"Yes, I believe I will be."

And I do. I believe in Jonah and his ability. I believe in his love and his commitment to getting me away from Dominick. I believe in us and our future. That's all I need.

"Thank you for telling me about Vince. I wish you'd told me earlier, but I don't know if I would have listened. He really had me fooled." She shakes her head.

"Just stay away from him, okay?" I lift my eyebrows, letting her know I expect an answer.

"Yeah! Of course."

I nod, but something deep in my gut tells me she's doesn't have the self-control to stay away.

She stands up and wraps me in a hug. "I'm sorry, Rave."

"I know. Me too." I pull back, breaking the hug. "I'll text you later tonight when you get off work. Are you sure you're okay being alone at your place? Jonah said you're welcome to stay in his guest room for as long as you want."

"Yeah." She waves me off with a flick of her hand. "I'm fine, but tell him thanks."

"I will." I walk out the door, but pop my head back into the office. "Don't kill anyone from the male species tonight."

"I'll try not to."

Leaving the restaurant, I can't help but sympathize with every man who crosses paths with Eve.

———

"Excuse me, miss? You aren't allowed in there unless you're on my list," a large rent-a-cop says as he taps his clipboard.

I'm stopped just short of the Training Center's doors. I knew Jonah had some of the local media coming to interview him today, but this is like trying to get backstage at a U2 concert.

"Oh, of course. Um, Raven?" I hope Jonah put me on the list or I'm about to feel like a complete idiot.

He pushes his mirrored aviator sunglasses up the bridge of his nose with the tip of his index finger. His gaze starts at my feet and slides up my body. I cross my arms at my chest as I'm visually violated.

"I'm going to need to see some identification."

He's really taking this door security seriously. It Llooks like someone didn't make the cut in cop school. I hand him my ID.

He looks at his list, checks my driver's license, studies my face, and is back to his list.

You've got to be kidding me.

"All right. You're all clear." He hands back my card.

I'm surprised he didn't need a blood sample. I nod in his direction and push through the doors.

The place is alive with activity. The murmur of voices hums in my ears as I gaze around the lobby. No sign of Jonah. I slide through the groups of people and down the hallway to the main training room. The guys are training as usual, but now they're surrounded by cameras and news anchors. I push through about a dozen people in suits, most of whom are talking or texting on their cell phones.

Stretching up on my toes to see over their heads, I search for Jonah. I see Rex and Caleb boxing with two trainers I've never met. Owen is talking on camera, a very attractive news anchor wearing a low cut v-neck shirt and a miniskirt, holding a microphone to his mouth.

"Baby girl." I jump and squeak at the sound of Blake's voice at my shoulder.

"You scared me to death." I place my hand over my heart.

His face is serious and thoughtful. No wisecrack come-ons or dirty jokes. He steps into my space, his green eyes boring down on me. "I heard about what happened last night."

"Last night?" Memories of being naked above Jonah flood my mind. My cheeks flame. I smack my head with my palm. "Oh, Vince." Of course, he would be talking about Vince.

"Yeah. Vince." His eyes narrow and jaw tenses. "What did you think I was talking about?"

"Nothing. Forget it." I blow it off with a disinterested shrug and pray the pink drains from my face.

He's still staring. Blake's never serious for this long. His face looks pained as he studies the space just above my head. I look up. Nothing there. What in the heck is he doing?

"Blake, you're freaking me out."

He looks at me, grief working behind his eyes before he blinks it away. "Look, I know…" He grimaces and stares at the floor, like he's gathering strength from it. "I know what it's like to have a no-good, asshole for a father. I've lived it. Still living it." He rubs his shaved head. "It's one thing to fuck with your son, but to fuck with a girl?" A half groan, half growl rumbles in his chest. His focus is fixed on me. "I guess what I'm trying to say is, I got your back. And Jonah's. You feel me?"

I rub my lips together, trying to smash the inevitable quiver. Whatever happened to Blake in his past is enough that the simple memory erases the man I know and replaces him with a scared, timid boy.

My eyes burn with forced back tears. This is too much. First Jonah and now Blake. They act like they would lay down their lives to protect me. That's crazy. And unfamiliar. It feels like …family.

"Yeah, I feel you."

His eyes sparkle and his cocksure smile returns. He leans toward me with his hand cupping his ear. "I'm sorry. Did you say you want to feel me?" He runs his hands over his chest. "Anywhere in particular or you want me to make suggestions? There's one place, down—Ow!"

I smack him in the stomach, happy to see the anguish wiped from his face.

He rubs the spot at his belly where I hit him. "We need to get you in the octagon. Damn, that hurt."

I shoulder bump him, and he takes his cue to pull me to his side. I don't say a word, afraid that my voice might show the deep emotions I'm feeling.

"Come on. I'll take you to your man."

TWENTY-THREE

RAVEN

Two days until fight day.

My mind is focused on installing a new timing belt on the Impala while the lulling voice of Al Green being so in love fills the air. I mentally inventory my progress. White wall tires, a paint job, and she's done.

Bent over with my head under the hood, I feel a tight grip on my hips. Jonah's touch has become a second skin, as recognizable as my own. I smile and gently press my backside into his groin.

"You wanna tell me what it is you're hiding from out here?"

He's managed to figure me out in the short time we've been together. Come to think of it, he seemed to read me pretty well after a few days.

I straighten from beneath the hood on a sigh. His hands slide from my hips to my stomach and I melt into him. His touch in any capacity renders me totally helpless.

"I'm not hiding. I'm processing."

With my hair pulled up high on my head, my neck is at his mercy. He kisses his spot before gently nipping. I shiver.

"You're freakin' out because that formal dinner is tonight and because my mom is coming into town tomorrow." His ability to read me can also be incredibly annoying.

"Yeah." *Can't a girl have a secret?* "I don't do well with parents. What if she doesn't like me? I'm sure she's really protective of you. I mean if you were my son I would be too. It's just ...I know how my mom feels about me..."

I'm unable to finish my thought, not wanting to hear the words out loud. The fact is I'm pretty sure my mom hates my guts. She must blame me for her horrible life. If she never had me, she would have been able to run away from Dominick and have a chance at a real life or love. How could she not hate me? Thinking about it makes me hate myself.

"She's going to love you, baby. She'll be charmed by you just like everyone else."

I wish I had his confidence.

"Besides, you don't know how your mom feels about you. I know her actions show that she doesn't care, but maybe she doesn't know how to show you how she feels. Maybe she thinks you hate her. Hell, you have every right to."

I usually brush off the subject of my mom when it comes up, but something deep inside tugs at me. His love has given me a safe place to fall. I can give him a piece of me. With his chest pressed to my back, I won't have to witness the pity in his eyes. *I can do this.*

"When I was a little girl, I used to sneak into her bed at night."

His arms tense and his chest flexes against my back.

"I would curl up next to her, desperate to feel the heat from her skin. I remember I would slowly inch my hand closer and closer, so afraid to wake her, until I could touch just the tip of my finger to her back or her arm. Sometimes I would just loop a strand of her long hair around my finger."

My voice drops to a whisper as I'm taken back to those nights. I feel small and insignificant. Crushed with sadness, my lungs struggle for a full breath.

"I usually only got a minute or two before she'd wake up. It was as if she could sense me, even in her sleep, like my very presence triggered an internal alarm system that told her to get away. She would make me go back to my bed. Some nights I'd be so angry and desperate I'd refuse to leave." My humorless laughter breaks with emotion. "She would get sick of telling me to get out, and she'd go sleep on the couch. She'd rather sleep on the couch than with her own daughter."

"Baby…" he whispers and kisses my head.

"The saddest part is that those nights were the best. I got to sleep the rest of the night surrounded by her smell. I would wrap myself up tight in her sheets and pretend they were her arms. I'd bury my face in her pillow, smelling her shampoo and night cream."

Hot tears drip from my jaw, and Jonah's arms tighten on my waist.

"Anyway, that's the reason I listen to old music. All those old tapes were my mom's. I took them when I left. I knew she'd be mad, but I also knew she wouldn't come for them." I wipe my cheeks and sniff. "Listening to this music, the music she had playing every day of my entire life, it's the only way I can be close to her."

The pressure at my waist is released and he turns me to him. I keep my eyes focused on his chest, not ready to confront the look on his face. His fingers beneath my chin pull my gaze to his. Bending down, his lips softly brush against mine and stay there as he speaks.

"Baby, I promise you that you'll never want for physical contact again." His big, strong hands hold my head and he leans his forehead against mine. "I'll always hold you when you're scared." He softly kisses my jaw. "Comfort you when you're sad." His lips brush against my cheeks. "Take care of you when you're sick." Tilting my head back, he kisses my forehead. He bends down and his hazel eyes narrow into mine. "I'll make it my life's mission to make up for every second you were neglected."

I'm captivated by his stare, which, like his hold on my heart, doesn't let go. I suck in a ragged breath, overcome with emotion.

"I know I say this all the time, but I love you, Jonah. So much."

"I love you too, baby. Thank you for telling me about your mom. There's nothing you need to keep from me. I want to know you, even the stuff you're not proud of."

"Okay."

"My gorgeous girl and her 'okays.'"

I bury my face in his chest, feeling lighter, having released a heavy burden from my past and placed it on the strong, capable shoulders of the amazing man before me.

"Now, as far as the formal dinner tonight goes? You have nothing to worry about. I won't leave your side, not even for a second." His dimples slowly appear as a smile creeps across his face. "I'll even take you to the bathroom with me." He kisses my neck. "That might actually make this stupid dinner worth going to."

I exhale as his playful words bring me peace. And the visual of Jonah and I having bathroom sex also helps to chase away the last of my nerves.

"I can't wait to see you in the dress you picked up."

I roll my eyes, remembering the day he shoved two thousand dollars cash into my backpack to shop. I planned on not using it, until I realized how expensive good formalwear is. I used all of it.

"Besides, if anyone should be worried, it's me," he says.

My brows pinch together and I study his smoldering eyes. "Why would you worry?"

"I gotta worry about all the assholes who'll be sniffing around you all night. Pretty sure beating someone's ass at this dinner in front of all the bigwigs would be frowned upon."

He's all dimples and beautiful white teeth as he looks from my eyes to my lips. My heart beats wildly and desire floods my veins. I lick my lips in anticipation and run my hands over his muscular chest, thumbing his nipples through his shirt. Feeling the sinewy ripples of his chest, I imagine his naked torso above me. Heat ignites my blood and flips my belly. I look up at him from under my eyelashes.

His smile fades and his eyebrows arch. "Again?"

It hasn't even been a week since I lost my virginity to Jonah, but my appetite for him is insatiable. I can't get enough, and from the frequency of our lovemaking, neither can he.

"Well, I guess if you don't want to, I can just go back to working on the Impala," I say teasingly.

I shift out of his hands and take a step backwards. He hauls me to his torso with a growl, his mouth at my ear.

"Oh, I want to. Seeing you out here, bent over this car, your sexy ass in those short shorts…" His words are lost as he possesses my mouth. He bites my lip and I moan against him. "That's my girl."

Bending down, he puts his big shoulder to my stomach and grabs me behind my knees. In one quick move, I'm thrown over his shoulder.

"Jonah!"

He smacks me on the bottom, and my mouth slams shut. I allow the sensations to penetrate my body.

Why does that feel so good?

JONAH

"It's six twenty-five, babe. You about ready?" I call out to my bathroom door, the same bathroom door I've been talking to for over an hour.

Raven locked herself in there with her dress and a bag full of girl crap and hasn't come out since. I've heard all manner of sounds coming from the other side, but still haven't gotten even the slightest peek at my girl.

"Okay. One more second." She's been telling me one more second for the past fifteen minutes.

I turn toward my full-length mirror to straighten my tie. Slipping my finger beneath the collar, I give it a yank, hoping to give my neck some relief. Monkey suits and a heavyweight's body do not mix. Even custom made, they feel like a glorified straight jacket. I lift my arms and bring them to cross at my chest. The fabric stretches to its limit making me claustrophobic. I can't wait to get this night over with.

The sound of something hitting the bathroom floor gets my attention.

"Shoot! I'm okay!"

I press my ear to the door. "You sure?"

"Yes, I just …um, these shoes are really high and your tile is slippery."

It's not right, but the thought of Raven, as hot and graceful as she is, sliding around off balance in the bathroom, makes me laugh.

"Are you ready? I'm coming out," she says, a nervous tremor in her voice.

There's a click from the lock, and I step back. The door slowly opens and the bright light from the bathroom bathes Raven's silhouette in an ethereal glow.

Holy shit. My jaw drops and I stare in awe.

She's dressed in a light purple, floor-length gown that has a slit all the way up the side. Standing with one leg slightly cocked, her entire upper thigh is exposed. My gaze follows the line of her tan leg to the sexiest pair of strappy silver stilettos. The dress is hot, but my mind imagines her in nothing but those shoes. I open my mouth to tell her how beautiful she looks, but the sight of her breasts robs me of the words—their full swells pushed up in offering, begging for my lips. My mouth goes dry.

"Do I look okay?" She runs her palms down the front of her dress self-consciously. Typical Raven. An absolute knock-out and she has no idea.

"Baby, you're a vision. I've never seen anything so beautiful in all my life."

Her eyes look down the length of her body then lock on mine. "Thank you." She takes a step towards me then freezes mid-step. "Oh, you haven't seen the back yet."

The back? There's no way the back could be better than what I'm looking at right now.

Her eyes sparkle and she gives me a mischievous grin. Slowly, she turns and my breath catches in my throat.

There is no back.

The birds in her tattoo fly in formation from her hip to her shoulder for all to see. Her hair is tied up loosely in an elegant, messy mass of shiny dark locks, giving me an unobstructed view. My eyes travel the expanse to the two dimples visible above her perfect ass. I reach down to adjust myself in my pants. Suddenly my collar isn't the only thing that's tight.

Placing her hand on her cocked hip, she looks over her shoulder. "You like?"

"I ...uh, yeah." I clear my throat. "I more than l-like. It's ... You're amazing. You l-look." To save myself from further embarrassment due to my sudden case of stutter-mouth, I shut up.

Stepping to her, I start at her hip and run my finger along the path of her tattoo. Mesmerized by the softness of her skin, I watch tiny goose bumps follow the line of my finger. I press my lips to her shoulder. She drops her head to the side, exposing the full length of her neck. I ghost a kiss against her skin, followed by my tongue. The combination of her sweet taste and pear smell makes me hungry for what's beneath the dress. My teeth scrape along her sensitive throat, and I bite with gentle pressure. She leans back and a moan bubbles up from her chest, escaping her lips in a purr.

"You are absolutely gorgeous," I whisper against the spot where I bit her.

"Mmm, thank you." Her voice has taken on a breathy quality that has me straining against my slacks. "You look very handsome too. I like the black on black. It reminds me of Clark Kent."

I kiss her neck once more, and pull back. "Clark Kent? He was a dorky news reporter. He wore starched white shirts with bow ties and shit. I think he even sported a pocket protector."

Giggling, she turns to face me. It's then that I notice her face. She usually wears minimal makeup, but tonight it's heavier in all the right places. Her eyes are rimmed with a smoky color that highlights the aquamarine. Her cheeks dusted with pink, and her lips. *Holy hell.* Those lips.

"Wait, I thought Clark Kent was the hot one."

I'm focused on her shimmering, pink glossed mouth as she talks.

"You know the one who wears black all the time and drives the cool car?"

"Huh?" I swallow hard, caught up in the sensory overload that Raven is dishing out in buckets.

She places her soft hand against my cheek. "Um ...Clark Kent?"

Fuck, that's right. I forgot what we were talking about.

"Bruce Wayne, baby. Batman."

"Yes! You're right. Bruce Wayne. He's the hot one that all the girls—"

I can't take it anymore and crash my lips against hers. Her blatant sex appeal and childlike innocence does me in. Her lip gloss tastes like marshmallow and her mouth like peppermint. I suck at her lips, and she buries her hands in my hair, holding me to her.

My girl.

I run my hands over the dress, feeling her nipples pucker beneath the fabric. My hands grip at it with impatience, gently tugging, knowing what's underneath is so much softer. There's no way we're going to dinner. Nothing is as important to me in this moment than getting my girl naked underneath me.

"Jonah," she says breathlessly between kisses.

"Mmm?"

"The door."

"Hmm?"

"The doorbell's ringing. Our ride's here."

"Don't give a shit," I growl and walk her backwards towards my bed.

Her legs hit the bed, stopping our progression. I hold her hips and grind my now painfully hard erection against her. She tilts her head and deepens the kiss. *Fuck yeah.* My girl, always so ready.

My phone is ringing in my pocket and the doorbell won't quit. I groan, annoyed, but never give up her mouth. This is happening. Now.

She laughs and presses her palms against my chest. Reluctantly, I pull back.

"Jonah, we need to stop." Her raspy voice and traveling hands betray her words.

"Not going anymore." I'm kissing her neck at my spot, hoping she gives up on the idea and gets naked soon.

"It's a limo, right?" There's a smile in her question.

I step back to meet her eyes. "Yeah, it's a limo." I smile. "Why?"

She shrugs her shoulders and drops her face, her cheeks flushed. I hook my fingers beneath her chin and bring her eyes back to mine, lifting my eyebrows.

Is she thinking what I think she's thinking?

"I just thought it might be …um …fun, you know? To make out in a limo?"

My body hums with excitement at the prospect of getting dirty with Raven in the backseat of a chauffeured vehicle.

I grab her hand and lead her to the front door. "Fine. But we're leaving right after dinner and picking up where we left off."

"Sounds good to me," she says through her giggles.

—

"Mr. Slade, it's a pleasure to meet you," the limo driver says while looking at us from the rearview mirror. "I've been following your career for years."

Ah, shit. I'm presented with the opportunity to shove my hand up Raven's dress in a moving vehicle, and we get chatty Charles the limo driver.

"Thanks, man. I appreciate your support."

Raven rubs my thigh with soothing strokes, and I consider moving her hand up six inches. Would Charles even notice? *Nah.*

"That fight in '07 against Hollander was incredible. How long had you been with the UFL when you fought him?"

I groan and curse the fact that I represent more than myself at times like these, but also my training team and the UFL. "Four ye—"

"Four years! That's how many. And three years before that you were undefeated against Santoro!" He slaps his steering wheel, his booming laughter filling the length of the car.

"Yeah, look we were hoping for a little private time to talk about some things. Do you think we could put up the privacy wall, so—"

"My cousin Junior is training with an MMA fighting league in San Antonio. He's been..."

Charles goes on and on, but my focus is on my girl whose face is bright red from holding back laughter. *Hardy fucking har har.*

I decide I've heard enough from Charles and tell him we'll continue after the dinner, but that I need some fucking alone time with my date. Shit.

Privacy window up and finally alone, I'm assaulted by her smell. I practically attack her, not that she's complaining. I almost get my hand up her dress when the limo lurches to a stop. *Shit!*

I tell Charles we need five minutes. Raven checks her face in a mirror, and I think about everything except what I'll be doing to her later tonight. Great, now I'm thinking about it again.

"You about done? If I don't get out of here soon, I'll finish what I started."

She gives me a sexy smile and tucks a couple loose strands of hair back into place. "I'm ready."

I laugh, shaking my head at her mixed message reply.

We exit the limo, and holding hands, we walk through Mandalay Bay Hotel's casino to the elevators. Raven fidgets at my side as photographers snap pictures and people start to gather.

"You look gorgeous, baby." I try to take her mind off being the center of attention to a bunch of strangers. She blushes and holds my hand tighter.

This dinner is held on the sixty-fourth floor of the hotel in a swanky restaurant called Mix. As soon as we exit the elevator, we're greeted by an older gentleman in a tuxedo.

"Ah, Mr. Slade. Your party is expecting you. If you'll follow me, I'll escort you and Miss…"

Her hand locks mine in a death grip.

"Raven," I say.

"Of course, Mr. Slade. Miss Raven. Please follow me."

Releasing her firm grip, she leans into my shoulder. "Thank you." Her whispered words are only for my ears.

I lift her hand, kiss her knuckles, and give her a wink. She never tells people her last name, afraid of being associated with Dominick. His name circulates among the richest of Vegas's philanderers. And a high-end place like this is bound to be familiar with the name if not the man himself.

We're led into a private dining room in the back of the restaurant. It's packed with roughly thirty people from the organization. I feel Raven's hesitation as we step into the crowd. I spot Owen and Nikki across the room and decide to stick close to them so that Raven will have someone to talk to.

Different people greet me with handshakes and hellos, but all their eyes are on my girl. This is going to be a long fucking night.

TWENTY-FOUR

RAVEN

I'm at one of the fanciest restaurants in town, I arrived by limo, and I'm wearing an outfit that cost more than I make in a month, bought for me by my rich boyfriend.

I'm Julia Roberts in *Pretty Woman*.

How appropriate.

No, Cinderella. I'm Cinderella out with my Prince Charming. Although, I'm pretty sure my Prince Charming would kick the real Prince Charming's butt in a fistfight. And now my nerves are setting up imaginary fights between cartoon characters.

Well, at least it's taking my mind off the fact that I'm totally out of my element. I may as well have written *I don't belong* on my forehead in black eyeliner. Everyone here is either rich, famous, influential, or a combination of all three. I need to pull it together.

I jump as Jonah places his hand on my back. I look up to see a tall man with sandy blond hair and blue eyes eyeing me.

"Raven, this is Taylor Gibbs, the owner of the UFL."

I gather my social graces. I've never seen so many high-powered people in one room. The place is practically vibrating with egos and money.

"Mr. Gibbs, it's nice to meet you. Thank you for having me."

"Raven, it's a pleasure."

He reaches out to shake the hand I've extended. Jonah tenses and pulls me closer to him, tucking me deep into his side. Mr. Gibbs brings my offered hand to his mouth, kissing it softly.

I press deeper into Jonah at the gesture. No one's touch feels welcome, except Jonah's. To keep from embarrassing him in front of his boss, I put on a brave face.

"I'm glad you could make it, Raven." His glare zeros in on Jonah and a whisper of tension charges the air between them.

My eyes dart back and forth between the two.

Jonah's brooding is directed at his boss. Mr. Gibbs smirks at me and releases my hand. I bring it immediately to Jonah's abdomen, hoping that the touch will help shake the creepy from my hand.

Mr. Gibbs starts in with Jonah about who he needs to touch base with at the party when a man walks up behind him. He's as big as Jonah in height and width, but where Jonah's ferocity is inviting, this man's is terrifying. He has dark hair and eyes that look almost black. His face is held in a permanent scowl with a scar over his left eye and one at his chin. He stalks toward us with the grace of a rhino.

"Well, if it isn't my own personal punching bag," he says, glaring at Jonah.

Jonah's grip tightens. "Del Toro. I thought they only allowed civilized people into this place. Not knuckle-dragging chimps like you."

Mr. Gibbs moves between the fighters. "Save it for the octagon, guys. No need to make a scene in front of the lovely Raven."

Del Toro's eyes swing to me and his head tilts to the side. He studies my face and a small smile tips his lips. His expression is animalistic, but not a chimp like Jonah chided. He looks more like a hungry lion.

Now I know what it feels like to be a zebra on the Serengeti.

"Raven, when you get bored with this loser, I'll show you how a champion does it." He steps forward, causing Mr. Gibbs to use his shoulder to keep him back.

Jonah growls so deeply that I feel it before I hear it. His eyes fix on Del Toro in the death stare to end all death stares. "You fucking talk to her again I'll put you in a coma right here."

Energy from years of animosity rolls off of them in waves. Jonah's jaw is tense, his icy glare fixed, and his fists balled at his sides. He's about to lose it. I can't let that happen.

I put on my sweetest smile and step in front of Jonah, placing myself directly between two of the biggest men I've ever seen. "You must be Victor Del Toro. Jonah's told me all about you. Six years as the Heavyweight Champion." I whistle through my teeth. "That's impressive."

Blinking, Del Toro takes his eyes from a seething Jonah and sets them on me. His face visibly relaxes, but not by much.

"Yeah, it's impressive, and I don't plan on giving up the title anytime soon."

"No, of course not." I bat at him with a girlie giggle that's so sweet it makes Del Toro smile. *Great. It's working.* "About your offer, I can promise you I'll never get bored with Jonah. But thank you for the compliment."

"You let me know if you change your mind, sweetheart." He glares at Jonah one last time and walks away.

There's a collective sigh of relief from two of the three people left. Jonah's still seething, but at least his fists are no longer clenched.

"Wow, you have a gift. I've never seen anyone who can talk down testosterone-fueled fighters that quickly. Must be those eyes." Mr. Gibbs winks at me before excusing himself.

Once he's gone, I turn to a still-frozen Jonah. Pressing my body to the length of his, I slide my hands around his neck. His eyes are unfocused, clinging to the edge of self-control.

"Hey. You okay?"

He makes a sound that's half grunt half groan. Hm. Not okay. I need to try a different tactic.

I press my breasts against his chest and kiss his chin. This gets me his eyes. Progress.

Making my way from there, I brush my lips against his jaw line slowly, allowing him to feel my breath on his face. His arms wrap around my waist, and his thumbs rub circles on the exposed skin at my back. Now we're getting somewhere.

I kiss below his ear. "You okay?"

"Better."

I lean away, but keep my hands locked behind his neck. "That was intense."

"I want to beat that guy's ass. I swear, Raven, I don't regret making that deal with Dominick. I'd do it a million times over," he whispers. "But, I'm really, *really* looking forward to beating the shit out of that asshole when I get another opportunity."

I try to comfort him with a smile, but it feels off. My chest aches. Guilt wars with gratitude. How can I do this to him? How can I not?

This must be torture: all this talk about being the next Heavyweight Champion, his undefeated record, and Del Toro antagonizing him. Instead of going out there on fight night, doing what comes naturally, he has to play possum.

I'm grateful for his sacrifice, but I didn't anticipate how much he would suffer. Turn his back on his instincts. Push down his nature. All for me.

I pull away and he releases me from his hold. His eyes roam the room casually, unaware of the internal struggle his words induced.

My lungs are tight. I can't breathe. The weight of all that's happened presses in from all angles. I turn to a nearby table and lean heavy against the chair. I knew what he was giving up on a hypothetical level, but seeing it with my own eyes, feeling the aggression electrifying the space between them, just made this *real.*

A group of people walk up to us, but I'm so lost in my head I don't pay attention. My mind whirls with excuses to get out of here. Bathroom. I'll just run to the bathroom, gather myself and—*What the hell?*

A gorgeous blonde in a skin-tight, bright red dress is standing way to close to Jonah. I watch in horror as the beauty queen wraps her arms around his neck. In sickening slow motion, she presses an open mouth kiss right on his lips.

Fuck that!

Adrenaline floods my veins.

"Hey!" My body moves before I think better of it and I'm right in her face.

Jonah's wiping his mouth with the back of his hand.

"Get your hands *off* my boyfriend."

She looks me up and down before pressing her body closer to his. Jonah takes a step to the side, but she winds her arms around his waist, sticking to him like a Siamese twin. "And if I don't? What are you going to do about it?"

Even her glare is pretty.

"Step away. Now." My voice shakes, but I stand tall.

Jonah gives her arms a final tug and she releases her hold.

She steps into my space. With her slutty shoes, she's a good six inches taller than me. Her strapless dress reveals cut muscles that are coiled and ready. "Do you have any idea who I am?"

"No. Don't care. But if you touch my boyfriend again, *you're* going to find out who *I* am."

An evil glint touches her crystal blue eyes. "I'm Camille Fisher. I fight for a living. You want to go there. Let's go there."

I'm sick and tired of people messing with me. She may be strong and trained, but I'm fed up and pushed past my limit.

I get right in her face and give her a smile that is most likely all teeth. "I'm Raven, Jonah's girlfriend. And I'm a mechanic."

She tosses her head back, her blond hair cascading around her shoulders, and laughs. "Mechanic. Scary." She says the last word in a sing-song voice and rolls her eyes. Her body closes in.

"Baby, leave it alone. Let's go." Jonah slides his hand around my waist.

"Yeah, you should be scared." I lean in until our noses are almost touching. "Every time you get in your car, I want you to think about how easy it would be for me to cut your brakes. I'm sure you have some overpriced piece of fiberglass built in some foreign country. Do you have any idea how simple it is to disassemble a car? A few missing bolts and the thing falls apart while you're driving down the freeway."

"You wouldn't."

"Try me, bitch."

Her eyes travel back and forth between Jonah and me.

"Forget it, Camille. Let's go," her friend says from behind her.

"Hey, hey, hey! What do we have here? I love a good cat-fight." Blake strolls up with a huge grin on his face, like he saw the entire thing and finds it hilarious. "They're way more fun naked, but then again..." He scratches his chin and looks at the ceiling before looking back at us. "Isn't everything?"

I bite my lip against a smile.

"Blake, this is Camille Fisher." Jonah introduces Blake, and I don't miss that he pulls me back a good two feet as he does.

Camille's eyes sparkle as she takes in all that is Blake. He gives her a visual once- over, like he's sizing up a meal. It's obvious where this will end up tonight.

"Camille, you've got quite a mouth on you." Blake's double meaning makes me giggle-snort, earning me another glare from the female fighter.

"Come on, baby. Leave her to Blake." Jonah guides me away from the group, still wiping red lipstick from his face.

"Here, allow me." I run my thumb along his full lower lip, rekindling my anger at the reminder that another woman pressed her mouth against his. "Where do you think she parked her car?"

He kisses my finger, smiling. "Don't know. But damn, watching you nut up on that bitch? Tough, gorgeous, and hot as hell."

I wrap my arms around his waist and kiss him. "There. All memories of her erased." My fingers absently run along the collar of his shirt. "I don't know what came over me. My tolerance tank was full and I snapped."

"Now you know how it feels to be me."

His words bring my thoughts back to earlier. As pissed as I was at Camille, Jonah must feel that a million times worse facing off with Del Toro. And there's nothing he can do about it.

"I'm going to run to the ladies' room. Wash all this red lipstick from my hand." I hold my hand up, and quickly drop it. I don't need to wash my hand, I just need a second to shake off my thoughts and get through the night.

"I'll go with—"

"No, it's fine. You've got people who want to talk to you here. I'll be back before you know it."

His questioning stare locks on mine, as if he's trying to read my thoughts. I avert my eyes, knowing he'll be able to if I give him enough time.

"All right, find me when you're done. Or I'll find you."

"Jonah, I'm fine. Really."

He doesn't look convinced, but I take my chance to leave before he changes his mind. I kiss his dimpled cheek, and slip from the room.

The maître d' directs me to the restroom at the other side of the restaurant. I welcome the distance and take the time to sort my head. Halfway there, something familiar catches my eye. I stop mid-step and squint. *No, it can't be.*

Sitting at an intimate table for two is a stunning woman with long black hair and a shimmering gold dress. She flips the dark locks in a playful manner, a bright smile lighting her face. She seems happy and carefree. If I didn't know better I'd say she looks ...in love.

"Mom."

TWENTY-FIVE

RAVEN

It's been two years since I've seen her. Part of me wants to run to her, hoping the sight of me will make her smile. I want her to tell me she's missed me and has been meaning to call, as most moms would do with a child they haven't seen in two years. But I'm frozen in place. Those thoughts are nothing more than the musings of a neglected child—one who wants what she'll never have.

I study her as she sips her wine, her eyes intent on the john across the table. She tilts her head and smiles. The softness in her gaze makes my heart pinch with envy.

I've never been on the receiving end of her smile. Her blank stares, those I know. The way her sparkling eyes go dead when she looks at me, I know that too. And she's certainly never looked at me with love. Indifference, yes. Resentment, maybe.

Love? No.

She wouldn't give me that. But here, for the right price, she gifts these things to a stranger. He's paid for it. He is deserving of it, but not me, not her own daughter.

My breath becomes short. Anger boils my insides. Tears launch their brutal attack without mercy. This time, I don't fight them. I savor the sting on my cheeks as the salty evidence of my neglect consumes me. I welcome the sadness and desperation as it spurs on my rage.

I've been such a fool. Daydreaming about what might be. I have no parents. They used each other to create a sick joke of a human being for their own selfish reasons. I've put up with the neglect and abuse for long enough. No more.

My legs begin a journey my mind hasn't caught up to. Before I know it, I'm standing at their table. My eyes lock on my mom. I sense the curious stare of her date from the corner of my eye, but I wait. I wait to be acknowledged by her.

It doesn't take long before her face turns to me with a polite smile, probably thinking I'm a waitress, and then falls instantly: blank stare, dead eyes.

No smile for me, mom? What a shocker.

Silently, our eyes locked on each other, my lips curl.

"Can we help you?" says the john.

I ignore him and speak directly to her. "How could you?" The acrid tone of my words makes her shift in her seat.

"Raven," she whispers my name like it's a dirty word. Her eyes dart around the room. "I'm on a date. Call me tomorrow and we can—"

"How fucking could you? You smile at him." I point an accusing finger at the john. "But you can hardly stand to look at me!" My fist slams against their table, shaking the china. "Your own daughter."

Eyes on the john, she shakes her head and shrugs as if to say, *I don't know what she's talking about.*

Bitch!

"I'm sorry about this, Mark. There must be some mis—"

"You're sorry, *Mark*?" My glare swings back and forth between Mark and my mom. "You're sorry, *fucking Mark*? You ruined my life!"

Mark jumps from his chair. "Watch your tone! We're having dinner, and if you know what's best for you, you'll turn around and walk out of here. Now."

I have no intention of walking out of here. Not without saying what I need to say.

"Did you know, Mom? Did you know what his plan was for me? Do you have any idea what it's like to have your dad tell you that he …that he…" I can't bring myself to say it, but the fear showing in her wide eyes tells me she knew. "He's come for me."

Her hand grips at her throat and her face pales. She leans to the side, squinting at something behind me. She wants to avoid what I'm saying. No, not this time.

I get right in her face and point. "You did this to me. Why? You ruined my life. I wish you never had me!"

Her eyes glisten before they drop to her lap.

"That's enough!" Mark grabs my arm and pulls hard.

Unfazed by Marks tightening grip, I intend on expelling the ugly until they throw me out. "Do you hear me, *whore*? I wish I was never born!"

"Get your motherfucking hands off her," a low, but authoritative rumble demands from my back.

Mark's eyes move to a towering figure behind me before he releases his hand. I don't have to turn around to know my savior as his strong arms wrap around my waist.

The sound of Jonah's voice and comfort of his touch trigger a sob from deep in my chest. *He's here. Thank God.* I lean into his embrace. I don't know how much he heard, but his presence reminds me of what I have and dulls the ache of what I never will.

"I've got you, baby. Let me take you home."

Home.

Jonah is my home now. He's the only one who ever cared enough to fight for me. He's my family. All that matters now is us.

Jonah turns me in his arms. I bury my face in his chest, and let the emotions overtake me. His soothing words are nothing but background noise to my uncontrollable sobs.

He walks us from the restaurant and back to our waiting limo. The tears begin to dry as I'm placed into the privacy of the car. I'm a mess of nerves, anger, and hurt as verbal vomit flows from my lips like a sorority girl on induction night. Sobs break with roaring words of devastation as twenty-one years of pain finally find release.

Jonah's eyes are wide, watching me kick and scream, throwing out every curse word that comes to mind. I'm not fully aware of what I'm saying, but Jonah flinches as the once foreign words tumble from my lips with ease.

Seconds turn into minutes before my heart rate slows and my muscles relax. Exhaustion sets in. Jonah slides to my side, wrapping me in his arms.

"You finished?" His question is tender and laced with meaning.

Finished crying? Finished with my mom? Finished fighting my future?

Nodding my head into his neck, he holds me tighter.

"I should've gone with you. I never should've let you leave after that shit with Camille." He sounds angry with himself, but none of what happened tonight is his fault.

A new wave of anger flickers at the mention of her name, but there's no fuel left to ignite it. I sink deeper into his embrace.

"Taylor wanted me to be seen in public with her to promote the Female MMA League. I told him I wouldn't do it, but I guess she didn't like taking no for an answer." His lips press against the top of my head. "Don't think she'll be hearing no from Blake."

Camille up against Blake. She doesn't stand a chance.

"I understand. It just caught me off guard. Del Toro, Camille, my mom..."

"Crazy night."

I nod.

"Feel good? Telling her off like that?"

My face heats, and I'm thankful it's dark so he can't see it; although, he can probably feel it through his shirt.

"How much did you hear?"

"Everything. You were yelling pretty loud. I'm proud of you, baby." His warm hand caresses my arm, reinforcing his words.

"Proud? I acted like an idiot in there. Made a fool out of myself, out of you."

"You stood up for yourself. Let your mom know what you've been keeping inside for way too long. What you did was really brave."

Once again, he gives, unknowingly filling my emotional cup to the brim. And then some.

"Please tell me no one from your team heard. Your boss? Your publicist? Camille!" My voice grows louder as hysteria returns.

"Shhh, they had no clue. I went to find you and saw you leaning over your mom like a bear about to attack. I told the hostess to give them the message that you were sick and I had to get you home. Did me a favor. I hate those stuffy dinners, everyone blowing sunshine up each other's asses."

The limo slows to a stop. I peer out the window to see we're in Jonah's driveway. Charlie, the limo driver, opens the door and Jonah gets out. I hear him mumbling something about not talking to the media followed by Charlie's emphatic agreement. Jonah reaches in to help me out of the car.

"Miss Raven, it's been a pleasure." Charlie's face looks concerned.

I wipe my eyes and smile. "Thank you, Charlie. It was nice meeting you."

Jonah tosses him a thick fold of bills and a chin lift and guides me to the front door. I beeline it to Jonah's room to take off my dress and wash my face.

Stepping into the bathroom, I flip on the light and recoil at my reflection. Walking closer to the mirror, I tilt my head and squint.

Holy heck.

Black eye makeup marks channel down my face like a road map of mayhem. Blotchy red marks on my cheeks and forehead highlight my bloodshot eyes. I look like a demented prom queen, minus all the blood. And Jonah held me like this, as I screamed every cuss word I could think of.

My hands fly to my mouth. He must think I'm a lunatic.

Words thrown from my hissy fit come rushing back. The memory of Jonah's hazel eyes, wide and set on me while ... *While I made a total fool out of myself.*

Hysteria swells in my chest. I roll my lips into my mouth and force back the maniacal laughter. A fluttering bubbles up from my chest as I recall my mom's face when I stepped to her table. Laughter explodes, ricocheting off the tiled walls. Mark's face when he saw Jonah has me doubled over. The sorry sack looked like he soiled his briefs.

The intensity of what happened sinks in. I muffle my frenzy into a washcloth, hoping its cool contact will ease the delirium. My cheeks hurt from smiling and I check out my blurred reflection. Crazy eyes, bleeding black tears, huge smile. Pure, certifiable insanity.

I collapse into a torrent of giggles, causing rivers to stream down my face. Tears born of laughter feel so much better than those born from pain. My jaw aches, but the howl continues to tumble from my lips.

My side cramps. I press against the pain and try to calm down with deep breathing.

It doesn't work.

My stomach muscles contract as I cackle without control. The sound fades in waves as I trade oxygen for lunacy. *Is it possible to die of laughter?*

I sense movement from the corner of my eye. Jonah is standing in the doorway, frozen and staring. Without the breath to speak, I hold up my palm and pray he gets the message. *Yes. I've officially lost it.*

"What the fuck?" he whispers.

I shake my head, pleading with him to stop. If he speaks another word, I'm pretty sure I'll cough up my kidneys from laughing.

He tilts his head, studying me. "Are you fucking kidding me?"

He didn't listen. I squeeze my eyes shut, and soundless laughter racks my body.

"I ...can't ...stop." I manage to get out the words before another wave of laughter brings me to my knees.

"Baby?" His lips are twitching like he's fighting the urge to join me in Crazytown.

He closes the distance between us in two long strides and he kneels in front of me. His face is fixed in a sexy half-grin; his eyelids are low and lustful. He grabs my face hard, not hard enough to hurt, but enough to get my attention. My laughter dies under the intensity of his stare. Blood races through my veins and my belly somersaults. Heat blooms in my chest and I lean in.

"There she is," he whispers.

My pulse surges with a furious passion that is anything but funny. Eyeing his full lips, I get closer, pressing my chest against his. My tongue slowly makes a pass along my lower lip, preparing for his attention.

"That's my girl," he growls before his lips cover mine.

Exploring his mouth, desire consumes me. I scrape my teeth along the inside of his bottom lip and swallow his answering groan. All the emotions from this evening are spiraling together to fuel the kiss and ramp up my need. I rip through his dress shirt, buttons bouncing off the marble floor. Pushing it from his shoulders, I run my hands down his rippled abdomen, digging my nails in as I go. His hands tangle in my hair to deepen the kiss. The smell of mint and aftershave permeate the air and seduce my senses.

His hand trails down my arm, leaving a wake of fire against my skin. With a gentle touch, he finds the slit of my dress, pushing the fabric aside at my hip. Still on my knees, I spread my legs in anticipation. He grips my hip then slides his hand down to where I need it most. I groan and roll my hips into his hand.

He stills. I smile.

"All night?" His voice is dark and hungry.

"Yes, all night." My answer is spoken through the satisfied smile that pulls at my lips.

His eyes lock on mine, wide and fascinated.

"What? You didn't expect me to wear panties with this dress, did you? It's too low cut in the back. I had to go commando." Who knew something as simple as not wearing panties could give me so much power? And power over someone as strong and commanding as Jonah is a potent aphrodisiac.

"That would have saved us a whole lot of trouble tonight. If I had known you were naked under that dress, I can guarantee you wouldn't have seen Camille or your mom. Hell, you wouldn't have seen much outside of my sheets."

I place a soft kiss against his lips and stand. His eyebrows drop low as he watches me with rapt attention. I turn my back to him, but peek over my shoulder and wink. He stares at me, a helpless look on his face.

Yes!

I slip a strap off my shoulder, making sure to keep my eyes locked on his. He licks his lips. I turn and glance over my other shoulder before sliding that strap down. His fists flex against his massive thighs. Inch by inch, I drop the dress lower in a lazy striptease. His eyes glaze over beneath heavy lids as I reveal the backside of my naked body in painstakingly slow steps.

Finally, with the dress pooling around my feet, I step out of the silken fabric. I'm left standing in my high heels. And nothing else.

Jonah rises to his feet. Still with my back to him, I'm attacked by a moment of self-consciousness and cup my breasts to hide them from his view.

He steps behind me. I can feel the heat from his body and smell the spice of his cologne, but he's not touching me.

"Turn around," he demands gently.

My head swivels his way, followed by my body. The clicking of my shoes against the marble floor is the only sound in the room next to my quickened breath.

His eyes take me in from hair to heels. With a feather light touch, he removes my hands from my breasts. "No hiding."

He runs his fingers from my hand, to my shoulder. They continue their journey down my spine to my bottom. I suck in a breath as he traces the line down between my legs and back up leaving a trail of heat that pools in my belly. He walks in a slow circle around me, never breaking his fingers contact with my flesh, skating around to my stomach, my hip, and back while he walks.

His gaze is dark and predatory as he stalks me. Gorgeously sculpted muscles painted in brilliant colors catch and reflect the light. I stare at him unabashed, watching his reflection in the mirror when his circle is complete and he's stopped behind me. His silence speaks volumes while he takes in my form.

"Leave the shoes on." The jagged edge to his voice sends a delicious tremble up my spine.

I turn toward him and grab the waist of his slacks. The evidence of his arousal is pressing against his fly, pushing the fabric past capacity. I run my fingers along his length, feeling steel beneath wool. His hips flex into my touch.

"Jonah—"

"Step back, baby."

I move back until the cold granite presses against my backside. His hands grip my waist and lift, setting me on the countertop. The heat from his kiss and warm hands at my breasts erase the chill of the icy rock against my bare skin.

He presses himself between my legs, gripping my hips with impatience. I fumble with his belt and zipper, his breath escaping on a hiss when I finally release him. I gasp as he slides a hand between my legs, forcing a tremble of need to slither down my spine.

"Jonah, the bed. Now." His barely-there touch and gentle coaxing has me begging for his possession.

A flash of his one-dimple smile and heavy eyelids almost push me to the edge. He works between my legs with magical fingers. With my hands braced behind me, I press against his hand.

"Not going to the bed, baby. I want to watch us."

His words are confusing, but I'm too lost in the sensations to ask for explanation. My heart races; pleasure coils deep in my belly. A moan falls from my lips. He moves his hand, and I miss it for a second before I feel his heat press against me.

"Yes," I whisper.

He buries himself deep and captures my mouth. With one thrust, my vision explodes in Technicolor sparks. Tingling shards of ecstasy flood my body. I call out his name, rolling my hips and riding out my release. He covers my neck and shoulder in wet kisses. Caught up in my free fall, I wrap my legs around his waist and rock against him, greedy for more.

"So fucking pretty." He runs his hands from my hips to my knees and behind him to my calves. "Love your shoes, baby. I want to feel them digging into my back. Wrap me tight."

A sagging puppet at his mercy, I lock my ankles behind his back. He braces his hands on the counter's edge, putting distance between our torsos. I watch in fascination as his eyes lower to our connection. I turn to our reflection in the mirror at the end of the double-sink countertop.

The visual of our bodies loving each other in an erotic rhythm has me memorized. His multi-colored biceps contract. Abdominal muscles ripple with every flex of his hips. My body sways in time with each delicious thrust, back and forth in waves.

For the first time, I see myself the way Jonah sees me: sexy, alluring, and even tempting. My long legs, tipped with stilettos, are wrapped tightly around his waist. Our eyes meet in the mirror. No smiles now.

Only scorching fire.

We watch our reflection and the pleasure builds. Our eyes lock in intimacy, liberating us of our need for words.

His gaze drops to my breasts, the driving power making them bounce. He bends forward, taking one into his mouth, and flicking the tip with his tongue. I grind into him harder, desperate for more contact.

A current builds, starting loose in my torso and condensing in my stomach. My lips part to accommodate my labored breath.

He pulls back, locks eyes with mine, and bites his lip. My hands sift through his hair and to pull his mouth to mine. A groan rumbles in his chest. His fingers dig into my bottom, the pinch against the sensitive flesh pushing me higher.

And like a lightning strike, I'm hit. My insides, once liquid, crystalize and shatter in pulses of euphoria. I throw my head back and moan. I fight to stay upright as my body enjoys the blissful indulgence.

He collapses on top of me before I feel his teeth sink into my shoulder. I tilt my head, and he groans against my skin, his body jolting from the power of his release.

My arms shake with the reverberations of my orgasm or from the strain of holding up our weight. He must sense my struggle and lifts his body to pull me to his chest.

Jonah holds me close, running his fingers through my hair while I come down and catch my breath. He places soft kisses on my face before we're drawn to our reflection.

He smiles. "That was hot."

I blush and agree. "Blazing."

"I'm buying you a pair of those shoes in every color they make."

"They're 500 dollars."

"Make that two pair in every color."

His expression is serious, and I burst into laughter. All of the stress and pressure I'd been feeling from earlier dissolve to a distant memory.

With a small effort, Jonah lifts me from the counter and places me on my wobbly legs. I look down and notice his pants are still around his ankles. He kicks them off and kneels in front of me. One by one, he slips off my shoes so that we're both standing naked.

He pulls me into his arms. "You doing better?"

"Yeah." I chuckle, remembering the state Jonah found me in earlier. "Guess I just needed the release."

His body shakes with silent laughter. *What is it with his sense of humor?* I pull back enough to show him my confusion.

"Guess you got your release …twice."

"Jonah!" I slap his arm and my face flames.

"Ow!" His humor fades and something serious works behind his eyes. "I Hhate seeing you like that."

"It's okay—"

"No. It's not. I can't wait for this shit to be over. For you to be free of…"

I rest my cheek against his chest and sigh. "Me too."

He reaches over and flips on the shower. The room fills with steam. "Come on. I'll get you all cleaned up. We have a big day tomorrow."

"Big day?"

His eyebrows hit his hairline.

My hand covers my mouth as realization dawns.

Tomorrow I meet his mom.

TWENTY-SIX

JONAH

"I think I might puke." Raven rubs her stomach, a grimace etched into her gorgeous face. She's made herself sick worrying about meeting my mom. I couldn't even get her to eat breakfast.

I wonder if any of her nerves this morning are leftover from her breakdown last night. I'd never seen a person go from ratshit mad to completely unglued. When I overheard her laughing in the bathroom, I realized she'd reached her breaking point. I knew I needed to bring her back—to pull her from her hysterics and place her gently back into her skin.

Her skin.

My dick twitches at the memory of her slowly sliding off that dress, each sliver of delicate flesh, beckoning for my touch—the way her body responded immediately to the slightest brush of my fingers, opening to my unspoken request. Erotic flashes of her legs wrapped around my body flood my mind. Heat radiates from the red marks on my back left by her shoes. Watching the reflection of our bodies tangled together is forever branded into my memory.

A groan bubbles up from my throat, and Raven turns her attention toward me with narrowed eyes, throwing me from my sexy daydream. Her eyes get big at the sound of a mumbled voice over the airport's loudspeaker.

"What'd he say? Was that it? Did they just announce her flight? I think that's her flight," she says, her eyes dart around the baggage claim carousel where we've been waiting for the last fifteen minutes.

Raven bounces on her toes like a kid who has to pee. My lips pull up. "Maybe you shouldn't have had that fourth cup of coffee this morning."

"She's not going to like me. She probably wants you with some sweet, homey girl who, you know, bakes or loves scrapbooking, not a car mechanic who can't even microwave popcorn." She looks around like she's mapping out an escape.

"You kick ass with a microwave, baby. Don't sell yourself short."

She glares at me, but her mouth ticks with the shadow of a smile.

"Baby, she's going to love you. Trust me. Now stop jumping around like a fucking pogo-stick and come here."

I throw my arm over her shoulder and she leans into me. Her muscles relax as my fingers trace along her skin.

"Excuse me, 'Assassin'?"

A tall, awkward boy in the throes of puberty approaches us. "Yeah."

He shuffles his feet and avoids my eyes. He's taller than Raven, but lanky. His messy brown hair hangs over his black-rimmed glasses. Printed in bold letters, his bright yellow shirt reads *Stephen King is my Homeboy.* I stifle a laugh.

"I thought it was you." He flips a pen in his hand. "I'm a big fan. I've seen all your fights." His voice cracks. "That take down against 'Pit Bull' Perez in oh-nine was the best I'd ever seen. I know you're going to beat Del Toro tomorrow."

Raven gasps, and her grip tightens on the back of my shirt.

"I can't wait to see the look on Del Toro's face when you hold up that belt."

You and me both, kid. Pride in my ability as a fighter and anger for my inability to prove it battle for dominance in my head.

"Thanks, man. I appreciate your support." This kid's got the height and the know-how. From the looks of his worn jeans, ratty shoes, and ...everything else, I'd guess he gets his fair share of assholes at school fucking with him. That's all any good fighter needs. Fuel. "You know your stuff. Any interest in fighting for the UFL?"

"Humph, I wish." He shrugs and runs the back of his hand across his forehead, making his glasses lopsided. "My mom says I'm too weak for sports." He scrunches his nose to straighten the frames on his face.

"What are you? About a buck fifty?"

"Just about."

"You start training, pack on a little muscle. You'd be a perfect welterweight."

His smile is so big that it looks as if it may break his face. "You really think so?"

"Think so? I know so."

"Wow. Thanks, 'Assassin.'" He stares at me, but his glazed eyes tell me he's in his head. Probably picturing himself as a fighter five years down the road. He blinks. "Oh! Can I get your autograph?"

He hands me a black sharpie marker and turns around, motioning for me to sign his t-shirt.

"Sure, what's your name?"

"Killian."

"No shit?" Great name for a fighter.

"Yeah." The backs of his ears turn bright red. "It's Irish."

I write a quick message on the shoulder of his shirt.

Killer Killian,
No one dictates your future but you.
"The Assassin"

I pop on the cap and hand Killian his pen.

"Good luck tomorrow night." He stands a little taller, his voice more confident.

"You start training, you hear me?"

He smiles, nods, then turns and walks away.

Raven's head burrows deeper into my chest. I instinctively pull her closer. Her arms wrap around my waist and she's no longer bouncing and jittery. "That was sweet. You're great with your fans."

I kiss her head. "Yeah, well, they've been really good to me."

But will they ever forgive me for letting them down?

"He seemed pretty confident that you'd win the fight tomorrow." Her voice is almost a whisper as her arms tighten around my waist.

I school my voice and try to be as convincing as I can. "Look, I don't want you to worry about this fight. Everything will go as planned. I'll get another shot at the title in a year, maybe two. It's just one fight. Okay?" The truth is I'm disappointed I won't be destroying Del Toro in front of a live audience tomorrow. But in this situation, the prize for losing outweighs the heavyweight title.

I search the room again for my mom. We fall into silence for a few minutes until I spot a familiar smile in the crowd.

"There she is." I lift my chin in her direction.

"Ohmygosh, ohmygosh, ohmygosh." It seems Raven's calm demeanor was nothing more than an intermission. She's back to bouncing.

"Joey, my baby!"

My mom rushes to us, dropping her bags and throwing her arms around my waist. At a generous five foot five, she's been hugging me around the waist since I was sixteen. It's been a few months since I saw her last, but she looks the same: Dark hair without a hint of gray, styled to perfection. Her stylish clothes, pristine makeup, and designer bag making her seem younger than her fifty-three years. Yep, hasn't changed a bit.

"Mom. This is my girl, Raven. Raven, this is my mom."

Pulling back, she takes a side step and grabs both of Raven's hands. "It's so nice to meet you, Raven. You're just as beautiful as Joey described."

"Nice to meet you too, Mrs. Slade."

"Please, call me Katherine."

"Thank you, ma'am …um, Katherine."

With Raven's hands still in her grasp, my mom looks at me. "You did good, son. She's beautiful and polite."

"Yeah, *she* is." I shake my head. "I still can't believe you thought I was gay."

Raven stares at me aghast while my mom shakes her head and smiles.

Dropping her hands, my mom slips her arm into the crook at Raven's elbow. "Come on, dear. Let me tell you about the time when my Joey was four and he ran around the front yard naked pretending to be a superhero called Super Weenie Man."

"Shit, Ma."

Raven giggles.

"Watch that mouth, Joey. You're in the presence of ladies."

Grabbing her bags, I walk behind two of the three women I love the most in the world.

"Jonah, wait up!"

I'm heading into the training center, after dropping my mom and Raven off at my house, when Blake's voice causes an about face. I have a quick training session and a short meeting I need to wrap up so I can get back to them for dinner.

"What's up, Blake?"

"Dude, we got problems."

We're standing on the sidewalk outside the training center's doors, and Blake looks around like he's checking for snipers.

"Ah, shit. What now?"

"Okay, I was at Zeus's last night and I ended up hooking up with this new girl, Sherry, or Terry ...Mary?" His eyes go skyward as he scratches his cheek and shakes his head. "Whatever. She mentioned that a guy—"

"Zeus's? I thought you tagged Camille last night?"

His body freezes. "Camille! I can't believe you unleashed that crazy..." He closes his eyes and rubs his temples as if to organize his thoughts. His eyes open and he glares at me. "We're gonna talk about that, but first the stripper."

I nod, unable to manage the smile that is wreaking havoc on my face. It's not often Blake has issues with girls.

"So, the stripper," he continues, "told me a guy named Dominick had offered her a job as an escort. I guess she thought that'd impress me." He rolls his eyes. "Anyway, she told me a few of the girls accepted his offer and—"

"You gonna get to the point where you tell me what the fuck this has to do with me?"

"Dude, listen. And stop interrupting. Shit." He folds his arms across his chest, hangs his head, and blows out a frustrated breath. "I asked her who accepted his offer. She said she wasn't sure, but that more than a few were interested."

"So? I don't give a shit what Dominick does. As long as he leaves Raven out of it."

"The new girl told me she overheard a convo in the dressing room. Dominick's hiring for a special job. One that takes place the night of the fight. At The Mandalay Bay Arena. You think that shit's a coincidence?"

"Maybe he needs some fresh girls for all the high-rollers that will be hitting up the fight. Dominick has to know better than to fuck with me on fight night. I'm going to be making him a rich man." Or, a richer man.

"I've got a really bad feeling about this," Blake mumbles.

There's nothing I can say. This whole situation sucks. The only thought that brings me peace is that, by Sunday, Raven will be all mine and we can move on with our lives. I rub my eyes and pinch the bridge of my nose to soothe the throbbing headache this conversation has brought on.

"Remind me when I decide to settle down to find a girl without baggage. Preferably one with no family." He holds up his hand and starts ticking off fingers with each stipulation. "No kids, ex-husbands, psycho dads, fucking skeletons in the closet. None of that shit."

"It's gonna take a special girl to put up with your ass, Blake. You got no room to be picky."

"I'm serious, man." He points at the ground. "I'd rather stay single my entire life, banging anyone who can keep up, than take on some chick with issues. You can tattoo that on my ass if you don't believe me."

The serious mask on his face tightens into a scowl. "Oh, and thanks a lot for pushing that crazy bitch Camille on me last night. I got her in the elevator, just about to do her, and you know what she said?"

I shrug. I'm still pissed at that chick for upsetting Raven, but I have to give her credit for freaking Blake out.

"She said if I wanted to get up in there, I had to prove myself." His voice pitches high. "She said I had to submit her to the ground before she'd let me fuck her. I'm looking to get off, and she wants jiu-jitsu foreplay. Who does that shit?"

Unable to hold it in a second longer, laughter bursts from my mouth.

"It's not funny, man. It's whacked. I had blue balls for two hours before Kerri, or whatever the fuck her name was, at the strip club got me off."

"I can't believe you couldn't get a submission on a girl. Maybe they can open up a spot for you on their team. Teach you a thing or two."

Blake's look of disgust only makes me laugh harder.

"Oh, real nice. You're a dick, you know that?" He stomps off and through the doors.

—

RAVEN

"So, Raven, tell me about your family. Does your mom live here in town?"

Water spews from my mouth. I choke and gasp for air.

"Oh, goodness, honey, are you okay?" Katherine hands me a dishtowel and pats me on the back.

She's been busy making dinner and filling me in on Jonah's milestones growing up. The subject change took me by surprise.

"Yeah, I'm good. Thank you. Just went down the wrong pipe."

"You scared me."

You think that scared you? Ask me again about my mom.

I'm not happy about opening the closet doors to my soul and revealing my dark secrets to the one person in the world

I want to like me. But, I can't lie to Jonah's mom either. She's going to find out eventually, and what will she think then? If I plan on being a part of Jonah's life, I need to be honest, upfront. What's that saying? The truth will set you free. *More like the truth will keep you single.* Maybe she'll forget if I change the subject.

She's cutting vegetables, oblivious to the fact that I'm about to drop a bomb directly on her sweet head. "So, you were telling me about your parents?"

Too late.

I'll talk around it. That will give her enough to be satisfied, and I won't have to tell her the ugly truth.

"My mom lives in town, yes, and so does my …um …my dad." Saying the word makes me want to spit to clean out the dirty.

"Are they still married?" Her questions are so casual and every day. Nothing more than a little small talk with the girl who's dating her son. *Boy, is she in for a surprise.*

Just get it over with! It'll be easier that way.

I bite my lip, working up my nerve. "Uh, no, they were never, um, married."

This sucks.

"Oh, that's too bad. What do they do? For work?" Her eyes are fixed on the task before her, chopping and dumping into a bowl.

"My mom is in sales." *Please, let that be enough.* My stomach churns. This already feels like a lie.

"What does she sell?

My shoulders slump in defeat. Might as well get it over with. I check the clock on the microwave. Jonah should be home soon. I wish he were here now.

"Herself. My mom is a call girl."

Her chopping ceases and she turns toward me, *the* question burning in her eyes. "Call *center* girl?"

I scrub my face with my hand. "Call girl."

Katherine's knife drops on the counter with a clang. Her eyes are huge and her mouth moves, but no sound comes out.

I'm not finished yet. "Her pimp …well, he's my …my uh … he got her pregnant."

She adds head shaking to the list of silent responses.

"I don't …or, um, never had a relationship with either of them." I exhale a long breath.

There. I did it.

My teeth rake over my lower lip. I count the tiles on the floor. Silent seconds tick. I prepare for the speech about my being trash and no good for her son. I straighten my spine, ready for her attack on my character. Dragging my eyes to meet hers, I lurch in shock.

Her eyes are the exact shade of Jonah's. And just like Jonah, filled with compassion. Not judgment. I relax a fraction under their gaze.

"That's an incredible story." Her voice is gentle and calms my nerves. "You must have been through a lot growing up. I can't imagine what it must have been like for you." She picks up my hand and holds it in hers. "You know what you are, Raven?"

I shake my head *no*, fearing that my voice will break the consoling cocoon her words provide. I'm desperate to know.

What am I?

"You're like that single wild flower that grows from the crack in the pavement: miraculous growth with no water source or fertile soil. A person walking by would step around that flower to avoid crushing it. It's not like the field of wild flowers you tromp through carelessly, crushing them under your feet, knowing that the next day will bring a hundred more."

She pauses to place her hand on my cheek. "You've managed a life through your obstacles. It may be a lonely life, but a life nonetheless. Surviving is nothing to be ashamed of. It's something to be *proud* of."

She sees me as worthy. Not a weight in Jonah's life, but special. A miracle.

I want to express what her words mean to me, but can't organize my emotions fast enough. Tears pool in my eyes. I blink, and they overflow as her speech runs on repeat in my head, leeching out the poison left behind in my soul.

She brings a kitchen towel to my face and wipes my tears. Her kind smile is more than I can handle and I sob.

"Oh, honey." She pulls me into her arms. I'm completely lost in her embrace. She holds me tight, speaking words into my hair about strength and release.

My cheek presses into her shoulder, soaking her shirt with my tears. I startle when a pair of strong arms pull me away from her. So deep in my sorrow, I didn't hear him come in. The familiar smell of citrus and spice relax my muscles, and I bury myself into Jonah's chest.

"Mom. What the fuck happened?" Anger laces his voice.

I can't see Katherine's face, but her whispered, "It's okay, Joey" has him relaxing against me. He takes a deep breath and holds me until I calm.

"Baby?" He kisses my head and rubs my back.

I lean away from Jonah, but he keeps his arms tightly around my waist. I wipe my face, feeling exposed and embarrassed. "Sorry. It's stupid—"

"No, Raven, don't do that. Don't belittle your strength with embarrassment. You have nothing to be ashamed of." Katherine's eyes are wet with tears.

I nod and simply say the only thing I can, "Thank you, Katherine."

Staring at Jonah's neck, I'm unable to lift my gaze, fearing what I might see in his eyes.

"Hey. Look at me."

I brave a glance.

He's smiling tenderly, bringing forth both dimples. "You okay?"

I nod.

"Right." He kisses my lips, then the tip of my nose, and finally my forehead.

"My son is lucky to have you, Raven. I'm very proud of him, and I'm equally proud of you."

Warmth floods my chest, flowing into my cheeks and pulling on my lips. I look from Katherine to Jonah.

"You girls have fun today?" He doesn't take his eyes from mine. His voice is soft and I appreciate the change to a happier subject.

We hang out in the kitchen while Katherine puts the finishing touches on dinner. Jonah steals pieces of food off the counter and she slaps his hand. For the first time, I see Jonah as a boy while he playfully teases his mom. I laugh as she reprimands him for drinking milk straight from the carton. She fills him in on his sister and her husband. He laughs at the stories about his nephews getting into trouble.

I'm nothing more than a spectator to this beautiful display of family. I watch in silence as envy piggybacks my happiness.

After a delicious meal, I excuse myself to clean the kitchen so Jonah and his mom can have some time alone. Drying the last dish and putting it away, I head straight to Jonah's garage for some quiet time with the Impala.

With my hair pulled back, I plug the iPod into the dock and allow the music to wash through my body, taking with it the multitude of conflicted emotions tumbling in my chest.

Some of the music from Jonah's iPod is familiar, but one song catches my attention. I read the name on the screen as "Halo" by Beyonce. It seems Beyonce knows a thing or two about my situation, as her words become my heart's anthem. I put the song on repeat and turn back to the car to bury myself in work.

Lost in the combination of my work and the music, I jump at the sound of the door opening. How long have I been in here?

"I knew I'd find you here." He wraps me in a hug. His body is warm and comforting.

"I wanted to give you and your mom some time alone. I thought I'd come out here until she went to bed."

He sits on the hood of the Impala, propping his heels on the bumper and pulling me between his legs.

"My mom is in love with you." He tucks a loose strand of hair behind my ear. "She flat out told me that if I didn't marry you she'd disown me. I think she likes you more than she likes me."

My cheeks warm. "She's incredible, Jonah."

"I'm glad you think so. You know, I was kinda hoping that someday she'd be your mother-in-law."

My eyes flash to his and a slow smile pulls at my lips. *Holy crud.* Is he asking what I think he's asking?

"Whaddya say? You feel like droppin' Morretti for good?"

TWENTY-SEVEN

JONAH

I'm not breathing. I'm waiting.

She's staring at me like I sprouted horns …and a tail.

I just asked her to marry me. Sure it wasn't your candle-light dinner, down on one knee, shed a tear kind of proposal. But it was a proposal. I don't know what came over me. It just came out. I don't regret the words, but fuck. What kind of a dick asks his girlfriend to marry him in his garage? I don't even have a ring.

I've known for a while now that I wanted to spend the rest of my life with her. I just haven't been able to focus on that. It's been more important that I focus on our immediate future and the fight.

But now, nothing's as important as her answer. Why isn't she saying anything?

I reach out and cup her face, running my thumb along her lower lip. "Baby?"

Her eyebrows pinch together. *Not a good sign.*

With a few rapid blinks, she focuses on me. "What if you win tomorrow night?"

Ah, fuck. Not this again.

No matter how many times I assure her that I can throw this fight, she's never totally convinced.

"I told you I'd lose it. I mean it. Now leave it alone." My words are terse and powered by irritation. I don't mean to be rude, but *fuck*. I just proposed, and this is the shit she wants to talk about?

I push both hands through my hair and take a deep breath. Her soft hand brushes my cheek. I look at her, my jaw cramping and eyes narrowing. She jumps, but quickly recovers, and places a lingering kiss on my cheek.

"I believe you can lose the fight, I do. But what if I say I'll marry you and then something happens? Something terrible, like you get hit too hard and flip the switch on Del Toro? Or what if, I don't know, he does something to forfeit the fight? You want to marry a prostitute? You want to share your wife with the wealthy men of Las Vegas?"

I grimace at the thought. No, I won't share my wife with other men. I'd fucking kill any man who came near her with those intentions.

Her expression goes soft and she nods. "That's what I thought. So what are our options? We could run, take off, live out our married days moving from place to place ...'til death do us part."

She brings both hands up to cup my face. "You deserve better than that, Jonah. Your mom deserves better than that."

"I don't want to live without you." Emotions surge within me making my voice rough.

A single tear trails down her cheek, betraying her smile. "And I don't want to live without you. Of course, I want to spend the rest of my life with you." Her expression hardens. "But I don't want to talk about the future. Not until we know, with one-hundred-percent certainty, that we have one."

So that's a yes. Right? A maybe? Shit.

"Nothing will keep me from you. I know what's going to happen tomorrow night. But if things don't go as planned, I'll take you away. Living a life on the run is better than living a life without you." I wrap my hand around the nape of her neck and pull her face close to mine. "*No one* can keep us apart."

"I love you, Jonah." Her hands run down my shoulders, and chest, settling on my abdomen.

My blood roars from the heat of her touch. I need her to understand that her life means more than my own. I'd give it all away: every dream, every accomplishment. Everything for her.

With a gentle tug, I tilt her head and hold her lips mere centimeters from mine. She closes her eyes and leans in for a kiss. I fist her hair tighter, holding her in place. A moan vibrates deep in her throat. We swallow each other's breath from our parted lips. Electricity buzzes between us. My teeth scrape against my lower lip with the urge to take her mouth. Her eyes dilate and her breath quickens.

She shifts and steps closer. The side of my mouth curls into a half smile. My girl. Always so anxious and ready.

She licks her full lips. Our mouths are so close I can almost taste the moisture her tongue left behind.

"Jonah—"

"Baby, you look so sexy right now."

She closes her eyes at my whispered words. I hold on tighter.

"Holding you like this, putting you close to what you want. It's hot, baby. You shift and rub your thighs together like you're trying to put out a fire."

She sucks her bottom lip into her mouth.

"You press into me, like you're hoping our bodies will melt together."

A whimper escapes her lips.

"Mmm. Love that sound." I flex my hips into her stomach.

Her eyes shoot open and plead with me to end to her suffering. Pissed or begging, smiling or crying, my girl is damn sexy.

My girl.

Dominick's words echo in my head. *I take care of what's mine.* His? The fuck she is. I don't care what I have to do tomorrow night to make it happen, but I will walk out of that arena with Raven under my arm and our entire future ahead of us.

I lean forward and brush my lips softly against her forehead. Her eyes flutter closed. I brush my lips against each of her eyelids, taking my time to savor the soft pear scent of her hair. Finally, my lips hover over hers.

"You're mine, baby. Always."

"Promise me." Our mouths are so close, her lips brush against mine with her words.

My chest cramps at the desperation in her voice. "I promise."

And that's all I can take.

I cover her lips with mine, and she immediately opens to me. Our tongues glide together in gentle strokes. I grab her hair, tilt her head, and delve in deeper. Soft, wet, and delicious. A groan pushes up from my chest and she takes it with an answering moan.

My ass planted on the hood of the Impala, I use my leverage to pull her tight between my legs. Her hands slide under the legs of my shorts and up my thighs. She pushes her soft fingers under the hem of my boxers and my hips roll into her touch. I let go of her hair with one hand and snake my arm behind her back.

"I love you." A storm of emotion and hunger swirl in my chest, making my declaration come out on a growl.

"I love you."

She pushes her hands the extra few inches to my throbbing hard-on. The muscles in my stomach contract as her touch sends waves of pleasure up my spine. With both hands, she grabs hold and strokes. I'm light headed. Her grip tightens as I rub and tease her breasts over her shirt. I want to go soft. Be gentle. But my hands claw at her clothes, itching to get to her skin.

Closer.

I break the kiss, grab the hem of her gray tank top, and pull it over her head. My eyes go wide at her bright red, lace bra. *Fuckin' hell.*

I slide off the hood of the car, mesmerized by her breasts as they strain against their lace cage. My hands cup her and squeeze gently. Her head falls back on a moan. I run my thumbs across her nipples watching how they react beneath the fabric.

My hands travel down her tight, flat stomach to the waistband on her shorts. With a swift tug, I pop the button and open to what I know is matching lace panties.

Raven shifts her hips and slides her short shorts down her long, tan legs. My head tilts as I take in her body from head to toe. Each sliver of soft skin, every curve of decadent flesh, all perfect and mine in every way. My eyes linger on the parts of her body I want to get to first, covered in red lace. I lick my lips.

"Your turn." She motions to my shirt with a tilt of her head.

I want her hands on me. "Uh-uh. You do it."

Her eyelids are heavy over blue-green pools of liquid heat. She slips her hands beneath my shirt, eyes locked on mine. Her fingernails drag against my skin as she runs her hands up to my chest. I suck air through clenched teeth as the bite of her nails sends pleasure straight down. I raise my arms and bend for her to pull my shirt off over my head.

 The weight of her stare on my naked torso shoots heat through my veins. She runs her hand along my arm to my shoulder while her other hand glides down to the button of my shorts. She stops there and slips her fingers inside the waistband of my boxer briefs, brushing against the tip of my dick.

My head falls back on a groan. I'm going to explode if I don't get inside her soon. I reach down to undo my pants.

Her hand covers mine and she pushes up on her tiptoes, placing her lips against my neck. "No, I got it."

Soft, wet lips part at my neck as she licks and nips while unbuttoning my shorts. They fall to the ground and I kick them off. I press her back against the Impala, placing her sexy, lace-clad ass on the hood. She lifts an eyebrow in question, but her crooked smile tells me she knows exactly what's about to happen.

She leans back, resting her weight against her elbows. I pin her with my eyes, plant my knee between her legs, and climb up.

———

RAVEN

His body covers mine, pushing me back. My stomach jumps at the thought of our naked bodies tangled together surrounded by the smell of oil and rubber. This scenario has run through my head a few times since I started working with Jonah. I rest my heels on the bumper as Jonah covers my face, neck, and shoulders with hot, wet kisses.

A fantasy come to life.

Just like his spontaneous proposal. Not at some romantic beach local or in some crowded restaurant. But here, in my sanctuary. No cheesy sonnets read down on one knee or even a ring. I don't need that. Any of it. All I need is him.

Sucking and nibbling, he makes his way down to my breast. He continues lapping at my skin before pulling my flesh into his mouth over my bra. The combination of his warm tongue and the friction from the lace make my back arch, pushing me further into his touch.

No one has ever claimed me like he has—stood his ground, willing to fight, just so he could have me. Our future depends on that fight. I may lose my future. I won't take his down with me.

His attention shifts from my breasts, and he kisses down my body. My knees fall apart. He settles himself between my legs, teasing my inner thigh with his tongue. I don't know what's going to happen tomorrow night, but for now, tonight, I am his and he is mine.

Completely.

With one finger, he traces the seam of my panties from my hip down. He slides the delicate fabric to the side and, without hesitation, dives in. A groan rumbles in the back of my throat. He slides both hands beneath my butt, pushing me deeper into his mouth. I rock my hips against him, unable to stay still.

My body ignites at his attention. With the slightest touch he brings comfort and, with a little more, intense ecstasy. But this time there's an extra layer of emotion. Belonging.

A powerful urge to bond rockets through my veins. Power, need, passion all mix into a potent cocktail and I'm overcome with desire to take him. I use my foot to push his shoulder back. He looks up at me, eyebrows pinched, hands up in surrender. Something that looks like concern etched in his face.

I want to give him a reassuring smile. Let him know that everything's okay, but animalistic yearning wins out.

With a quick flip of my thumb, I unhook my bra, sliding the straps down my arms and tossing it across the room. I lie back and lift my hips to rid myself of my panties. His eyes go dark, forehead dropped so he's looking at me from beneath his thick eyelashes.

If I don't move fast, he's going to pounce.

Hopping from the hood, I reach for the waistband of his boxers. He watches as I slide the cotton down his sculpted thighs to his ankles, where he kicks them to the side. In a crouch on the floor, I take advantage of my position and take him deep into my mouth.

"Aww, damn." He groans and rakes both hands into my hair.

I look up from my position on the ground and watch the ripples of his muscles contract with every thrust of my mouth. Here on my knees, in a position of submission, I've never felt more powerful. His body responds to every flick of my tongue, every pull of my mouth. My heart swells with the love I see in his face as he looks down at me.

"Baby, enough." He hauls me to my feet.

My hands on his chest, I press him back to sit on the hood of the car. He's stronger than I am and capable of protesting, but he allows my control. And if I'm not mistaken, I think it's turning him on.

With his back against the hood, I climb above his body, and straddle his hips. He cups my breasts. I give him a moment to play before I take his wrists in my hands and push them above his head. He smiles at me as if my attempt at domination is cute. I give him the wettest, sexiest kiss I can muster, wiping that smile right off his gorgeous face.

"Fuck, baby." He runs his hand through my hair, and rests his hand at my throat. "You're amazing. My sexy, shy girl one minute, sex crazed vixen the—"

I take him in my hand, lift up on my knees, and bury him. He groans so deeply it vibrates our connection.

"Mine." My possessive claim tapers off into a moan.

And with that, my dominance is over. His hands tangle into my hair and his back leaves the car. His kiss is deep, proving the word I've just said.

Yes. I'm yours.

Exultant tears burn the behind my eyes. I fight to hold them back. My hips roll in waves and Jonah matches my pace. I kiss his jaw, neck, and shoulder, pushing him back against the hood. Bracing my hands on his brawny chest, I thrust harder, pressing down deep, reaching.

"You're so beautiful, baby. I love watching when I'm inside you."

I'm beyond words as pleasure coils in my belly. His thrusts become urgent and powerful, spurring on my frenzy. My body is overflowing with sensations, begging for release.

His eyes spark beneath heavy lids. "Let yourself go, baby."

My body obeys his command. Tiny explosions fire from low in my belly and shoot up my spine. I grip his shoulders and throw my head back. He holds my hips steady as reverberations rock through my limbs.

Lost in the foggy aftershocks of my climax, our positions flip. I lie flat on my back on the hood of the car, and absorb the heat from where Jonah's body was. My heels brace on the bumper, my knees fall open. I bring them back up, but lack the strength to keep them there.

Jonah leans down and drops a tender kiss on my lips. I kiss him back with lazy strokes of my tongue.

He straightens and grips my hips. Entranced, I watch the slashes of his muscles roll as he finds his release. He bites his lip, and I gasp at the blissful pinch of his fingers digging into my skin.

His pace quickens moments before he groans my name. Goose bumps race across the planes of his chest and ecstasy floods his face. He slows to a glide, sending delicious sensations to my belly. He falls forward, braces himself with his arms, and kisses me.

This kiss isn't fast or deep, not a beginning to a desperate end. His lips are firm, molding against mine. We explore each other's mouths in tender strokes. Patient and meaningful, expressing the love between us with every swipe and passing nip.

He breaks the kiss and looks at me. His eyebrows knit together and he looks over his shoulder.

"How many times has this song played?"

My face heats as I try to think of a way to get out of having to explain my song choice and the fact that it's been on repeat. Your iPod must be broken. I accidently hit a button. I don't know why the same song keeps playing. Remember, I only own tapes. The list of excuses keeps growing. I settle on indifference. "I think it's Beyonce." I shrug.

His eyes narrow at me. *Darn it!* He sees right through me every time.

"Yes, I know who it is. I remember putting it on the iPod for you." His eyes dart to the side as he listens to the words. He hits me with the deadly one-dimple smile. "I guess you like it?"

I nod and turn my face away. Avoiding his eyes will help the red coloring my cheeks to fade.

"I like this song. It…"

"It what?"

The softness in his voice tells me he's well aware of why I like it. Why does he need to hear me say it?

I exhale a heavy breath and meet his eyes. "It reminds me of you. You're my saving grace, Jonah. My angel." I wiggle my arms between our bodies and cross them over my chest. "Happy?"

His teasing smile dissolves. His dimple is replaced by a slight tick in his jaw. He doesn't look angry. More like, confused.

I feel stupid and exposed after my sappy comment. "Can we go inside now?" I hope to get that intense look off his face or at least get me out from under it.

He blinks and his expression softens. "It's funny, this thing between us." He flicks his finger back and forth from me to him. "Every concern or emotion we feel, it's mutual." He laughs in a short burst. "Here you're thinking I'm saving you, when all this time it's been *you* who saved me."

My heart swells to the point that I'm choking on it. "Jonah—"

"I was cold. Dead on the inside from the time I heard about my dad's accident. Never felt anything outside of kicking ass or a killer hit in the octagon. Fighting gave me my breath, but you brought me back to life."

I whimper and cover my mouth.

"This whole time I thought I was living. But the day I met you, the lights came on. You fill me with things I thought I'd never feel again." His hand tugs my at my wrist, freeing my gaping mouth. He kisses my lower lip. You're *my* angel, baby."

With my world split in two, ultimate devastation runs parallel to blessed elation. And I'm stuck in between. My future uncertain, staring into the hazel eyes of everything I've ever dreamed about. And more. More than I deserve, but I'm taking it.

I'll hold on with a grip so tight, that even if they take my body, they'll never take Jonah from my heart.

TWENTY-EIGHT

RAVEN

"What're you doing here, Ray?" Leo walks into Guy's office as I'm putting my stuff in a locker. "Thought you'd be spending the day with your man? Big fight tonight."

I suck in a shaky breath. Big fight is right. That's why I'm here on my day off. Jonah has to go to the training center, and there isn't enough work left to do on the Impala to keep my head in a good place until tonight.

"Nah. He's got official UFL stuff to do all day. I'm going to meet up with him after the fight." I put on my most unaffected face and stroll past Leo into the garage. "What have we got?" I motion to the few cars in the bay.

"You can run a diagnosis on the Tahoe. Said it's making some clinking noise. Check the alternator." He goes back to working on a Toyota.

Greatest thing about working with guys, they never ask too many questions.

I start work on the Tahoe, my hands moving through the procedures, but my head wrapped up in tonight. Flutters of nervous energy turn my stomach and tighten my chest. My phone rings in my pocket, making me jump three feet in the air, and earning me a lowbrow look from Leo.

"Hey, Eve." I greet my friend loud enough for Leo to hear. He rolls his eyes and disappears back beneath the hood of the car.

"Rave. Ugh, I'm so pissed right now." Her voice sounds genuinely pissed, and she's huffing and puffing like she's just run a marathon.

"Why? Are you okay?" I head back to Guy's office, close the door, and flop down in his chair.

"Hillary came in two nights ago with the stomach flu. I told her to take the night off, but did she listen? Noooo." She grunts loudly and I hear something heavy drop. "So here I am, forty-eight hours later with six, *six* people short for dinner service tonight. On one of the busiest nights of the summer."

I know where this conversation is going. My nervous flutter turns into a throbbing pound. She's not coming.

"I have to work. There's no way around it."

Darn it.

"I understand. It's a bummer, but you're the manager. What can you do?"

"Um ...I could kill that bitch Hillary for starters." More banging.

"What are you doing? It sounds like you're trashing your house."

"Oh, what am I doing?" Her voice is high and dripping in sarcasm. "I'm setting up the bar. By myself! I have one bartender tonight. One! Man, I need a drink."

I rub my forehead. How am I going to get through this night without my best friend?

"Where's the after party?" Her question gets my attention.

"After party?"

"Well, yeah. Duh. The heavyweight champion throws an after party following a big win. Jeez, Rave, how long have you lived in this town?"

"Right. Um …okay." There will be no big win, therefore, no after party, but she doesn't need to know that.

"I'll be off by eleven and I'll meet you guys out. Just make sure to have Mr. Pecs-n-Abs put me on the list."

Her mention of being put on the list reminds me of Vince. "Hey, have you heard from Vince?"

Her throat clears followed by an even bigger bang that has me pulling the phone from my ear. "Nope."

One word answer. Translation: *I don't want to talk about it.*

"You okay?"

"Fine."

One word again.

"I'll text you after the fight."

"Sounds good. And Rave, I'm really sorry."

"No worries. I'll see you tonight."

I end the call as a new layer of dread falls on my shoulders. At least I'll have Katherine there with me. He's going to lose this fight. Everyone will be devastated, but at least I'll be free for us to be together. That's all that matters.

I punch out a quick text to Jonah.

Eve called. Emergency at work. She's not going to make it. ☹

I'm holding the phone in my hand when it chimes seconds later. New text.

Sorry, baby. Ask Guy? xJ

I never thought to ask Guy. He'd love to go to a UFL championship fight, and I'd love the extra support, even if he has no clue what's at stake.

Great idea! ☺ I love you.

I'm already dialing Guy's phone number from the garage line when my phone chimes again.

His ticket will be at will call. See you in a
few hours. I love you more. xJ

—

JONAH

My drive to the UFL Training Center is silent. Usually on fight day, I surround myself with deep, bass-hitting music. It always helps me to get pumped up, ready to destroy my opponent. Not today. I'm lost in the weight of my thoughts. My strategies for the fight play in my head on an endless loop.

Stay away from the jaw. Take him to the ground, lock him down. Keep moving. Do not get hit in the face.

My pulse pounds with adrenaline for the fight. But tonight I'm amped for a different reason.

After tonight, this mess with Dominick will be over. Raven will be free and clear to live a long happy life.

That's if I avoid flipping the switch. I've never, not once, been able to control it from happening. A groan rumbles in my chest. There's too much on the line for me to doubt myself. I will control it tonight.

Before I know it, I'm pulling into the lot at the training center. I jump out of the truck and head to the door in a daze. My head is a whirlwind. I focus on my pre-fight checklist to keep my mind off the emotion.

Weigh-in, strategy meeting, warm up, arena.

I quicken my pace through the parking lot as a few photographers snap pictures.

"'Assassin,' you ready for the fight tonight?" The reporter has a microphone at the end of his outstretched arm.

With a tug to drop my baseball hat lower, I ignore him and keep walking.

"Is it true that fighters never have sex before a big fight?" another reporter shouts.

Fucking idiots.

"Do you have a lucky charm of some kind? Dirty socks or a jock strap?"

Do they really expect me to stop and give them an answer? I force a smile their way, pulling off a sneer at best.

Pushing through the doors, I'm hit with cold air that prickles my skin. Blake's sitting alone in the lobby, obviously waiting for me.

"Blake."

He stands and meets me halfway to the hall. His eyes work the room before coming back to me. "You ready for this shit, man?"

I nod.

"All right, dude. I got your back. We do this as planned, shouldn't be any problems. You're home in bed with your girl, naked if you're lucky, by midnight."

A grin pulls at my lips. "Got it."

Blake drops his signature crooked smile and his jaw goes hard, eyebrows dropped low. "Let's fucking do this shit!"

He claps me on the shoulder and leads the way into the locker room. My entire team is there huddled in the back, waiting. I'm greeted with fist bumps and chin lifts.

Guilt eats away at my insides. My crew has worked just as hard as I have to get me this fight. They've trained with me non-stop, taken punches, suffered injuries, all for me. I'm letting them down by not going out there and giving it my all.

I sit on a bench, elbows on my knees, focusing on the ground. I force myself to pull an image of Raven to the forefront of my mind: her wide, innocent, aquamarine eyes. That's it. I need to keep my mind right here.

"You ready?" Owen says as he plops down at my side.

"Ready as I'll ever be." I fix my eyes to the floor. It's a dick move, but I'm hoping he brushes it off to me getting in the zone.

"Good enough. Let's warm you up and get you to weigh-in."

My body moves through all of the pre-fight bullshit, but my mind is absent. I pop in my earbuds and listen to music, mentally walking myself through every round. The guys don't talk to me much, only direct me where to go and what to do. Every now and then I catch a look from Blake. His jaw set, eyes cold, but knowing. We seem to share the same thought. Let's get this shit done.

We load up into a white van and head to the arena. The streets are lined with tourists, fans, and paparazzi. I'm grateful for the dark, tinted windows and the inconspicuous car that allows us through without hassle. The driver avoids the front entrance and turns down a ramp to a private parking garage where he parks beneath the arena.

Blake turns around in his seat. "It's show time."

We unload from the van where we're met by a man in a suit. He introduces himself as the event planner and takes us to our assigned dressing room.

The space is about half the size of the locker room at the UFL Training Center. Two large leather couches line the walls with a coffee table in between. The floor has been covered with padded, interlocking mats that provide cushion for a grappling warm up. A heavy bag hangs in the corner, along with some boxing mitts. A small refrigerator sits in the opposite corner, probably stocked with water and a variety of sports drinks.

I drop my bag of gear next to a couch and take a seat while the guys on my team talk to the planner. Blake turns from the group, stalking toward me. His face is hard. Shit. Once he reaches me, his hand motions to his ear for me to pop out my earbuds.

He points to the door. "Motherfucker's sending in chicks."

A woman in this room would cause the exact opposite environment that I need. Before a fight it's all about relaxation. A relaxed mind is a sharp mind. The last thing any of us need is some chick in here kissing ass.

"The fuck you say?"

I shift to the side on the couch to look behind Blake. My team is hovering over the event planner, pointing in his face. The poor suit looks like he might shit his pants. I sit back, shrug, and lock eyes with Blake.

"It's probably just something the networks orchestrated for ratings. They come, they sit in the corner and keep to themselves. They keep the fuck away from me."

"Been fighting here for years and never had chicks in the dressing room." Blake's eyebrows lower over his eyes. "Gibbs knows we need calm before a fight. Why would he agree to this shit?"

"No clue. But lately this publicity shit is leading him around by his dick." First Camille, now this. He seems less about the fight and more about the ratings.

Blake nods then turns back to the team and the suit. I pop in my earbuds, drop my head back, close my eyes, and pull up my girl's face.

The couch dips next to me. I look up to see Blake mouthing something at me, and squint to read his lips.

"…fucking told you that dick was up to no good."

I catch something out of the corner of my eye that makes me do a double take.

Candy.

What the hell is she doing here? Before the question registers in my mind, it's answered.

Distraction.

Candy and a girl I've never seen saunter around the room, asking if there is anything anyone needs. They're both wearing what amounts to Hooter's uniforms, minus the owl. Their red shorts look like they're painted on and their tank tops look more like sports bras.

Fucking Dominick.

"Wes!" My blood is boiling and I'm itching for a fight. I shake my head, half furious and half impressed with Dominick's play.

If he can't distract me, he'll piss me off enough to want to kill someone then put me in the octagon.

My head trainer turns and walks to me. "What's up, Jonah?"

I stand and meet Wes eye to eye. "I want those girls out of here. Now." My voice is a low growl.

He looks over his shoulder and back to me, his eyes narrow. "Those girls?" He tilts his head, motioning to Candy and her sidekick.

"Yeah, Wes. Those girls." I throw my arms out and look around the room. "Who the fuck do you think I'm talking about? They're the only fucking girls in the room!" Blood pounds in my ears and a low buzz rattles in my head.

"Get 'em out of here, Wes. Seriously." Blake's voice is low and threatening at my side.

Wes steps over to the girls and says something I can't hear. They both look my way, and I spear Candy with a glare that I hope sends fear through her veins.

Her smile disappears and her eyes hit the floor. The girl with her is going into some long explanation about something and Wes listens. After a few minutes, he makes his way back to me.

"They can't leave. They've been assigned to the room. If they leave, they're afraid they'll get fired."

"That's bullshit!" Blake turns toward the girls. I grab his elbow.

Fuck it. I don't have the brain space to worry about this shit right now. I'm falling right into Dominick's trap by getting fired up. He wants me half-cocked before I get to the octagon. I won't give him the satisfaction.

"It's cool, Blake. You just keep that bitch away from me."

I suit up and hit the heavy bag. Every punch and kick relieves some of the anger polluting my focus. Blake and I move through some grappling techniques, and I feel the last of my tension dissolve.

Dominick thought he could goad me? Wrong.

Feeling back to myself, I go back to my place on the couch. Owen hits me up with the twenty-minute warning. Finally.

Behind my closed eyes, I play memories that make me relax. My dad and I playing ball in the front yard, him hugging my mom in the kitchen when he'd come home from work. Raven's face alight with laughter, her peaceful expression when she's deep in sleep—

A small hand brushes my knee then shoots straight up my shorts. My eyes fly open. I grab the hand and still its progression. Pressing it to my inner thigh, I pin the offender with my stare.

Candy is sitting on the coffee table, her body between my knees. She's leaning forward in her barely-there clothes, her palm against my skin under my shorts. And I'm holding it there with my hand. Fuck.

The room is almost empty except for a couple guys, who are currently being distracted by Candy's friend.

I rip her hand from my leg and stand, towering over her. "Nice try, bitch. Next time you put your hand on me, I'll break it."

She pulls free from my grip, fear working behind her eyes. She schools her features. "Whatever. Can't blame a girl for trying."

It's time to end this.

TWENTY-NINE

RAVEN

My knees are bouncing like the pistons on a Ferrari. I have a burning urge to run laps around this arena, but the fear that grips my gut keeps me planted in my seat.

I'm grateful for the executive car Jonah had pick us up. I don't think either of us could drive with these nerves.

The driver made sure to get us here just before the title fight, opting to forgo the opening fights at Jonah's request. He feared they might freak me out. He's right.

Where's Guy?

Last time we spoke, he said he'd be here for the opening fights. He's not.

I grab my phone. No missed calls. I call Guy again. No answer. *Darn it.* Maybe his phone battery died, or he left it at home.

"Still no answer?" Katherine is beside me, her hands folded tightly in her lap. She must be nervous too.

"No." I shove my phone into my pocket. "I can't imagine what's keeping him. He seemed really excited to come tonight."

Katherine rubs my back then re-knots her hands in her lap. "I'm sure he'll be here soon."

My fingers drum against the plastic seat of my folding chair, a furious beat that matches my racing heart. I scan rows of

people surrounding the octagon. The crowd hums with anticipation, bloodthirsty. So close to the octagon floor, no doubt
I'll be able to hear the thud of fist on flesh at this distance. My
stomach plummets.

I check the glowing digital numbers on the clock above the
octagon. Eighteen minutes and thirty-seven seconds, thirty-six,
thirty-five. They tick down, one by one, just like my freedom.
Numbered in minutes. I wipe my sweaty palms on my jeans.

A warm hand stills my twitchy leg. "Calm down, honey.
He'll be okay." Katherine misinterprets my anxiety.

Watching Jonah get hit in the octagon will be difficult, but
I'm more concerned with his acting skills than his fighting
skills.

I nod, smile, and fix my eyes back on the clock. *Where is
Guy?*

The seats in the arena fill up quickly as people return from
their bathroom and concession stand breaks. The air is heavy
with energy and aggression. It could be my imagination, but
the smell of blood and sweat seem to linger in the air from the
earlier fights. As the main event draws near, the arena comes
alive, chanting.

"Assassin, Assassin, Assassin…" Over and over, ratcheting
my tension.

I wonder if Jonah can hear this from his dressing room. I
wish so badly I was with him now, allowing the warmth of his
skin and soothing words to comfort me. My arms wrap around
my body. He'd hold me close. Probably tell me to breathe and
relax. He'd tell me everything is okay and he's going to take
me home tonight as his, for good.

Jonah's corner is empty. No familiar faces in sight. I look up
the aisle. They must all be in the back with him. The thought
brings my heart rate down and the muscles in my shoulders
ease up their grip. We'll be together soon enough, but for now

it's good he's surrounded by his team. I'd probably only make him worry.

Eight minutes, four seconds.

"Hey, Raven. This seat taken?"

My back stiffens at the grating voice. Candy. Swift air brushes my arm as she sits in the seat to my right. I turn to look at her, certain my face conveys my shock. My jaw falls slack as I take in her clothes. Not clothes, more like a modest bikini.

I'm speechless.

"Hello. Are you Raven's friend?" Katherine reaches her hand across my lap towards Candy. "I'm Katherine Slade."

Candy leans in, pressing her hard, fake boob into my arm, making me cringe and recoil. I stare in amazement as an angel and the devil shake hands. In my lap.

"Yes, I am." Candy's tone nauseates me. "It's nice to meet you, Mrs. Slade. I'm also friends with your son. We're very close." Her words are said to Katherine, but the way her eyes slide to mine, they're meant for me. *Bitch.*

"Oh, really, you know Joey?"

"Yes, I do. We've been close for a while now." Her saccharine smile and overly painted face lean towards Katherine. "As a matter of fact, I just left him backstage."

My heart cramps violently. I lock my narrow eyes on her. She was with him?

"I don't understand. You were with him just now?" Katherine sounds as confused as I feel.

A wicked smile stretches across Candy's face, and I wouldn't have been surprised if she had fangs. "Yes. He's doing great. A little tense, so I rubbed his shoulders forever." She draws out the last word as she rubs her hands and flexes her fingers. "My hands are killing me."

Fucking bitch!

Shocked, I meet Katherine's eyes. She looks …disappointed. She believes Candy. Well, I don't.

With my elbows resting on my knees, I drop my head into my hands, rubbing my temples. This is not happening. If I get into it with Candy, that will only upset Katherine. But if I don't call her out, then Katherine will think her son is a low-down, dirty dog. What do I do?

I love Jonah and I trust him more than anyone. Candy is lying. I bet she wasn't even back there with him. For the first time, the familiar creeping doubt that normally seeps in is absent. He's putting everything on the line for me tonight. Putting everything he's worked for aside for me and our future. I'll be damned if I'm going to let Candy make him out to be anything less than the hero he is.

My shoulders relax and I sit up straight. I turn into Candy's face as she forces an innocent expression, and fails.

"You know what, Candy?" I'm ready to unleash on the evil slut.

"So, Raven, what are you doing here anyway?" Candy starts talking as if I hadn't even opened my mouth. "Jonah told me you weren't able to come. Something about, hm, what was it?" She snaps her fingers. "Oh, yeah, something about getting a new job with your father? Dominick?"

Katherine gasps, and my jaw locks down, making my teeth ache.

How does she know about Dominick? Jonah and Blake are the only two people who know. My head spins. How else would she know that unless she was back there? Talking about me. They would never do that.

None of this makes sense.

Unless?

She's working for Dominick.

My heart pounds and I want to scream. Adrenaline fists my hands. I can't lose it here. Not in front of her. I won't give her the satisfaction. But one thing's certain: I need to get out of here.

"Excuse me," I mumble and stand to leave.

"Raven?" Katherine stands next to me, her eyebrows pinched together.

"I'm fine, Katherine. I'll just be a minute."

I scoot past Candy into the aisle, grasping my hands together to keep from backhanding her. She coughs to cover her snicker. I whirl to face her, giving up my restraint. *One slap. Then I'm out of here.*

The lights go dark. The room explodes in a fan-crazed roar. I'm frozen in place, unable to see in front of me. A spotlight cuts through the darkness. The top of the stairs illuminates a group of very large men. A man wearing a black shirt that says "Crew" in yellow across his chest ushers me back, telling me to take my seat. Back in place, Katherine grabs my hand.

"Ladies and gentlemen, welcome to UFL one-ninety-eight." The announcer's voice fills the room.

The crowd roars and my shoulders tighten with tension.

"Six-time Heavyweight Champion, Victor 'The Bull' Del Toro, will defend his title against the undefeated Jonah 'The Assassin' Slade."

A mix of boos and cheers ring in my ears. Katherine's grip tightens. The driving bass of Jay-Z's song "Niggas in Paris" fills the dome-shaped arena, sending the fans into a frenzy. The air electrifies my skin, every hair standing on end.

"Let's welcome our challenger. Ladies and gentlemen, put your hands together for Jonah 'The Assassin' Slade." The announcer's voice draws out his name and my body breaks out in goose bumps.

A bright light flashes to the top of the stairs. My eyes squint and burn trying to make out a familiar face. Out in front of the group are Rex and Caleb, but I've never seen them like this before. Their faces are masks of concentration. Their bodies are taut and unforgiving. They descend the stairs with the bravado of well-trained soldiers. I struggle for breath, suffocated by the anticipation in the air.

As the group walks down the steps, each member of the team comes into view. Wes walks behinds Caleb and Rex, then Blake. His teasing eyes and easygoing smile are replaced by determination. I search for Jonah's face in the group. Fans stand on their chairs, yelling and reaching to get to Jonah in the center of his crew. Security guards line the aisle, holding people back.

My hand squeezes Katherine's tighter and I push up on my toes. I get a quick glimpse of the tips of dark mussed up hair.

There he is.

His face comes into view and I'm completely floored. He looks positively deadly and more beautiful than ever. My heart almost beats out of my chest. His eyebrows are low in a fixed state of focus, making his eyes look black. His full lips are held in a tight, straight line, framed by his set jaw. The muscles under his colorful skin seem bigger as they flex under the light. I suck in a breath and throw my hand over my gaping mouth.

I've seen Jonah train and he seemed lethal then. But now, he looks homicidal. I say a silent prayer that this is all an act, because the way he looks now, he'd snap at slightest provocation.

They move down the stairs, passing rows of screaming fans. His team is circled around him protectively. They reach the bottom and walk down the aisle of our section. Then the group stops short. Right at our row.

I'm frozen, my eyes burning and stuck on Jonah's face. He turns his head towards me as if he's responding to my call. His eyes don't search, but land right on my face. Caught in the ferocity of his stare, I hold his gaze. A one-dimpled smile touches his face just long enough for me to see before it disappears and the focus is back.

That's it. He's letting me know that this is an act. I take a deep breath and smile back, huge. He gives me a wink and throws a quick look to Candy. His intense glare makes her cower.

Take that, bitch.

And with renewed hope, I watch the group continue down the aisle and into the octagon.

—

JONAH

"...sixth time returning Heavyweight Champion Victor 'The Bull' Del Toro."

Standing in my corner of the octagon, I wait for Del Toro to make it down the aisle. I find my girl in the crowd. She's holding my mom's hand. *Thank you, Mom.*

And why in the hell is Candy sitting where Guy should be? Maybe he couldn't make it? But that doesn't explain why Dominick's slut-bot is in his place.

It was one thing to see Candy waltz into my dressing room like she belonged there, but seeing her standing next to Raven is unsettling. I thought I scared her enough to get her to back off. Apparently whatever Dominick is paying is worth her continued humiliation. Candy spent the entire time in my dressing room, sitting in the corner on a plastic folding chair. Blake even made her and her slutty sidekick face the wall just to make a point.

I force my thoughts back to Del Toro and the fight. Nothing can throw me off my game. Not one fucking thing. Ten minutes. I need to stay up for the first two rounds. After that, game over. My eyes slide back to Raven like they're magnetized.

"Get your head in the fight, Slade. Your girl's still gonna be there when it's over," says Owen from behind me.

I nod. He's right. I need to focus on the fight and keep the buzzing in my head down to a minimum. Candy works for the enemy, and seeing her so close to Raven makes me wish I'd locked my girl in the bedroom. Maybe I shouldn't have had her come tonight. I could have set her up somewhere, far away from here, until the outcome was determined. But I need to see her face to stay grounded, to control the rage that'll be riding me hard.

Del Toro stands in his corner, giving me the stare-down. I'd give almost anything to knock that confident look right off his scarred face. Almost.

The ref motions for us to meet in the middle of the octagon. He gives us the speech they always give before a fight about no hits below the belt and make it a clean fight. His words may as well be spoken in Japanese as much as I'm paying attention. Instead, I'm locked eye to eye with Del Toro. The ref yells something and then repeats it. It's on the repeat that I hear he wants us to tap knuckles. Fuck that.

"You're going down, you little bitch," Del Toro growls as he takes his fighting stance.

He has no idea.

I raise my fists and we face off. My blood sizzles with restrained aggression.

The ref waves his hand between us. "Fight."

Del Toro and I circle each other, sizing each other up, fists at the ready. I focus on his hands, keeping his legs on radar. The crowd roars over shouts from our cornermen. Mine yell, "Take a hit!" His shout, "Take him down!"

Del Toro turns his fist, palm up, taunting me. "Come on, pussy. Take a shot."

My jaw grinds against my mouth guard. This cocky fuck thinks I can't lay him out. I have to let him take me. I mock swing. He flinches. *Yeah, fuck you.*

"Get movin', guys," the ref says. "Fans didn't pay to watch two fairies circling the maypole—Fight."

No more milking the clock.

I drop my guard. He throws the quick left. I dodge it. The crowd cheers. We circle again, and his right leg sweeps at my feet. I jump back. I feel the buzz in my head. My muscles coil. I find my groove and right jab a heavy body blow. He doubles, winded, but recovers. His fist comes at me. I duck. Shit. If this fight goes to decision, I'd win. I need to get hit.

I rush Del Toro and slam him against the fence, holding him in a clinch. A barrage of punches hammer my back.

My leg snakes around one of his, keeping him off balance. He attempts a knee to my thigh, but my hold locks him down. He tries for a chokehold. I bury my shoulder deeper into his chest. My body constricts around his. The clock ticks on.

"Break it up!" The ref pushes us apart.

Arms raised, I stand back. The ref waves his hand between us. Fight's back on.

Del Toro comes at me, head down, aiming for my gut. His signature move. He's going for the take down. The split second before he hits, I check the clock. Thirty-two seconds left. His shoulder slams into my abdomen, taking us both down. I land on my back, my lungs contracting for breath, and he straddles my leg in half guard.

Shit. Not good.

He rears back for the ground-and-pound. I throw my head to the side and cross my arms to protect my face. Blow after blow pounds against my forearms. Pain rockets through my body. The buzz a steady hum in my head. Adrenaline shoots through my veins.

With my free leg, I brace my foot against the mat. The blows continue. Ringing in my ears, the buzz goes nuclear. I need to get to my feet.

My heel digs deep. I thrust my hips, bucking Del Toro off. I've got the mount. I pull back, landing a blow that sends blood to the mat. My instincts want blood, but I can't knock him out. Instinct versus Raven.

A horn sounds and the black-and-white striped shirt of the ref is in my face.

Round one over.

I jump to my feet and head to my corner. My head starts to clear. Shit, that was close. My cornermen shout orders at me while I rinse my mouth out. Blake stands back, and my eyes meet his. He raises his eyebrows and tilts his head. He knows what happened. I came seconds away from flipping the switch. I nod. He holds up one hand, all five fingers splayed. Five more minutes. I need to hold it together for five more minutes. He drops his hand and motions to the octagon.

Round two.

Del Toro's bleeding. Fuck, I need to get hit more. Focus. Concentrate on the end game. My girl.

In the stands, Raven covers her mouth. She looks scared. Five more minutes, five more fucking minutes and she's mine.

"Round two," the ref yells. "Fight."

Focus. We move close, fists raised. Del Toro throws a hard right. I don't block it. It connects with my jaw. Lightning shoots down my neck. The buzz in my head is now a battle cry. I'm gonna kill this fucker.

I hit him with double strikes to his stomach. He steps back, gasping for breath. He comes at me with a quick jab to my ribs. Pain blasts through my side. I double over, but stay on my feet.

We circle each other. He throws a left. I dodge it. He's open. One right hook would knock him out. I punch his ribs.

He stumbles. I'm dying to finish this. I could take him down right now. Easily.

My eyes lock on his fists. He sweeps at my leg and connects. Pain throbs in my calf. I hop to regain my balance.

I unleash my restraint, my right fist slamming into his reddened ribs. He grunts and doubles over. My hands drop to my sides with a satisfied smile. Fuck, that felt good. I lock eyes with Raven. Hers widen, flick past me. I spin. His right knee flies up, I move back, but it's too late.

Two-hundred-fifty-seven pounds of force slam into my head.

Pain explodes at my ear. Bright white light flashes behind my eyes. My vision recedes. I stagger. My body hums. My mind empty, but for one thought.

Annihilate.

Del Toro steps into my space. I throw a right. My haymaker connects with the sweet spot on his glass jaw. His mouth guard flies in an explosion of blood and spit. He goes down.

Rag-dolled.

Game over. *Oh, fuck.*

THIRTY

RAVEN

"Ladies and Gentlemen, your new UFL Heavyweight Champion, Jonah 'The Assassin' Slade." The announcer's words reverberate in my soul, raising the hair on my skin.

He won.

I drop to my seat as everyone around me stays standing. The voices of the fans are slow and slur in my ears. Their faces contort with the force of their excitement. I blink and grip the sides of my chair.

He won.

Katherine leans down and hugs me. My body shakes as she continues to jump up and down. She says something, but submerged in my misery, I can't understand her. I absently nod, my focus distant, as I force my brain into action.

What do I do now?

I can't think of anything. Except him. My body aches for him, wanting to be held, to cry in the safety of his arms. Together.

As long as we're together, we can face what Dominick has planned. It's not too late to run. I could go somewhere remote, live low for a few years until Dominick loses interest. Tiny sparks of hope flare. That's what I'll do. I need to get to Jonah and get out of town. Now.

A jolt from my hip sends me to my feet. I press the pocket of my shorts to feel it vibrate. My phone. Who would be calling me now? I check the caller ID. New text from Guy? Guy doesn't text.

> Hello, Darling. If you want to save his life, you'll follow Candy. Failure to comply will end him. Slowly. You have five minutes. –D

He has Guy. Holy shit!

That's why he never showed. Dominick has him. My breath catches on a sob. I grip at my neck and swallow hard. He'll kill him if I don't cooperate. I don't have time to get to Jonah.

"Four minutes and counting." Candy grips my arm firmly.

I glare at her hand. She's in on this. Lying bitch.

Katherine continues to cheer as she glories in her son's victory. Her love for her son shines in her radiant smile. That same love that poured over onto me, even if only for a day. And now it's over.

Candy tugs my arm.

"Get your fucking hand off me!" My demand is firm, but soft enough for only her to hear. "I'm coming." I rip my arm from her grip. "Just let me say good-bye." I don't give her an opportunity to respond and turn to Katherine.

I let the love in her face reflect in mine and muster a smile before leaning in to be heard over the crowd. "Candy said Jonah wants me back in the dressing room. She has a pass so she can take me back." I lean back from her to look in her face.

"Oh, of course, honey. You go congratulate our boy. I'll meet you guys at home." The pride in her smile aches in my chest.

I throw my arms around her neck and hug her good-bye. "Thank you, Katherine, for everything." My throat swells as I muzzle the emotion that fights for release.

"Oh, well," Katherine says, seeming surprised by my sudden burst of affection. "Thank you for making my Joey so happy."

Released from the hug, she smiles, her face shadowed with concern. I nod with a smile then face Candy. My smile dissolves.

"Okay. Take me back."

My legs are heavy as I trail behind Candy up the stairs. We pass through the double doors and into a long hallway.

This is it. I'm being kidnapped. But my life is a small price to pay to ensure Guy's safety. Katherine and Jonah's safety. I should have known better than to fight destiny. Fight Dominick.

We stop at a single door. Nausea claws at my stomach. A rowdy group down the hall walks towards us. I wonder if it's Jonah and the guys headed back to their dressing room. If he saw me with Candy, he'd never let me go. Panic surges in my veins. If he sees me, Guy dies. I drop my gaze, my hair hiding my face.

Two quick knocks and the lock clicks. Candy moves forward and I follow through, head down.

Once in, I turn my focus to the room. The door slams behind me, and I'm plunged into darkness.

I gasp. My hands reach out for something to hold onto.

"Hello, darling."

I whirl around toward the direction of the door. My body slams against something solid. Arms wrap tightly around me. I struggle against the hold. Deja vu stills my body and stifles my scream. Why is this so familiar? Flashes from the night in the parking lot of Club Six spark my memory.

Oh God, no. Vince.

"Fancy meeting you here." Vince's low chuckle vibrates against my back.

"No. Dominick, please don't do this." I search desperately around the room for a face to plead with, but the dark is too thick. "I won't run. Just please, leave Guy alone."

Vince tightens his hold. Air is pushed from my lungs on a whimper.

"And I'm supposed to take your word for it?" Dominick laughs and brushes his hand against my cheek. "Don't you worry, Raven. I will take what is rightfully mine. What I created. You can't run far enough or hide deep enough to escape me."

I jerk my head aside, away from his touch. Vince shakes me roughly then loosens his grip.

Responding to his words with pure instinct, I suck in air to yell. A soft cloth is pressed to my face. Stinging vapors pull deep into my lungs, my eyes roll back in my head. I kick and jerk. I'm going to die. My muffled screams echo in my ears. Darkness creeps in. Jonah, help me. Then, everything goes black.

—

JONAH

A tornado of applause whips and swirls around my body. Static roars in my ears along with my hammering heartbeat.

Del Toro is down. The ref yells, "Knockout."

Failure rocks me, weakening my knees. I drop to the mat. Only a minute and a half left in the round, and I would have had it. I watch in slow motion as my team climbs the chain link. They rush toward me, faces alight with victory.

I search out the one member of my team still standing on the outside. Blake. His glare meets mine. Whatever he sees brings life to his body, spurring him into action. He hops the fence, pushing his way through people. I'm detached, a bystander in my own skin. My conscious mind struggles with reality. It ended so fast. I just …snapped. I won the title, but lost the prize.

Desperation brings me back. Voices go from static to clear as I regain my senses. I need to find her. I sit back on my heels.

My eyes magnify the faces around me, like binoculars, bringing into focus my surroundings. I search the crowd. A mob of people block my view, jarring me from all angles. They yell, patting my shoulder. My back. My head.

"Find her." The mumbled words are a weak command to my body.

Blake drops to his knees in front of me, his hands on my shoulders, forcing my attention.

"Do not lose your shit, man. Lock it down, you hear me." His voice is commanding, his words a touchstone to my sanity.

I hold his eyes and fight against the tide of crippling emotions that pull at my soul.

"There ya go. Hold your shit, man. Stay focused on me."

I look at him, but don't see him. Instead visions of my future flicker through my mind. Raven in white. A little girl with aquamarine eyes and my dimples, pigtails and pink ballet shoes. My girl in my bed, every night, forever. Everything I just lost.

Blinking away the burn, I swallow hard. I lurch forward, on all fours, fighting the rising bile. A stabbing pain rocks my midsection, and I spit my mouth guard to the mat.

"Don't do this now, man. Not here."

"I lost her." My voice grates against my throat as I force out the words. I can't believe it. I couldn't save her.

"No. *You* don't lose. 'The Assassin' does not lose." He grips my shoulders, pulling me to my feet.

Breathing deep, I force a nod. My skin feels tight surrounded by people in my space. I need to get out of here. I can't think straight.

I need Raven. To touch her and remind myself that she's real and …still here. Her birthday isn't until tomorrow. We have a few hours to get out of town. Disappear. At least until we can come up with a better plan.

On a visceral quest, I push through the crowd. No faces, no familiarity, just bodies. Obstacles that stand between me and Raven.

At the octagon's perimeter, I search the arena, scanning the crowd. Where is she?

A microphone is shoved in my face. "'Assassin,' how does it feel to be the new UFL Heavyweight Champion?"

"No questions." Blake's voice draws my attention. He tilts his head towards the octagon's exit.

From there, I scan the seats where Raven was sitting. People crowd around the octagon. Security pushes them back. My eyes pick apart each person, and, still, no Raven.

"Where is she?"

Blake grips the chain link, focused and scanning. "They're gone. They were right there." He points to the row of seats they were in just seconds before the fight ended.

My hands rake through my hair. No. This cannot be fucking happening. My aching muscles contract as my fists tighten. She couldn't have gone far. I continue to scan the area, hoping her face will appear in the crowd. Still nothing. I'll pick this entire place apart, one motherfucker at a time, until I find my girl.

"'Assassin!' Great fight! Can you tell us what it feels like to have won—"

Blake shoves the reporter in the chest, sending him back and landing ass to mat. "No fucking questions." Blake towers over the downed reporter before turning back to me. "Shit." He sounds annoyed as if the guy was nothing more than an obnoxious mosquito.

He looks over my shoulder.

"There's your mom." Blake's voice rises above the roar of the crowd. I follow his stare.

She's standing at the floor of the arena, on tiptoes, eyes searching. In a few long, purposeful strides I'm in her space.

"Mom, where's Ra—"

"Oh, Joey, you were great! Congratu—" She moves to embrace me, but I catch her wrists, forcing her eyes to mine.

"Mom. Where's Raven?"

Her smile falls and her eyebrows pinch together. "Raven? Honey, Candy took her back to your dressing room, just like you asked her to."

Dread drops in my stomach, threatening to bring me to my knees.

"Fuck me. I knew that skanky-ass ho was up to no good," Blake says from behind me.

Mom's face pales and her eyes implore mine. "Jonah, what's going on?"

My feet burn with unspent energy. I don't know what the fuck's going on. But I'm sure as shit going to find out.

I race up the stairs two at a time. Weaving my way through the crowd, I shove people aside when they don't move fast enough. I burst through the double doors and run down the corridor to my dressing room. My foot hits the door with the force of a battering ram, splintering the wood frame.

"Raven. You in here?" I rush through the room in search of my girl. But even as my hopeful eyes continue their search, I know she's gone. This was Dominick's plan all along. Send Candy in for distraction and extraction. Like placing the last piece into a puzzle, everything now makes sense.

I flip the coffee table upside down. "Fuck!"

Raven is in the hands of a madman. My hands rip through my hair. I should have known Dominick would pull some back-handed shit. Now my girl is with a psycho who uses his own daughter as a pawn in his sick games.

Resolve burns deep in my chest. My heart pounds with intent. The buzz between my ears throbs and floods my body.

My veins surge with revenge in lethal potency. A plan forms in my head. My lips curl as my teeth clench.

I'm going to get Raven back tonight. I don't care who I have to kill to do it.

———

RAVEN

I float in a void, a black hole, tossed on waves of dark smoke. No feeling. Just …nothingness. A faint sound taunts me. Calling me to its comfort. I want to move towards it, but can't grip consciousness enough to move.

An urgency to fight the dark fuels my blood. I push against the fade. The sound gets louder. The soothing vibrations tickle my ear as I try to place it. The sound is as familiar as my own name. I concentrate harder.

An engine. A small one, sedan maybe.

I push harder and hear a moan deep in the distance.

Is that me?

The engine is joined with the rhythmic beat of music. I strain to hear it and surface from the murky depths. Feeling returns to my body in sections of warmth like a hot towel lying on bare skin. I orient myself. I'm on my side. My eyelids are heavy as I push to get them open.

I wiggle my fingers and roll my wrists. They're tied together. My mind struggles to place myself. I remember Katherine. My heart cramps. The fight. Jonah. The text. Candy.

Fucking Candy!

Adrenaline fuels my muscles and I force open my eyes. I'm in the backseat of a car. The driver is a man; that much I can tell from the back of his head. No other passengers. I swallow what feels like razor blades. How long have I been out? I clear my throat to speak, getting the attention of my driver. His head whips around and I muffle a scream.

I'll be happy to make it your business …all night long.

"Good morning, sleepyhead. Have a good nap?" His wicked laugh crawls over my skin, making me curl into myself.

Faced forward, he tilts the rearview mirror, his eyes on me. They glow in the light of the dashboard. He looks demonic.

"Where—" I clear my throat. "Where are you taking me?"

His reflection glares at me. "We're going on a little road trip."

"What happened? Where's Jonah?"

"I have an idea. Why don't you go back to sleep or pretend to be asleep so I don't have to hear your voice? Or better yet, you shut your fuckin' mouth, or I'll climb back there and shove something in it."

Tears burn my eyes and my throat clogs with emotion. I nod and vow to keep quiet for the rest of the trip.

An orange glow draws my attention. I peer through the gap in the front seats. A clock. The numbers ground me—give me something to hold on to. Just like before the fight, I watch the minutes tick away, along with my future. As the minutes stretch by, I make myself sick. Every imaginable horror comes to mind. Jonah doesn't know where I am. I'm alone with someone who hates me enough that killing me would be kind.

As many times as Jonah has swooped in like an angelic warrior to rescue me, my predicament is impossible. No one will help me now. If I'm going to get out of this, I'm going to have to do it myself.

The car turns. I tilt my head to look out the window from my back seat bed. My view is a wall of pine trees. We're in the mountains, and from the sound of the creaking suspension and gravel assaulting the wheel wells, on a dirt road. After another twenty minutes, the car slows to a stop.

Vince exits the car, giving me seconds of relief before the back door swings open and he grabs me by my bound ankles. He throws me over his shoulder like a dead animal. It's completely black outside. Darkness like I've never seen having lived in the city my whole life. There's a source of light ahead that penetrates the night. Vince heads toward it. He walks up a few wooden steps before we go through a door and into the living room of a cabin.

He turns left and I'm airborne. My wrists bound, I'm unable to break my fall and my head slams into something solid. Stabbing pain pierces my skull and I swallow an agony-riddled cry. Warm liquid oozes down my face, pooling in my ear. My vision swirls.

Vince's footsteps against the wood floor disappear behind me.

I squint against my throbbing head. I'm on a couch with wooden armrests. I worm my body around and face the direction we came in. Plain wood flooring and log walls are all I see. This place isn't set up for a long-term guest. More like a place for a weekend hunter. And here I am tied up like prized kill. How ironic.

A door slams shut, making me jump. My muscles coil tight, every sound amplified. Heavy footfalls sound down the hallway getting louder. Closer.

Please, God. Help me.

Dominick and Vince appear from the mouth of the hallway. Their fine suits and coiffed hair are a morbid contrast to the natural wood of the cabin.

"Raven, darling, I'm sorry about your head. Vince is great muscle, but tends to be a bit brutal."

Vince smiles and licks his lips.

"As I'm sure you've figured out, your boyfriend won, or lost as it was, so now you belong to me." He kneels and places his lips just inches from my ear. "Between you and me, win or lose, I had no intention of releasing you."

My eyes burn. I stare at the man before me whose eyes are identical to mine. The man whose blood runs through my veins, and I feel nothing but pure, concentrated hate.

He reaches into his pocket, and with a flick of his wrist, he's holding a knife. I kick and pull at my restraints. No!

"Calm down." He sounds bored and not at all impressed by my fight. He points the knife, gently pressing the tip into the soft skin beneath my ear. "You be a good girl now or I will cut you. Do you understand?"

I nod frantically, forcing the tip of the knife farther into my skin. A whimper leaks from my lips. He watches as a trickle of blood makes a trail down my neck.

"So beautiful." He swipes at the blood with his fingertip and puts it in his mouth. "You are going to make your Daddy a very rich man."

Every inch of my body shakes in violent bursts. He slides down the couch to my feet and cuts my binds. Then follows with my wrists.

I flex and roll my ankles and wrists. Sitting up, my head swims. I steady myself, blinking away my nausea. Something tickles my cheek. I swipe at it and see blood on my hand. *I'm going to be sick.*

"Dominick, may I use the bathroom?" My voice quakes with fear.

He tilts his head and studies my face. I focus on his neck so he can't read my intentions in eyes. He must be satisfied with what he sees and nods.

I push up, ignoring my sore wrists and throbbing head, and search for a bathroom. The first door in the hallway is open. I rush in, shut the door behind me, and try to find the lock. Dammit! No lock.

Panic and fear collect in my stomach, sending me to the toilet an on my knees. I gag and cough, arching my back with every painful heave. Bile-flavored spit coats my dry mouth, making me retch harder. The smell of my own blood flips my stomach again. A violent heave rocks my body until my stomach surrenders. I try to catch a breath, allowing the tears to fall freely. I sob with my head resting on the toilet seat. My hand does a quick search of my pockets for my phone. I knew it wouldn't be there, but desperation has me grasping anyway. I'm stuck. Out of options.

What's going to happen to me?

THIRTY-ONE

JONAH

"Open the door!"

Nothing. I knock harder.

"Dude, calm down. You're gonna scare the piss out of her." Blake's leaning against the brick wall outside Milena's house while I bang the fucking door down.

I pound wood again. "Milena. Open up!"

Blake's expression sours with disapproval. "Yeah, Milena. Open up for the enormous scary guy beating the shit out of your door." He tacks an eye roll onto his sarcasm.

Shit. He's right, but we're running out of time. Dominick has my girl, and she could be getting farther away with every minute that passes. They could be in fucking Mexico by now.

After leaving the arena, we went straight to Raven's place. We let ourselves in with the spare key I kept after having her door replaced. It didn't take long for us to find what we were looking for. Who knew an old bank statement would mean more than the Title belt. Finding that felt like winning the lottery and being the first man on the moon all wrapped up into one. The address on that statement led us here.

Milena. She's our only hope. If this doesn't work, I don't know what else to do but go to the police. And if Dominick finds out, which he will with all the moles he's got planted in the department, Raven's as good as dead.

Resolve thickens my blood and brings my fist back to the door. I hold it back and breathe. Calm. Just one minute of her time is all I need. I flex my fist and knock lightly.

Nothing.

I swear to shit if she doesn't open this motherfucking door, I will bust the fucker down and drag her ass out. Ah, hell. So much for calm.

"Milena, it's Jonah. I'm…" I squint against the vicious buzz pounding in my head. "He's taken her. Do you know where he would have gone with her?" My forehead rests against the door. "I need to find her tonight. Just, please, open the door." Seconds of silence feel like hours. What am I going to do?

A click of a lock jolts me back. The door cracks open. Milena's eyes are cautious as she peers out just beneath the protective chain. My breath catches in my throat. She looks so much like Raven. I rub my chest to squelch the burn.

"He took her?" Her voice is soft and carries the hint of a Latin accent.

"Yes. From the arena."

She stares through me with unfocused eyes.

"I need to know where he might have taken her. Anywhere you think he might be. Addresses would be great, but a general vicinity is fine too."

She blinks and meets my eyes. "Come in."

The door closes enough to unhook the chain and opens slowly. I walk in with Blake at my heels. Milena's eyes widen when she sees I'm not alone.

Before I can introduce Blake, he's in her space.

"I'm Blake." He extends his hand to her. She places her small hand in his, but locks eyes on me. I nod.

Her shoulders drop along with her eyes. "Milena." Her apprehension isn't unexpected. I imagine working for a man like Dominick hasn't instilled much trust in men.

"We're going to need your help in getting our girl back. You up for that?" Blake must've come to the same conclusion, his voice the equivalent of kid gloves.

"Mm-hm." She nods and Blake releases her hand.

As crude as he can be, the guy has a side that evokes trust, especially in women.

"Please, sit down." She motions to a couch in the living room. We head in, but I'm too antsy to sit.

I survey my surroundings, surprised by the lack of hominess. The house I grew up in has family photos all over the place, along with knickknacks picked up from family vacations and trophies won by my sister or me. This place feels more like the waiting room of a doctor's office than a home. Cheap, decorative art hangs on the walls, matching throw pillows arranged on a couch that looks like it's never been sat on. And Raven grew up here? My chest cramps.

"Milena, I know you don't know me."

She backs into the couch and sits, her hands obsessively picking at the hem of her sweater.

"But, I'm in love with your daughter. I need to get to her. I can't call the police—"

"No." Her eyes focus on me, her one word confirming that the police won't do shit.

"Right. You're the only one who can help me. Please."

She stares across the room. I turn to Blake. He points to his watch. We're running out of time. Milena has retreated into herself. It was just like the photo Raven took of her the day she left home.

I squat to her eye level. This woman has caused the girl I love more pain than I can stomach. I see-saw between wanting to scream at her and wanting to worship at her feet. She holds the key to my future.

"Look, I know you and Raven have ...issues. And I don't know what you've been through or why you did the things you did. But I know your daughter. She doesn't want this life. If you feel anything for her, if you care for her at all, then please help me."

Her gaze swings to mine. "There is a place. In the mountains. He takes some of the girls there after..." She looks to her lap. "Girls in my profession sometimes get pregnant. He takes them there to have the procedure done and for recovery."

My stomach lurches. That sick-ass motherfucker! These girls, scared out of their minds, he takes to a non-medical facility so some hack doctor can scrape out their insides. I rub my head to numb the buzz that roars between my ears.

"It's where she was born." Her voice is just a hair above a whisper. But the words ring like they came from a bullhorn. "The cabin. He'll take her there." Her eyes bore into mine with an intensity that I can't argue.

"Where is it? Do you have an address? Name of a town?" The questions roll from my head in rapid fire.

She jumps to her feet and heads to the kitchen. Seconds later, she returns with a piece of paper and a pen. Frantically, she starts sketching.

"It's off the Interstate towards the ski resort. You'll pass through a small town with a diner on the side of the road. The sign looks like a wagon wheel. After that, maybe fifteen minutes or so, there will be a turn off on the right-hand side. Take that until you hit a fork in the road," she explains while drawing it out. "Right at the fork and follow that." She hands me the paper. "It's the only thing out there. You can't miss it."

I bolt through the living room to the front door. Blake meets me there, door open and waiting.

"Jonah!"

I stop and turn to Milena, her eyes brimming with tears.

"Bring her home safely, and," she looks at the floor and my heart breaks as the gesture reminds me of Raven, "tell her I love her."

"When I bring her back, you tell her yourself."

———

RAVEN

The dark is contagious. It spreads from the simple absence of light to something bigger. Something that seeps in through your eyes and multiplies until it takes you over. Starting with your mind, it works its way through until it extinguishes the last spark of hope you have hidden deep in your heart.

Everything is dark. The moonlight spilling through the window is only bright enough to illuminate a square on the dirty floor. The smell of wood rot matches the creeping dread that fights to become my only companion. But I won't lose hope. Not yet. Sooner or later, their guard will drop. I'll run and live in the woods like that boy who was raised by wolves. If it means having my life back, Jonah back, I could do that.

I've watched the moon square move across the floor. Dark stains pepper its surface. Is that blood? What happens in this room? I race to the window and push up on the lever to open it. It doesn't budge. Again. Fear floods my body. Air rushes in and out of my lungs in erratic bursts. A sob crawls into my throat. I hold it back. I won't let him win. I push it down, numbing myself from the inside out. Detach. Separate my mind from my body. That's the only way to survive.

I lie back on the bed, the only piece of furniture in the room. Calm, deep breathing, eyes closed. I imagine the bed beneath me is Jonah's. He's next to me, his arm thrown over my stomach. My heart rate slows. His breath kisses my cheek as he whispers how much he loves me. My muscles relax. He twirls a strand of my hair around his finger. The corner of my mouth lifts.

Footsteps. I'm thrown from my fantasy. My body sits up ramrod straight, eyes wide.

Each step is tentative, like someone sneaking down the hall. They sound close as the wood floor creaks outside my door.

My heart races. Could it be Jonah?

I rush to the door and press my ear to it. The knob to the door jiggles and twists. I walk backwards until my legs hit the bed. Hope and relief surge through me in waves.

Tears build at the joy of seeing Jonah again. My skin itches for his touch. I'm practically bouncing on the balls of my feet. The door inches open, revealing the tall, dark figure of a man.

I squint into the dark. "Jonah?"

"Nope, but you can go ahead and pretend. Won't bother me at all."

Vince. My stomach plummets. Terror snakes through my veins.

He shuts the door behind him and locks it with a key. With a slow strut, he comes toward me. He passes through the moonlight square, illuminating his face. His eyes work my body, making his intentions clear. I want to scream, but dread freezes my most primitive reaction.

"You thought I could let you go after what your boyfriend did to me in that parking lot?" He runs the tips of his fingers from my shoulder down to my breast. "It's payback time."

No. My head moves from side to side, unable to articulate the words. Fear, exhaustion, and anxiety get the best of me.

He shoves me onto the bed. I scurry backwards as fast as I can. He grabs my neck, pushes me down, and climbs on top of me. I whimper. It's not much, but it gives me hope.

React, fight, something.

"You be quiet and I'll take it easy on you. If you fight, I'll enjoy that, but you won't."

Holding my wrists together over my head with one hand, he reaches down and unzips his pants.

Oh God, please no.

He pins me to the bed with his hips. I kick and buck to get out from under him.

"Fight it is." He licks my neck and bites my earlobe, hard. "This'll be fun." His breath smells like liquor. I turn my face to avoid it.

"Stop." It's weak, but as the word comes out so does the will to survive. "Get off—"

His hand silences me. My arms ache. My struggle is pointless.

He presses himself between my legs. Twisting and tugging, I try to rip my arms from his grip. Pain rips through my elbow. The only thing keeping him from his goal is my shorts. His weight crushes my body. He anchors me tighter to the bed. His mouth crashes against mine, drowning my screams. I fight and thrash, forcing myself deeper into the bed. *Jonah, I need you.* My mind screams for him to burst through the door.

Break his arm, baby. Arm bar. Remember, Raven. Fight.

I squeeze my eyes shut as Jonah's voice stills my racing thoughts. Tears trail down my temple. It may be panic or some innate survival response, but my lesson on the arm bar comes back in brilliant clarity. I can do this.

That's my girl.

Waiting for the opportunity is going to be the hardest part. I need to stop fighting so he can free his hands. I breathe deep and stop squirming.

"Change your mind? Not going to fight me anymore?"

I shake my head no.

"Yeah, I knew you were a whore."

He slides his hand over my breast to the button of my shorts. With one hand, he pushes them down my thighs. Unable to get them past my knees, he lets go of my wrists and sits up.

Opportunity.

I say a prayer for strength and move quickly. I grab his right wrist with both hands. His eyes dart to mine. I throw my leg over his arm, straddling his shoulder. He jumps in surprise. Bracing my weight on my shoulder blades, I cross my legs at my calves. His arm runs the length of my body, from knees to chest.

He struggles and grabs at me with his free hand. "You little bit—"

One powerful thrust of my hips turns his words into a scream. I pull his arm tight and flex my hips deeper into the hold. I feel and hear a sickening snap at his elbow. Vince howls in pain.

I did it.

With a tight hold, I refuse to let go. I keep my hips thrust forward and he continues to yelp. Power surges through me. He's crying out for me to release him. I'm locked down with an unrelenting grip. He kicks and hollers on the bed.

Light pours into the room, blinding me. I push my hips harder, making Vince cry out. Something wraps around my neck …hands. They clamp down, choking me. I gasp and writhe. My vision adjusts to the light. I stare into the blue-green eyes of Dominick. His face is red with anger, jaw clenched tight.

And he's not letting go.

THIRTY-TWO

JONAH

My truck eats up highway as we blaze down the interstate. Hands vise-gripped to the wheel. Eyes scanning. Exit signs fly by in a blur of green and white. Blake is silent beside me. His head dips to the hand-drawn map then forward and back again.

I play out my strategy. No more polite conversation and deal-making. I know Dominick won't give up Raven easily. Not after what he went through to get her. He had this planned all along, including hiring Candy to do his dirty work. I should have known.

Inwardly, I berate myself for buying into his bullshit. How could I have been so stupid? Well, that shit ain't happening again. There are only two ways this confrontation will go. Dominick beaten into a bloody pulp, left begging for his pathetic life, or Dominick dead. And I'll have to accomplish this while keeping Raven safe, or more importantly, alive. *Fuck.*

"Turn left here." Blake's direction calls me from my thoughts.

A quick turn and we're on an unpaved road. I hit the four-wheel drive and lay heavy on the gas. Dirt and rocks spit from my back tires as we weave through the narrow mountain roads. My eyes focus on the path ahead.

"Fork in the road." Blake points ahead.

I don't have to look at the map to know which way to turn. Milena's handwritten instructions are branded in my mind.

"Pull off. Park in the trees." He drops the directions on the dash and grabs the handle for a quick exit.

"Pop the box and grab my Eagle." I toss him the key to my glove box.

Within seconds the cold metal of my fifty-caliber Desert Eagle warms my hand.

I check the clip. Fully loaded. We hop from the truck and hustle back to the dirt road. I shove the gun into my waistband at my back.

We jog down the tree line, making sure to keep to the shadows. The cool mountain air invigorates me. It's close to two in the morning. The title fight was only a few hours ago. It feels like ages. I should be exhausted, but I've never felt more alert.

We cross to the other side of the road where a small light shines like a beacon through the trees.

"That's got to be it." I don't wait for Blake's response, and take off toward the light.

The rickety A-frame cabin stands alone in the mass of pine trees, a one-lane dirt driveway leading to it. It's small, probably two bedrooms at most. This shit shack looks like it's made of scrap wood and spit. If I weren't convinced Raven was inside, I'd drive my truck full speed through the front fucking door.

We step closer, cautiously keeping to the dark in the trees. She has to be here. Some deep part of me whispers she may not be, but I choose to ignore it. This is my only chance of getting her back.

Something catches my eye from the side of the shack. I creep closer, tucking in behind the trees. *Bingo.*

"They're definitely here." I motion to the hundred-thousand-dollar Benz parked in the trees next to a black Lexus sedan.

"What do you want to do? Just knock on the door and start busting caps in his pompous ass?" Blake's idea would usually make me smile, but there isn't a hint of humor in his voice. He's dead fucking serious.

"Let's check out the windows first, try to get an idea of what we're dealing with. If I can't get a handle on what's going on in there, I'll kick the motherfucking door down."

"Sounds like a plan." Blake moves toward the cabin.

I grab his shoulder, needing to say something before we do this. "Whatever happens in there, you get her out. Understand?"

His eyebrows drop low. "If shit gets ugly, I'm not leaving you—"

"Don't worry about me. Just get her out and far away."

Blake puts his hands on his hips and drops his head, a string of curses flowing in a whisper.

"Promise me."

He meets my eyes, his jaw tight. He shakes his head.

"Blake, please."

His gaze swings to the treetops for a second then back to me. "All right. I'll get her out."

"Good." I nod. "Now let's take this fucker out."

We run low to the ground to the cabin. I motion for Blake to take one side of the shack, whispering for him to check the windows. We'll split up and meet in the back.

I edge up under the first window and peek inside. An empty living room. No furniture except for a wooden-framed couch. The embers from an old fire smolder in the fireplace. My eyes scour the area. No sign of Raven.

With my back to the wall, I slide to the next window. It's frosted glass, probably a bathroom. I press my ear to it. Nothing.

In a few more steps, I'm at the back of the cabin. Blake is just rounding the opposite corner. We meet at a single window, our backs against the wall on either side. The low vibration of angry voices rumbles against the glass, but the words are indecipherable. With a nod, we glance inside.

"Holy shit," Blake whispers through clenched teeth.

It's dark in the room, but light from the open door is enough to illuminate the scene. Vince and Dominick surround a small bed. They're hunched over, like vultures picking away at their prey. I don't have to see who they're holding down to know who it is.

Adrenaline shoots through my body, injected by a rocket launcher. The roar of my pulse pounds between my ears. An instinct to kill rushes down my spine, juicing up my muscles. My skin vibrates with lethal energy.

Get the fuck off her!

I need to draw them away, redirect their attention. I grab my gun, point it at the assholes. *No.* I can't risk hitting Raven.

With a flip of my hand, I use the gun's butt, and smash the window. Glass shatters, cutting through the silence and causing Dominick and Vince to spin around.

"Well, fuck. I guess it's on now." Blake's words ring from behind me as I race to the front door.

I kick it open. The walls rattle.

Pop.

Light flashes. I stumble back. Pain explodes in my shoulder and down my arm. I blink, pushing against the nausea and agony that threatens to take me down. The fucker shot me.

"Shit. You okay?" Blake's question is nothing more than static to my main concern.

Where is she?

I scan dimly lit room, blinking away the floaters from the flash of gunfire. Standing at the mouth of the hallway is Dominick and Vince. Both with guns raised. Vince's is smoking.

"No, Jonah!" Raven's voice comes from the hallway. *Thank God, she's alive.*

The confirmation sends renewed strength to my mind and muscles.

I straighten from my tortured huddle, sucking air through my teeth. *Fuck, this hurts.* Then point my gun with my good arm. "Let her go, Dominick." My voice sounds stronger than I feel.

"You broke into my home, Mr. Slade. I could kill you right here, in cold blood, and get away with it." Dominick's voice cracks with anger or frustration. I'm not sure.

"Dominick, please don't." Raven's appeal ends on a whimper.

Is she hurt? I search in her direction, but can't make her out in the dim light. She's blocked in the hallway behind the bulk of the dicklicks who brought her here.

"Not true, asshole. In order to get away with it, you'd have to stay alive. And I can promise you, if I go down, so will you." My aim is steady, head clear. I breathe deep and heavy, working past the pain.

"Well, we can put that to the test, although, I'd rather not have to deal with hiding dead bodies tonight." Dominick's tone sounds genuinely put off.

"Cut the bullshit." I step closer, making sure to speak slowly so he understands. "I will not leave this place without her."

His lips curl back over his teeth. "Oh, but you will. We made a bet. You lost."

Waves of failure wash over me. "You had no intention of letting her go, did you? If I'd lost the fight, you'd just walk away?"

A chuckle rumbles from deep in his chest. "Brains and brawn. Impressive. And here I thought you were just a dumb jock."

I fucking knew it. This guy plays by his own rules. I can't believe I fell for it.

My injured arm moves on its own accord to steady my aim.

"You're de—" *Dammit.* Pain blazes at my shoulder.

Vince snorts with laughter. "Not so strong now, are ya? You may have taken me down in a surprise attack at the club, but I dare you to come at me now."

Blake pulls a large hunting knife from the back of his pants. He spins it in his hand before he takes a fighting stance. He gives me a quick chin lift and focuses on the men across the room.

"Let me go." Raven pushes at her captors, trying to get past.

My blood screams to get to her, to throw her over my shoulder and kill anyone who stands in my way. It's my only option. I move. Dominick yanks her to his front, his gun at her head. I stop mid-stride.

"Not one more step, Slade." His gun is pressing against her temple, her head turned away from the weapon, eyes screwed shut. Her chest heaves with heavy breaths or possible hysteria.

I push the urge to kill down deep. Right now, I need to make sure she's unharmed.

"Baby?" I need to see her eyes, read in her expression that they didn't hurt her. *They better not have hurt her.* "Baby, look at me."

My gun is on Dominick. His on her. Vince's moves back and forth between Blake and me.

"Jonah…" Desperation laces through my name as her words trail off. She blinks open her eyes and turns toward me.

Her stare is wild, the aquamarine almost glowing against their red rims. A large, bleeding gash cuts through her eyebrow. White-hot fury explodes deep in my chest. Visions of what could cause that kind of wound flash before my eyes. None of them good. I mentally shake away the possibilities of what would've happened if we hadn't gotten here when we did.

Going rat-shit crazy won't help anyone and may jeopardize her safety. I need to focus on keeping her safe.

I lock eyes with her, hoping to God she sees something there that makes her listen. This shit is about to get ugly, and I need her as far away from it as possible.

"Baby, are you hurt? Anywhere besides your head?"

She shakes no. "I want to go home. Jonah…" Hysterical cries burst from her lips.

My stomach twists. "I know, baby. I'm here to take you home." I pin Dominick with a glare. "Let her go."

"Not a chance." Dominick pushes the gun harder into Raven's head, making her wince.

My finger twitches against the trigger.

"You don't know what they did…W-What they were going to…" The sound of her soul-shaking sobs rip through the small room.

"I'm finished talking, Slade. Walk away. Now. Or she dies."

I ignore Dominick. "Raven, everything's going to be okay." The look of terror in her eyes has me inching closer to comfort her.

The movement sends Dominick's gun in my direction. *Good.*

Vince closes in. Blake follows suit. Tension boils in the air like acid. It's a four-way standoff. Whoever shoots first, wins.

Blood drains from my shoulder in a steady drip. My vision blurs at the edges. I need to end this before I pass out. "Raven, baby." I stagger a step. *Shit.*

"He tried to rape me." Her words are spit at Vince.

Dominick drops his head with a muttered curse.

My eyes are drawn to her shorts, opened and unzipped. *Oh, fuck no.* Fire flares in my gut. My vision returns with crystal accuracy, but all I can see is blood. I should have ended him that night in the parking lot. He may think he knows what pain is, but I'm about to give him a lesson in agony.

I swing my aim to Vince, step close, point blank range.

"I'm going to fuck you up, you no-good piece of shit." My words shake with the force of my anger.

"You better start apologizing, asswipe. My friend here's about to put a bullet in your brain." The rage in Blake's voice tells me he's walking a thin line of control.

Vince and I face off. My gun to his face, his to my chest. I'm vaguely aware of the other people in the room, but right now I've got sniper vision and Vince is in my crosshairs. Kill first, explain later.

"Just fucking end this, Dominick." Vince's gun shakes in his hand. I notice he's not using his other arm to brace the weight of his weapon, but instead has it cradled to his body. "Give me the go ahead to take this guy out. It's the least I could do after what that whore did to my arm—"

I lower my gun to his groin.

Pop.

"Aargh!" His scream of agony has him dropping to the floor along with his gun. He curls into the fetal position whimpering.

I kick his weapon away. "I warned you."

Blake scoops it up and aims it at the miserable mound of flesh on the floor. "Won't be using that tool ever again, eh Vinnie?"

Vince writhes once and then goes still. Probably passed out.

"Big mistake, Slade." Dominick shouts and the sound of Raven's cries fill the room.

I swing my gun toward him. His arm visibly flexes around her waist, making her gasp for air. I take aim, but feel my confidence draining along with the blood that flows down my arm.

"You don't get it. She's mine. You want to shoot me? Go ahead. But if I die, I take her with me." He moves toward the door, dragging Raven with him.

I move to block him. It's a risk, but after everything, I don't believe he would kill her now. He thrusts the gun hard, forcing her neck to an awkward angle. *Fuck.*

Losing her once was a pain worse than death. I will not lose her again. I take another step.

"He's gonna kill her, man." Blake's words speak to the raging beast in my head.

My shirt and jeans are soaked in my blood. I fight for consciousness. Blinking hard, I force myself to think clearly. Plans, ideas tumble in my head. My head feels heavy on my shoulders. I'm running out of time. There's only one option left.

"Fine." I lower my gun to the ground, then stand, palms forward in surrender. "You win."

"You too." Dominick motions to Blake to drop his weapons.

"Jonah?" Blake's eyes dart from my shoulder to my face, asking the question, *Have you lost your mind?*

I nod for him to drop his weapons. He shakes his head.

"Do it. He'll kill her." I hope my voice sounds desperate.

Blake drops his weapons and gives me a I-hope-you-know-what-you're-doing look. *Me too.*

Dominick tries to move past me. I stagger into his path, blocking his way.

"Wait. I just need to say one thing before you go." My words are a string of slurs.

I shut down my rational thinking. Or what's left of it. I'm firing on pure instinct. Using the one thing that has yet to fail me. I'm going to fight.

My head drops forward. Weakened from loss of blood, I gather my remaining strength. I'm not looking to beat him, only to buy enough time for Blake to get Raven out of here.

Dominick moves his gun-holding hand around her waist, and digs in his pocket for something. Car keys maybe.

Raven's sobs tighten my chest, making it hard to swallow.

Hang in there, baby. I have a plan.

"No time for parting words, I'm afraid. If you boys will get the fuck out of my way, my daughter and I—"

"She's *my* daughter!"

—

RAVEN

My mom is here. She said I'm her daughter. The ferocity of her words shakes the deepest corner of my soul.

"Milena." Dominick's voice sounds bored, but his muscles tense at my back. "What the fuck are you doing here?" He looks between her and Jonah. "You brought them here?" He aims the gun at her. "You stupid, bitch!"

She doesn't flinch.

"I won't let you take her." She steps closer, her back straight, conviction burning in her eyes. "Let her go."

"And if I don't? What are you going to do about it?" He shakes with laughter. "Look at you. You're pathetic and weak."

"Not anymore." Her voice is firm, not the slightest tremble. "I'm not that naïve girl anymore." She pins Dominick with a glare. "Do you remember that night? Twenty-one years ago to this day. Just a few yards from where we're standing."

I was born here?

His grip loosens and he leans toward her. "Of course, I remember. You gave her to me then. You didn't want anything to do with her. Wouldn't even hold her."

I twist my neck away from his devastating words. Heartbreak slashes through my body, threatening to drop me to the floor.

"Raven?" My mom's voice is tender.

Her soft expression contradicts the torture that works behind her dark brown eyes.

"I'm so sorry. I'd lost my parents." She exhales a quick breath and drops her head. "I couldn't bear to lose you too. It's no excuse. I know that now."

Tears stream down my face as her public apology seeps into my soul.

"You ungrateful bitch, I've given you everything. You were nothing when I saved you from your shitty life." Dominick shouts across the room, throwing his words like weapons.

She sneers in his direction. "I would rather live a thousand lives with nothing than the one I've lived with you. You used my fears against me to get what you wanted." Her voice cracks. "Raven was my baby." The room reverberates with the emotion behind her words.

Her baby. Warmth blooms in my chest. I stare, shock and amazement freezing my voice.

"But she was never mine, was she? You made that clear from the beginning."

Goose bumps race over my skin. She was protecting herself. This whole time I thought she hated me.

"I created her—"

"She's a human being, Dominick. You're messing with people's lives. She doesn't want this." She takes a step towards us, her shoulders tall and her expression fearless. "Let her go."

She's here. Fighting. For me.

Dominick's gun stays aimed at her. Blake and Jonah stand close, muscles tense, eyes darting.

She lifts her chin in defiance. He's going to kill her. And she's willing to die to free me.

I can't let that happen.

I fight the tears that brim in my eyes. It took strength for her to come here and risk her life. I won't repay that with fear. I've waited my entire life to feel my mom's love. And now that I have it, I refuse to lose it. We can fight to save each other.

"Your time is up, Milena. And who better to replace you than your own daughter." He runs the cool metal of his gun down my cheek. "She looks like you. Moves like you." He grabs a handful of my hair and pulls it, making me cry out. "She probably even fucks like you."

"Piece of shit!" Jonah's voice rumbles through the room.

"You stay the fuck out of this, Slade." Dominick points his gun at my mom.

"Don't worry, darling. I'll take good care of her." He kisses my cheek. I lean away from him. His grip tightens. Gun cocked. "Good bye, Milena."

Jonah moves fast. I'm thrown to the floor. My head smacks the hardwood. Pain lances through my skull, and bright stars flash behind my eyes. I struggle to sit up, blinking. Jonah has Dominick on the ground. They push and pull for the gun in a deadly tug-o-war.

Oh, God.

Blake pulls me up. "Baby girl. Let's go."

He drags me to the door, hooking my mom around her shoulders, and pushing us out.

"No!" I squirm in his hold. "I'm not leaving him."

Blake's biceps tighten. He's too strong. "Please, Blake. Let me go!"

He drags us down the stairs. Every step escalates my need to run back.

"Can't. I promised—"

"Please, Blake! I won't lose him." I'm kicking and flailing.

His steps slow.

"I can't live without him." I continue to claw at Blake's arms. I will never give up my fight for Jonah.

A deep groan rumbles from his chest. "He's going to kill me." His words are mumbled beneath his breath.

And then I'm free. My will to save Jonah burns in my muscles as I sprint toward the cabin.

I dart into the room. Jonah and Dominick are still locked in a vicious battle. I slide across a slippery pool of Vince's blood.

There's commotion, yelling. I look up to see Dominick's gun pointed at Jonah's face. I need to move faster.

A gun. I scurry on all fours. Blood covers my hands. Tears blur my vision. I fumble with the weapon. Crawling toward the fight. Jonah locks eyes with mine. His features twist in undiluted panic. Dominick's arm gets loose. The gun presses below Jonah's chin. *No!* The gun slips from my grip, I scramble for it with shaking hands. I get it, raise my hands to aim, and pray I'm not too late.

Pop-Pop-Pop.

THIRTY-THREE

RAVEN

The room is still. Pain radiates from my arms, seeping into my shoulders. People are yelling, but it sounds as if I've got cotton balls in my ears. Muffled and incoherent. White noise rings in my head, along with my hammering heartbeat.

I push myself up. The weight of the gun drops from my hand. Dominick is down. His body still. His chest void of the rise and fall of breath.

Dead. I killed him.

Someone pulls at my arm. They want my attention, but I can't look away from the morbid scene before me. Out of the corner of my eye I see Jonah. He's sitting up. Blake is shouting in his face, but I can't hear what he's saying.

Jonah's gaze swings to mine. The red blood splattered on his face is a gory contrast to his pallid skin. His eyebrows are low and his face pinched. I watch his mouth move, able to make out the single word. *Baby.*

My breath hitches. It's over. I'm free.

As if summoned by my thoughts, he rushes to me and I'm in the safety of his arms. The gentle sway of his body rocks me, and I clutch his blood-soaked shirt. He cups my cheek with his good arm, holding me to him. I feel the pressure of his mouth against the top of my head. His lips move against my scalp, but his words are vibrations. I pull away and watch his lips.

I love you.

A smile tiptoes across my face.

I love you too. My lips move, the cadence of my voice hums in my throat, but I can barely hear it. He pulls me back to his chest.

I can't force myself to look away from Dominick, his expensive-suited corpse lying in a pool of his own blood, a grim reminder of what I've done. What I had to do to save Jonah and my mom. And myself.

I search the recesses of my heart for regret, guilt, horror. Nothing. I've just killed my dad, the man responsible for my life. And all I feel is …relief.

———

JONAH

"You guys okay?" Blake walks up from my truck to the steps of the cabin where Raven and I sit.

As soon as I could, I dragged Raven out of there. It was the only way to get her to stop staring at Dominick's dead body.

I haven't left her side, except to run in and clean Dominick's filthy blood off my face.

"Better. We're starting to get our hearing back." I run my lips along the top of Raven's head, breathing in deep. "You make the call?"

"Yeah. Made it on my way to the truck. They should be here soon." Standing on the lower step, Blake leans against the banister. "Need anything?"

I give Raven a squeeze. "Baby?"

She shakes her head.

Milena is sitting on a rock nearby, but she keeps her distance, probably not sure how Raven feels about her. What she did tonight redeems her in my book. I owe my entire life to Milena. But ultimately, forgiveness is Raven's to give.

Minutes tick by before sirens and bright lights descend on us. An ambulance, fire truck, and a handful of police cars pull up to the cabin. Paramedics and cops unload in a hurry until we're surrounded by uniforms.

"Mr. Slade, I'm Kevin." One EMT that rushed out from the back of the ambulance meets us on the steps. He pulls back the fabric of my shirt to examine my shoulder. "Can you walk?"

"Yeah. Take care of her head. I'll wait." I motion to Raven who is slumped against my good side.

Kevin sidesteps and pulls back Raven's hair to check out her forehead. "Ma'am, are you injured anywhere else?"

She glares at me, but doesn't argue. "No. Just the cut on my head."

A smile pulls at my lips. I look forward to a lifetime of dirty looks from her.

"All right. Mr. Slade, let's get you into the ambulance and get some IV fluids started. I'll have Roger come and take care of…"

"My wife." I glare at Kevin. "Make sure Roger knows."

The sound of Raven's giggle is better than any pain medication.

"Yes, sir, Assasin. By the way, great fight tonight." The eager EMT is a fan. *Good to know.*

"Yes, it was." I lock eyes with Raven. "Best fight of my life."

Kevin puts his hand out to help me up. I'm tired and dizzy from blood loss, but this guy looks like a noodle in scrubs. I shake him off and push to standing. *Oh, shit.* Gripping the handrail, I squeeze my eyes shut, willing the vertigo away.

Raven presses into my side, using her body as support until my head stops spinning.

She walks me down the few steps to the dirt. I pull her in for a hug before we're dealt with by our assigned EMTs.

The angry mark above her head is no longer bleeding. I run my knuckles down her cheek, grateful that a cut is all they got on her. "Get your head taken care of." I kiss her longer than I should for the audience we have, but fuck 'em.

A team of EMTs rush into the cabin. Roger scurries up with some kind of a field medical kit and gets to work on Raven's head.

I drag my body to the ambulance where Kevin asks me to climb inside.

"Mind if you treat me out here?" There's no way I'm letting Raven out of my sight. It should be comforting being surrounded by cops, but with Dominick's far reach, I need to stay alert.

"Oh, I don't—"

I spear Kevin with a glare that has him nodding.

"Yeah, sure thing, 'Assassin.' I'll just pop a stretcher up here."

"Thanks."

Kevin moves some equipment to just outside the ambulances back doors. He moves around my shoulder doing some shit. I don't pay attention, but instead keep my focus on my girl. I pull my eyes away from her to watch them wheel Dominick's sheet-covered corpse from the cabin. Vince is next. It looks like they've got him awake and talking. *I should have aimed higher.*

A cop with a note pad asks me questions. I answer them until he's satisfied and walks away. He moves to questioning Raven next. Milena jumps to her side.

"Hey, man. How's the shoulder?" Blake plops down next to me at the back end of the ambulance.

"It's all right." I'm not concerned about my fucking shoulder.

Both Milena and Raven talk and nod as they most likely retell the night's events. I wish I could hear what they're saying.

"She's going to be okay, ya know."

I don't take my eyes off my girl. "How do you know that? She just killed someone."

Blake shrugs. "Cops said they'd been looking for something on Morretti for years. The guy's operation was locked up tighter than a Royce Gracie shoulder hold. This little situation was the Golden Goose taking a big fat dump right in their laps."

I don't say anything, but God, I hope he's right.

"Guess ole Vinnie started singing like a canary the second they got him conscious. Fucker gave away everything. Even told them he roughed up Guy and stole his cell phone."

"He roughed up Guy? Is he okay? Wait, does Raven know?" I watch Raven. Her body language is relaxed. They must be finishing up.

"Yeah, he's good. A few bruises and a gnarly concussion. That's how they got Raven out of the arena. They sent her a text from Guy's phone. Fucking assholes. Threatened to kill him if she didn't cooperate with Candy."

The name grates on my nerves. "And what about her? They gonna arrest her?"

He leans back, crosses his arms over his chest. "Yup. She'll go down for kidnapping and whatever else the prosecutor can scrape up."

I exhale a long breath. Guess keeping Vince alive was a good thing.

"Don't you let her cry one tear for that dick." Blake looks to the ambulance that holds Dominick's body then back to Raven. "She's a sweet girl, and sweet girls feel shit for shitty people. Don't let it eat her up inside. She saved your life."

I turn a glare on my friend. "Yeah, she did. And don't think I've forgotten about your broken promise, ass."

"Dude, she forced me. I got her out, but she threatened to tell the women of Vegas that I've got a needle dick." He throws his hands up in mock surrender. "I can't let that happen. I've got a reputation to uphold."

"How hard is it to keep a fucking promise?"

He shrugs, but has the decency to look embarrassed. "Your girl can be persuasive."

"Dick." I chuckle and turn back to Milena and Raven, making a mental note to take it out on him in the octagon once my shoulder heals.

"Milena's fucking hot as hell." There's a smile in his voice.

I glare at him, but can't help the curl in my lips. "Are you seriously talking about my girl's mom? Sick fuck."

"What? I know hot when I see it, and Milena's smokin'." He stands and holds out his hand. "Keys. I'll follow Milena home in the truck and bring it by in the morning. I'm assuming you'll be riding down the hill in this." He motions to the ambulance. "I'd offer to take Raven home, but knowing you, you ain't letting your girl out of your sight for …well, ever."

I toss him my keys. "Thanks, man."

He looks away and nods. Guy code for, *no problem, you'd do it for me.* Fuck yeah, I would.

Blake turns on his heel.

"Hey, B. You keep your dick to yourself around Milena, ya hear?"

He stops, looks to the ground, and shakes his head. He continues walking and turns over his shoulder. "I don't do chicks with kids, remember?"

I laugh to myself and watch as Raven finishes up. She turns away from the group of police who frantically fill their note pads and heads in my direction. She has a blanket from the

EMT wrapped around her shoulders. He head wound is clean and covered with a butterfly bandage.

Standing, I pull her into my arms. "Hey." I push the blanket down to kiss her neck at my spot. "You okay?" She curls in tight, just like she always does, as if she was carved from my own form.

"Yeah. I'm great." The smile in her voice is unmistakable.

"Mr. Slade, it's about time we get going," Kevin says from inside the ambulance.

"Come on. Let's get this over with so we can go home." I move to help her inside the vehicle.

"Oh, no, she can't come." Kevin wags his finger as I one-arm lift Raven into the ambulance. "But if she wants to, she can meet …you …um…"

Raven and I are inside, settled on a stretcher, completely ignoring his rant.

"Well, okay. I guess she can come." He must finally realize that he'll be riding in another vehicle before she does. Smart kid.

"Thanks, Kevin." I pull Raven into my arms and kiss her head. "I appreciate your flexibility."

Raven's body jumps with silent laughter as she hides her smile in my chest. I wrap her up tighter, thinking about how close I was to losing this. Losing her.

The ambulance fires up and we head back to Vegas. Raven's breathing slows to the rhythm of sleep. Even with my shoulder on fire, tired as hell, and minus a shitload of blood, I don't sleep. Instead, my mind conjures plans—plans for the future we now have sealed. And I'm not wasting a single second.

"Kevin, I need you to do me a favor."

"Sure thing, 'Assassin.'"

"I need to make a phone call."

—

RAVEN

Beep-Beep-Beep.

The gentle sound brings me back to consciousness. I blink several times into the dark before lifting my head from my warm pillow. I observe my surroundings, thankful to see the lights of medical equipment rather than log walls. I'm not in the cabin, but in the hospital with Jonah.

My head swirls with the events from this morning. The cops told me that Guy was safe. They even gave me a phone so I could call him. He apologized for not being at the fight to protect me. I reassured him that Dominick was out to get his way, no matter what.

Katherine showed up and sat with my mom while Jonah was poked and x-rayed. The doctor said that that the bullet went straight through without injuring anything vital, but they had to do surgery. Three hours later, we were put in a private room. I assured Katherine and my mom that I was okay. There was no way I was leaving Jonah's side. I traded my bloody clothes for a pair of clean scrubs, crawled in bed with Jonah, and fell asleep.

A yawn crawls up my throat and I lie back down in the crook of Jonah's uninjured shoulder.

"Good morning." His sexy, sleepy voice does delicious things to my body. Even laid-up and hospitalized, he's irresistible.

"Good night, you mean." I walk my fingers to his abdomen, pulling his hospital gown up to slide my hand against his rippled muscles.

He reaches for my face but drops his hand with a groan. "Shit, that hurts."

I look up at him and smile. "Looks like you're going to have to keep that hand to yourself."

"Not a fucking chance. Come here." His demand is firm and sexy.

I lift my face to his and brush my lips against his chin. "Thank you, Jonah. Thank you for finding me."

"And thank you for saving me."

My cheeks heat and I bury deeper into his chest.

"How're you holding up? You know, with everything?" His hand traces soothing patterns on my back.

"Um …I'm good. I feel like I should feel something, ya know? Guilt or …remorse. I just don't." I huff out a breath. "The cops said this morning that no charges are being filed. Justifiable homicide and all that."

"You want to talk about what happened with Vince?" His muscles tense against my body.

"Not much to tell. He tried to—"

A deep growl rumbles in Jonah's chest.

Yeah, probably best to skip to the end. "You told me to break his arm. So I did." I hear the words, and even I think they sound crazy. But it's the truth.

"I told you?"

I circle his belly button with my finger. "Yeah. In my head. You told me to fight. You said *arm bar*." I shrug. "You weren't even there yet, and you were protecting me."

"I'll always protect you." He hugs me to him. "Not that you need it. My girl's tough as nails. I'm proud of you."

Inwardly, I smile. I'm proud of myself.

"Fuck, I wish I'd killed that son of a bitch."

"Nah. He deserves to live the rest of his life behind bars. Death is too easy."

He laughs in a quick burst then groans. "Ugh, remind me not to do that again."

Starting at his neck, I trail soft kisses to his jaw. "Poor baby." I push up to meet his eyes. "I love you."

His hand slides up my back into my hair. "I love you too. So much."

He takes my lips in a brutal kiss that I feel in my toes. I moan into his mouth as our tongues glide against each other. Desire floods my veins as I explore his mouth. His strong lips dominate mine, molding them to his will. I roll his nipple between my thumb and forefinger. He groans and his hips flex off the bed.

Pushing up, I press my breasts into his chest, tilting my head and delving deeper into the kiss.

He breaks away with a hiss. "Fuck."

The whispered curse sends me back and sitting up. "Shoot, did I hurt you?" I touch him and jerk my hand away, afraid of hurting him again.

"No, but if we don't take this home, I'm afraid I'll be forced to give the good doctor and his unsuspecting nurses a visual aid in sex education." He shifts and adjusts the blankets to camouflage his arousal. It doesn't work.

A giggle bubbles up from my chest, and my hand covers my mouth. Something rough on my finger rubs against my lips. *What the heck?*

My mood sobers as I examine my hand, palm down, fingers splayed. It's on my ring finger. A gold band composed of tiny diamonds with one large round diamond in the center. The setting is old-fashioned, understated, and absolutely perfect. I stare in awe.

The cool air burns my eyes. I'm unable to blink. I force my eyes to Jonah who's smiling his thousand-watt smile: all teeth, two dimples, and shining eyes.

"Jonah?" I whisper, my eyes asking the question my words can't form.

"The ring was my mom's. My dad gave it to her when they got engaged, and she wore it every day, until this morning. She brought it by when you were sleeping." He pulls my hand to his chest and nimbly spins the ring on my finger.

"Raven, I fell in love with you the second I saw you. I thought I had my life mapped out, thought I had it together. Then you came along and flipped my world on its head. You make me want things I never knew I needed. This ring is more than a symbol of my love. It represents family. Our family. The one we'll build together. You said you didn't want to talk about our future until you knew we had a future to talk about. Well, now we do. So? Will you marry me?"

Our family. Our future. Now that we have one.

He stares at me, his eyebrows raised. I taste the salty tears as my lips curl at the edges. A slow smile creeps across his face.

I study the perfect ring then lock eyes with him. "Okay."

His face splits into a smile. "Okay." He kisses me deep and hard, possessive.

My insides turn to liquid. I explore every curve of his rippled stomach, and his muscles flex beneath my touch. My nails dig into his skin and drag down lower, until they're under the blankets that lie across his hips. He flexes into my touch, showing me what he wants. *Me.*

"Oh, one more thing." He breaks the kiss enough to speak, but his words are said against my lips.

An embarrassing whimper escapes at the loss of his mouth. "Yeah?" I lean into him.

He rubs his thumb across my aching lower lip. "Happy birthday, baby."

The words are barely out before I'm on him again. Desperation takes over my rational mind and I pull at his gown. *Too many clothes.*

A voice clears from the end of the bed, popping the love-driven sex bubble we'd created. I curl into Jonah's body, hoping to disappear from whoever caught me making out with my injured boyfriend. Fiancé.

"Well, well, well. Looks like someone's feeling better," Blake says from the foot of the bed, motioning to the pile of thin hospital blankets at Jonah's crotch.

I say a quick prayer of thanks that it's Blake and not Katherine. "Hey, Blake."

"What's up?" Jonah acts unaffected as he twirls a strand of my hair.

"Just came back from the police station. Dominick's operation is under intense investigation. Thought you two would like to know Vince and Candy are going to be looking at the inside of a jail cell for the foreseeable future."

Jonah and I take a collective breath.

Blake grimaces. "Vinnie should be the most popular guy in his cell block. They couldn't save his dick so they gave him a pussy. Boys in prison should love that."

"Blake!" I attempt to sound offended, my hysterical laughter ruining any chance I have of being taken seriously. Besides, that's the least he deserves for what he did to Eve, me, and probably loads of other women who weren't lucky enough to get away.

"I see you got a decent piece of ice there on your finger, baby girl."

I hold up my hand and admire the ring again. "Yeah." Jonah kisses my head at my breathy reply.

"Right on. I'll leave you two lovebirds alone." He holds up his hand. "Word of caution, the doc is on his way in to check on your shoulder. You might want to keep Mr. Moby on the down-low." He looks at the bed then back at us. "Looks like it's too late for down-low, so …under wraps."

"Dude, you mind keeping your eyes off my dick?"

He flashes his cocky smile. And even in the arms of the man of my dreams, his smile makes me giggle like a teenage girl. He winks then turns on his heel and heads through the draped dividers.

"Catch you two later. Got a hot little nurse who's waiting to give my dick an oral exam."

I laugh hard, trying to keep my body from shaking at its intensity. "He's so funny."

"Yes, so you've said." Jonah's deadpan tone makes me grin.

"Ooh, are you jealous?" I touch the end of his nose with my fingertip.

"Hmph. No."

I slide my lower lip out in an exaggerated pout. "Oh. That's too bad. I was going to prove my feelings for you …physically." I kiss the sensitive skin below his ear.

"Is that right?" I can hear the smile in his voice.

"Mm-hm. I like you jealous."

"Get used to it, baby." He groans when I pull his earlobe between my teeth. "You know you're mine now? To have and to hold 'til death do us part."

"I do."

EPILOGUE

*Two months, five days, and
twenty-two hours later...*

JONAH

"Forty-two *million* dollars?" Owen's palm slams on the bar, his jaw slack, eyes wide.

I pop the bottle cap and place the fresh beer in front of him. "Projected. It'll take awhile to liquidate all of Dominick's properties." We knew Dominick was loaded with dirty money, but finding out about his multiple luxury high-rise condos and commercial properties was a surprise.

Rex leans in, his pierced eyebrow raised high. "No shit? What're you guys going to do with all that money?"

"Y'all should buy one of them private islands. Like Oprah." Caleb motions one of the caterers over and pops a bacon-wrapped shrimp in his mouth.

"Forty-two million dollars." Owen repeats himself, sounding no less shocked. "Fuck the island. Kick some cash to your boys, man."

"Dominick Morretti dies and you guys get all his money? Fuck…" Rex shakes his head. "I wish my dad was a dead-piece-of-shit pimp." He throws back the dregs of his beer.

"Raven was his next of kin. It's her money. She's got plans for it."

Caleb stands from his barstool. "Between her money and your money, y'all could buy up half of Vegas."

"Nah. My title-fight winnings look like pennies in comparison." I flex against the stifling confinement of my jacket. I can't wait to get this tux off. Raven is excellent with formal-wear removal. My blood heats and has me searching her out.

She's on the dance floor that the party planners put in my backyard. Blake spins her around, her white wedding gown swirling at her feet. The strapless top pushes her breasts up in an enticing way. I absently tug at the collar of my tuxedo. It's loose, reminding me that I took off my tie and unbuttoned the top button while ravishing my wife in the limo on the way home. I can't wait to peel that dress off her.

"So what's she going to do with all that money?" Owen pulls me from my fantasy.

I take a swig of beer. "She bought her mom a house. And she started Raven's Nest."

"Yeah, I know that, but what about the other thirty-something million?"

"She plans to funnel it all into the foundation as it comes in."

I look for Milena in the crowd. Since that night at the cabin, she's been the kind of mom Raven's always wanted: attentive, loving, hands on. The other day, I walked in to find them flopped on the couch watching Overhaulin'. Their eyes were riveted to the screen while Milena twirled a strand of her daughter's hair.

Between Milena, my mom, and Eve, Raven has been able to get Raven's Nest open and running. The foundation provides rehabilitation, job training, housing, and counseling for prostitutes getting out of the business. The place is already packed with the girls from Dominick's stable.

"That's some cool shit, man." Rex toys with his lip ring.

"What's cool shit?" Her voice draws my attention. No longer the girl who can't curse, Raven can drop bombs with the best of them. She strolls up with Blake at her side.

"I believe they were talking about me, baby girl." Blake grabs a beer. "Don't know if you've noticed, but I'm cool as shit."

Caleb stands from his barstool and pushes it toward her, offering her a seat. "We're talking about Raven's Nest."

Blake plops down on the barstool, earning a glare of Caleb. "Thanks, dude."

She steps in beside me, champagne in hand. A slight blush colors her cheeks. "Oh."

I wrap my arm around her tiny waist and hug her to me.

"You're in the running for sainthood with that move, princess." Owen shakes his head. "Don't know if I'd be able to give away that kind of money."

Eve slides in between Blake and Rex at the bar. "Raven's not about money. Hell, she'd give away every last cent if it meant taking care of someone else." She grabs the open beer I just set down in front of Caleb and takes a swig. "Thanks, Caleb."

"Shit, man," Caleb mumbles in frustration.

Raven sips her champagne and shrugs. "That money isn't mine. It belongs to those women. They sold their bodies and he reaped the benefit." She checks the clock and turns back to the guys at the bar. "I'm just giving it back to them."

The guys all grumble to themselves, probably still shocked that Raven didn't keep even a few million for herself.

Eve shakes her head, a knowing smile on her face. "Anyone up for a twirl on the dance floor?" Her eyes rake across the available dance partners. "Come on, Blake."

"Shit, woman. I just got off the dance floor. Give a guy a second to reboot." Blake kicks back, resting his feet on the bar.

Eve's face lights with a wicked smile. "Ah, yes. That's right. Most guys can't go all night long. The weak ones lack, ahem, stamina." She looks at me. "How about you, Jonah? You look like the kind of guy who—"

"That's for shit." Blake jumps to his feet. "I got way more stamina than he does." He motions to me with a thumb over his shoulder. "Dance floor now, woman."

Eve winks at Raven and takes off with Blake.

I turn Raven to me and pull her in for a hug, chest to chest. The guys redirect their attention to the TV. I run my finger along her bare shoulder and up to her neck, pushing her long hair to her back. "These earrings your mom gave you look amazing. They're almost the same color as your eyes." I kiss her neck at my spot.

She touches the diamond and aquamarine studs. "She told me they were my grandmother's. I love them. They're perfect. This whole day has been perfect." She smiles. "I still can't believe we got married by Liberace."

"Hey, you chose him. We could have had the Asian Elvis, or the Marilyn Monroe drag queen."

She laughs and leans into me. I wrap my arm around her and kiss her head.

"It was the rhinestone suit that got him the job. Every single inch of that thing was covered."

"Only in Vegas."

"Did you see Guy dancing with my mom? I think he's got the hots for her." She scrunches up her nose in an adorable way.

"It was nice of him to give you away today. He's a good man. Milena could do worse."

Her huge blue-green eyes look up at me. "You don't think…"

I shrug, my lips twitching. "They'd make a cute couple."

"Eww. That'd be like—"

"Like your mom and your dad hooking up."

Now it's her turn to shrug. "Good point."

"Did you save me a dance, Mrs. Slade?" My whispered words in her ear cause her to tremble. I trail a line of kisses down her neck.

"Um, sure." She tilts her head, opening up for me. "But it's five."

I pull back and lock eyes on her. "So?"

She looks to the sixty-inch flat screen hanging on the wall behind me. Her forehead drops a fraction, and she looks up at me from beneath her batting eyelashes.

"Even on your wedding day?" I cross my arms over my chest. I have every intention of giving this girl anything she wants as long as we both shall live. But I do enjoy watching her squirm.

"Hey, you've been watching ESPN. Same difference." She finishes with her hand on her sexy hip.

I lean in and kiss her forehead at my new spot. The slight scar that slashes through her eyebrow does nothing to mar her gorgeous face. "You win."

With a flip of the remote, I switch ESPN to her show. She kisses each of my dimples and finishes at my lips.

"Overhaulin'? Fuck yeah! Coolest wedding reception ever." Caleb rounds the bar for a better view.

"Oh wow." Raven sips the last of her champagne. "It's a '66 Ford Fairlane GT." She doesn't take her eyes from the screen.

Overhaulin' on her wedding day makes her giddy. So easy to please.

I wrap my hands around her waist and hoist her up to sit on the counter. She kicks her white, Chuck Taylor clad feet back and forth.

Owen leans in, his head resting on his hand, eyes to the TV. "Who's this Chip Foose guy?"

My lips fight a smile as Raven goes into a detailed biography of the automotive designer. I hand her a fresh glass of champagne and a piece of wedding cake the waitstaff passed out earlier.

"Ooh, yum." She takes the glass and a bite of wedding cake. "Thanks, honey."

I groan at her calling me honey and kiss the frosting from her lips. She started doing that after the night at the cabin. I thought nothing could sound as good as my name from her lips. I was wrong. "You're welcome, baby."

"Uncle Jonah," Eric and Aiden call in unison from the pool. The six-year-old twin boys jumped in about an hour ago.

I leave Raven to her show and walk to the pool's edge. "What's up, rug rats?"

"Come swimming with us," Aiden says before disappearing underwater.

"Yeah, do that thing where you throw us across the pool to the deep end." Eric spins in a circle, making speedboat sounds.

"Boys, your uncle can't swim tonight. He has guests to entertain," my sister calls, walking toward me.

"Your mom's right, guys. But I promise I'll swim with you all day tomorrow. Deal?"

"Deal," they answer before swimming off to the other side of the pool.

Beth leans into my side and I throw my arm around her shoulder.

"I'm really happy for you, big brother. I gotta say I never thought you'd settle down."

I laugh and give her a squeeze. "You're not the only one."

"She's really special, Joey. I've only known her for two days and I'm in love with her."

"She has that effect on people." I kiss her head. "I'm glad you guys are here. I know it was short notice."

"We wouldn't miss it for anything." She sips her drink. "I will say it was a rather short engagement."

I nod. "When God hands you a gift, you don't push it away and tell him 'later'."

She smiles up at me. "Dad would be proud of you. You've grown into an amazing man. Just like him."

Emotion burns my eyes. I swallow hard, absorbing the weight of her words and let the silence speak for me.

"I'm going to go find my husband and make him dance with me." She breaks the silence, and with a quick hug, she walks away.

I turn back to watching my girl from a distance. She laughs in the center of a bunch of muscle-head fighters, as if she was born to be there. I'd like to think she was.

My heart swells with pride. There's just a shadow left of the shy auto mechanic that walked into my house with her head down. This courageous woman confronted her life head-on. Faced her demons. And won.

And she's not hoarding that strength, but choosing to share it with others. Giving them a chance to beat back the circumstances of their lives and bend it to their will. I've never seen that kind of beauty. Until now. And she's wearing my ring.

———

RAVEN

It's late. I don't know what time it is. I'm swaying on an empty dance floor with my husband. Our guests are long gone, leaving us alone at last. Jonah's strong arms and broad chest cradle me to him. Content and relaxed, I replay the day in my head.

My mom helping me into my dress, wrapping me in her arms, telling me she loves me. It's as if Dominick's death cut some invisible tie that held her back, and now she's able to love freely, without restraint or fear of loss. To love me the way she's always wanted to. Or possibly to show the love she's always felt.

Guy walking me down the aisle. His snort and eye roll when he saw the flamboyant impersonator, only to get tears in his eyes when he gave my hand to Jonah.

And my Jonah. The intensity of his stare as he said his vows. As if hearing the words weren't enough, he wanted me to feel them.

Our first kiss as husband and wife, his hands traveling down my body to cup my bottom in front of everyone. Okay, that was a little embarrassing—hot—but embarrassing. My body didn't hate it. That was obvious when I had to hold onto Jonah as I waited for my legs to start working again.

It was perfect. Every single second.

Jonah's sister and mom have been staying here with us, but they insisted on getting hotel rooms for the night. We had the option of getting the hotel room, but decided we'd rather spend our first married night at Jonah's house—our house.

So here we are, alone beneath the stars, locked in each other's arms. Jonah's heart beats against my ear. We stop and kiss then go back to the gentle sway. Time stands still.

"Baby?"

"Mm-hmm?" I swallow a yawn.

"I'm ready to take you to bed now." He stops moving as if to punctuate his words with a stop-dancing-and-get-your-ass-in-our-bed exclamation point.

My pulse quickens and excitement wakens my body. I stop swaying and look up at him. His eyelids are dropped low with want. I inwardly smile at my effect on him. I lock my hands behind his neck and push up on my tiptoes while pulling his mouth to mine.

Electricity hums between us as our lips connect. Sparks explode beneath my skin with every touch. Ever since the cabin, everything between us is more intense, like we're sucking every second out of life as we feast on each other's bodies.

His hand slides up from my waist, over my ribs, and stops just beside my breast. I moan and arch my back in an attempt to get him closer, but his hand stays put.

With long, deep pulls, I suck his tongue into my mouth. His answering groan tells me he's at the edge of his restraint.

He dips down, scooping me into his arms and heads for the house, never breaking the kiss. The spice of his cologne, all masculine and sensual, liquefies my need. My fingers sift and grab at his silky hair, pulling him down.

Two steps into the house, he stops and lays me on the couch.

"Can't wait." His husky voice vibrates against the tender skin of my neck.

I toe my shoes off just before he pushes the skirt of my dress up to my waist. A groan rumbles in his chest as he takes in what I'm wearing beneath my wedding gown. I prop up to my elbows, enjoying the view of Jonah on his knees studying my bridal lingerie.

"Do you want to see the rest?" My voice is deep and dripping with desire.

He caresses my legs, every swipe of his callused hands sending heat straight between my legs. "There's more?"

With a teasing kiss, I stand. Giving him my back, I unzip, and slowly peel the fabric from my body.

A hiss slips from between his teeth as my dress drops to the floor. *He likes it.*

I peek over my shoulder to see him sitting, his eyes fixed on my bottom.

He stands up and steps into my space, so close I can feel his heat against my skin. "Turn around."

I do just that, but step back, out of his reach.

With a slow sweep of his gaze, I'm trembling.

His eyelids drop low and a predatory glint flashes across his eyes. "Come here, Mrs. Slade."

My legs burn to obey his every command. But I withhold. "Uh-uh. You're going to have to come and get me."

His eyes lock on mine, fire burning behind their hazel depths. He tilts his head to the side, eyebrows raised. Yeah, he likes the challenge.

"You want to be chased." He steps toward me.

I step back.

Like a shot, he moves, swiping at me with his powerful arm. Anticipating his move, I wheel around and dash toward the hallway. Excited giggles bubble up from my chest, flying out on a squeal. I make it to the hallway entrance before his strong arms wrap around me from behind.

"Gotcha." The word is spoken at my ear.

I moan in response. He carries me the few short steps to our bedroom door. He releases me, and I flip around. His eyes are dark and hungry. My stomach flips and drops low.

He advances on me, and with every step forward, I take one back. My legs hit the bed. He closes in. I roll my lips, eager for his contact. He traces the top of my white corset with a barely-there touch. My breasts push against the lace, overflowing at the top. He trails his fingers down the center of each breast where the dark-skinned tips show through the delicate fabric. He circles them with slow, agonizing motions.

I part my lips to accommodate my quickened breath. He cups my breasts, finally giving them the attention they so desperately need. Bending down, he sucks my nipple into his mouth, a torturous ecstasy that drops my head back with a moan.

"Jonah." The urgent plea falls from my lips.

His hands move down the ribbing of my corset to my hips. He slides his fingers beneath the barely there fabric of my g string. My body warms as he loves me with his touch.

Feather-light kisses cover my neck as he slides his hand into my panties. A moan catches in my throat. My legs wobble.

"Lie down, baby." His words are spoken against my skin, my body obeying his command. There's nothing I wouldn't do for him as his fingers push me to the edge of my control.

I lie on the bed. He pulls my panties down to my knees, but doesn't take them off. They're stretched taut between my bent legs, keeping them from falling wide open.

He works between my legs, my body bending to his every whim. I need more. I pop my breasts from their lacey restraint and arch my back, offering them up to him.

His eyes lift and widen. "Greedy little wife."

I roll my hips against his hand, affirming his words.

His mouth locks around my nipple. Blood races through my body, muscles clenching in euphoric satisfaction as I cry out my release. Weak with satiated bliss, my legs strain to fall apart. He continues to nip at my breasts.

I grab at his shirt, pulling at the buttons.

"You first." He rolls me to my side and unlaces the crisscross ribbon at my back, removing my corset. I kick off my panties, and he pulls his white dress shirt from his body.

I suck in a breath as my eyes take in the circular scar at his shoulder. The evidence of his heroism. His bravery worn like a badge, forever imprinted on his skin, like his tattoos. A smile tugs at my lips as I study his newest. Right over his heart, my name in script with beautiful black wings extending from either side.

"I love you, Jonah."

He doesn't answer with words, but instead kneels between my legs. My knees fall open wide. He moves over me and lies in the cradle of my legs, the fabric of his dress pants rubbing against my bare flesh.

He braces his weight above me with his muscled arms. "I want you off the pill, baby."

"Huh?" I'm not sure what my face looks like, but it feels as if it's gaping.

"I know it's soon. But, since when do we do things on a timeline? I want to start our family." He kisses my neck then bites me gently. "What do you say?" His mouth continues its torment.

"Mmm."

"That a yes or a no, baby?"

A real family. One that we make together. "I'm ready." I flex my hips.

With shining eyes and his two glorious dimples, he gives me a smile that nearly stops my heart. "Really?"

"Yes."

Without another word, he releases himself from his pants and in one thrust, buries himself completely. I lock my legs around his hips, our chests pressed together so tight I can feel his heart beat against mine. His hands cup my face and I place my hand on his jaw.

He moves, slow and beautiful, loving me in a gentle rhythm that brings tears to my eyes. His gaze locks on mine, and the affection pouring between us threatens to overwhelm me.

I watch the pleasure build. His perfect white teeth dig into his lower lip. His eyes fight to stay open against the mounting frenzy. Pleasure coils deep my belly. I arch my back and dig my feet into the mattress.

I don't want it to be over too soon. I lock down his hips with my heels.

He stops and takes a deep breath. "No need to hold back, baby. We have forever."

Forever. The word echoes in my head and I release him to move.

I'm free. Free to live happily with Jonah. No more threats to our future. Free to fly.

His pace quickens, and his muscles tighten with each stroke. I lift my hips, searching for more, deeper, harder. Passion, trust, and love spiral together until it explodes from my body, and I cry out his name. He groans into my neck, biting down on my shoulder and his pace intensifies. With one last thrust, his body relaxes onto mine.

Our chests heave in unison, the soft moans from the aftermath of our love-making fill the room.

He slides in and out in lazy strokes. "Sorry our first time as husband and wife was …um …fast. I blame the dress. And the stuff you had on under it."

I run my hands through his hair, forcing him to look at me. His shy smile makes him look younger and almost embarrassed. "We have forever, remember?"

He closes his eyes and leans into my touch. "Yeah." His eyes flutter open and he turns to look over his shoulder.

"What?" I lean to the side and look down our joined bodies to the end of the bed. "I guess someone's feeling left out."

Dog is curled up in a ball at Jonah's feet. He gives us a sleepy meow.

Jonah turns back, shaking his head. "I can't believe you talked me into bringing that thing home."

"Jonah. He's my responsibility. I couldn't just leave him to fend for himself like some kind of—"

"Alley cat?"

"Ugh. You know what I mean." I give Jonah a playful shove and he rolls off and to my side. His fingers draw invisible patterns on my stomach. "I'd be sick if I moved away and no one was there to take care of him. Everyone needs someone."

"I never thought I'd have anything in common with a mangy cat." His lips curl at the edges. "We both need you." He moves from my stomach to my forehead to trace my scar. His smile falls. "I almost lost you."

"No, never. I would've fought. However long it took. I'd never give up until I was free. You're my life, Jonah. My family, my love, my best friend. Nothing, not even destiny, could keep me from you."

He leans forward and brushes his lips against mine. "Okay."

THE END

A NOTE TO MY READERS

I hope you enjoyed Fighting for Flight. Please take a moment to leave a review on Amazon.

The next book in this series will be *Fighting to Forgive.*

Fast and hard, just the way he likes it. Blake Daniels flies through life the way he burns through women: on his terms, no regrets.

His fighting career in full swing, he has no need for attachments. He knows what he wants, but when a haunting secret from his past threatens his future, he teeters on the edge of sanity.

She's through with men. After the fifteen-year marriage that never should have happened, Layla Moorehead moves on to start a new life—one that focuses on making amends for the irreparable damage she's caused her sixteen-year old daughter.

Saddled with shadows from their past, their lives come crashing together in a violent mix of passion and betrayal.

Is love enough to overcome history?

Or will they be left *Fighting to Forgive?*

ACKNOWLEDGEMENTS

There are so many people to thank, make sure to look for your name. It's probably on here.

To my husband and my girls, thank you for allowing me the time to write this book with minimal complaints and guilt trips. You guys are my world. I love you.

To my mom, Gale West, your love and support gave me the confidence to give writing a try. Thank you for believing in me.

To Evelyn Johnson, thank you for listening over a glass of wine as I first voiced my idea. Your excitement for the story gave it wings. Your companionship while doing my research in Vegas was invaluable. I'll be forever grateful for your encouragement.

Thank you to my family and friends for believing in me. You know who you are.

To the amazingly talented Elizabeth Reyes, thank you for taking time out for newbie writer and pointing me in the right direction. You have a forever-fan in me.

To Jenny Aspinall, and Gitte Doherty. Thank you for championing my idea to write a MMA romance.

Thank you to Chris Letts who never stopped encouraging me from start to finish.

To my friend and Las Vegas connection, LeAnne Zinke, thanks for the inside scoop.

To all my amazing critique partners, Jacki P, Travis Casey, Hijo, Carroll "Sully" Sullivan, and Kaci Persnell, each one of you contributed something different and invaluable to this story. You guys kick serious ass.

Thank you to my amazing critique partners and betas, Claudia Handel and Nicola Layouni. You girls rock.

To my gorgeous Sister Wives of Writing, thank you for all the times we stayed up late messaging about anything and everything, I'll be forever grateful.

To Cristin "C-Spice" Harber, thank you for never saying no when I needed a riding partner on the Pity Train. Your steadfast attitude, constant encouragement, and faithful friendship kept me sane. You've taught me so much about writing, and I'm honored to have a front row seat as the world of publishing opens its doors to your talent.

Sharon "Shexy" Cermak, my Sister from Another Mister, from prologue to epilogue, you've been a guiding force. I'm forever indebted to you for your commitment and support.

To Amanda Simpson at Pixel Mischief, thank you for book. You have an amazing gift.

A huge thank you to Theresa Wegand for her superhuman editing skills—thank you for saving me from looking like a complete idiot. Your keen eye and attention to detail is exceptional.

And finally, to you, my readers, thank you for giving me a shot at storytelling. It truly is a pleasure unparalleled. I hope you come back for more.

–JB

ABOUT THE AUTHOR

JB Salsbury lives in Phoenix, Arizona with her husband and two kids. She spends the majority of her day as a domestic engineer. But while she works through her daily chores, a world of battling alphas, budding romance, and impossible obstacles claws away at her subconscious, begging to be released to the page.

Her love of good storytelling led her to earn a degree in Media Communications. With her journalistic background, writing has always been at the forefront, and her love of romance prompted her to sink her free time into novel writing.

Fighting for Flight is her first novel in the MMA romance series.

For more information on the series or just to say hello, visit JB on Facebook or Goodreads.

http://www.facebook.com/JbSalsbury?fref=ts

http://www.goodreads.com/author/show/6888697. Jamie_Salsbury

Printed in Great Britain
by Amazon.co.uk, Ltd.,
Marston Gate.